I0762290

The Crystal Dynasty

The Quest Begins

Abigail Mader

Caspian Ocean
Dunes of Decessus
Darlington
Ringwick Lagoon
Belmont
Belshire
Middlebeck Farm
Sleights
Temple
Wittleshire
Stowden
Geraldton
Renlands
Snowy Mountains of Azend
Falmouth

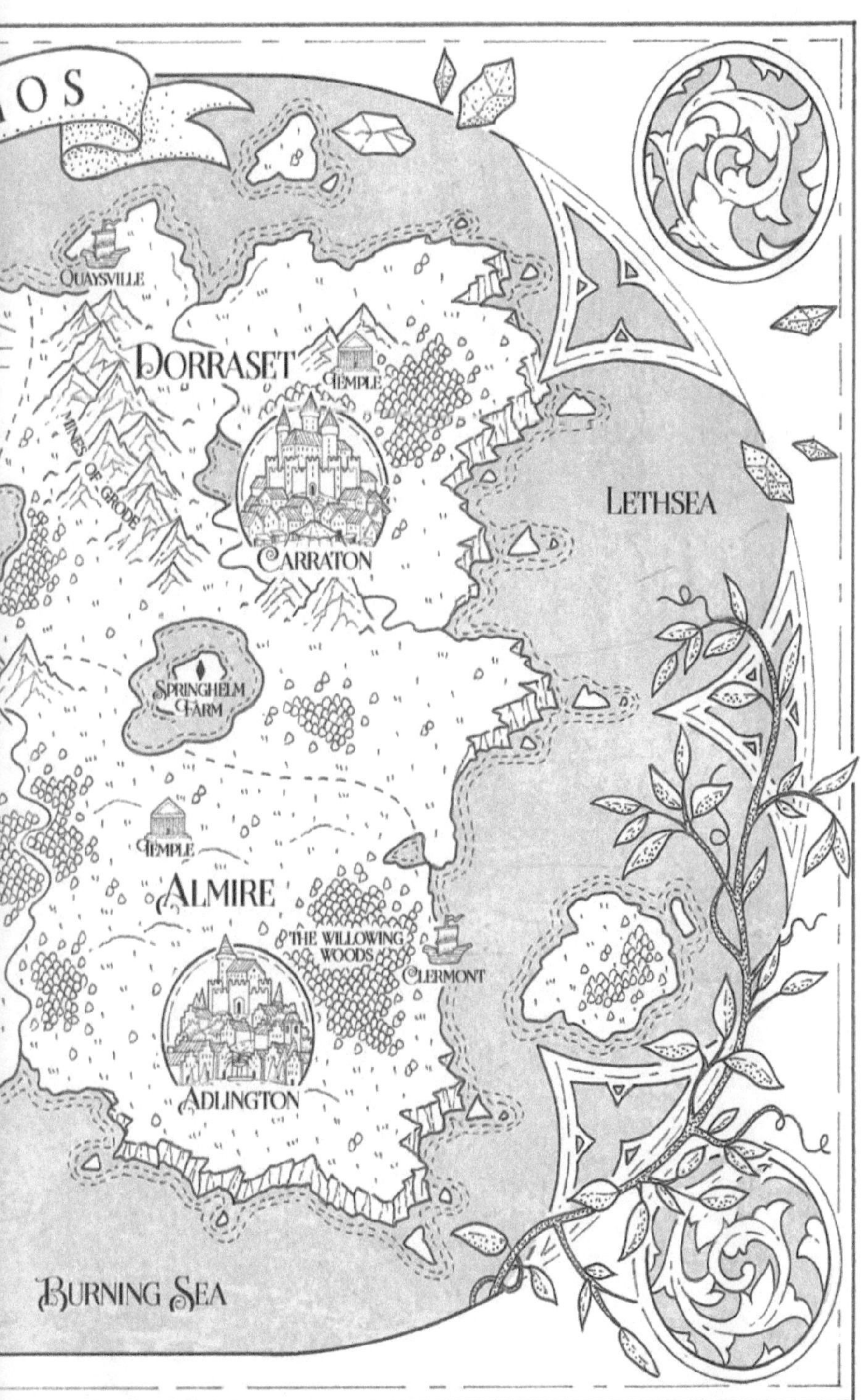
OS
QUAYSVILLE
DORRASET
TEMPLE
MINES OF GRODE
CARRATON
LETHSEA
SPRINGHELM FARM
TEMPLE
ALMIRE
THE WILLOWING WOODS
CLERMONT
ADLINGTON
BURNING SEA

ISBN: 987-17635740-4-5

Dedication

To all the readers who loved fairy tales as children but found the villains more fun to read.

This is for you.

Enjoy!

Content Warnings

A couple of open-door spicy scenes at the end of chapters 5 and 21.

Detailed birth scene

Detailed descriptions of torture

Mentions of unaliving children

On page death

Table of Contents

Prologue

The chamber was dimly lit, shadows dancing on the ancient stone walls. A figure cloaked in darkness stood before a shimmering pool, its surface rippling with images of what was and what would come. It had been a long time since they last gazed into this body of water, and the visions they had seen in the past were now nearing completion.

"We are on the edge of a precipice of what is about to happen," a voice echoed behind them, filled with concern.

"I know," replied the figure, their tone calm and resolute. "Trust that I have it all under control. The children are going to succeed. I'll make sure of it. Elinor cannot continue to rule much longer. They are safe in their grandfather's care, and before long, I shall step in and ensure they receive the guidance they require."

The voice softened, almost wistful. "You have been watching over this land all this time, even now, you strive to see the world righted once more."

The figure nodded, though their face remained hidden. "Always. And I will continue to do so and guide those who need it. The hour has come for the crystal shards to reunite."

A heavy silence fell over the chamber, broken only by the distant sound of water flowing from above and cascading into the pool below. With a slight turn, the figure revealed a celestial pendant shaped like a star, its soft, otherworldly light radiating an aura of her divine power.

"The prophecy is clear. The children are the key to restoring balance. We must be patient."

The voice, now filled with a renewed sense of hope, responded, "Then we shall wait. And when the time comes, we will be ready."

The figure turned back to the pool, watching as the visions shifted and changed. Images of battles fought and sacrifices made flickered across the surface. The weight of the past and the uncertainty of the future pressed heavily upon them, yet their resolve remained unshaken.

"Remember," they said softly, "we are not alone in this. Allies will arrive from unexpected places, and together, we shall restore what has been lost."

The voice behind them whispered, "And the children? Do they possess enough strength?"

"Yes, they do," the figure replied with unwavering confidence. "They carry the legacy of their ancestors and the hope of our people. They will rise to the challenge."

As the final words echoed through the chamber, the figure stepped away from the pool, the celestial pendant glowing brighter with each step. The path ahead was fraught with danger, but they were ready to face it, knowing the fate of Ethos rested in their hands.

Chapter 1

Eight Years Later

Even after eight long years, that dreadful night remained vivid in Aevah's memory as if it had happened yesterday. It had been the most terrifying evening of her life, and the days that followed were equally harrowing until they finally reached the safe haven, they now call home. She remembered their grandfather waking her and Jacob, and quietly leaving the castle in the chilly, dark hours. She had heard the cries of people, unsure of what was happening around them.

That brief night at the temple had been their only solace, a fleeting moment when they believed they would return home come morning. Little did they know, an arduous journey lay ahead, one that would change their lives forever. While travelling by horse for what seemed like weeks, Aevah had often felt disoriented as she tried to piece together fragments of conversation exchanged between her grandfather and his dear friend, Sean.

The knowledge that they were being pursued kept her on edge throughout the journey, no matter how much they tried to put her and Jacob at ease. She still remembered those times when they had almost been apprehended. The terror had gripped her heart, leaving her paralysed with fear at the thought of being taken away.

The fear of what lay ahead had been just as frightening. Anxiety consumed her thoughts as she wondered what awaited them. *Where were they going? Where were her parents?* It hadn't been until they reached the quaint little cottage of Middlebeck Farm that she managed to calm her nerves. Slightly. Her heart broke when her grandfather finally explained what had happened and why they had to leave.

It was one thing to imagine the possibilities but hearing them spoken aloud made everything painfully real. Aevah could no longer pretend that life would return to normal. Instead, she had to confront the harsh reality. The grim truth was that her father had been killed by his own sister while her mother was imprisoned and locked away.

She had known then that she would never return to the home she remembered. No, the day she did would be a dark one indeed. Nothing would be the same when she walked through those familiar hallways.

But she vowed that her old home would be hers again. She promised herself that she would go back and reclaim it from her aunt. Someday, they would all return and live as happily as they could in the place that once belonged to them.

Her grandfather had done his best to turn this dwelling into a home – to make it welcoming – a place where they could grow up and simply be children. In the beginning, it was exactly what she and her twin brother, Jacob, needed. Two small, frightened children. That's what they had been at first. Despite her grandfather's constant reassurances, it had taken them a long time to feel safe enough to venture beyond the cottage's boundaries.

Now, Aevah yearned for more than the safety of this place. She ached to leave, to explore the unseen world, to meet her people, and to discover lands yet unknown.

She longed to return to the castle, to the familiar hallways and gardens where she used to play. To walk the well-trodden paths and visit the friends she had once known. It would never be the same without her parents, but she still yearned to see those places again.

She missed her father's bear-like hug – the way he had enveloped her in warmth and safety, the scent of wood and leather clinging to him as he held her close, refusing to let go until she wriggled free.

Her mother, as far as she knew, was alive but in hiding, or so her grandfather always said. Aevah clung to the hope that this was true and longed for the day she could embrace her again. To breathe in the floral scent of her favourite perfume and sit together, brushing each other's hair before the day began.

Holding onto these memories kept her going, especially those of her father. She cherished the few recollections she had of him, wishing they had been given more time together. The life they could have had was taken from her. He would never meet the person she would grow to become, never teach her the lessons he was meant to, nor share the adventures they could have had. All of it was lost to them both because of one.

She still held onto hope that she would one day be reunited with her mother, that they could return home and begin anew, as best they could, as a family once more. Yet deep down, she knew that even if she found her, things would never be the same. That fateful night had upended their lives in ways they could never have imagined.

Over the years, their grandfather had explained to them the lore of their land – the secrets of the four crystal shards, the divine spirit, and the power deep within themselves. When they were younger, these stories had felt like nothing more than fanciful tales. But now, it turns out everything they had been told was real, and the very existence of the people of the country was about to be put in jeopardy.

The power of the shards was being sought after, and in the wrong hands, they could bring destruction to the land and its inhabitants. It was up to her and Jacob, as the true heirs, to find and reclaim them before anyone else could – especially before their aunt.

As much as she felt ready to move on, the thought of leaving their haven was daunting. The idea of retrieving the crystal shards seemed almost impossible. But this was what their grandfather had been preparing them for all along. They had to take their kingdom back, or there might be no realm left to save if their Aunt Elinor succeeded with her plans.

From what they had been told, some of the Lords of the land also sought control for themselves, wanting the shards to claim the crown and rule. Yet the power of the shards carried a darkness, and anyone with a corrupt heart would inevitably fall victim to its whims. Their aunt, not long after taking the throne, had nearly succumbed to that darkness herself, killing many innocents in the process. It was only with the help of the priestesses that she overcame the hold of the shadows.

If any of the shards bonded to a person driven by greed, the consequences could be catastrophic. For now, the shards remained safe, hidden by a charm cast long ago. They couldn't be found without being told by the person who held the charm's link. Grandfather was the current holder, but he had warned them that the magic was close to breaking. The charm needed to be renewed, but no one alive today knew the original enchantment to perform it once more. Once the charm broke, the remaining shards would become easy to detect – for anyone with access to the power.

With her aunt's control of the power, she would easily locate the remaining three shards. The secret notes written long ago, detailing their hiding places, would no longer be necessary. Their only hope was to begin their own hunt now and retrieve the shards before she could.

Over the years, their grandfather had shown them the maps and riddles tied to the hidden crystal shards. Yet, no matter how hard they studied, the exact locations eluded them. Even their grandfather couldn't say where they were. He had never been told. The map was ancient – so old that many of the places marked on it no longer existed. At best, it provided hints of where to begin. The rest would depend on their ability to uncover the hiding spots themselves.

Aevah recognised it was time to leave. However, a small part of her hesitated – a part filled with fear. She was terrified of the unknown, of not knowing what to do, what to expect, or whom to trust. But she knew she wouldn't face it alone. She had Jacob. Together, they could confront anything.

They were sixteen now, having celebrated their name day only a few days earlier. It was now or never. Things would only get worse if they stayed hidden away.

With confidence and determination etched on her face, Aevah set out to find Jacob and her grandfather. She needed to tell them it was time to leave before her courage faltered and she delayed their departure. She hoped Jacob felt the same, so they could begin this journey of theirs, wherever it might take them.

She found both outside, tending to the animals. As she approached, they stopped what they were doing and turned to look at her. Serious expressions marked their faces, as though they already knew what she was about to say.

"It's time," she said.

Her grandfather stepped towards her, looking grave but calm. "Are you sure?"

"Yes."

"Then let's prepare to leave."

Beside him, Jacob nodded in agreement. He, too, was ready, though his anxiety was evident. The telltale sign of fear was the rhythmic tapping of his fingers, a nervous tic that he couldn't suppress. Many times, he had drummed his fingers on a table or his own body, trying to quiet his nerves. Even when his face appeared calm, his restless movements always revealed his true emotions. Right now, the fingertips of his left hand were strumming against his leg.

With the decision made, their grandfather led them back inside and helped pack what they would need. He offered advice as it came to mind and patiently answered their many questions.

In her room, Aevah rummaged through her belongings, sorting clothes and daily essentials she thought she might need. By the time she finished, her rucksack was bulging. Anxiety coursed through her as she moved like a whirlwind, her thoughts racing with fear that she had forgotten something important.

Forcing her rucksack closed, Aevah headed downstairs. Their grandfather bombarded them with even more information until their minds were abuzz. Still, they were as ready as they could be to begin their journey.

As Aevah stood at the threshold of the charm surrounding the cottage, everything suddenly became very real. Packing to leave and actually leaving were two entirely different feelings.

Saying goodbye to her grandfather, the man who had raised them for the past eight years, pulled at her heart.

A part of her doubted they could do this. Overwhelmed by emotion, she threw her arms around him and clung to him tightly, tears streaming down her face. He held her just as firmly, his own tears falling silently. Before either of them could let go, Jacob joined them, and the three of them shared a heartfelt embrace.

Eventually, their grandfather pulled away and offered what Aevah was sure were pearls of wisdom, though her mind barely registered his words. What she heard was probably the most important thing to her at that moment, and that he loved them both and believed in them.

With a gentle nudge, he directed them to their horses, encouraging them to mount. Aevah climbed onto her horse, giving him a final wave before setting off down the road with Jacob at her side. As they rode away, she cast a last glance over her shoulder, watching her grandfather riding off into the distance. Her shoulders slumped as the realisation settled in – this might be the last time she would see him for a long time.

The weight of their task pressed down on her, but she took a deep breath, straightened her posture, and steeled herself. She had to be strong, for Jacob and for herself.

As they rode, they gradually realised they were unconsciously heading towards Sleights. Though Aevah would love to go there, she knew that without their grandfather's help to change their appearance, the villagers would not recognise them.

Neither of them wanted to return as strangers to people they had known most of their lives. Reluctantly, Aevah suggested they stop and figure out exactly where they should go. Veering slightly into the woods and away from the dirt road, they dismounted. She pulled out the map, and the two of them looked at it carefully. After a few moments, Jacob pointed to Burford. It wasn't far from the suspected location of one of the shards, making it a logical place to begin their search.

With their destination decided, they mounted their horses once more and set off along the track, the first leg of their journey stretching out before them.

***

Hearing Aevah's words sent a jolt of panic through Jacob's body. He had known this day was coming, but the finality in her voice shattered any illusions he had been clinging to. This was the end of the childhood he knew and the beginning of something unknown – a new chapter he wasn't sure he was ready to face. Still, he masked his unease, putting on a brave face, and followed her lead as they raced upstairs to pack.

In his bedroom, Jacob scoured his belongings, his heart pounding and his mind racing with scattered thoughts. The reality of their departure loomed, and he moved in frantic circles, unsure of what to pack. Grabbing a few fresh clothes, he hurried to their shared bathroom for toiletries, shoving them hastily into his bag. After layering himself in extra clothing and pulling on his cloak, he searched for his bedroll, certain it was somewhere nearby.

He tossed whatever else he could find into his rucksack, though his movements felt aimless. This wasn't a typical overnight trip to the village; it was something far greater. A journey unlike any other – a quest to save their home, protect their people, and reunite their family once more. *But what does one pack for a life-altering adventure filled with uncertainties?*

When his rucksack was finally full, Jacob paused for a moment, taking in the room that had been his sanctuary for the past eight years. Standing at the threshold of his childhood, he felt the weight of what he was leaving behind. With a heavy sigh, he closed the door, knowing in his heart it was likely the last time he would set foot in the cottage he called home.

His steps felt heavier as he trudged outside and saddled up his own horse as Aevah and their grandfather did the same. He watched as his grandfather meticulously double-checked their horses, adding extra supplies and handing each of them a bag of gold.

They walked silently to the edge of the magical barrier, where the air seemed thick with tension, anticipation, and unspoken goodbyes. The three of them stood still, unwilling to say the words that would sever the last ties of comfort.

It was Aevah who broke first, throwing her arms around their grandfather in a fierce embrace. Jacob, not wishing to miss that moment, joined them. The three clung to one another, none of them wanting to let go.

Their grandfather was the one to pull away first. His glimmering eyes spoke volumes, but his voice remained steady as he addressed them both.

"Goodbye, my little ones. We will meet again. You are stronger than you realise, and you can do this. Stick together and there's nothing you can't overcome. Remember everything I have told you."

Jacob watched as his grandfather climbed onto his horse, his words sinking in. Out of the corner of his eye, he saw Aevah mounting her horse, and he quickly followed suit, swinging himself into the saddle. With a final wave and goodbye, they parted ways – Jacob and Aevah heading in one direction, while their grandfather rode off in another.

As they rode, Jacob's heart ached, the distance between them and their grandfather growing with each passing moment. He couldn't help but wonder when, or if, they would ever see him again. The thought clung to him as they travelled down the familiar path.

It wasn't long before it dawned on them that they were subconsciously riding towards Sleights. Aevah seemed to notice it at the same time, and they exchanged a glance. As much as he wanted to visit the village, he knew it was impossible. Without their grandfather's help to change their appearance, the villagers wouldn't recognise them.

The thought of returning as strangers to people they had known most of their lives sent a pang through his chest. They veered off the road, moving slightly into the woods, where they dismounted. Aevah pulled out the map and spread it between them to look at.

"Where do we go?" she asked, her eyes searching his for guidance.

Jacob leaned closer and took in the land's layout. He let his thoughts settle as he recalled the advice their grandfather had given them.

"We need to travel to Burford. We should take this road here if we want to avoid Sleights." He traced his finger along the map, pointing out an alternative route. "It's a little further, but not by much. We will get there before dark."

As he looked up, he caught Aevah's expression. She looked just as uncertain as he felt. His chest tightened, but he forced himself to stay calm. This was the first time either of them had ventured beyond the village without their grandfather, and its enormity pressed down on him. Memories of the past, of being pursued and nearly caught, gnawed at his resolve. Still, he reminded himself that the odds of anyone recognising them now were slim. They had both grown and changed in the years since. Their mother alone would know them at a glance.

"Okay," Aevah said, interrupting his thoughts. "Let's go."

Jacob nodded, and they mounted their horses once more. Riding side by side, they silently contemplated what lay ahead. The familiar landscapes of their childhood gradually gave way to the unknown, the road stretching out before them like a challenge they couldn't refuse.

Neither of them knew what awaited them, but they were determined to succeed. This journey would test them in ways they couldn't yet imagine, but Jacob clung to the hope that they would emerge stronger. Together, they would face the dangers ahead, driven by the shared dream of reuniting their family and protecting their land.

Chapter 2

Saying Goodbye

George's heart pounded in his chest. He didn't want to say farewell, but he had no choice. He had protected his grandchildren for as long as he could, and now it was their turn to play their part while he fulfilled his own. As they sat atop their horses, watching him with weary eyes, he could sense the twins' reluctance to leave. The air between them was heavy with unspoken words.

George hesitated, knowing he needed to make the first move. At last, he managed to utter a quiet goodbye, his voice quivering with sadness. Without waiting for a response, he turned away and rode on. Yet, after only a short distance, the urge to see them one last time overwhelmed him. Reining his horse, Dusty, to a halt, he turned in his saddle and watched until they disappeared from view.

His chest tightened as he sat there, a nervous wreck. He was leaving them to fend for themselves, but he reminded himself that he had done everything possible to prepare them. He had faith in their abilities. They were ready. They had to be.

Over the years, he had poured his heart into teaching them all he knew – wisdom about the power, battles, and politics. He had ensured they were well-prepared for the challenges of ruling, along with the practical skills of self-defence, swordsmanship, and archery. If he thought they needed to know something, he made sure they learned it. Between the two of them, they possessed every skill necessary for success.

But George's primary concern had always been their safety. He had shielded them from harm for as long as he could, but now the time had come for them to embark on their journey into the real world. He wasn't abandoning them entirely, though. He had no intention of that. To help them further, he needed to find their mother and complete his own task.

With a deep breath, George gave Dusty a gentle nudge, urging him into a canter. The road ahead was long, and Adlington was still miles away. He hadn't visited Cecilia, the twins' mother and his daughter, in far too many years. The thought of facing her made his stomach churn. He had kept them safe, but now he had sent them off on their own. He bore the brunt of the blame for their absence from her life. Still, the visit was overdue, and he knew he had to face whatever welcome – or reproach – awaited him.

When he disappeared, he hadn't shared his whereabouts with anyone but Sean, fearing the consequences for anyone who knew where to find him. His caution had been justified. Even from his distant refuge, rumours reached him about the horrors Elinor inflicted on those innocent people – his friends – those she suspected of aiding him. He was glad he had told no one else.

He had often planned to send word or even risk a visit to Cecilia with the children once the dust had settled. But every time, fear held him back. He couldn't risk his grandchildren's lives like that. Not for any reason.

So, he bided his time, dedicating himself to teaching and training them for the moment. And that moment had finally come. With the best preparation he could give them, his grandchildren set out on their own mission: to secure the crystal shards. Meanwhile, George focused on thwarting Elinor's plans and convincing Cecilia to gather an army of rebels. If Elinor were defeated, Aevah and Jacob would be safe. They could return home with the united shards, and one of them could take their rightful place on the throne.

No matter what, the crystal had to be reunited. George was the last link, keeping the shards hidden. Someday, he knew he would die, and when he did, the protective charm would be gone. The shards would then light up like beacons to anyone with a trace of power in their veins. If Elinor used the shard already in her possession to search the land, it would guide her to the others with ease. Shards sought shards, drawn to reunite as one.

If the crystal were restored to its rightful place in the tower and protected by those pure of heart, there might still be hope to save the country from greed and destruction. George had instilled this knowledge in his grandchildren, and now the responsibility rested on them. While they hunted down the shards, he would devise a plan to destroy Elinor once and for all.

No matter what the cost, he was determined to stop her before she could discover his grandchildren's whereabouts or their mission. He would go to any lengths to keep them safe, even if it meant sacrificing his own life.

As that thought settled in his mind, George reined in Dusty, halting abruptly. An idea struck him, sharp and clear. A wide grin spread across his face. He patted Dusty's neck and spurred him into a gallop, heading back to the cottage he had just left.

Once there, George dismounted and set to work, creating a deliberate message meant for Elinor, should she ever find the place. When he was satisfied with his efforts, he remounted his horse and continued his journey towards Adlington, towards Cecilia, and towards the demise of the woman who dared to call herself queen.

***

Adlington had been Cecilia's sanctuary for the past eight years, a place that offered safety and a fresh start after her harrowing escape. The torment she endured in the castle still haunted her, but she had clung to the hope that reaching the temple of the priestesses would solve all her problems.

It hadn't. While she was safe, she was no closer to discovering the whereabouts of her father or her children. Her father, ever cautious, had shared his location with no one. Thanks to the kindness of the priestesses, Cecilia had been directed to a modest but functional house they owned in Adlington. Yet, in those first few weeks, anxiety consumed her, struggling to devise a way to locate her family.

She had briefly considered reaching out to her uncle, Lord Goodman, but news of his death shattered that possibility. With no other relatives who might know the secluded cottage's location, she was left grasping at fragments of memories. She was certain her father had taken refuge in a quaint little dwelling somewhere, far removed from the rest of the world, but the specifics eluded her.

The last time she had been to the cottage, she had been a child. Those memories, tied to a time when her mother was still alive, were like scattered puzzle pieces. Fleeting glimpses of the place surfaced in her mind, but none offered a clear sense of where it was or what its surroundings looked like.

As months passed and her funds dwindled, Cecilia chose to remain in Adlington. It might have seemed an odd decision, given that Elinor had previously lived there for almost a decade before ascending the throne. But in hindsight, Adlington proved to be the perfect hiding place. Since becoming queen, Elinor had shown no interest in returning to the city. She had all her belongings sent directly to the castle in Carraton, leaving her former manor under the care of Lloyd and Victoria Roberts. Cecilia had very little contact with them over the years. These individuals were used to a life of luxury and opulence, avoiding the less glamorous parts of the city. Instead, they preferred to spend their time in upscale markets, mingling with wealthy socialites who were living the high life.

This distance ensured Cecilia was safe from any unexpected encounters with people from her past. With her dyed jet-black hair, simple clothing, and understated demeanour, she blended seamlessly with the other local women seeking employment. A change of name and a slight alteration to her accent further disguised her, securing her a job as a kitchen hand at a local inn. The skills she had once learned in Carraton now served her well in her humble role.

Cecilia knew that anyone searching for her would never think to look in Adlington. It was the last place they would expect – the lion's den itself. Hiding in plain sight, she had transformed her life into one of anonymity. Though far from easy, her new existence provided her with safety and distance from those who might recognise her. The Queen she had once been gone, buried beneath layers of disguise. Here, she was just another face among the crowds, unremarkable and utterly unrecognisable.

Thanks to her job at the inn, Cecilia often overheard conversations about the affairs of the country. The steady stream of travellers and locals kept her informed of Elinor's latest actions and any developments that might hint at her children's whereabouts. While no news of her children ever surfaced, she found a strange comfort in that silence. It meant they were still hidden, still safe. The gossip she heard was little more than the usual talk of Elinor's questionable decisions and her grip on the kingdom. But there was never any mention of power plays involving the crystal shards. That absence of any news never told Cecilia much about Elinor's goals – whatever plans she had for the shards remained elusive.

Every day without change brought a measure of relief. For now, the delicate balance of her life remained intact. But deep down, Cecilia knew it was only a matter of time before something shifted.

"That's as clean as this place's gon' be. Off with ya, lass, and call it a night," Beth said, her voice warm and tinged with the local dialect. The stout, middle-aged woman had a cheerful smile, her flour-dusted hands still busy wiping away remnants of the day. Her frizzy yellow hair was as untamed as her humour, which Cecilia had grown to appreciate over the years.

Cecilia folded her cleaning cloth and hung up her apron. "Twas a busy one for sure, Beth. Let's hope it'll be quieter on the morrow."

"Ha! We can hope, lass. We can hope. Now, on with ya, and don't forget that ham. It needs eatin'."

"Aye, I've got it. Till the morrow."

With a nod to Beth, Cecilia picked up her basket, tucked the leftover ham inside, and slipped out the back entrance of the inn. The cobbled streets of Adlington greeted her with the cool, crisp air of early evening. Behind her, the inn had come alive with the sounds of clinking tankards and boisterous laughter as travellers and locals settled in for a night of drinking. Cecilia had learned through experience that the lively tavern was best avoided once the drinks started flowing.

She stuck to the busy, well-lit streets as she made her way home, keeping a safe distance from the drunkards who spilt into the thoroughfares. Her neighbourhood was a quiet one, and she always felt a sense of security walking through it. While it was wise to avoid the bars and shadowy alleys after dark, this part of Adlington remained peaceful during the day and tolerable at night.

Summer breathed new life into the area. Workers toiled under the sun in the fields, weeding and harvesting the season's first crops. As Cecilia turned onto the next street, she found herself in a charming lane lined with two-story houses on either side, with a quaint cobblestone road running between them. She made a left turn and followed the bumpy path until she arrived at a grey stone house featuring a slate roof and a striking red wooden door, a common sight among the homes in this area.

Numerous homes like hers were scattered across the county – safe havens maintained by the priestesses for those in need. Whether sheltering their own on the move or providing refuge to individuals facing misfortune, these houses offered temporary sanctuary. Yet, no one typically stayed as long as Cecilia had. The locals, however, were blissfully unaware of the true ownership of the property. To them, she was just another person living on the street, unremarkable and unassuming.

Cecilia reached the red wooden door and set her basket on the ground. Fishing the key from her pocket, she prepared for her nightly battle with the stubborn lock. No matter what she tried, the door was always a challenge. With one hand, she twisted the key as far as it would turn, and with the other, she gripped the doorknob tightly. The mechanism finally gave a loud, reluctant *click*. Bracing herself, Cecilia threw her shoulder into the doorframe, forcing it open with a jolt. As always, she stumbled forward as the door gave way.

Steadying herself, she brushed off her dress with practised ease, pocketed the key, and retrieved her basket once more. Once inside, she closed the door behind her and walked through the modest living area into the equally small kitchen. The house was cosy, with just enough space to meet her needs.

In the kitchen, Cecilia placed her basket on the wooden table with four chairs. Carefully, she took out the pins from her hair, letting her fingers glide through the strands as her locks cascaded free. Tilting her head to one side, she savoured the sensation, the tension in her scalp easing at last.

Beth's words about the ham echoed in her mind, prompting her to begin slicing it for her evening meal. The rhythmic motion of the knife against the cutting board felt almost meditative as she moved on to the carrots and potatoes. Roughly chopping the vegetables, Cecilia worked quickly, lost in her thoughts. She turned to place the prepared vegetables in the oven – then froze, her heart leaping as her eyes landed on the tall man approaching her.

"Need a hand?"

"Adrian!" Her voice was sharp with surprise, though a smile quickly followed. "You startled me. I didn't realise you were home."

Without missing a beat, she slid the tray of vegetables into the oven and closed the door. Turning to face him, she studied him for a moment, still marvelling at the twists of fate that had brought him into her life. If someone had asked her eight years ago to picture her future, the man standing before her wouldn't have even crossed her mind. Yet here he was.

Her life had taken such an unexpected turn that the man who had once been her sworn enemy was now her greatest ally – and someone she dared to call a friend.

When she had escaped the castle, it had been Adrian who let her go, despite the risk to himself. He could have so easily returned her to Elinor and the torment that awaited, but he hadn't. That choice had changed everything.

Thinking back, Cecilia recalled that day with a clarity that still sent chills down her spine.

Months had passed since she had arrived in Adlington, and life had settled into a rhythm. The inn was bustling as usual, filled with the chatter of patrons and the clatter of dishes. Amidst the chaos, Cecilia barely noticed the cloaked stranger sitting alone, nursing a tankard of ale. With his head covered and his ragged brown cloak blending into the background, he was easy to overlook.

It wasn't until he ordered food that her world tilted. She approached his table, carrying a steaming bowl of stew, and placed it before him. When he lowered his hood, her breath caught in her throat. Had she not already set the bowl down, she was certain she would have dropped it. His amber eyes, sombre and piercing, locked onto hers, and every painful memory she had worked so hard to suppress came rushing back.

"I need to speak with you," he muttered before turning his attention to the food.

All Cecilia could manage was a stiff nod before retreating to the kitchen, her mind racing. Fear wrapped itself around her like a shroud, tightening with every passing moment. *What could she do? There was no one to confide in, no one who would understand. She was not who her fellow workers thought she was.*

Her hands shook as she moved aimlessly around the kitchen. Her thoughts were a chaotic swirl. She didn't even realise what she was doing until she caught herself about to place fresh bread into a sink full of water. Beth's sharp voice jolted her back to the present.

"Do ye be sick, lass? Ye don' look yersel'," Beth said, pressing a flour-dusted palm to Cecilia's forehead.

Seeing no other way out, Cecilia feigned illness. Within minutes, she found herself being escorted home by Faye, another kitchen hand. When they reached her house, Faye handed her a small pouch of medicine Beth had insisted on and reminded her to rest. Once alone, Cecilia's fear erupted into frantic action. She checked and rechecked every door and window, locking each one tightly. Only when the house was secured did she blow out the candles, leaving herself in darkness.

She curled up in the corner of the living room, her knees pulled to her chest, rocking back and forth as her mind buzzed with questions. *If Adrian had found her, who else knew where she was? Had she been foolish to think she was safe all these years?*

Cecilia felt paralysed with fear at the thought of returning to work. *She knew she could only pretend to be sick for so long, and what if Adrian already knew where she lived?* Since he was aware of her workplace, it was reasonable to assume he also knew where she was living as well.

Her heart pounded, and her stomach churned with dread. Suddenly, the sound of the door rattling shattered the silence. She froze, her breath caught in her throat, and her palms grew clammy. The rattling grew louder. Each sound was a thunderous blow to her already frayed nerves.

When the door burst open with a bang, Cecilia jumped to her feet. Terror etched into her wide eyes. She grabbed the nearest object – a heavy candlestick – and held it above her head. Her knuckles turned white from the strength of her grip. She stood there trembling, waiting for Adrian to find her.

As light footsteps echoed on the hardwood floor, Cecilia remained frozen in place, prepared to defend herself. She even channelled the power, as feeble as her own strength was, hoping for anything to give her any advantage against him.

"Cecilia? I know you are home. I'm not here to hurt you. I just want to talk."

Adrian's voice cut through the tension, calm but firm. Her breath came in shallow gasps as she listened to his soft footsteps drawing closer. When his shadow appeared in the doorway, she swung the candlestick, catching him across the shoulder. He stumbled but quickly grabbed her arm before she could strike again.

"I deserved that," Adrian said, releasing her and raising his hands in surrender. "Please, hear me out. I swear, if you want me gone after this, I'll leave, and you will never see me again."

"After everything, do you really think I would give you an ounce of my time willingly?" Cecilia snarled at him, pointing the candlestick directly at him.

"Please, just one conversation," he pleaded.

Cecilia's glare burned into him, her heart pounding as memories of the past warred with the desperation in his eyes. For a moment, her resolve wavered. Slowly, she lowered the candlestick, though her grip remained strong.

"Fine," she said, her voice still tinged with suspicion. "You have five minutes. Make it count."

Fortunately for her, he wasn't there as a villain sent to retrieve her. Instead, he was like her – a traitor to the crown. He recounted what had happened and how he had escaped after witnessing the devastation left by Elinor, with all the innocents killed. He wanted no part of it and couldn't understand how blind he had been to the truth. Even with his confession, it took considerable effort for him to convince her to believe him. She had heard rumours of his betrayal of Elinor but hadn't dared to trust them. He was her only confidant all those years.

After countless hours of discussion and weeks of mistrust on her part, she finally believed his story to be true, and a truce was formed between them. It felt good to have someone with whom she could talk to and be her authentic self with, even though there were many others she would have preferred to be with. After learning everything that had happened since her escape, even Cecilia struggled to comprehend the depths to which Elinor had sunk. While she understood the effects of the power, she wasn't entirely surprised. Instead, she felt a deep sadness over the loss of so many innocents. She mourned both her family and friends, particularly Mistress Katelyn, who had always been a true friend to her. Then there was dear Sean and Anita – both wonderful people who had deserved so much better. Words couldn't express the anguish she had felt at their passing.

Over time, she and Adrian had grown closer as they settled into life together in Adlington. They continued to seek out her father and children while trying to find a way to stop Elinor. Today, their bond involves being more than friends. He had come to hold a special place in her heart. For a long time, she had denied her feelings for him, but eventually, she realised that James would have wanted her to find happiness – even if the person she had chosen wasn't someone he might have imagined.

In the present, Cecilia moved towards Adrian, wrapping her arms around his waist and pressing a gentle kiss on his lips. He returned it with a warmth that made her heart flutter. Pulling away, she smiled softly, her eyes sparkling.

"You can get the fire started. A chill has set in."

Adrian nodded, smiling back, and headed to the living area. Soon, the warmth of the fire filled the house, and they sat together for dinner, a quiet moment of peace between them.

Chapter 3

Deceit in the Realm

No matter how hard she tried, Elinor couldn't shake the feeling that her entire world was on the verge of being turned upside down. The gossip about the twins and their survival was swirling more fervently than ever, no doubt because their sixteenth name day had just passed. She was no fool and still heard the whispers of those select few who clung to the hope of their return.

Ordinarily, such rumours rolled off her like water off a duck's back. The throne was hers, and no one had seen the twins since the day she took the crown. But now, a part of her couldn't ignore the unease gnawing at her. There was an intuitive sense that something monumental was imminent, an event poised to change the course of everything. She could only hope that whatever it was would work in her favour and not theirs. Assuming, of course, that they were even alive. Though she often tried to convince herself they were no longer a threat, deep down, she knew better.

And then there was George. If he decided to act on the events of that night, she knew she was woefully unprepared to stop him. The thought of being defenceless made her feel vulnerable in a way she had never experienced before. Her guards were loyal, but their presence couldn't compare to the raw, electrifying power she once wielded – the darkness that had flowed through her veins.

She still had some of that strength, yes, but it was nothing compared to what she had possessed for that short time. Pure, unbridled magic at her command had made her the most powerful being in the land. She had been unstoppable. Whatever she willed had come to pass.

Now, with only a fraction of that power remaining, she could put on a convincing show to keep others in line, but the days of wielding utter destruction were gone. For that, she would forever resent the high priestess and her sanctimonious circle of priestesses. They had stripped her of her magic, leaving her diminished. Unfortunately, with their elevated status and untouchable temples in their sacred lands, they were beyond her reach and control.

Since the day they robbed her of her powers, she and the priestesses had crossed paths only during the annual bonding ceremony. Even that once-a-year encounter was one too many, in her opinion and attended solely out of duty. Yet, as queen, she maintained the façade of respect, adhering to protocol as was expected of her.

Unbeknownst to the priestesses, Elinor was still secretly working to locate the crystal shards. After discovering Cecilia had swapped the real shard in the castle for a fake, her first priority had been to recover it. To her surprise, the task had been easier than expected. Cecilia's connection to the power was pitiful, even by Elinor's current diminished standards, and within days, she had traced the shard to a poorly hidden hole beneath a large tree.

After retrieving it, Elinor returned the shard to the tower and added her own wards of protection. If anyone other than herself tried to remove it, she would know. She wouldn't make the same mistake twice. Nearly losing everything once had been enough. It was through sheer determination, the support of her husband Bradley, and – though she hated to admit it – the intervention of Lord Stone that she had held onto her throne and her life.

In the years that followed, the fear of betrayal never left her. She lived as though walking on eggshells, always bracing for something, or someone, to turn against her. The possibility of being stripped of her remaining power, or worse, losing her kingdom, loomed over her like a shadow.

Lord Stone, in particular, remained a source of unease. On that fateful night, he had made it clear she owed him, and while he appeared content with his quiet life in recent years, rarely venturing beyond his home, Elinor never let her guard down. The moment she did, she knew he would seize any opportunity to strike.

Then there was Adrian. The traitor. He had fled the castle that same night, confirming her suspicions that he had been in contact with the high priestess, and brought them to her home to strip her of everything. His disappearance served as a constant reminder that no one could be trusted. Despite her best efforts, Adrian remained elusive. Countless men had been dragged before her, claiming to have captured him, but it was always a mistake.

Between Adrian and George, she felt plagued by thorns buried beneath her skin, each attempt to remove them only driving them deeper. She needed to find them both. Only then would the persistent annoyance be eradicated, which involved first finding the crystal shards. These shards would restore her power and make sure no one could control her. However, it also required locating and eliminating George – a task that was slowly nearing its conclusion.

For now, she bided her time, listening carefully to the whispers circulating through the court. Every rumour, every scrap of information, was examined for hints of a plot against her or news that George was on the move. She couldn't escape the certainty that he would come for her eventually, and she had a feeling it would be soon. Her guards remained vigilant, ever watchful for that inevitable day. A day for which she was ready.

Until then, Elinor governed the kingdom with the unwavering support of her husband, Bradley. His contributions were invaluable in maintaining order in Ethos and securing the allegiance of the other lords. Trust was a rare commodity in her life, but Bradley had proven time and time again to be one of the few she could rely on completely. In the aftermath of that night, he had stood by her, picking up the pieces and bolstering her authority. His calm reassurances and deft disputes of the high priestess's claims helped steady her subjects' loyalty.

Marrying Bradley had been the wisest decision she had ever made. That evening was etched in her memory. The day had passed quickly, yet certain moments distinctly stood out.

She remembered standing before the grand mirror, her breath catching as she took in her reflection. Her golden gown flowed like liquid sunlight, its intricate embroidery capturing the light in a dazzling display. The tiara on her head sparkled delicately, accentuating her glowing skin and regal presence. She truly felt like a queen – graceful, powerful, and beautiful.

As she walked to the altar, her heart pounded with a mix of excitement and anticipation. Bradley waited for her, resplendent in a golden suit that perfectly complemented her gown. His expression, filled with pride and unwavering love, never faltered as their eyes locked.

When they exchanged their vows, the moment became uniquely theirs. Eschewing tradition, they had written their own, turning what could have been a formality into something deeply personal and heartfelt. The kiss that followed sealed their promises, binding them together as partners in life and in rule.

The celebration that evening was one of pure joy. Laughter, music, and the clinking of glasses filled the air. Guests feasted on sumptuous dishes, drank wine freely, and danced abundantly. The festivities reached their pinnacle with their first private moment as husband and wife – a tender, intimate beginning of their shared journey. Elinor often thought back to that day, knowing there had been no better one since.

In the years that followed, their marriage was a strong partnership. Bradley occasionally left to sail the seas and tend to his family's business, but he spent most of his time by her side, helping her rule the kingdom. Together, they made an exceptional team, their ideals aligning seamlessly as they ruled with purpose and unity.

Their only point of contention was the topic of children. Bradley, eager to start a family, often broached the subject, but Elinor was in no rush. She understood the necessity of an heir to secure their lineage but felt no urgency. As the one who wielded the power, she had the luxury of time – more so than Bradley. Unlike him, she would age more slowly and have a bit more time on her side. After lengthy discussions, he agreed to wait, which delighted her.

Together, they spent the past few years shaping Ethos into something extraordinary. Their combined efforts forged a kingdom that reflected their vision, making them a force to be reckoned with in the realm.

"Your Majesty."

Elinor turned towards the doorway to find Julian standing there. He bowed deeply, a gesture of respect that reflected his unwavering loyalty. Rising from the bow, he stood at attention, waiting to be addressed.

Julian was one of the few who had stood by her side when she had nearly lost everything at the start of her reign. His allegiance wasn't just to the crown but to Elinor herself – a bond forged through shared hardships and a deep mutual respect. Professional to a fault, his dedication was evident in every task he undertook, no matter how challenging or insignificant.

"Ah, Julian. To what do I owe the pleasure of your presence this evening?" Elinor gestured towards the chair opposite her by the window.

He moved forward and sat, though his posture remained stiff as if he felt uncomfortable in the plush velvet chair. Elinor studied him closely, waiting for him to speak. When he stayed silent, she gave him a small nod, urging him to share his news.

"Your Majesty, it has come to my attention that someone is working to sabotage you."

"Is that so?" Elinor's relaxed posture stiffened, her back straightening as her sharp gaze locked onto his.

"Tell me, what makes you think that?"

"Those recent ships of your husband's, the ones carrying trade materials. I have reason to believe they weren't lost at sea because of storms."

Julian's words made Elinor tense, her hands curling into fists. "Why do you suspect this?" she asked, her voice clipped.

"Bradley's vessels have not returned, yet the market is still abundant with goods matching those supposedly lost at the bottom of the ocean. I suspect someone has seized the ships, stolen the cargo, and destroyed the vessels to cover their tracks."

"Do you have any suspects?" Elinor's tone turned icy.

"I have ideas," Julian replied, meeting her gaze steadily. "But I need more time to investigate before I can be sure."

Elinor stood and instinctively clenched her hands tightly at her sides as she turned to the window. Her mind raced. *Who would dare to betray her like this?* It had to be one of the lords. Bishop came to mind – his obsession with wealth made him an obvious contender. Then, there was Lord Stone, a man with more than enough motive to undermine her at every turn. Whoever was responsible, their treachery would not go unpunished.

She turned back to Julian, her expression hard with determination. "Find out who is responsible for this. Use whatever resources you need. I want to know who dares to steal from us."

Julian rose, bowing once more. "As you wish, Your Majesty."

With that, he left, leaving Elinor alone with her thoughts. Whoever was behind this would pay with their life. All other concerns faded from Elinor's mind as she summoned a guard to find Bradley. He needed to know what was happening. It was his business being targeted, after all.

It wasn't long before he arrived, his face tense with concern as he moved swiftly towards her.

"What has happened? The guard said it was urgent."

"It is," Elinor replied, gesturing for him to sit. "We need to talk."

She relayed Julian's report, her tone steady but her eyes focused. Bradley listened intently, and as the truth of the situation sank in – that his cargo was reaching Ethos without his ships or men – his shoulders slumped. For a moment, he simply sat there, his head in his hands.

Elinor waited silently, allowing him the time to process the news. She understood this was more than a financial blow to him.

Bradley was a man of the sea, someone who thrived on the open waters despite the risks. He loved sailing, accepting its perils as part of its allure. The sea was lawless, its storms indiscriminate, claiming lives and ships alike without care. Such losses were mourned but understood – they were acts of nature, not malice.

This, however, was different. The idea of pirates or bandits seizing his ships, stealing the cargo, and sinking the vessels along with their crews violated everything he stood for. His men hadn't died battling the mistress of the seas; they had perished for another's greed, abandoned to the ocean's depths.

When he finally looked up, his hands clasped together, his eyes burned with determination. "I need to know who did this."

"Julian is already working on it," Elinor assured him. "Seek him out and work with him. I'll do what I can on my end."

She placed her hands over his, grounding him for a brief moment. Bradley nodded, his resolve clear, before standing and leaving. No doubt, he was heading to find Julian and begin his own investigation.

As for Elinor, this required a more calculated approach. It was time to summon the lords for a meeting, though she knew they wouldn't come willingly under suspicion. No, it would need to be under the guise of an enticing event – something none of them could refuse.

A tourney.

The thought brought a wicked smile to her lips. No lord would decline an opportunity to showcase their court's strengths before their peers, particularly with a generous monetary prize awaiting the victor. It would be the perfect pretence to gather them all in one place while she worked to uncover who among them was responsible.

Her mind raced with the details. The event needed to happen sooner rather than later, and preparations had to begin immediately. Five weeks would suffice, but only if the invitations went out today. Elinor's smile deepened as her plan solidified.

No one would dare decline, and soon, she would have them all right where she wanted them.

With a plan firmly in mind, Elinor made her way to the study, having summoned a scribe to meet her there. Settling into a comfortable chair near the grand desk, she awaited their arrival, her thoughts racing with the details of the tourney.

When the scribe arrived, she greeted him with a warm yet purposeful tone. "Soren, thank you for coming so promptly. I have a marvellous idea to host a tourney. I would like you to compose an announcement for me and send it to the cities and lords alike."

Soren bowed respectfully. "What a wonderful plan, Your Majesty. It would be my honour to assist." He seated himself at the desk, arranging his parchment and quill with precision.

Elinor rose from her chair, her hands clasped behind her back as she paced the room. "We must ensure the event is well-attended," she began. "Write this: 'By the queen's decree, a grand tournament shall be held…"

Soren nodded as he began to transcribe her words. "Shall I include details about the jousting and archery competitions, Your Majesty?"

"Yes, and mention the lavish feast that will follow, as well as the monetary prizes," she replied. "We want to make this an event they cannot afford to miss."

Soren worked diligently, capturing every nuance of her instructions. When he finished, Elinor reviewed the document, her sharp gaze scanning each line. Satisfied, she dismissed him with instructions to send the announcement to the local messengers and arrange for carrier pigeons to deliver it to distant cities and lords across the kingdom. In each city, heralds would proclaim the news to the people, ensuring no corner of the realm remained unaware.

With the tourney soon to be announced, Elinor turned her attention to the meticulous planning required. For this monumental task, she summoned Lord Roland, the trusted seneschal renowned for organising grand events, and Lady Chloe, her loyal lady-in-waiting. Roland's expertise in orchestrating gatherings of state – including her wedding – had proven invaluable, while Chloe's keen eye for detail and connections within the community made her indispensable and more than capable of the role.

Julian would have been her choice for overseeing logistics, but his focus was needed elsewhere – on the investigation into the missing ships and identifying those responsible. The tourney itself was a clever ploy to gather her suspects in one place, where she could unmask the traitor and exact justice.

Elinor waited in the study, making notes about her vision for the event when Chloe arrived.

"Ah, Chloe, come in and take a seat," Elinor said, gesturing to a chair.

Moments later, Lord Roland appeared, his expression calm and professional. Elinor greeted him warmly as a maid entered, serving tea and a plate of delicately arranged cakes.

"Thank you both for coming," Elinor began, her tone resolute. "I have summoned you to discuss the organisation of a grand tourney."

Roland inclined his head. "Your Majesty, we must ensure this tourney is the most splendid event the kingdom has ever witnessed."

"Precisely," Elinor agreed. "I trust your expertise, Lord Roland, to bring that vision to life."

She turned to Chloe, whose eyes gleamed with excitement. "Chloe, I'll need you to coordinate with the local craftsmen and merchants. We'll require market stalls and repair stations for the knights' armour and weapons. Your attention to detail and your network will be critical to his effort."

Chloe leaned forward, her enthusiasm palpable. "I shall begin at once, Your Majesty. Everything will be perfect."

"Excellent," Elinor said, smiling at her trusted aides. "Let us make this tourney an unforgettable spectacle."

With clear instructions and unwavering determination, the discussions flowed seamlessly. Plans began to take shape, promising an event that would not only dazzle the kingdom but also serve Elinor's deeper purpose of unmasking those who dared to conspire against her.

Chapter 4

New Guests

Elinor prepared for bed after a busy but productive session planning for the tourney. A knock at the door interrupted her routine. Chloe answered and returned moments later to inform her that Julian had arrived with news. Elinor nodded, requesting a moment as she wrapped a silk dressing gown around herself. With a flick of her wrist, the candles on her dresser flared to life, bathing the darkened room in a warm glow.

At her invitation, Julian entered her chambers, his expression grave.

"Julian, please, take a seat," she said, gesturing to the chair across from her. "From the look on your face, I gather you have bad news for me?"

"Not the best, Your Majesty," he replied, his voice tight. He sat stiffly, gripping the arms of the chair as if to steady himself.

"Speak plainly. What have you discovered?" Elinor leaned back in her chair, attempting an air of calm. Yet her posture betrayed her unease as she awaited his response.

"I traced the names of the ships that sank the king's consort's cargo and identified the pirates involved. However, the culprits have returned to the seas. No one seems to know their current location."

"Well, that's a start," she said curtly, her narrowed eyes revealing her frustration. "Keep at it. Use whatever resources you need. Bradley has an extensive network in the sailing and trading world. Make use of it. I'll have him assign his own team to assist and ensure they share all their findings with you."

"Thank you, Your Majesty."

"I have the utmost faith in you. I suspect Lord Stone is behind this, but I need proof." Rising, she escorted Julian to the door, where they exchanged brief thanks before parting ways. As Julian left, Bradley entered the room.

Elinor quickly relayed what Julian had uncovered.

"I'll make some inquiries and track down those ships," Bradley said. Before she could respond, he disappeared into the night.

Elinor sighed, feeling her weariness envelop her like a heavy cloak. She climbed into bed, pulling the sheets around her and leaning back against the pillows. Sleep eluded her as she tossed and turned, her mind consumed with thoughts of the missing ships and her suspicions of Lord Stone.

Seeking distraction, she reached for the book on her nightstand. She tried to read, but the words blurred as her thoughts raced. She must have skimmed the first few lines a dozen times, yet her mind couldn't focus on the text.

Finally, admitting defeat, she blew out the candles next to her. As she leaned into the pillows, she felt too high up, so she removed the top pillow and let it drop to the floor beside her. Then she looked towards the burning candles on her dresser. With another wave of her hand, she extinguished them.

As she lay in the quiet darkness, her thoughts turned bitter. The power she still possessed made life easier, but it was only a fraction of what she once wielded. The high priestess and her coven had seen to that. One day, they would pay for what they had done.

Shaking her head, Elinor pushed the vengeful thoughts aside. She focused instead on the brighter days she hoped were ahead. Slowly, she drifted into an uneasy sleep, waking only when she felt the warmth of Bradley's body as he returned to her side.

His arms enveloped her, and she reached out, her fingers caressing his arm. His lips pressed firmly atop her head.

"Any news?" she murmured, her words laced with a yawn.

"Not yet," Bradley replied. "I have sent messengers to my trusted allies and given them full authority to act as needed. I also let them know Julian is a loyal ally in this matter, so they'll keep him informed. We're working together on this."

“Then we wait,” Elinor said softly. “The truth will reveal itself soon enough.”

Cocooned in Bradley’s warm embrace, she closed her eyes and surrendered to sleep, her worries momentarily forgotten in the comfort of his presence.

***

As the weeks passed, responses to Elinor’s tourney invitations poured in. Every lord confirmed their attendance, each accompanied by a list of eager participants. The numbers were impressive, a mix of chivalrous knights, lords, and nobles, all vying for glory. Bradley was among them, determined to compete. From the moment the event was announced, he and the cavalry under her command began rigorous training.

Every day, the training yard buzzed with activity as the knights honed their skills. Elinor stood on the balcony now, her sharp gaze fixed on the men below, assessing their archery practice firsthand. Victory was her goal, and she spared no effort to ensure it. The finest blacksmiths in the city had been commissioned to forge armour and weapons of unparalleled quality for her house. Only the best would do.

Her eyes followed the swift movements of the knights as they lined up their bows. The rhythmic twang of bowstrings and the solid *thud* of arrows meeting their targets filled the air. Determination was etched on their faces, and Elinor took silent pride in their precision and focus.

Sir Miller, ever the perfectionist, stood nearby, coaching a younger knight with calm authority. He adjusted the lad's grip and stance with practised ease.

"Keep your elbow higher, Thomas," Sir Miller instructed, his voice steady but firm. "You need to maintain a straight line from your shoulder to the tip of the arrow."

Thomas furrowed his brow, nodding in concentration. "Like this, Sir?"

"Better," Miller replied, stepping back to observe. "Now, focus on your breathing. Inhale as you draw the bow, exhale as you release. Let the breath guide your shot."

Thomas inhaled deeply, pulling the bowstring taut. With renewed determination, he released the arrow, watching it fly true and land near the centre of the target.

"Excellent," Sir Miller praised, a rare smile breaking his otherwise stern demeanour. "Remember, consistency is key. Practice this until it becomes second nature."

From her elevated perch, Elinor felt a swell of pride as she observed the knights' progress under Miller's expert guidance. Satisfied, she turned to leave but paused when she noticed Bradley striding confidently into the training yard.

He moved with an easy arrogance, his fine leather armour hugging his form. Over his dark blue tunic, emblazoned with the royal family's wolf emblem, he wore a casual air of self-assurance. He stopped before a target and inspected his bow.

Bradley glanced up at Elinor, a mischievous glint in his eye, and winked. He adjusted the bowstring with deft fingers before nocking an arrow. With a sharp focus that stilled even the breeze around him, he drew the bow, his body a picture of perfect poise. A heartbeat later, he released.

The arrow flew straight and true, landing with a satisfying *thud* in the bullseye. Bradley's grin spread wide as he met her gaze. Without hesitation, he fired off arrow after arrow, each one striking its mark in a flawless ring around the first.

Looking up at Elinor once more, he called out, his voice tinged with playful confidence.

"Not bad, I think. What says Her Majesty?"

"Bravo, my love. Not overconfident at all, I see," Elinor remarked, her tone light with a hint of teasing.

Bradley responded with an elaborate bow, a playful grin lighting up his face. Elinor rolled her eyes, but the corners of her lips betrayed her, twitching into a smile at the look he gave her.

"Enjoy your practice," she called as she turned to leave. "I have a few tasks to complete, but I shall meet you later. In the meantime, try not to trip over your own ego..."

"I can't promise anything!" he replied, his laugh echoing across the training yard.

Elinor shook her head at his arrogance but couldn't suppress a small chuckle. As she walked away, she reflected on the knights' progress. She felt confident they would do well in the tourney – Bradley included. Unlike other competitors, he wasn't taking part as a member of his family's house but as a representative of Maycott and the crown. Competing as the king's consort was a role he accepted with pride.

Though he was only participating in the archery event at her request, Elinor had no doubts about his success. Bradley was a natural marksman, and his skill was undeniable.

She hadn't yet seen many of the other contestants in action, but she wasn't concerned. Of the six houses competing, only two posed any real challenge in her mind: Lord Stone's and the Woodlock's. The Malins and the Bennetts were close seconds. With Bradley being a Woodlock competing under the Maycott house, it would be intriguing to see how his house's knights responded. She expected a few playful jousts were likely to happen, but there was no denying they had lost one of their best archers for the games.

The planning for the tourney was nearing completion. Thanks to the combined efforts of Lord Roland and Lady Chloe, accommodations for attendees and participants were arranged. The city thrummed with life and activity, bustling as preparations reached their peak. The event promised to significantly boost trade, not just within the city but throughout the surrounding regions – a welcome benefit for the queen.

Yet amidst the excitement, Elinor's mind remained burdened by the unresolved matter of Bradley's sunken ships. As the days and weeks went by, information had begun to surface. Reports pointed to a culprit who, if her spies were correct, would soon dock in Quaysville. Her men were already stationed at the port, ready to arrest the captain and crew as soon as they arrived.

Now, it was simply playing the annoying waiting game – a test of patience Elinor detested. Fortunately, Julian was due to meet her shortly, and she hoped he brought news.

As she made her way to her study, the sound of hurried footsteps caught her attention. Turning, she saw Julian approaching at a brisk pace, his expression resolute. In his hand, he clutched a roll of parchment.

"My queen," he said, his voice even but urgent. "This is it… the news you have been waiting for."

"Come, let us speak in private," Elinor commanded, her heart pounding as she led Julian swiftly through the castle hallways. The tension in her chest tightened with each step, but hope flickered within her. She couldn't help it – this had to be the update she had been waiting for.

Once inside her study, she turned to him, her voice edged with urgency. "Well? Have they docked? Have you captured the pirates responsible?"

"Yes, to both questions, my queen," Julian replied, his expression breaking into a triumphant smile. "Their ship arrived early, and our guards apprehended them without delay. They are being brought here as we speak. They should arrive by the end of the week at the latest."

"Excellent. Have they been interrogated yet?"

"The men questioned a few of them, but they refused to divulge much. They were informed, however, that they would face you directly and that your methods leave no room for defiance."

"Indeed, they won't," Elinor said, her tone firm. "Thank you, Julian. You've done well. Keep me informed of their progress. I want to know the moment they arrive at the city gates. I plan to welcome our new friends personally."

"Of course, Your Majesty."

Satisfied, Elinor dismissed him with a nod, then made her way to the cells. The guards snapped to attention as she entered, clearly having been caught slacking in their duties. Not that anyone could escape.

The chilling echo of her footsteps resonated through the dim hallway as she ventured deeper into the corridors. She signalled one of the guards to open the questioning rooms for her inspection.

Each chamber was a masterpiece of torment, identically designed to extract secrets and shatter the spirit. Large racks dominated one side, their rollers poised to stretch the victim's body to unbearable limits. Nearby, a pulley system awaited, its ropes ready to hoist prisoners from the ground by their wrists, dislocating shoulders with excruciating precision.

Elinor's gaze lingered on the trapdoor – a personal favourite among her tools. Beneath it lay a claustrophobic, coffin-like space where prisoners were confined in utter darkness for days at a time. The stale air, the crushing isolation – it was akin to being buried alive. It was a terrifying experience that left prisoners broken and desperate. The effect on those who had endured this torment was a testament to its effectiveness.

She had first experimented with this method over eight years ago when Cecilia had disappeared. Katelyn had been her initial subject. The results, even after just a few hours, had astonished her. Over time, Elinor began sending those who defied her into the darkness for increasingly prolonged periods. She ensured they received food and water – enough to keep them alive – but days spent in that oppressive void had a profound effect.

It broke them.

When they emerged, they were hollowed-out remnants of their former selves. Their eyes were empty, their bodies flinched at every sound, and they became puppets she could control without resistance. The fear of being left in that darkness indefinitely gripped them so tightly that they would say or do anything to earn their release. Physical torment had its limits; pain ended eventually, and some proved adept at masking their true intentions. But mental torture – breaking the mind and eroding the spirit – was a far more effective tool. When their will shattered, their strength became hers to command.

She vividly remembered the first time she witnessed this transformation in Katelyn. The defiant woman who had entered the chamber was not the same person who emerged. Katelyn's spirit was broken, and her once fiery determination had been completely under Elinor's control. There had been no resistance left in her – only obedience. It had been a revelation.

Since then, Elinor had honed her methods. Each session taught her something new, each victim refining her technique. She watched as even the strongest, most resolute individuals crumbled. What remained were shells of people who would never dare challenge her again.

Her methods were ruthless, but they were necessary. In a world where power reigned supreme, she couldn't afford the luxury of mercy. Her rule depended on absolute control, and she was willing to go to any lengths to maintain it.

As she walked through the interrogation chambers, she took in the meticulously arranged setup. Each room held a sturdy table and chair designated for the interrogator. Leather rolls were laid out neatly on the tables, each holding an array of tools designed for breaking bodies and spirits alike. She unrolled one, examining the gleaming implements inside. Sharp blades, pliers, needles, thumb screws, hooks, and so much more were polished and ready for use.

The final, most crucial features of the chambers were the shackles bolted to the walls, ceiling, and floor. These restraints ensured that her victims remained immobilised, unable to escape or resist. The cold, unyielding metal glinted under the dim light as she inspected each set. She tugged on the chains, testing their strength and making sure they were secure.

Satisfied that everything was in perfect order, she paused for a moment, allowing herself a grim sense of accomplishment.

These chambers were not just rooms – they were fortresses of control. Every element had been carefully chosen and positioned to break the body and mind of anyone who dared defy her.

Turning to the nearest guard, she spoke in a commanding tone. "I'm expecting guests for these rooms soon. Make sure our best interrogators are on standby and see that everything remains in perfect working order."

"Yes, Your Majesty."

With one last glance at the chambers, Elinor departed the cold, oppressive cells and returned to the warmth of the castle. A wicked smile played on her lips as anticipation surged within her. The pirates would soon arrive, and their fates were already sealed.

Chapter 5

Getting Answers

With news that the pirates who had sunk Bradley's ships would arrive in the city by mid-morning, Elinor's spirits soared. Her eyes sparkled with excitement, a stark contrast to Bradley's unease. He barely touched his food, his knees bouncing beneath the table as though charged with restless energy. He was a live wire, his tension practically vibrating off the walls.

"Relax, my love," Elinor said as she placed her hand over his. The gesture stilled him, and he sank back into his chair with a deep sigh, his shoulders slumping. But his reprieve was brief. Moments later, he straightened abruptly, leaning forward with his hands clasped tightly on the table.

"I'm simply anxious," he admitted, his voice low. "What if they refuse to speak? We'll be no closer to proving it was Lord Stone."

"Fear not," Elinor replied smoothly. "They will talk. We shall make sure of it. Besides, I have already taken precautions in case they fail to name the one who hired them."

Bradley's brows shot up at this revelation. "Oh?" he said, tilting his head.

"In time, my love. Be patient, and all shall be revealed."

"Then I guess we wait for our guests to arrive," he muttered, leaning back once more. He took a long sip from his glass, though the tension in his posture remained.

After finishing breakfast, they stepped outside together. Elinor, determined to keep Bradley's mind occupied, led him through the blossoming garden. The air was heavy with the scent of summer, the sun-drenched flowers in full bloom, adding vibrant splashes of colour to the winding paths.

As they strolled, Elinor deftly shifted the conversation to the upcoming tourney. It wasn't long before Bradley's thoughts were distracted, his earlier anxiety temporarily replaced by an animated discussion of the events and competitions.

By the time they looped back towards the castle, Elinor caught sight of Julian waiting at the garden's entrance. The sight of him caused Bradley to stiffen, his arm going taunt beneath her reassuring squeeze. As they reached Julian, Elinor offered him a curt nod, granting permission to speak.

"Your guests have arrived, Your Majesty," Julian announced, his tone measured. "They are awaiting your presence in the questioning room."

"Excellent. We shall head there shortly. Are the interrogators prepared?" Elinor asked.

"They are in the rooms, awaiting your orders," Julian replied.

"Tell them to begin. We won't be long," she instructed. Julian nodded and left to deliver her message. Elinor turned to Bradley, her eyes meeting his.

"Are you ready for this?"

"Yes," he answered firmly. His posture was straight, and his eyes focused.

"Then let's go. We will get that information, no matter what it takes." She linked her arm through his, and together, they strode through the castle hallways with heads held high, their footsteps echoing off the stone walls. Soon, they stood outside the first questioning room.

Inside, six men awaited their fate. Five were chained to either the walls or the floor, while one groaned on the rack. His body contorted in agony. Their appearance was pitiful – gaunt, bruised, and battered. The arduous journey to the castle had clearly taken its toll. Unfortunately for them, Elinor thought with cold detachment.

She and Bradley positioned themselves by the table when a shrill cry erupted from the man being tortured. His back arched as the veins in his arms and legs bulged under the strain. Elinor scanned the room, her expression unwavering.

"Which one is the captain of their ship?" she asked, her voice sharp and commanding.

The interrogator, a grizzled man known only as Smith, jabbed a thick finger towards the far end of the room. "The one on the end." Without further ceremony, he cranked the rack again, wrenching another scream from the prisoner.

Smith was a towering figure, broad-shouldered and strong as an ox. His anonymity and love for inflicting pain made him ideal for this grim task – at least in Elinor's eyes.

Her cold smile returned as she approached the captain. He stood chained to the wall, his posture straight despite the restraints. Scars marked his sun-weathered skin, and his hardened gaze carried an air of defiance. Even now, as his comrade writhed on the rack, he barely flinched.

"Tell us who paid you to sink the king's ships," Elinor demanded, her voice like ice.

The captain locked eyes with her, his tone calm as he replied, "You think a few threats will compel me to talk? I have faced worse than you."

Elinor's smile vanished, replaced by a flicker of irritation. "Very well," she said coolly, stepping back. "Perhaps some persuasion is in order."

She closed her eyes, embracing the surge of power that began to ripple through her veins. The candles began to flicker, casting eerie shadows across the stone walls. The air grew heavy, charged with an unnatural energy. As the essence of darkness filled her, Elinor let out a quiet, euphoric sigh. It had been too long since she had felt this.

Though her power was diminished, it was enough for what she needed. She opened her eyes, now gleaming with a dark intensity, and raised her arms. Tendrils of black smoke unfurled from her fingertips, slithering across the room before striking the pirates in their chests. Each man jerked against his restraints, their faces contorting with pain and terror.

They cried out, bodies stiffening and twitching as torment radiated through them. Elinor held the sensation in place for several minutes before the power ebbed from her. That was the extent of what she could manage for now – but they didn't need to know that. Fear was everything, and she wielded it like a weapon. Lowering her hand, she addressed the room with a cold smile.

"That was but a taste of what I can do. Now, let's see what Smith is capable of. Keep going until the captain breaks."

Elinor moved to a nearby chair, reclining as though this was merely another day's work. Smith wasted no time methodically moving between the prisoners. Each scream was met with indifference from Elinor, although her gaze never left the captain. His defiant expression remained unchanged, even as his comrades suffered.

Whenever she felt her strength return, Elinor unleashed another burst of agony, catching the men off guard. Their cries echoed off the stone walls, a symphony of torment. Before long, Bradley joined Smith, adopting his techniques with alarming enthusiasm. He worked with meticulous precision, his sadistic smile growing wider with every scream he elicited.

Elinor's eyes flicked to her husband, drawn by the glow of excitement in his expression. He had forgotten the questions, immersed in the thrill of pushing the prisoners to their limits. Watching him take such pleasure in their suffering sent a shiver of exhilaration through her.

Not wanting to miss out, she sent another wave of agony directly at the captain. His jaw clenched, and his body stiffened, but he refused to cry out, holding fast to his defiance.

"Is that the best you can do?" he taunted, his voice dripping with contempt.

"Not at all," Bradley replied smoothly, stepping towards him with unnerving calm. "Torturing your men seems to have little effect on you. Let's see how you fare when it's your turn."

Bradley gripped the captain's chin firmly, forcing him to look up. With deliberate slowness, he picked up an evisceration spoon from the table, holding it level with the man's gaze.

"Let's start with your eyes. Which one first… one or two? You choose." He pointed to each eye in turn, his tone eerily casual.

"You're mad!" the captain spat, his voice cracking as he tried to pull free from Bradley's grasp.

"One," Elinor called out, her voice laced with amusement.

"One it is," Bradley replied without hesitation. He slammed the captain's head back against the wall, his grip tightening around the man's throat. With his free hand, he guided the spoon towards the captain's right eye.

The pirate thrashed against his restraints, but before he could resist further, Elinor unleashed her power again. Dark energy coursed through him, immobilising his body and filling him with the sensation of burning pain. The captain's defiance crumbled as his screams filled the room.

Elinor leaned forward, a smile spreading across her face as Bradley worked with cold precision. The captain's pleas for mercy only delighted her further. Moments later, his eye gave way, falling from its socket with a sickening squelch and landing on the floor.

The other pirates sat in stunned silence, their faces pale with terror. Fear paralysed them, the realisation of Elinor's ruthlessness sinking in. None dared speak. Their resolve shattered as they witnessed just how far she was willing to go.

"Take the second one now," Elinor commanded as she rose and moved towards Bradley.

"No!" the captain cried, his voice trembling. "I'll tell you what you want to know. Just make it stop!"

Elinor smirked, releasing the burning sensation she had been sending through his body. His muscles slackened, and he slumped against the restraints, wheezing in pain.

"Speak," she said coldly.

"Lord Stone," the captain gasped, his voice ragged. "It was Lord Stone. He's the one who paid us."

Elinor's smile widened, satisfaction glinting in her eyes. "Thank you," she said smoothly. Then, turning to Bradley, she added, "The other one now."

With a swift, practised motion, Bradley gripped the pirate's face once more. His movements were efficient, almost mechanical, as he removed the man's remaining eye. The bloodied orb fell to the ground with a wet plop, and the captain's scream tore through the chamber, sending shivers down the spines of everyone present.

When the cries subsided, the room fell silent save for the captain's ragged breathing and stifled sobs. Tears of blood streamed from the empty sockets as he whimpered, "I told you what we know, Your Majesty. Please… no more. Let us go."

Elinor laughed as she looked at his eyeless face and then spoke. "Oh, but why would I do that? You're not going anywhere," she said, her tone growing more commanding. "I'm hosting a tourney soon. I'm sure you have heard about it. You will all be presented to Lord Stone at the right moment. Mark my words. He will rue the day he dared to cross me and my husband."

Satisfied with the confession, she turned to Smith. "Put them in the cells for now, but have your fun in the meantime. Remember, none of them are to die. I need them alive for the tourney."

Smith nodded, a sadistic grin spreading across his face as he resumed his work. Elinor and Bradley left the room, the screams of the prisoners trailing behind them.

In the next questioning room, Elinor repeated her instructions to the other interrogator. This man shared Smith's love for inflicting pain, though he preferred to taunt his victims as he worked. One prisoner was already howling in agony while the others begged for mercy.

As Elinor was about to leave, Bradley grabbed her wrist, his grip strong but not harsh.

"You go on," he said. "I'm staying here. These lowlifes robbed me and cost me money. I intend to make them pay." A wicked glint shone in his eyes as he looked at the pirates, who recoiled under his gaze.

"Have fun, my love," Elinor replied with an approving smile. "But remember, no killing. I need them alive to ensure Lord Stone gets what's coming to him."

Pride swelled in her chest as she left Bradley to his work. Returning to her chambers, she drew herself a bath. Clean and refreshed, she settled at her desk and spent the evening going over her plan. It was spectacularly devious, a masterpiece of vengeance. She could already envision the look of horror on Lord Stone's face when the moment came.

Hours passed as she refined every detail. Finally, as she prepared to retire for the night, Bradley entered the room. His clothes were soaked in blood, his smile dark and sinister – the expression of a man utterly pleased with himself.

"That was exhilarating," Bradley said as he strode towards her, gripping her and pulling her into a deep kiss. Their tongues intertwined, a fiery dance of passion. Elinor leaned into him, pressing her body firmly against his, her fingers weaving into his hair and tugging gently, forcing his head back.

"I'm delighted to hear that," she muttered, her lips brushing his as she spoke. "It sent a thrill through me, witnessing your delight in their suffering." She kissed him again, their lust and longing igniting like a spark to dry tinder.

The knowledge of what they had just done fuelled a surge of fervent desire between them. Elinor eagerly threw herself into Bradley's arms, her hands roaming his body with unrestrained hunger. He responded with equal intensity, his hands gripping her nightgown and tearing it away with ease, revealing her bare form. Her hardened nipples brushed against his chest as he guided her towards the wall, pinning her there with an urgency neither could suppress.

Their yearning for another raged unrelentingly, the desire consuming them. Elinor's hands moved quickly to undo Bradley's pants, pushing them to the ground. As his hands cupped her behind, lifting her, she wrapped her legs tightly around his waist. He bit her neck, the sharp sting making her gasp, but her nails dug into his back in response, leaving red trails in their wake.

Bradley's mouth explored her body, his lips and teeth teasing her sensitive nipples, alternating between biting and sucking, a mixture of pleasure and pain that sent shivers down her spine. Her moans filled the room, each sound a testament to the raw energy between them.

Her body craved him, every fibre of her being begging for fulfilment. She moved rhythmically against his hardened shaft, urging him silently to take her. Bradley didn't hesitate. He pushed himself deep inside her, eliciting a cry of ecstasy from her lips. The pleasure surged through her, radiating from her core as he thrust into her with growing force. His hands gripped her hips tightly, anchoring her in place, their movements perfectly synchronised.

The intoxicating scent of their mingled sweat and desire filled the air as their bodies collided with rhythmic intensity. Elinor arched her back, her fingers clawing at his arms as each thrust sent shockwaves of pleasure through her. She felt the tension building within her, a crescendo that left her trembling.

When she finally let go, her body convulsed in waves of pure ecstasy, her cries echoing off the walls. Bradley's movements grew more frenzied as he neared his own release. His hand closed around her throat, the pressure causing her breath to hitch. The mixture of fear and excitement sent a shiver down her spine, heightening her pleasure. Her wide eyes locked with his, the unspoken connection between them electrifying.

As she gasped for air, every sensation sharpened, the balance between desire and survival pushing her closer to the edge. When her second climax hit, it tore through her, leaving her breathless. Bradley followed moments later, his muscles tensing as his release consumed him. He pressed her harder against the wall, his breathing ragged as he let go of her throat, stepping back slightly.

Still caught in the afterglow, he grabbed her arms and raised them above her head, his lips capturing hers in another searing kiss.

"Well, that was just what I needed," Elinor said with a satisfied smile as she leaned into him for support.

"And I," he responded, scooping her up effortlessly and carrying her to the bed. He laid her down gently, brushing a stray lock of hair from her face. His eyes, filled with tenderness, lingered on her for a moment before he climbed in beside her.

Elinor turned her body towards him, letting her gaze roam over his features. His strong jawline, shadowed with a hint of stubble, gave him a rugged charm, while the way his hair fell slightly over his forehead added to his allure.

He smirked, catching her looking. "Wanting more, Elinor?" he teased, raising an eyebrow.

She slapped him playfully on the chest, rolling her eyes. "No, I'm more than satisfied right now."

She curled up close to him, her fingers idly tracing the tattoo on his chest. He pressed a soft kiss to her forehead, murmuring, "If you say so," before closing his eyes.

They lay there in comfortable silence, Elinor watching him as her thoughts swirled with the night's events. A happy tingle coursed through her, leaving her heart light and her body warm. Tonight had been a night she would never forget.

Chapter 6

A Full Castle

With only a few days until the event began, the city and the castle were bustling with activity. Word of the tourney had spread far and wide, attracting crowds eager to witness the spectacle or take part in it. This influx of people proved advantageous for the crown, as the additional visitors meant a significant increase in revenue. Workers in Carraton had been tirelessly preparing the venue, while nearby farmers and locals with available land erected tents and makeshift shelters near the site.

Elinor had yet to see the final setup and was now making her way to the grounds for her first glimpse. The event was being held in a field belonging to the crown, just outside the city. She felt a thrill of anticipation as she imagined the progress made. Although the tourney had been conceived as a ploy to root out those against her and Bradley, Elinor couldn't deny the infectious excitement that had swept through the city. The vibrant atmosphere was impossible to resist.

Now that they were certain Lord Stone was behind the stolen cargo and sunken ships, Elinor viewed the upcoming days as a personal game. She relished the thought of toying with him, letting him believe he was safe, only to expose his treachery and orchestrate his downfall in front of everyone. It would be the perfect revenge.

Meanwhile, as lords, knights, and their entourages began arriving, both the castle and the city hummed with anticipation. Elinor was eager to observe the participants as they prepared for the competitions. From her knowledge of the contenders, she had even placed a few unofficial bets on who might win specific events. Naturally, Bradley was one of her picks. Though she was confident in his skill as an archer, she couldn't be entirely certain how he would fare against the kingdom's other elite marksmen. Still, she wouldn't dream of wagering against her husband.

Over the course of four days, participants would compete in a variety of events, including archery, jousting, foot combat, melee, a contest of strength, and, of course, the grand pageantry to mark the tourney's opening. The schedule promised an impressive lineup. Day one would commence with a grand display and feast in the arena, featuring music and heraldry to set the tone for the days ahead. Day two would showcase archery and foot combat, providing a stage for archers to demonstrate their precision and fighters to engage in thrilling hand-to-hand battles to determine the best among them.

Day three would feature the jousting and a strength contest, challenging knights to unseat their opponents successfully and then demonstrate their might through various feats.

The concluding day would showcase the Melee. A free-for-all where participants would engage in foot combat with blunted weapons, displaying their skills and using battle tactics to outlast their rivals without causing serious harm. Hopefully.

To honour those who participated and triumphed, a celebration and awards ceremony would follow. Scores would be tracked throughout the games, and winners would receive their prizes during the festivities. Though preparations unfolded in a whirlwind, the event promised to be spectacular. With Lord Roland and Lady Chloe's meticulous planning, Elinor felt confident the occasion would proceed flawlessly.

That evening, Elinor had arranged a dinner to welcome the participating families of the court. With all the lords in attendance, it presented the perfect opportunity to begin laying her trap and luring Lord Stone into a false sense of security. A warm reception would likely put him at ease, allowing her to gauge his behaviour towards both her and Bradley. His interactions might inadvertently reveal more than he intended, further tightening the noose around him.

Beyond her strategic manoeuvres regarding Lord Stone, Elinor looked forward to reconnecting with others, particularly Lady Victoria and Lord Lloyd. Though she trusted few, she regarded these two as genuine friends over the years. Their presence would provide a comforting contrast to the evening's underlying tension. Trust was scarce among many houses, and gatherings such as this often felt like navigating a razor's edge. The dinner would demand a careful blend of courtesy and subtle manipulation. A challenge Elinor was well-equipped to manage. This was the kind of environment in which she thrived.

"We are here, Your Majesty," Julian announced as the carriage came to a gentle stop. He swiftly dismounted and opened the door, extending his hand to assist her.

"Thank you, Julian." Elinor accepted his aid, gracefully lifting her skirts with her free hand as she descended the steps. She turned towards the field, following Julian's gesture. As she approached the site, Elinor slowed to a halt, her breath catching at the sight before her.

The usually plain meadow, reserved for the horses, was being transformed into a scene of grandeur. Wooden lists encircled the area, creating a protective perimeter. Near the centre of the grassland, clusters of vibrant, oversized tents stood tall, offering participants spaces to prepare and rest between events. Banners representing the participating houses fluttered in the breeze, each one a vivid proclamation of anticipated victory.

Elinor's gaze fell upon the royal boxes. Elevated on raised platforms like thrones, they were draped in rich crimson velvet and adorned with the wolf emblem of Carraton, a proud symbol of lineage and power. From these lofty seats, she and her guests would witness the entire spectacle: the clash of swords, the thunder of hooves, and the triumphs and defeats of the knights and champions.

The air crackled with anticipation. Elinor could almost taste the fear of the men about to face their opponents, their breaths held and eyes wide as they prepared for combat. She imagined the triumph of the victors, the roars of the crowd as they bested their rivals. The ground would be soaked with literal blood, sweat, and tears of warriors who fought not only for victory but also for their place in the court.

It wasn't just the main setup that captured her attention. Surrounding the lists, colourful stalls were being arranged to offer viewers scrumptious food, ale, and fine wines, as well as trinkets to commemorate the occasion. Elinor swirled around, her eyes bright and hands clasped to her face.

"Oh, this is just wonderful, isn't it, Julian? It's better than I could have imagined."

"It's splendid, my queen. I can't wait to see this place on the day."

"It will be one to remember, an event that won't be forgotten. Why, I have no doubt this tourney is destined to go down in history," Elinor mused.

As they continued to take in the scene, something unusual caught Elinor's eye. Near a larger tent, a group of craftsmen were busy assembling an intricate wooden structure. It was grand, and unlike any she had seen before, adorned with elaborate carvings depicting scenes of past tournaments and legendary battles. The craftsmanship was exquisite, and each detail was meticulously rendered.

Elinor walked closer, her curiosity piqued. "Julian, look at this. The detail is astonishing."

He nodded, equally impressed. "Indeed, Your Majesty. It seems they have spared no effort in making this event truly remarkable."

Admiring the intricate carvings, she stepped back, watching as the craftsmen pieced the structure together. There was something about art and its ability to tell stories. Histories long past could be remembered through the delicate strokes of a brush or, in this case, the chiselling of wood. Each detail spoke of a time and place of people who had lived, loved, fought, and triumphed.

She could almost hear the whispers of bygone days, the echoes of ancient voices carried on the wind. The stories of heroes and villains, of battles won and lost, were all captured in the intricate designs before her. It was a poignant reminder of the legacy she was a part of and the lineage she carried forward.

Elinor's thoughts were interrupted by Julian's voice. "Your Majesty, the preparations are nearly complete. Shall we continue?"

She nodded, tearing her gaze away from the craftsmanship. "Yes. Let's see what else awaits us." Elinor's eyes widened as she took it all in, walking a lap around the area.

Back at the carriage, she looked out one last time, soaking in the scene as a smile curved her lips. With the dipping sun on the horizon, she gazed out, knowing she stood on the cusp of something extraordinary. In a few days, the field would erupt with cheers and the magic of chivalry. For now, though, it lay quiet – a canvas waiting to be painted with valour and a battle for greatness.

With the anticipation of the impending events and the multitude of guests awaiting her at dinner, Elinor followed Julian back to the carriage. As they rode home, a faint smile remained etched on her face. She was looking forward to what was to come.

Chapter 7

A Dinner for the Lords

Elinor and Bradley had dressed and were ready for dinner. Elinor wore a floor-length silk gown in a deep blue hue, the fabric shimmering under the light like liquid sapphire. A silver tiara encrusted with diamonds rested elegantly on her head, while a matching statement necklace complemented the ensemble, lending her an air of regal sophistication. Bradley, too, made an impression with his coordinated blue tunic and surcoat adorned with intricate embroidery. Their outfits harmonised perfectly, a subtle yet deliberate display of their unity.

When they entered the grand ballroom, the space was already teeming with guests. Laughter and conversation filled the air, but an undercurrent of anticipation lingered beneath the surface. The attendees, despite their outward smiles, radiated tension. As Elinor and Bradley stepped further into the room, heads turned, and all eyes were drawn to them. Elinor's warm smile illuminated her face as she scanned the crowd, her gaze lingering briefly on the familiar and unfamiliar alike. Guests bowed or curtsied in deference as the couple passed, their respect evident in every gesture. The two exchanged polite greetings with those nearby before parting ways to mingle individually.

Drinks flowed freely among the guests, and Elinor felt certain that the evening would prove to be eventful. She resolved to engage in small talk with the lords before dinner, hoping to gauge the mood and intentions of her peers ahead of the tourney. Lord Stone's thinly veiled disdain for her and Bradley weighed on her mind, and she was eager to discern whether the others shared his views or harboured similar ambitions to undermine her authority.

As she moved deeper into the room, her eyes fell upon Lord Christopher Malins and his wife, Lady Evelyn – steadfast allies since the beginning of her reign and among the few families she truly trusted. Their residence, Ravenswood Manor, lay on the outskirts of Adlington, where they oversaw the region's vital fishing operations, supplying fresh fish to Almire and Dorraset. With them stood their two sons, Kane and Mitchel, both poised to compete in the upcoming tournament.

Elinor approached with a gracious smile. "Good evening, Christopher, Evelyn. How are you both?"

Christopher bowed respectfully. "We are well, Your Majesty."

Lady Evelyn offered a warm smile of her own. "It's always a pleasure to attend these gatherings. The boys have been looking forward to this for weeks.

Elinor's eyes sparkled with warmth. "I'm glad to hear it. The thought of participating in their first tournament must be thrilling," she said, shifting her attention to the two young men.

The brothers nodded in unison. "It's an honour to take part in such an event, Your Majesty," Mitchel replied earnestly.

"I look forward to seeing how you fare," Elinor replied, her gaze shifting back to Christopher. "It has been some time since we last spoke. Tell me, how is the fishing industry faring in Almire?"

Christopher's expression grew serious. "We've had a good season so far, Your Majesty. The waters have been generous, and our supplies to Almire and Dorraset remain steady."

"That's excellent news," Bradley interjected, stepping beside Elinor with a warm smile. "Your efforts are vital to the kingdom's prosperity."

"Indeed, they are," Elinor added, accepting a glass of wine Bradley handed her. "And it is a contribution we deeply appreciate."

"You honour us," Christopher said with a respectful bow. As Bradley continued chatting with Christopher and Evelyn, Elinor excused herself, her attention drawn to Lord Wesley Bishop, who had been casting furtive glances in her direction. His demeanour suggested he was eager for a conversation.

As Elinor made her way towards him, her keen eye took in the woman clinging to his arm – a woman who was decidedly not his wife. It seemed Bishop had brought one of his mistresses to the tournament, likely in an attempt to impress her while he competed. Beside him stood Daniel Cole, another schemer of dubious reputation, whose presence only reinforced Elinor's weariness. Daniel's enthusiasm for the event stemmed from the prospect of winning – or swindling – a fortune before the tournament concluded.

Bishop's reputation preceded him. Hailing from Belmont, a land notorious for breeding cunning opportunists, he was known for his self-serving nature. His actions this evening only emphasised that trait. While his wife was bedridden with illness at home, he indulged himself in the company of his mistress. His family oversaw the fishing operations in the Belshire region, supplying Belshire and the Renlands with fresh fish – a fitting role for a man as slippery as the commodity he managed.

"Lord Bishop," Elinor greeted with a pleasant smile, though her tone held a subtle edge. "How lovely to see you again. It's unfortunate that your wife couldn't join us. I received her apologies and heard she was unwell."

"The pleasure is mine, Your Majesty," Bishop replied smoothly, offering a slight bow. "Yes, she has taken ill with a fever, and our physician strongly advised against her travelling."

"A shame," Elinor said with a hint of coolness. "I hope she makes a swift recovery." Her gaze shifted to the woman at his side. "It seems you're not without company, however. I don't believe we've had the pleasure."

Bishop's smile faltered ever so slightly before he introduced the woman. "Indeed not, Your Majesty. May I present Selene Hall, my guest, for the tourney."

Selene curtsied deeply, her cheeks flushing under Elinor's scrutiny. Elinor's smile remained polite, but her posture stiffened imperceptibly, and her eyes narrowed slightly as she regarded the woman. Her voice, though cordial, carried an unmistakable note of steel. "A pleasure, I'm sure."

Without waiting for further conversation, Elinor's gaze moved beyond Lord Bishop to Lord Lloyd and Lady Victoria Roberts. She bid Lord Bishop a pleasant evening and strode purposefully towards the Roberts, one of the few couples she considered true allies.

The Roberts, like Bishop, hailed from Belmont, but unlike him, their loyalty had proven unwavering. They had been instrumental during Elinor's rise to the throne, offering their cunning and connections in exchange for positions of influence. Elinor had no illusions about their motives – they valued power above all else – but their skills had been invaluable, and they had yet to betray her trust.

In gratitude for their support, Elinor had rewarded them handsomely. They now resided in a manor in Adlington and held the responsibility for managing the farming and timber supplies of Almire and Dorraset. Their rise had come at the expense of Lord Johnathon Goodman, whose treachery had earned him a swift and decisive end at Elinor's hand.

It was a calculated relationship but one that served both parties well. And as Elinor approached, their warm smiles reminded her why they remained within her inner circle.

"My dear friends, how are you both this evening?" Elinor greeted warmly, placing an affectionate kiss on Victoria's cheek.

"We are well, Your Majesty, and greatly looking forward to the tourney. It promises to be a grand event, judging by the turnout," Lloyd remarked, his gaze sweeping across the bustling room. "I hear the city and surrounding areas are packed to the rafters already," he added with a knowing smile.

"It is, which is fantastic for us, for obvious reasons," Elinor replied, her voice filled with enthusiasm. "I can't wait for it to begin. The games are sure to be splendid… I'm confident. And with the rivalry brewing between many courts, it promises to be quite entertaining."

"Indeed," Victoria agreed, her tone lowering as she leaned closer to Elinor. "We are also aware of your recent troubles with the sunken ships. Know that we have been making inquiries on your behalf."

Elinor inclined her head slightly in gratitude. "We shall converse later," she said in a quiet, measured tone before returning to a more conversational volume for others nearby to hear. "Enjoy the evening. Excuse me, though. I have a few more guests to greet before dinner begins."

With that, Elinor made a mental note to arrange a private conversation with the Roberts later. She then moved towards

William Bennett and his wife, Roweena. The Bennetts resided in Wittleshire, near Belmont, where they managed farming in the region and oversaw the wood supply for Belshire and the Renlands. Accompanying them were their two sons, Galrick and Nicholas. Galrick, at twenty-two, was a participant in the tournament, and William's pride was evident in his beaming expression as he rested a firm hand on his eldest son's shoulder. Nicholas, being only sixteen, would simply observe the event alongside his parents.

"William, Roweena, a pleasure to see you both, as always," Elinor greeted with a nod.

"We're thrilled to be here for the tourney," William replied proudly, motioning towards Galrick. "And, of course, to watch our Galrick compete."

Elinor turned her gaze to the young man. "You must be excited to take part in such an event," she remarked.

"It's an honour, your Majesty," Galrick said earnestly. "To be included in something so grand is a privilege."

"I'll be watching with immense interest," Elinor said, a warm smile gracing her features. "I expect great things, knowing your family's legacy."

"He will do wonderfully," William interjected, his pride shining through.

After exchanging pleasantries and engaging in brief small talk, Elinor's attention was drawn to Thomas Stone, her most significant rival, standing among the lords. Their relationship was complex – a mix of necessity and veiled animosity. Neither particularly liked the other, but they had long accepted that cooperation was a requirement for maintaining their respective positions. Stone had proven helpful in the past, offering his aid when Elinor needed it most, though always with an eye towards what he could gain from it.

For the sake of appearances, they maintained a cordial front, but their conversations never strayed beyond the realm of work. Tonight, however, the fragile truce between them teetered on the brink. His recent interference with Bradley's ships wouldn't go unanswered.

Stone stood with his wife Felicia, whose icy demeanour mirrored her husband's. Elinor had little reason to interact with her and preferred to keep their exchanges minimal. The Stones resided in Geraldton, a region near the Renlands known for its hardy crops that thrived in cold climates. Root vegetables and brassicas were their primary harvest, but the area also specialised in raising livestock suited to the snowy terrain. In winter, snowshoe hares were among the meats they provided, filling a seasonal gap when other game animals hibernated.

Despite his official responsibilities, Stone was rumoured to dabble in clandestine trades, a practice he had expanded during James's reign as king. However, since Elinor's rise to power, she had systematically curtailed his illicit operations, doing so subtly enough that he might not suspect her involvement. His recent actions against Bradley's vessels, however, suggested he might have uncovered the truth – or at least harboured suspicions.

As Stone turned and caught sight of her, Elinor moved closer, determined to address him directly.

"Lord Stone, wonderful to see you. I trust your journey wasn't too long?" Elinor greeted him with a polite smile.

"Not at all, Your Majesty. The trip was worth it to witness such a grand event," Stone replied smoothly. "Although a bit more notice would have been nice. I had to leave certain matters in the hands of my clerk to make it here on time."

"Yes, my apologies for that. It was rather a spur-of-the-moment idea that I put into action," she admitted lightly, her tone unapologetic.

"As are most things you seem to do," Stone muttered under his breath, though it was loud enough for her to catch.

Elinor's eyes narrowed slightly, her smile turning sharp. "Careful, Lord Stone. One can never predict what the whims of your queen may lead to next," she warned, her voice cool yet laced with unmistakable authority.

Before he could muster a response, Elinor held his stare for a lingering moment. When Lord Stone finally looked away, turning back to his wife, Elinor moved on, satisfaction flickering across her expression. Felicia Stone, who had been silent through the exchange, immediately leaned in to whisper to her husband, no doubt sharing her opinions on the interaction. Elinor suppressed the temptation to glare back. Soon enough, she thought, she would put the pair of them firmly in their place.

Shaking off the annoyance, she made her way towards her mother-in-law, Lady Constance Woodlock, her sister-in-law, Adina, and Adina's wife, Fleur. The trio stood out with their warm presence in the crowd.

Bradley's father had passed a few years prior, leaving Adina to take charge of the family business. With Bradley's focus on helping Elinor run the kingdom, his sister had taken up the mantle with confidence and skill. Adina's wife, Fleur, whom she had met during her travels in Caldoria, proved to be a steadfast partner in both business and life.

Elinor liked them both immensely. They possessed passion, drive, and ambition in abundance – traits she deeply admired, particularly in traders who needed to navigate the cutthroat world of commerce.

After greeting them warmly, Elinor ensured all her guests were seated as the dinner was prepared to be served. The servants entered the ballroom with synchronised precision, carrying platters laden with an impressive feast. Plates of wild boar, venison, grilled fish fillets, roasted vegetables, and freshly baked bread were set down in front of the guests. The aroma of the food filled the air, mingling with the spiced notes of wine and mead, creating an atmosphere of indulgence and celebration.

As the guests dined, murmurs of appreciation and the occasional burst of laughter filled the room. Servants moved seamlessly around the table, refilling goblets and ensuring that no one waited for anything. Once the meal was well underway,

Elinor took the opportunity to steer the conversation towards the reason for their gathering.

"I'm thrilled to have you all here for the tourney," Elinor said, her voice carrying across the room with warmth and genuine excitement. Her guests responded enthusiastically, expressing their anticipation for the events and praising the efforts of their knights in preparation for the competition.

"So, tell me," Elinor continued, her tone inviting, "how many competitors do each of you have participating?" She directed her gaze around the table, waiting for each to answer in turn.

The first to speak was Christopher Malins, who sat proudly with his family. "My house has fifteen knights participating, Your Majesty, including my two sons here," he said, beaming as he gestured towards Kane and Mitchel.

Elinor turned to the young men with an encouraging smile. "How wonderful! I look forward to seeing how you both perform. Is this your first time competing in an event like this?"

"It is Your Majesty," Kane replied, his voice steady despite the faint flush of nerves in his cheeks. "We are both eager and will do our name proud."

"I'm sure you shall," Elinor said warmly before turning her attention to Lord Stone, who sat further down at the table. Her smile dimmed slightly as she addressed him.

"And how many competitors does your house have in the tourney, Lord Stone?"

Stone straightened in his chair, his expression composed. "My house has twenty-five knights ready for the events," he announced confidently. Then, with a deliberate pause, he added, "I had considered participating in the archery competition myself but ultimately decided against it." His gaze shifted pointedly to Bradley. "Aren't you competing in that event, My Lord King?"

Bradley's expression intensified, but his voice remained polite. "Indeed, I am."

"Well then," Stone said with a faint smirk, "you might stand a chance."

Bradley's jaw clenched and leaned forward as his eyes locked on Stone. "If you are skilled as you imply, Lord Stone, why didn't you sign up? It's easy to boast from the sidelines and critique those who are actually involved," he said, his tone cool and cutting.

Stone bristled at the challenge. "I recant what I said," he declared, his voice loud enough to draw attention. "I will participate in the tourney. Specifically in the archery competition. If only to wipe that smug smile off your face."

"Good luck. You'll need it," Bradley retorted, leaning back in his chair with an arrogant expression. He watched Lord Stone with a hungry gleam in his eyes, casually sipping his wine.

Elinor glanced between the two men. Her face was impassive as she glossed over their heated exchange. Internally, however, she was gleeful. Bradley had succeeded in goading Lord Stone into taking part, which would not only make the tourney more intriguing but also align perfectly with her own plans for him.

Continuing her round of the table, Elinor asked each lord about their participants. The Roberts had eight knights entered into the competition. Bishop boasted ten, including himself. Bennett claimed fifteen, with his son Galrick among them. Elinor's own house had the largest contingent, fielding thirty knights, with Julian proudly serving as her personal champion. Bradley's household of Woodlock contributed twenty-five, though, as king consort, he was competing under the Maycott banner on behalf of the crown.

With so many competitors from across the houses, the tourney promised to be a glorious event. The conversation naturally shifted towards the events themselves, with lively debates about who might be best in the various challenges. Elinor listened attentively, occasionally chiming in as the lords and ladies began placing bets and sharing playful jabs.

As the platters emptied and the wine flowed freely, the mood grew even more jovial. Talk gradually shifted from the tourney to political matters within the realm. Elinor was pleased to hear that most regions were thriving, though not all news was cheerful. The southern region of Almire faced challenges with its crops, as a late frost had delayed planting. Only time would tell if the harvest would be sufficient.

The Renlands, meanwhile, were dealing with an influx of wolves and other beasts coming out of the mountains in search of food. The cause of the attacks remained unclear, as the crops in the region were reportedly flourishing. She hoped the monitoring efforts she had ordered would prevent the situation from escalating. It had been years since wildlife had posed such a problem, and she was determined to avoid a full-blown crisis.

Through it all, no one mentioned Bradley's sunken ships. Elinor had half-expected a sly remark from Lord Stone, but he remained conspicuously silent on the matter. He carried himself with his usual arrogance, showing no outward signs of suspicion. This reassured her that he likely remained in the dark about her involvement.

Satisfied with how the evening was unfolding, Elinor rose to her feet and raised her goblet high. "To friendship, to unity, and to a glorious tourney ahead!" she declared, her voice clear and commanding.

The hall erupted in a resounding cheer as the guests lifted their glasses, the clinking of goblets echoing through the room. Spirits were high, and the excitement for the coming days was palpable.

As the night wore on, the atmosphere became even livelier. Laughter echoed through the grand hall, mingling with the melodic strains of a string quartet performing in the corner. Servants glided gracefully among the guests, refilling goblets and offering trays of tempting desserts.

Elinor moved through the crowd with ease, engaging in light-hearted conversation and basking in the festive energy. She saw the anticipation in the eyes of the young lords, their eagerness for the challenges ahead practically brimming over. Everywhere she looked, there was joy and excitement.

Eventually, Bradley joined her, slipping his arm around her waist as they stood watching the revelry unfold. "You've done well, Elinor," he murmured, his voice filled with quiet pride.

She glanced up at him, her lips curving into a knowing smile. "It's only the beginning," she replied softly. "Soon, the real games will begin."

As the evening wore on, the guests began to take their leave, their laughter and chatter gradually fading into the quiet night. Elinor and Bradley lingered in the now-empty hall, savouring the rare stillness and the quiet anticipation of what was to come.

Chapter 8

The Tourney

The day had finally arrived. The castle buzzed with activity as workers hurried back and forth, putting the final touches on preparations for the tourney. Guests filled the halls, making their way to the great hall to greet the knights of the realm before the games began.

Elinor stood atop the raised platform, her gaze sweeping over the crowd as they mingled, their conversations brimming with anticipation for what was to come. Bets were already being placed, coins exchanging hands with eager excitement. The competitions and their participants had been announced, and this gathering marked the final meeting before the events commenced. As queen, it was her duty to oversee the proceedings, declaring the champions and, when necessary, resolving disputes where no clear victor emerged.

Beyond the contests, the celebrations promised an abundance of feasting and drinking. The festivities would culminate in an awards ceremony, where prizes and gifts would be presented – not only to individual winners but also to the house that earned the most points. Among the rewards, a unique *gift* awaited Lord Stone, reserved for the final moment – a gesture of particular significance.

With a few hours to spare before the official start of the tourney, Elinor and her lady-in-waiting, Chloe, ventured beyond the castle to explore the field. The vibrant sights and smells of the festival greeted them as vendors called out from colourful stalls, hawking roasted meats, spiced ale, and trinkets. Each item offered a promise of the merriment to come.

One stall caught Chloe's attention – a display of ribbons in a dazzling array of colours stretched across the tabletop. She picked one up and held it out to Elinor.

"Look, this one has the royal crest."

Elinor stepped closer, taking the ribbon in hand. Its red and black hues gleamed in the sunlight, and at its centre was the intricately woven wolf emblem of Maycott. Her eyes drifted across the table, noting that each ribbon bore the symbol of a different house, all beautifully embroidered with remarkable craftsmanship.

"These are fantastic," Elinor said, her tone admiring. "They are wonderfully crafted."

The vendor, a young woman, blushed deeply under the queen's gaze. "Thank you, Your Majesty. I made them myself."

"You are very talented. How much for this one?" Elinor asked, holding up the ribbon.

"For Your Majesty? Nothing at all," the woman stammered.

"Nonsense," Elinor replied firmly. "Your hard work deserves payment." She nodded to Chloe, who promptly retrieved the purse she carried for such occasions.

"And I would love one, too," Chloe added, selecting a ribbon. She handed the woman a silver coin, insisting she keep the change after they agreed on a price.

Elinor tied her ribbon to the front of her cloak, its vibrant colours standing out boldly for all to see. With a smile of satisfaction, she turned her attention back to the stalls, eager to discover what other treasures awaited her.

As they approached the event grounds, the mingling scents of hay, leather, and polished steel filled the air, weaving a sensory tapestry of anticipation. The thought of knights and champions clashing for glory loomed large in everyone's minds. Spectators packed the stands, excitement buzzing through the crowd as participants prepared for the contests. Though hours remained before the main events, the seating areas and vendor stalls were already bustling, guests soaking up the vibrant atmosphere and embracing the festive spirit.

In the arena, Elinor moved among the competitors, greeting them with warm words of encouragement. Today, being dedicated to the parade and feast required minimal preparation. The knights and their workers busied themselves in their tents, polishing armour, mending small dents from training sessions, and ensuring every detail was in order. Everyone was in good spirits.

"Lloyd, how are you? Is your house ready?" Elinor asked, approaching him with a warm smile.

"Your Majesty, I wasn't expecting to see you here in the trenches!" Lloyd replied, his tone tinged with surprise. "I'm well, thank you. Just making sure everyone is organised before the parade. I want them to look their best and make Adlington proud."

Elinor nodded approvingly. "I'm sure they will. I wanted to soak it all in from every angle before declaring this tourney open. Your men will bring honour to your house."

Lloyd grinned. "We'll give it our all, Your Majesty. The knights are eager to showcase their skills."

As they spoke, a young squire approached, carrying a freshly polished helmet. He bowed respectfully. "Sir, the armour is ready."

"Thank you, Dale," Lloyd said, taking the helmet and inspecting it closely. "It looks perfect. Make sure this goes to Sir Cedric and organise the others."

Elinor watched the interaction with a smile. "It's good to see such dedication. I look forward to watching your knights in action."

Leaving Lloyd to finalise his preparation, Elinor made her way towards the royal box, where she would officially open the games. As she reached the entrance, she saw Bradley and Victoria deep in conversation. Victoria's young daughter, Rose, stood beside her, looking utterly charming in a mustard-yellow velvet dress, her bright red hair adorned with matching ribbons.

"Well, don't you look sweet, little Rose?" Elinor said, crouching to meet the girl's eye line.

Rose curtsied and twirled, beaming under the queen's attention. "Thank you, Your Majesty."

"She certainly looks beautiful," Victoria added, her pride evident. "Everything appears magnificent. I, for one, can't wait for the games to begin."

"It's going to be one to remember," Bradley said, a sly smile playing on his lips.

"Indeed. Victoria, I need to catch up with you and Lloyd after dinner. There's much to discuss," Elinor said.

"I'll be sure to find you. I'm eager to hear what's been happening." Victoria smiled, her voice full of curiosity, before being gently pulled away by her daughter and disappearing into the crowd.

As they left, Bradley leaned in towards Elinor, his hand resting lightly on her waist, whispering in her ear.

"When will you call the crowds to attention? I believe the houses are ready to begin with the parade."

"Perfect. Let's take our seats, and I'll make the announcement. It will give everyone a chance to find a good spot to watch from," she replied. Together, they made their way to their seats in the royal box.

From her vantage point, Elinor looked out over the arena, which was packed with bodies, the hum of voices rising like a tidal wave. Realising her words would be drowned out by the noise, she used her power to amplify her voice, ensuring it carried all the way to the farthest corners of the space.

"Ladies and gentlemen, may I have your attention?" Her voice rang out clear and commanding, cutting through the noise and silencing the crowd in an instant. "The tourney will begin shortly, so please make your way to a viewing point."

Elinor sat down beside Bradley as her ladies began filing into their seats below her. Chloe took the spot on her other side while several members of the court settled nearby in the royal box. Around her, the hum of small talk and gossip resumed, with speculation swirling about the participants and their chances of victory. Bets were still being placed, silver coins exchanging hands as the excitement grew.

Moments later, a messenger came forward, bowing low, before delivering the news that the houses were ready to begin. Rising once more, Elinor stepped forward to formally open the event. This was her duty as queen; while heralds and attendants would oversee the scheduling and announcements, it was she who declared the games officially started.

"Esteemed guests," she began, her voice resonating with regal authority, "welcome to my first tourney as your queen. Today, I'm honoured to witness the valour and skill of our noble knights. This is not merely a display of prowess but a celebration of the spirit of chivalry and camaraderie that unites us all. May the contests be fair, the victories honourable, and the memories everlasting. To all participants, I wish you luck. And to those placing wagers, may fortune smile upon you. With that, let the games begin!"

The crowd erupted into thunderous cheers, and the fanfare of trumpets announced the parade's commencement.

The announcer stepped forward, calling for House Malins to lead the procession. Their knights rode into the arena straddling magnificently adorned horses, their banner – a white-and-green standard emblazoned with the sigil of a bear – fluttering proudly. As they advanced, the riders displayed impressive horsemanship, weaving through intricate manoeuvres before staging mock charges and pretend sword fights, eliciting cheers and applause from the spectators.

When their demonstration concluded, each knight passed by the royal stand, where Elinor acknowledged them with a nod and a gracious smile.

One by one, the other houses followed in kind. House Bennett entered next, their white-and-blue banner bearing the sigil of a horse. They were succeeded by House Stone, whose fox emblem gleamed against an orange-and-black backdrop. Then came House Roberts, their bronze-and-green banner featuring a soaring eagle, and House Bishop, whose serpent sigil slithered across their green-and-black standard.

Finally, Bradley's own House Woodlock entered the arena, their knights riding beneath a striking banner of blue-and-black, adorned with the sigil of an albatross.

Behind Elinor, Bradley's sister, Adina, and her wife, Fleur, erupted into cheers, their voices cutting through the noise of the crowd. Adina's face glowed with pride as she waved enthusiastically while Fleur clapped with unrestrained excitement, her smile wide and joyous. The vibrant banners of House Woodlock rippled in the breeze, their colours adding to the lively atmosphere.

Elinor turned towards them, her own smile widening. "I love the enthusiasm, ladies! I hope to see some great competitors from your house."

"Oh, we have brought plenty of experienced knights," Adina replied with playful confidence. "Even if you did steal our best archer." She shot a teasing look at Bradley, a glint of amusement in her eyes.

Elinor laughed heartily. "Yes, I did. And while I would love to apologise, I'm afraid I'm not the least bit sorry."

Bradley chuckled, shaking his head. "You know, Adina, we might have to negotiate a trade. Perhaps we could send you one of our finest swordsmen in return."

Adina grinned mischievously. "I'll hold you to that, brother. But don't forget… we have the most skilled warriors."

"Oh? Care to wager on it?" Bradley teased, his tone challenging.

"Only if you're looking to lose all your money," Fleur chimed in with a playful grin. Laughter rippled through the group, but any further teasing was interrupted as Elinor's house, Maycott, entered the arena. Their banner stood proudly, a striking display of a wolf's head in red and black, outlined in gold for added effect. The crowd erupted in cheers, their attention captivated by the regal display.

Once all the houses completed their demonstration, they engaged in a series of jovial games designed to entertain the spectators. Knights and squires participated in a spirited tug of war, while falconers showcased their skill with birds of prey. Falcons and eagles soared above the crowd before returning to their handlers, who also brought tame birds for the younger audience members to interact with and feed.

Fleur, ever the adventurer, wandered over to the falconry station. Donning a protective glove that extended to her elbow, she held out her arm. An eagle landed with a grace that belied its size, its sharp eyes scanning the gathered crowd. Fleur fed it with a steady hand, her expression a mixture of wonder and delight. The audience watched in awe, charmed by her natural affinity for animals.

Meanwhile, Bradley decided on a whim to join the tug of war, finding himself on the opposing team to his rival, Lord Stone. The crowd's excitement surged at the sight of the two men squaring off. The teams gripped the rope, muscles straining as they pulled with all their might. Mud churned beneath their boots as they dug in, each side determined not to give an inch.

"Come on, Bradley!" Elinor called out, her voice ringing above the crowd.

The two teams battled fiercely, the rope creaking under the strain. Bradley glanced towards Lord Stone, whose face was flushed with effort, his jaw set in grim determination. Summoning one final burst of strength, Bradley and his team gave a mighty heave, dragging Lord Stone's side over the line.

The crowd erupted in cheers, and Bradley grinned as he wiped the sweat from his brow. He strode over to Lord Stone, who leaned forward with hands on his knees, catching his breath and looking thoroughly defeated.

"Well fought, Lord Stone," Bradley said, extending a hand.

Stone eyed him warily but eventually clasped his hand in a firm shake. "Until next time," he muttered.

Elinor clapped her hands, her face glowing with pride. "That was fantastic! Well done, everyone!" Her voice carried above the crowd, and the competitors and spectators responded with cheers of camaraderie and laughter.

As the games wound down, performers took to the field, enacting mock duels and skirmishes that depicted historical battles. They wove stories of legendary heroes and bygone eras, their dramatic retellings captivating the audience. Elinor watched with rapt attention, her eyes tracking the actors' every move as the clang of swords and the cries of battle filled the air. The tales transported her to a time of valour and glory, leaving her deeply engrossed.

The crowd burst into applause when the performances ended, their cheers echoing across the field. Elinor joined in enthusiastically, her appreciation evident as she clapped alongside her guests.

The evening transitioned into a grand feast back at the castle. Lords and ladies gathered in the great hall, which was adorned with the banners of each house. Chandeliers cast a warm glow over the space, illuminating the long tables laden with sumptuous dishes: roasted meats and delicate pastries. The sounds of minstrels playing lively tunes filled the air, adding to the festive atmosphere.

Elinor and Bradley took their seats at the head table, overlooking the revelry.

The opening day of the tourney had been a resounding success, and Elinor found herself thoroughly enjoying the festivities. As night deepened, stars glittered in the sky, and the fires scattered throughout the grounds burned brightly, their crackling flames casting a warm glow against the darkness. The air was rich with the aromas of spiced wine and roasted meats, mingling with the sounds of laughter, music, and the occasional burst of hearty cheer.

Elinor and Bradley stood together, watching as the revellers danced, shared stories, and revelled in the joy of the day's events. The merriment was infectious, and even Elinor, who bore the weight of her crown, felt utterly at ease.

As the celebrations reached their peak, a hush fell over the crowd. A herald stepped forward to announce the schedule for the following day. Archery contests and foot combat, featuring thrilling one-on-one duels, promised an action-packed spectacle that had the crowd buzzing with excitement.

Shortly after the announcement, Elinor and Bradley excused themselves, making their way to the study for a meeting with Lloyd and Victoria. Their daughter had left earlier with the nanny, prompting them to also leave for the evening, saying they needed to check on her. When Elinor and Bradley entered, they noticed that Lloyd and Victoria were already seated, so they took seats opposite them. Once everyone was settled, Elinor began to share what had been happening recently.

"I would say I'm surprised, but it's exactly the kind of thing Lord Stone would do," Lloyd said, shaking his head.

Victoria leaned forward, a knowing look on her face. "So, I assume you're planning to confront him soon?"

Elinor nodded, her expression firm. "At the end of the tourney, once the winners have been announced and the rewards presented. I've prepared a particularly special 'gift' for him. One I doubt he'll appreciate."

"But one he deserves," Bradley added with a sly grin.

"And then some," Elinor replied. Her tone turned sharp with determination. "I'll also be adding an extra precaution to make sure he falls in line."

Victoria's curiosity was piqued. "Ooh, do tell," she said, her eyes sparkling with intrigue.

Elinor shook her head, smiling slyly. "This one, I'm keeping to myself. But I will say this: once it's done, I doubt Lord Stone will dare to step out of bounds again."

As the conversation continued, Elinor leaned back in her chair, her eyes heavy with exhaustion. The day's events were catching up with her. Unwilling to risk falling asleep mid-discussion, she stood, glancing between the others.

"I'm ready to retire for the night. How about you?"

Lloyd rose as well, stretching his arms. "Yes, I think we all need a good night's sleep before the games begin tomorrow."

Victoria followed suit, smoothing her skirts. Together, the group left the study, walking down the dimly lit corridor. When they reached the point where their paths diverged, they exchanged a few last words.

"Goodnight, Lloyd, Victoria. Rest well," Elinor said warmly.

"Goodnight, Your Majesty," Lloyd replied with a respectful nod.

"Sleep well, Elinor, Bradley," Victoria added, her eyes twinkling with anticipation for the coming days.

Elinor and Bradley walked hand in hand towards their chambers, the weight of the day settling comfortably around them. As they reached their door, Bradley turned to her, a mischievous smile tugging at his lips.

"Are you still not planning to tell me what this twist for Lord Stone is?"

Elinor raised a brow, her smile teasing. "And spoil the surprise? What do you think?"

"No?"

"No," she repeated, grinning as Bradley laughed softly.

"I can't wait to see what you have up your sleeve," he said, his voice filled with both admiration and amusement.

"You're going to love it," she promised, leaning closer. "Just wait."

With that, they disappeared into their chambers, the anticipation of the days ahead hanging between them like a pleasant secret.

Chapter 9

Let the Games Begin

After the parade the day before, the excitement in the air for the tournament's events was unmistakable. By early morning, people were already making their way to the field, eager to witness the opening archery competition. Bradley, participating in the event himself, had left early to get in some practice, leaving Elinor to enjoy a peaceful breakfast and a leisurely start to her day.

Feeling more tired than usual, Elinor allowed herself the rare indulgence of sleeping in and eating in bed. With the tournament in full swing, there were no meetings to attend or pressing duties to occupy her time. It seemed as though everyone had unofficially declared the week a holiday in honour of the games, and Elinor was determined to savour the reprieve before her responsibilities resumed. After finishing her meal, her ladies helped her prepare for the day. Once dressed, she joined Chloe in the carriage, the buzz of excitement for the tourney palpable as they made their way to the venue.

By the time they arrived, the field was already teeming with spectators eager for the competition to begin. Elinor made her way to the royal stand, where many of the noble ladies had already gathered. Among them was Lady Stone.

"Good morning, Your Majesty," Lady Stone greeted her with a curt nod.

"Lady Stone," Elinor replied, her tone measured. "I see our husbands will be competing against one another today."

"Yes," Lady Stone said, a small smile playing on her lips. "I suppose it's a case of letting the best man win."

"Indeed," Elinor replied, her eyes narrowing slightly. "Although I believe there's little doubt as to who that will be."

Lady Stone's smile faltered for a fraction of a second, though her expression remained poised. "I agree. Though I suspect our interpretations of 'the best man' may differ."

Elinor returned a tight smile. "Well, we shall see soon enough."

The brief exchange left a charged silence between them. The distant sounds of the tournament's preparations filled the air, an audible reminder of the stakes. Lady Stone broke the silence by taking her seat, and Elinor followed suit. Shielding her eyes from the bright sunlight, Elinor scanned the field below.

It was a gloriously cloudless day – perfect for the tournament but potentially challenging for the archers, depending on the alignment of the targets. To her relief, the targets faced away from the sun, ensuring optimal visibility. She settled in her seat, her anticipation growing as she thought of Bradley's role in the competition. Just as she adjusted her posture, the announcer stepped forward and rang a bell to capture the crowd's attention.

"Ladies and gentlemen, esteemed guests and noble participants," the announcer bellowed, "I declare the commencement of today's events: archery and foot combat!"

The announcer paused as Elinor stood up, allowing her to officially declare the start of the tourney when she exclaimed, "Let the games begin!"

The crowd erupted in cheers, and the first competitors – archers from House Bishop and House Roberts – stepped onto the field. Over the course of the morning, each house would field four archers, with points tallied to determine the overall victor.

As the event unfolded, the knights displayed impressive sportsmanship, exchanging polite gestures regardless of their scores. However, the dynamic shifted noticeably when Bradley and Lord Stone took to the field. Positioned beside one another in the same time slot, their rivalry was unmistakable. From her vantage point, Elinor couldn't discern their words, but their body language suggested tension, likely peppered with veiled insults.

Elinor straightened in her seat. Her attention was fixed on Bradley as he approached the line for his first attempt. The crowd fell silent, holding its collective breath as he notched his arrow and drew the bowstring taut. After a moment of precise aim, he released the arrow, which sailed gracefully through the air and struck the target just shy of the bullseye. The crowd cheered, and while it was an impressive shot by most standards, Elinor knew Bradley wouldn't relax until Lord Stone had taken his turn.

True to form, Bradley stepped back with a composed demeanour, his focus now shifting to his opponent. Lord Stone, with a smug smile, took his place and readied his arrow. Elinor's breath hitched as she watched him release his shot. When the arrow landed, it was clear his aim had faltered, missing Bradley's mark by a noticeable margin. Elinor cheered quietly, her relief evident. Bradley's eyes flickered with satisfaction, though he quickly masked it with a neutral expression.

The announcer's voice rang out again. "Round two! Prepare your arrows!"

Elinor's heart raced as Bradley and Lord Stone readied themselves for the next shot. The tension between the two men was apparent, each determined to outdo the other. Bradley inhaled deeply, his eyes narrowing as he took aim. The crowd once again fell silent, their anticipation building with every passing second.

As Bradley released his arrow, Elinor's gaze followed its trajectory. It struck true, hitting the bullseye with precision. A wave of relief swept over her, but she reminded herself that the competition was far from over.

Lord Stone stepped forward, his movements sharp and deliberate. With an air of practised confidence, he notched his arrow and took aim, his face a mask of concentration. The crowd held its collective breath once more as he released the arrow. It sailed through the air, landing just shy of Bradley's mark.

A collective gasp rippled through the spectators, quickly followed by cheers and applause. Elinor allowed herself a small, satisfied smile, her confidence in Bradley growing with each passing round. The competition continued in this pattern for several more rounds, with Bradley's arrows consistently landing closer to the bullseye than Lord Stone's. By the final match, the frustration on Lord Stone's face was evident. His hand trembled slightly as he aimed, and when he released the arrow, it struck the outer rim of the target.

His failure was unmistakable, and rage overtook him. Shaking with fury, Lord Stone stormed off the grounds, leaving Bradley to wave graciously to the cheering crowd.

Elinor rose to her feet, unable to contain her excitement. She clapped enthusiastically, her joy mirrored by the roaring audience. When Bradley caught her eye, he gave her a deep, theatrical bow before exiting the field to make way for the next set of competitors. Elinor returned to her seat, her heart swelling with pride for her husband, and continued to watch the remaining participants. Her house was performing well overall, though she left the task of tallying scores to the official scorers.

One competitor who caught her eye was a young man named Galrick from House Bennett. His skill was undeniable, and he gave even the more seasoned knights a serious challenge. During his pairing with Bradley, the two seemed evenly matched, much to Elinor's surprise. What stood out most to her was Galrick's humility – a rare quality for a lord's young son. At his age, they were often arrogant and spoiled, but Galrick's demeanour was refreshing and admirable.

As the last match concluded, Elinor made her way to her house's tent. Inside, she found Bradley reclining with a drink in hand, exchanging playful banter with the other knights. When she entered, the men immediately stood and greeted her with respectful nods.

"Please, as you were, gentlemen," she said warmly. "I'm here to congratulate you all on an excellent performance today. Especially my dear husband." With a smile, she took the seat beside Bradley. At her words, the knights relaxed and resumed their conversation, their camaraderie filling the tent. A young squire quickly brought her a glass of wine, and Elinor joined in the lively banter.

"Lord Stone didn't seem too pleased at losing to you, Bradley," Sir Miller remarked with a smirk.

"No, he smashed his bow into the ground back at the tent," Sir Perkins added and then chuckled. "He's always been a sore loser."

Laughter erupted among the group, and the knights continued their playful teasing, pointing out both the flaws and merits of their peers. The jovial atmosphere was infectious, and even Elinor found herself laughing along with their jokes.

As midday approached, Elinor arranged for food to be brought to the tent. Platters of hot meals were set before them, and the group enjoyed their feast together, sharing stories and laughter. Soon, the knights began to prepare themselves for the next competition: foot combat.

After finishing her meal, Elinor wished the knights luck in the upcoming competition. She then retreated to her private tent to freshen up before returning to the royal stands. Upon arriving, she noticed Bradley engaged in conversation with a group of men. Offering him a polite nod, she took her seat. A few minutes later, he joined her just as the announcer stepped forward to address the crowd.

"With the first event of the day complete, prepare yourselves for the next challenge: foot combat!" the announcer proclaimed, ringing the bell. The competitors began lining up on the field, ready for the gruelling matches ahead. The organisers paired off the participants, each house contributing six challengers. The chosen weapons for the event were swords and poleaxes, raising the stakes and adding to the intensity of the battles. Each match promised to test the contestants' strength, strategy, and skill.

The first match featured two formidable knights – Sir Edmund of House Malins and Sir Gregory of House Roberts. Sir Edmund, renowned for his agility, faced Sir Gregory, whose strength was unmatched. The two warriors circled each other, their gazes locked, before clashing in a furious exchange of blows.

Elinor leaned forward in her seat, her heart pounding with each strike. Sir Edmund's nimble footwork allowed him to evade Sir Gregory's powerful swings, but Gregory's unrelenting force kept Edmund on the defensive. The knights fought fiercely, neither willing to yield, and the match remained evenly balanced as the tension in the crowd grew.

The announcer's voice rang out, cutting through the noise of battle. "A splendid display of skill and valour! Who will emerge victorious in this clash of titans?"

Finally, Sir Edmund executed an unexpected manoeuvre, deftly disarming Sir Gregory and sending his sword flying across the field. The crowd erupted into thunderous cheers as Sir Edmund was declared the victor of the first match. Elinor let out a breath she hadn't realised she was holding, her excitement growing for the contests yet to come.

As the competition progressed, Elinor found herself once again captivated by the prowess of young Galrick. He moved across the field like a force of nature, wielding his sword with a combination of grace and power that left his opponents reeling. Despite his youth, Galrick dispatched seasoned knights twice his size with remarkable ease, earning the admiration of the spectators.

His next opponent was a knight from House Stone, and Elinor felt a surge of anticipation as she watched them face off. She silently prayed to the divine spirit for Galrick's victory, her confidence in his abilities unwavering. The stage was set for another thrilling match, and Elinor couldn't wait to see how the young warrior would fare against his formidable adversary.

The two combatants lined up in the arena, each clad in plated armour for protection. Their helmets were securely fastened, visors lowered, and swords gripped firmly in hand. Both assumed defensive stances, muscles coiled, as they waited for the bell to signal the start. When the sharp ring echoed across the field, they sprang into action, moving swiftly on their feet and striking at one another with precision.

The match was evenly balanced, though the knight from House Stone appeared to have the upper hand. He pressed his advantage relentlessly, his blade flashing in the sunlight as he delivered a series of precise, calculated strikes. The clang of steel reverberated through the arena, but Galrick proved to be no easy opponent. With a deft parry, he deflected the knight's sword and countered with a powerful strike of his own, forcing his rival to step back.

Sensing his moment, Galrick kept up the pressure. His strikes were unyielding, driving his opponent to the brink. The knight struggled to maintain his defence, unable to block every blow as Galrick's attacks came faster and harder. Even as the knight rallied and launched a fierce counterassault, his blade a blur of motion, Galrick's agility and unmatched skill allowed him to dodge and weave effortlessly. Spotting an opening, he delivered a decisive strike, sending the knight sprawling to the ground.

The audience erupted in a cacophony of cheers and applause as Galrick stood victorious, his chest heaving from exertion but his armour unscathed. Elinor watched in awe, her admiration for the young warrior growing. Glancing towards the crowd, she caught sight of Lord Stone's furious expression as he hurled his glass to the ground in anger. A triumphant smile spread across her face as she stood, cheering loudly for Galrick.

"Bravo, young Galrick!" she called out. "You display remarkable strength and skill, outmatching men with far more experience. You are truly someone to watch, and I eagerly await the moment you face one of my own knights."

Galrick bowed deeply in response, his voice carrying across the arena. "Thank you, Your Majesty. Your praise is an honour."

Both Galrick and his defeated opponent exited the arena, making way for the next two combatants. Elinor resumed her seat, anticipation gleaming in her eyes as she awaited Galrick's next match. Although her praise had been partly intended to rile Lord Stone, she couldn't deny that the young warrior's talent was exceptional. Her curiosity about how he would fare against her knights grew with each passing match. Skilled fighters were always in demand, and Galrick could very well be an asset worth employing.

"It seems you struck a nerve, my dear," Bradley remarked with an amused chuckle.

"Oh?" Elinor replied, arching an eyebrow.

"Lord Stone stormed off after you praised Galrick," Bradley explained. "He truly is a sore loser. And yet, his house is performing well overall, so he really has nothing to complain about. Unlike House Roberts… they haven't won a single event so far."

"Perhaps they need a bit of encouragement," Elinor mused, her gaze sweeping across the crowd. "Or perhaps a new strategy. Strength alone won't secure victory. Wit and determination are equally important. Just because House Roberts is small doesn't mean they should lose everything."

Bradley nodded in agreement. "True. Look at House Bennett. Modest in numbers, yet they are holding their own—and that's largely thanks to Galrick. He's not only skilled but intelligent and driven, a rare combination. He's remarkable."

Elinor smiled. "Indeed, he is. I'm eager to see how he continues to surprise us."

The bell rang once more, signalling the start of the next round, and the royal couple turned their attention back to the field. After a brief break for food and refreshments, they returned to their seats. Elinor's heart quickened as the knights took their places for the next match. This was the moment she had been waiting for: Galrick against Sir Aldric, one of her knights.

Sir Aldric was an imposing figure, standing over six feet tall and stocky, with a broad chest that spoke of years of hard-fought battles. A seasoned knight with a reputation for being nearly unbeatable, he held his helmet in one hand as his sharp eyes scanned his opponent. His gaze reflected a mix of curiosity and disdain, sizing up the young challenger before him.

Opposite him stood Galrick, slimmer and less physically intimidating, though still of considerable height. What Galrick lacked in sheer size and strength, he more than compensated for with agility and quick reflexes – traits that had carried him to victory thus far. But whether those would be enough to defeat a queen's knight remained to be seen. This match promised to be a captivating clash of experience and raw talent.

Elinor leaned forward on the edge of her seat. Her eyes fixed on the two men as they took their positions. Sir Aldric placed his helmet over his head, lowering his visor before unsheathing his sword. Galrick, already in his stance, gripped his blade with practised confidence, his eyes locked on his formidable opponent.

The crowd fell silent, the arena blanketed in anticipation. All eyes were on the field, waiting to see if the young warrior could hold his own against such a renowned adversary. When the bell rang, the knights sprang into action, and the crowd erupted in cheers as steel clashed against steel.

Sir Aldric's strikes were precise and overwhelming, each swing forcing Galrick to retreat step by step. The older knight's experience and control were evident in every calculated strike, feint, and parry, his dominance slowly pushing Galrick towards the edge of the arena. The younger fighter dug his heels into the ground, refusing to yield despite the relentless assault.

Galrick's focus sharpened as he studied Sir Aldric's movements, seeking patterns and weaknesses. With agility and cunning, he began to anticipate the knight's attacks, darting in and out of range. His quick counterstrikes began to chip away at Sir Aldric's defences, each blow calculated to test the older knight's endurance.

"Oh, nice move!" Bradley called out as Galrick narrowly dodged a crushing overhead strike. Despite being knocked off his feet moments earlier, he rolled clear of the attack and sprang to his feet with remarkable speed. Darting to the side, he seized the opening to land a strike against Sir Aldric's back, causing the knight to stagger forward with a frustrated grunt.

Facing one another again, the two knights resumed their clash, the crowd growing louder with each exchange. The match wore on, and both combatants began to tire. Their movements slowed, their strikes less forceful as fatigue took hold. Galrick faltered briefly, stumbling to one knee.

Sensing victory, Sir Aldric raised his sword to deliver what seemed to be the final blow. But just as the blade descended, Galrick sprang up like a fox, his sword flashing upward to halt inches from Sir Aldric's exposed throat. Time seemed to freeze as the crowd collectively held its breath. Recognising his defeat, Sir Aldric released his grip on his sword, letting it clatter to the ground.

The arena erupted in thunderous applause, the unexpected victory electrifying the spectators. Elinor stood with her hand pressed to her chest in amazement. In the field below, Galrick, still breathing heavily, extended a respectful hand to Sir Aldric. The defeated knight, though visibly disappointed, nodded in approval and accepted the gesture, shaking Galrick's hand firmly.

"Oh, bravo to you both!" Elinor called, her voice carrying over the cheers. "What an extraordinary performance! A grand battle between two worthy opponents. Galrick, your talent is exceptional… outstanding enough to best one of my most admirable knights. Congratulations. I confess I wish to be upset with you for defeating Sir Aldric, yet your skills leave me in awe."

"Thank you, Your Majesty," Galrick replied, bowing deeply. "Your praise means everything to a young warrior like me."

Elinor turned to Sir Aldric with a warm smile. "Well fought, Sir Aldric. Though victory escaped you today, you brought honour to me and the House of Maycott. I am proud."

The knights bowed once more before leaving the arena as the next competitors prepared to take the field. Elinor resumed her seat, though the matches that followed paled in comparison to what she had just witnessed. The crowd remained enthusiastic, but to her, the subsequent battles felt anticlimactic. She clapped and cheered when appropriate, her thoughts drifting back to the remarkable display of skill she had just seen.

Before long, Bradley squeezed her hand gently, drawing her out of her reverie. "Ready to leave?" he asked.

"Yes," Elinor replied with a soft smile. "I feel quite tired after today's events."

Taking his arm, she rose, and the two made their way out of the royal stands. Along the way, they exchanged polite conversation with some of the lords and ladies in attendance before climbing into their waiting carriage. Elinor leaned back against the cushioned seat, closing her eyes as Bradley settled beside her, his hand resting reassuringly over hers.

"I don't know about you, but I feel like I could curl up in bed and sleep until morning," Elinor murmured, her voice heavy with fatigue.

"Then you should, my darling," Bradley replied, his tone warm and understanding. "It's been an exhausting few weeks for you—preparing the tourney, managing the guests, and dealing with Lord Stone and his constant transgressions. It's no wonder you're more tired than usual."

"Hmm," Elinor muttered softly in response, her eyelids growing heavier as she began to drift off. The rhythmic motion of the carriage lulled her into a light sleep. She woke only when Bradley gently shook her shoulder, his voice calm as he helped her out of the carriage and guided her to their chambers.

Still dazed, she climbed into bed, her movements slow and uncoordinated. Bradley removed her shoes and carefully slipped her dress off before pulling the blankets over her. As her face pressed into the velvety softness of the pillow, her eyes closed completely, and sleep claimed her in an instant. She didn't stir again until the morning light streamed through the windows.

Chapter 10

A Special Guest

Before Elinor headed to the field for the third day of events, she spent the morning in her study, signing a few pressing documents. She had assumed that the tourney would put routine matters on hold, but her clerk informed her of a handful of urgent issues that required immediate attention. The recent attack on Bradley's ships and cargo had galvanised her resolve to prevent such incidents in the future.

Among the documents was one guaranteeing safe passage for travelling merchants within her lands, as well as provisions for overseas trade. For the latter, she had already sent word to neighbouring countries with whom her realm traded, proposing an agreement to establish secure routes for sailors transporting goods. She also broached the question of penalties for those who disrupted trade for personal gain.

In her domain, the punishment for such acts was unequivocal: those found guilty would forfeit their lives. The complexity arose when addressing crimes committed at sea, where jurisdiction often depended on whose waters the offences occurred in. Elinor had awaited responses from several kings across the ocean, urging them to adopt similarly severe measures, including the death penalty, to deter such acts.

To her relief, the replies she received were favourable – each ruler agreed to uphold strict penalties against anyone interfering with trade operations. With this consensus, Elinor signed the prepared documents, which would be copied and sent to the relevant countries. These agreements safeguarded not only commerce but also her position. If pirates attempted anything similar in the future, she would have the legal foundation to act decisively without risking unintended consequences.

The last thing Elinor wanted was to provoke a war by executing someone of importance from another land without a prior agreement. Thieves or not, the lack of a formal accord could spark conflict, even if her actions were justified.

With her work concluded, Elinor left the study and joined her guests in the great hall for a celebratory breakfast. She dined with the remaining knights and other attendees, all of whom were in high spirits, eager for the day's events.

After the morning meal, the jousting would begin. Knights from each of the six houses would compete against one another, earning points to advance through the rounds. The tournament would continue until only two knights remained, jousting for the coveted title of the greatest jouster in the land.

In preparation for the joust, every house had adorned their horses with caparisons bearing their house colours and sigils. The knights were clad in heavy plate armour, ensuring maximum protection during the contest. Lances crafted from sturdy oak were lined up along the lists, ready for use. Each house had brought an ample supply, knowing how often they shattered during the competition.

The first match pitted House Bennett against House Woodlock, with each house fielding two knights for the event. The first pair of competitors were already mounted, awaiting the order to begin. Their chosen lances were handed to them by their squires. At the sound of the signal, the knights spurred their horses forward, charging down the list towards one another, their lances poised for the strike.

House Woodlock's knight aimed to strike true against House Bennett's, while his opponent sought to return the favour in kind. Woodlock's lance connected with Bennett's shield but glanced off its edge, deflecting with a sharp twist as Woodlock's knight turned his body. Bennett's knight struck out with his lance, only to meet empty air.

Reaching the end of the track, both knights wheeled their horses around to face each other again, eager for the next pass. After a quick check of the lances, the signal was given, and the knights prepared for another charge. As the trumpet sounded, they launched into motion, thundering down the list with renewed determination.

This time, House Woodlock's lance struck true, hitting the centre of his opponent's shield with a resounding crack. The force of the blow unseated Bennett's knight, sending him crashing to the ground with a heavy *thud*, his shield and lance scattering to either side.

With the match decided, the judges declared Sir Young of House Woodlock the victor. The announcer's proclamation brought the crowd to its feet, cheering enthusiastically for the triumphant knight. Meanwhile, the defeated knight's squire rushed to help him to his feet. Though uninjured aside from his pride, he bowed respectfully to Elinor before retreating to the tent prepared for him.

Sir Young took a seat on the sidelines, watching as the next set of contestants prepared for their bout.

Elinor remained in the stands, closely observing the matches as they unfolded. She cheered with particular fervour whenever her knights competed, especially when they faced Lord Stones's team. If her knights emerged victorious, she allowed herself a smug glance in his direction, a gesture he reciprocated when the tables were turned. The rivalry between them only added to the charged atmosphere of the games, which grew more electric with every pass and every triumph.

By the final round, only two knights remained – one representing Maycott and the other Woodlock. This was particularly notable as they hailed from the courts of Elinor and Bradley, respectively. Both were fiercely competitive, each determined for their house to claim victory.

The crowd murmured with anticipation as the knights took their places. Sir Reginald, the pride of Bradley's house, sat tall atop his magnificent white steed, his polished armour gleaming in the sunlight. He held his lance steady, his gaze fixed firmly on his opponent. Opposing him was Sir Wood, the champion of Elinor's house, mounted on a powerful black stallion that pawed at the ground, its energy barely contained. Sir Wood's lance was poised, and his sharp eyes never left Sir Reginald.

The announcer stepped forward, and a hush fell across the field. "This is a momentous occasion, as knights of the Queen and the King Regent prepare for the final charge! Let the strongest triumph and bring glory to their house!"

All fell silent as the knights adjusted their positions, waiting for the signal.

"This is it, my love. May the best knight win," Bradley said with a smirk.

"Good luck to yours. He will need it," Elinor replied coolly.

"Ha! We shall see."

Both monarchs were on the edge of their seats, their eyes fixed on the knights. Elinor's foot tapped restlessly, her thoughts consumed by the hope that Sir Wood would emerge victorious.

At the sound of the bell, the knights spurred their steeds forward, the ground trembling beneath the pounding hooves of the horses. Dust swirled in the air as they closed the distance with remarkable speed.

The first pass was swift and intense. Sir Reginald's lance struck Sir Wood's shield with a loud, resounding *thud*, earning Bradley's house the first point. Sir Wood's lance, however, glanced off Sir Reginald's armour, leaving him scoreless.

The knights returned to their starting positions, their movements precise and measured as they prepared for the second pass. When the bell sounded again, the intensity only heightened. This time, Sir Wood aimed true, his lance striking Sir Reginald's shield dead centre, evening the score. Sir Reginald's lance also struck its mark, but the blow lacked the same power, leaving the two knights tied.

All eyes turned to the final charge, the decisive moment of the match. The tension in the air was palpable as the knights readied themselves for one last run. The crowd held its collective breath as the bell tolled. With a thunderous burst of speed, Sir Reginald and Sir Wood charged towards one another.

This time, Sir Wood's lance hit Sir Reginald's shield with such force that it sent him tumbling from his horse. The white steed slowed, riderless, as Sir Reginald hit the ground with a heavy *thud*. For a brief, tense moment, he lay still, and an audible gasp rippled through the crowd. A hush fell as everyone waited to see if he was unhurt. Then, Sir Reginald raised a hand, waving to the onlookers, and removed his helmet.

Sir Wood dismounted immediately and helped his opponent to his feet. Once it was clear that Sir Reginald was unharmed, the crowd erupted into deafening cheers. The herald stepped forward, his voice ringing across the field as he proclaimed the victor.

"Victory to Sir Julian Wood of the Queen's House! Glory and honour to House Maycott!"

Elinor and Bradley rose to their feet, joining the crowd in applause. Both were proud of the courage and skill displayed by their knights. Though defeated, Sir Reginald accepted his loss with grace. He approached Sir Wood, offering a firm handshake and a friendly clasp on the shoulder before leaving the field, allowing the victor his moment of glory.

"Well, it seems you've won," Bradley said with a wry smile.

"You sound surprised," Elinor teased. "Of course, my knights are better than yours. Oh, and don't forget, you owe me ten gold coins."

As Sir Julian Wood approached the royal stand, Elinor's expression brightened.

"Julian, may I congratulate you on your excellent showmanship today. You've done both me and House Maycott proud."

"Thank you, Your Majesty," Sir Julian replied, bowing deeply.

"Rest well before the next game, but make sure to celebrate this victory tonight. I certainly will." Elinor cast a smug glance at Bradley as she dismissed her knight, sending him off to enjoy his triumph.

With the final event of the day still hours away, Elinor and Bradley returned to the castle for lunch. After a light meal, fatigue caught up with Elinor, and she dozed off in her chair. Bradley woke her gently, shaking her shoulder.

"My love, it's time to return," he said softly.

"Already?" she murmured, rubbing her eyes. "Give me ten minutes to freshen up. I'll meet you at the steps."

True to form, Elinor took closer to twenty minutes, but she eventually arrived, standing by the carriage as Bradley finished a conversation with the guards.

"Look who's making who wait now," she joked as he opened the door and helped her inside before following her.

"Apologies, my love. I got caught up with the men."

"Anything interesting?" she asked, amused.

"Just talk about who might win the strength games—and who has lost the most money so far. Apparently, Dimmock is losing coin fast."

Elinor laughed at that as the carriage carried them back to the field. They returned just in time, taking their seats as the next round of contests began.

Following the jousting, knights from every faction gathered for the strength contest. The events included wrestling, shield lifting, hammer throwing, the stone put, and carrying a log the farthest. Each activity drew a mix of participants, testing not only physical strength but also strategy and determination.

As the competition began, each house was eager to showcase its skills and prove its mettle. The wrestling matches were fierce, with participants grappling in close quarters, using a combination of brute strength and tactical mind games to outwit their opponents. Bloody noses and bruises were common, yet the knights persevered, spurred on by the deafening cheers of the crowd celebrating each victor.

In the shield-lifting event, the knights demonstrated incredible stamina and physical power, hoisting massive, heavy shields high above their heads and holding them steady for as long as possible. The crowd marvelled at the endurance displayed, their admiration growing with each passing second the shields remained aloft.

The hammer-throwing contest captivated the spectators as knights hurled enormous hammers through the air, aiming for both distance and accuracy. Elinor found herself impressed, watching in amazement at the sheer force and skill it took to send the hammer soaring.

The stone put tested the raw, explosive strength of the participants as they heaved massive stones with all their might. Each throw reverberated with a heavy *thud* as the stones landed, a testament to the knights' determination and unyielding effort. The competitors pushed themselves to their limits, continuing until their arms trembled with exhaustion, forcing the stones to drop at their feet.

The final event, the log-carrying challenge, demanded not only strength but also strategy and resilience. Knights struggled under the immense weight of the logs, balancing them on their shoulders as they staggered across the marked distance. It was clear this was the most gruelling of the games – postures bent under strain, faces glistening with sweat, and muscles bulging as they fought to maintain their footing.

Despite the fierce competition, camaraderie was evident throughout the games. Elinor noticed the shared cheers and encouragement from the knights and their supporters, regardless of house allegiance. It was a heartening sight, showcasing a unity that transcended rivalries. As the evening set in, the game concluded, and Elinor rose to address the gathered participants and onlookers.

"Knights and noble houses," she began, her voice carrying across the field, "today we have witnessed not only a display of remarkable strength and skill but also the true spirit of camaraderie. Though the competition was fierce, the support and encouragement you showed one another transcended house boundaries."

Her gaze swept across the crowd, her expression warm and proud. "It warms my heart to see such dedication and sportsmanship. Each of you has given your all, and I look forward to seeing what tomorrow brings. As the sun sets on this glorious day, let us congratulate not just the victors of the games, but the spirit of fellowship that makes our kingdom strong. I am proud of each and every one of you. Now, go and celebrate your victories."

At her words, a roar of cheers erupted from the crowd. The knights bowed to their queen, offering words of gratitude and respect as they began to disperse. Laughter and celebration filled the air as the participants headed off to enjoy the evening's festivities. Elinor, too, made her way to the waiting carriage, her heart light with satisfaction at the day's success.

Elinor rode back from the tourney alone, Bradley still at the grounds celebrating with the participants. As her carriage arrived at the castle, one of her trusted guards, Cole, was there to greet her. He stepped forward, extending his hand to assist her as she descended the carriage steps onto the pebbled ground.

"Your Majesty, I trust you had a pleasant day," he said, his tone respectful yet warm.

"I did, thank you, Cole. And how about yourself?" she asked as they walked into the castle together.

"Splendid, Your Highness. I managed to watch a few events earlier. The tourney seems to be going wonderfully," he said, a hint of pride in his voice.

"It is indeed. I'm glad I had it organised. It's doing wonders for the city's morale," Elinor agreed, a small smile gracing her lips. Her gaze sharpened slightly as she added, "But I sense there's more to your presence than simply chatting with your queen."

Cole straightened, his expression turning serious. "Yes, Your Majesty. I regret to inform you that your special guest is being rather… difficult. Additionally, there's the matter of our other guests to attend to, given their important role in tomorrow's proceedings on the final day of the tourney."

Elinor sighed softly. "Ah, yes. I'll handle our troublesome guest personally. As for the others, would you be so kind as to make the necessary arrangements?"

"It would be my pleasure," Cole replied with a bow.

"Thank you, Cole. I don't know what I would do without you," she said with genuine gratitude. As Cole departed to manage the pirates, Elinor made her way to a dusty, narrow storage room deep within the castle.

The room was unremarkable at first glance, its shelves cluttered with old bottles and rusted buckets. Elinor knelt down and pulled back a tattered, worn rug, revealing a heavy wooden trapdoor. Her fingers found the concealed latch, and with a soft creak, it unlocked. She lifted the door, exposing a dark, narrow staircase spiralling down into the depths. Grabbing a lantern from the shelf, she lit its candle with a wave of her hand. As she descended, she flicked her wrist, and the trapdoor above her closed, the rug sliding back into place as though untouched.

The room was protected by a powerful charm, one that allowed only a select few access. Any intruder who dared to enter uninvited would find the air stolen from their lungs, death coming swiftly to those who lingered. Aside from Elinor, the only others with entry were Bradley – though he had yet to set foot here – Julian and Cole. None outside this circle even knew of the chamber's existence.

At the bottom of the stairs, a narrow corridor lined with six small cells awaited her. Only one of the cells was occupied. The prisoner inside wasn't used to such conditions, and if Cole had described them as 'difficult', then Elinor resolved to make sure they understood the consequences of disobedience.

Shadows danced along the walls as the faint orange glow of her lantern illuminated the space. Elinor's presence seemed to amplify the oppressive darkness that clung to the chamber. She stepped inside, her power radiating through the room as she closed the door behind her.

"Hello, dear," she said, her voice smooth but laced with menace. "I hear you've been giving my men a hard time. That simply won't do. Perhaps a little lesson in obedience will change your mind."

The lone figure in the cell shrank back, their muffled screams barely audible through the gag covering their mouth. Elinor raised a hand, unleashing her magic. The prisoner's body writhed in agony, their muscles spasming uncontrollably as pain surged through them. Elinor watched coldly, releasing her power in measured bursts, conserving her strength for a final display of dominance if necessary.

When the muffled sobs grew louder, Elinor stepped closer. Unable to make out the prisoner's words, she reached down and removed the gag.

"Please… let me go," the woman begged, curling into a ball as if trying to shield herself from further torture.

Elinor crouched beside her, brushing a strand of hair from the prisoner's face. "Not until you've served your purpose," she replied. Her tone was calm, almost gentle, but it carried a chilling undercurrent. She sent a wave of pain through the woman, whose screams echoed through the chamber as her body convulsed violently. Elinor watched as their bloodshot eyes pleaded for mercy. Their expression contorted in agony. Her mouth twisted in a silent scream, and every muscle in their visage reflected the unbearable torment.

When Elinor finally withdrew her power, the woman sagged to the floor, and her sobs filled the oppressive silence. "You have a purpose, my dear, and all will be revealed soon. Unless you wish for me to return, I suggest you behave for my men," Elinor warned, her words dripping with authority.

Satisfied, she rose and left the cell. The echo of the woman's wails followed her as she ascended the staircase. At the top, she nearly collided with Cole, who was carrying a tray of food for their guest.

"She's all yours," Elinor told him coldly. "If there are any further problems, let me know, and I'll deal with her again."

"Yes, Your Majesty," Cole replied and nodded.

Exhausted from the day's events, Elinor returned to her chambers to rest. Yet, despite her fatigue, sleep eluded her. Her mind buzzed with anticipation for the final day of the tourney, a day she knew would be filled with excitement and triumph.

Chapter 11

End of the Tourney

On the morning of the fourth day, all the contestants assembled in the field for the melee. The participants were divided into teams, each consisting of members from different houses mixed into four new groups. Unique colours distinguished these groups: Team A wore red, Team B green, Team C blue, and Team D yellow. The competition followed a round-robin format, with each group battling fiercely against the others until only two teams remained. The final clash would determine the ultimate champion, bringing glory and honour to the victorious knights.

Once the teams were organised, Groups A and B entered the arena, ready for the opening match. Each contestant sported armbands in their team's colours, and flags bearing their respective hues fluttered behind them. Clad in full armour, they stood poised, gripping their weapons as they awaited the signal. When the trumpet sounded, the knights surged forward. There was no hesitation – both sides charged as one, their voices echoing across the field in fierce battle cries.

The clash was immediate and chaotic, a storm of bodies and weapons colliding in a frenzy. After the initial charge, the combat splintered into smaller skirmishes. Knights broke off into groups, engaging in intense hand-to-hand combat with swords, maces, and shields. Each team employed distinct strategies to tip the battle in their favour. Team A relied on brute strength and disciplined formations, using coordinated pushes to isolate and overwhelm their opponents. Team B, on the other hand, focused on agility and precision, darting in and out of the fray with swift, calculated strikes.

The contest was exhilarating and hard-fought, but Team A ultimately emerged victorious. Their relentless pressure forced Team B back over the boundary line, and most of Team B's members were eliminated, having been deemed 'dead' or 'fatally wounded'.

With the first match concluded, the field was swiftly prepared for the next bout, which proved just as thrilling as the first. Elinor watched from the sidelines, captivated by the spectacle, as were the gathered onlookers. By the end of the tournament, the knights were exhausted yet jubilant, their faces streaked with mud but lit up with smiles. The crowd erupted in cheers when Team C was declared the overall victor, their triumph celebrated by all.

"Congratulations to group C! What a splendid display of teamwork and skill from you all," Elinor declared. "The melee was the final event in this tourney, and to celebrate all who participated, as well as the victors of the games, a wondrous feast will soon begin in the great hall.

"But before we proceed, I would like to extend my heartfelt gratitude to all the contestants who have demonstrated such bravery and honour. Your efforts have not only entertained us but have reminded everyone of the valour and chivalry you embody daily. Let us raise our goblets to the spirit of camaraderie and the pursuit of excellence. To the knights, to the victors, and to the glory of our realm!"

Elinor raised her goblet high, her voice ringing clear above the gathered crowd. Everyone cheered and toasted as the sounds of jubilation echoed across the field.

After the speech, Elinor made her way back to the castle. Once in her chambers, she quickly prepared herself for the grand feast. She was certain many were already gathered in the great hall, celebrating with food and drink, but she was determined to look every bit the regal queen when she presented the awards. She donned a sweeping silk gown in her house colours of red and black, its elegant train trailing behind her. Her long, wavy hair was crowned with the royal tiara, a gleaming symbol of her authority and grace.

When she entered the great hall, the air buzzed with merriment. Bradley was already among the knights, laughing and raising his goblet in a toast. Drinks flowed freely, and the tables were laden with appetisers, which were eagerly devoured by the lively crowd. Many lords were deep into their cups, while some ladies, Elinor suspected, were still freshening up before joining the festivities.

The room fell silent as her guards announced her arrival. Heads turned towards her as she stepped into the hall, her presence commanding instant respect.

"Please, don't stop celebrating on my account," she said with a gracious smile. "This is your night, after all."

The crowd resumed their chatter and laughter, and Elinor made her way towards Bradley, who greeted her with a warm smile and a kiss on her hand. He swayed somewhat as he spoke, his voice cheerful.

"There you are, my dear," he said, his words slightly slurred.

Elinor chuckled softly. "You might want to eat a little more food, my love. You seem to have got an early start to the festivities."

As the music began to fade, a group of dancers dressed in vibrant colours moved to the centre of the room. With fluid movements, they arranged themselves into position. Lively melodies filled the air, and the performers launched into an intricate routine that captivated the audience. Their dance told a story through motion, each step and gesture adding to the narrative.

When the performance came to an end, the hall erupted in applause, only to fall silent as heralds stepped forward, their trumpets blaring a triumphant tune. Anticipation rippled through the crowd. The scores had been tallied, and the victors of the events were to be announced – both those who earned the highest points and the crowd favourites.

Elinor, like the rest, was eager to hear the results. She had her suspicions about who might win, based on what she had witnessed, but no certainty.

The heralds were tasked with announcing the winners, but it was Elinor who would present the prizes. The awards were laid out on a large wooden table, an impressive display of swords, bows, shields, coins, and more. She positioned herself near the table, her poise unwavering, waiting for the announcements to begin so she could bestow the prizes upon the deserving champions.

"Ladies and gentlemen," the herald's voice rang out across the hall, "it is time to reveal the champions of the tournament!" A hush fell over the crowd, anticipation thick in the air. As each victor was announced, the room burst into jubilant cheers, the walls echoing with applause and shouts of celebration.

Elinor stepped forward with regal grace, presenting each winner and runner-up with their prizes: finely crafted swords, high-quality bows, lances, decorated shields, hammers, belts, and gleaming gold coins. These rewards honoured the best house, the finest competitor overall, and the most promising newcomer. With each presentation, she offered heartfelt congratulations, even to the typically stoic Lord Stone, whose stern expression softened briefly in her presence.

The champions and runners-up were as follows:

For archery, Lord Bradley Woodlock of House Maycott claimed victory, with Lord Stone of House Stone taking second place.

For foot combat, Sir Edmund of House Malins emerged as the champion, followed closely by the young Lord Galrick of House Bennett.

For jousting, Sir Wood of House Maycott secured the top spot, while Sir Reginald of House Woodlock was named runner-up.

For the strength contest, Sir Aldric of House Maycott proved his might by taking first place, with Sir Miller of House Bishop in second.

For the melee, after an intense battle, Group C triumphed, displaying exceptional teamwork and spirit.

In the final tally, Sir Aldric of House Maycott was crowned the tournament champion, while the title of most outstanding newcomer was awarded to Lord Galrick Bennett.

Elinor's heart swelled with pride, not only because her house had secured first place overall but also because young Lord Galrick had earned the well-deserved recognition of the best newcomer. His performance throughout the tournament had been nothing short of exceptional.

She approached Galrick with a warm smile, extending the elegantly crafted sword that served as his prize. "Congratulations, Lord Galrick. I watched your performances with great admiration. Your skill and determination were truly remarkable. You have a bright future ahead of you."

Galrick bowed deeply, his expression both humble and proud. "Thank you, Your Majesty. Your words honour me, and

I shall treasure this gift. I am profoundly grateful for the opportunity to compete and for your kind recognition. I will strive to work hard and bring prestige to House Bennett."

With all the prizes presented, the hall erupted into renewed celebration. Elinor took her seat at the high table, observing the revelry with satisfaction as the feasting and drinking resumed. Yet, her attention often strayed towards Lord Stone, who sat among his companions, laughing and sharing a drink.

A mischievous smile played on her lips as she glanced in his direction. Rising from her seat, she tapped her goblet with a silver spoon, the clear chime silencing the room.

"May I have everyone's attention?" she called, her voice commanding. As the hall quieted and all eyes turned towards her, she continued, "I wanted to congratulate our winners once more and present one final, unique prize."

"Lord Stone, congratulations on being the runner-up in the archery competition. Come forward… I have an extra special gift for you," Elinor announced, her voice carrying a tone of mock cordiality.

At first, Lord Stone smiled, but his expression faltered at her words, replaced by a flicker of confusion. Elinor's smile didn't waver. Instead, it deepened, her eyes gleaming with a knowing intensity that made his face pale. Rising slowly, he moved towards the long table she gestured to, each step cautious, the table was draped in pristine white linen, and atop it rested a series of covered silver platters. Stone's brow furrowed as he tilted his head, scrutinising the mysterious setup.

"A special feast?" he asked hesitantly.

"Oh, it's certainly unique," Elinor replied, her tone almost teasing. "But I'm not sure you'll have the stomach to eat what lies beneath those trays."

With a nod from the queen, the guards removed the covers from the twelve platters in unison. A collective gasp swept through the hall, followed by a ripple of murmurs. Lord Stone stood frozen, his face ashen, and his eyes filled with horror as he stared at what lay before him.

On each silver tray rested a severed head, the flesh still fresh from its grisly fate. These were the heads of the main crew responsible for sinking the ships – a crime Elinor intended to expose fully.

"I believe you recognise these gentlemen?" she asked, her voice sharp.

"This is my first time seeing them," Lord Stone replied, his voice barely above a whisper.

"Really?" Elinor's brows arched in mock surprise. "Because they certainly knew you. Each of them had plenty to say about the great Lord Stone who hired them to destroy Lord Woodlock's vessels… for a tidy profit, no less."

"I swear to the divine spirit, I've never laid eyes on these men before, Your Majesty. I would never do such a thing. Especially not to the king consort."

"Funny," she said with an even icier tone, "because every one of these men gave detailed accounts of what you asked them to do. And I believe them. Seeing as my questioners and I tortured the truth out of them. A little pain in the right place can make even the most loyal dog confess."

Her sharp gaze pinned Lord Stone where he stood. His face had turned ghostly white, and beads of sweat began to trickle down his temples. He looked as though he might collapse at any moment.

"My Queen—" he started, his voice trembling.

"Save it, Lord Stone." Elinor cut him off coldly. "Now, as for your punishment., I considered simply having you executed. It would have been swift and easy. But then I thought of something much better."

Stone's body began to tremble as Elinor approached the table, her steps deliberate. She gestured to one of the heads.

"This one," she said, her voice calm yet laced with malice, "screamed so beautifully. A combination of my power and the rack made him sing like a bird between his pleas for mercy."

She moved to another. "And this one was particularly amusing… desperate and willing to do *anything* for freedom. He even offered to kill you and your family."

At that, Lord Stone flinched, the faint movement not escaping Elinor's sharp eyes. She smiled, a lopsided grin that dripped with menace, and continued her slow walk around the table.

"But this one," she said, pausing before a head with grizzled features, "the captain himself gave you up the moment Bradley removed his eye. He offered the rest of your plan when we took the other… for fun."

Elinor stopped opposite Lord Stone. The severed heads lined between them like a macabre display of justice. "No," she said softly, her voice deceptively calm, "killing you would be far too easy."

Stone gulped audibly, his hands trembling at his sides.

"First," Elinor began, "to help cover the loss of earnings and the destroyed ships, you will forfeit your winnings from the tourney. Seems fair, I think. That money will go to the king consort as restitution."

Lord Stone's face was hard, betraying no reaction.

"Secondly," she continued, "you will turn over the profits you gained from this little scheme. Refuse, and I'll simply invent a number and take what I want—from your land, your coffers, and your titles."

This time, Stone flinched visibly, though he tried to mask it. Elinor's smile returned sharp and knowing.

"And lastly," she said, her voice dropping to a dangerous whisper, "if you ever attempt anything like this again, or should you think to test my hand, I will harm her however I see fit."

At her signal, a guard stepped forward, dragging a trembling young woman into view. Her hands were bound, her mouth gagged, and her dirty blonde hair hung in matted clumps around her pale, tear-streaked face.

Elinor grasped the girl's hair, pulling it back to reveal her downcast eyes to the room. "Recognise her, Lord Stone? You should. She'll be the one to suffer if you cross me again."

Stone's face twisted in fear, with every line etched by worry. The crowd murmured uneasily, their eyes darting between the queen and the broken man before her.

"Rosalind. Release her!" Lord Stone cried, his voice laced with desperation. Elinor's smile widened, a cold satisfaction glinting in her eyes. She knew she had him now.

As he moved towards his daughter, the queen's guards swiftly stepped in, pointing their weapons at both him and Rosalind. Stone froze mid-step, unwilling to risk her life. Lady Felicia, however, was not deterred. She rushed forward, only to be struck down by another guard. With a cry, she collapsed to the floor. As she struggled to rise, Elinor's voice rang out, sharp and commanding.

"Stay where you are, or you'll join her."

"Let her go," Lord Stone pleaded, his voice cracking.

"Oh, I will," Elinor replied, her tone dripping with menace. "But only when I decide you have learned your lesson. For now, she is mine to do with as I please. So tread carefully, both of you. From this moment forward, it's your daughter who will bear the price of your actions."

With a wave of her hand, Elinor signalled her guards. They dragged Rosalind away towards the hidden cells as Lord Stone watched, his face a mask of anguish and helplessness.

"You won't get away with this," he muttered.

Elinor tilted her head, her smile unfaltering. "Is that a threat? Because my evening is wide open, and so is Rosalind's. I'm sure she would love to play my little games with me. I might even let you watch. I wonder how long it would take her to break from the never-ending pain. You've already seen the effects of just a few hours with me."

Stone fell silent, but his jaw clenched in visible rage, much to Elinor's delight. Both he and Lady Felicia stormed out of the hall, their gazes full of daggers aimed at the queen. She simply laughed as her guards covered the severed heads and carried the table away.

The crowd, unsure of how to respond to what they had just witnessed, remained silent. Elinor addressed them with a composed yet commanding tone.

"My esteemed guests, champions, and knights of the realm," she began, "do not let this incident dampen the spirit of the evening. Take heed, however, that attacking the crown is a criminal offence, and Lord Stone is paying in kind for his grievous error. Now, I bid you goodbye. Please, stay and enjoy the offerings I leave you."

As she concluded, a new wave of food, wine, and entertainment filled the hall. Smoking pipes and dancers were brought in to distract and delight the guests. Slowly, the crowd's unease began to shift into indulgent revelry as they gravitated towards the diversions.

Elinor left the hall with Bradley by her side. Listening to the renewed hum of the crowd behind them, Bradley leaned towards her. "Do you think he got the message?"

"If he didn't," Elinor replied, her voice cool, "he soon will when he realises I'm serious and when his daughter begins to pay the price."

"A cunning idea, my dear. But do you not worry, he'll try to free her tonight?"

Elinor smirked. "He might try, but he won't succeed. He won't find her. I made sure of that."

"Oh?"

"Come. Let me show you."

Elinor led Bradley to the storage room and closed the door behind them. The dimly lit space smelled faintly of old wood and damp stone. She knelt and pulled back the tattered old rug, revealing the hidden hatch. Bradley raised his brows as he watched her unlock it. She started to lift the hatch, but Bradley jumped in to open it for her, exposing the staircase.

"How long has this been here?" he asked.

"It's always been here, but I've had no need of it until now. I did add a little trickery of my own to the room. Anyone who enters without my permission will suffocate as their lungs are starved of oxygen."

Bradley peered down the staircase beneath the hatch. "What if someone stumbles in here by accident?"

"They won't," Elinor assured him. "This entrance is hidden by the power and known only to a select few I trust. Only a tracker could find this space, but they wouldn't last long inside it."

Bradley followed her down the narrow staircase. The air was damp and heavy in the secret cells. When they reached Rosalind's cell, she scurried back against the wall at the sight of them, pressing herself into the shadows as if to disappear.

Elinor stood in the doorway, holding the lantern aloft. Bradley entered with deliberate steps. He crouched before Rosalind, who hugged her knees to her chest, trembling and refusing to meet his gaze. Gently, he lifted her chin, forcing her to look at him.

"I remember her," he said, studying her pale, tear-streaked face. "Pretty little thing. Though not nearly as devious and cunning as her father." He stood, glancing at Elinor. "She seems to be a cowering mess now. Your handiwork, I presume?"

Elinor smirked. "She was not cooperating, so I made sure she behaved herself. I won't keep her down here much longer, just until Lord Stone leaves, and I'm convinced she's broken enough to behave. A few more nights should suffice. After that, I'll place her under Mistress Fleur's supervision in the castle. If she misbehaves, I'll visit her again until she learns her place."

Locking the cells behind her, Elinor and Bradley ascended the stairs and returned to their quarters for the night.

True to her word, Elinor visited Rosalind each evening for the next few weeks, subjecting her to relentless torment until she was certain the young woman's spirit was broken. Once satisfied, she placed Rosalind under Mistress Fleur's watchful eye, setting her to work during the day and keeping her locked away at night.

Lord Stone made several futile attempts to find his daughter over the following days, but when Elinor threatened her life again, he reluctantly departed within hours. Though he left, Elinor harboured no illusions: she knew he would return and try to free her.

For now, however, Rosalind belonged to her. Gone was the fiery, independent young woman. In her place was a hollow shell – obedient, trembling, and apologising at every misstep, terrified of the consequences. With Rosalind under her control, Elinor knew she had Lord Stone exactly where she wanted him.

Chapter 12

Family Time

A few days after the tourney, the castle had returned to its usual rhythm, and Bradley spent the morning with his sister before she and Fleur were about to sail away. He had to admit he sometimes envied their carefree lifestyle. He missed the seas – the wonder, the adventure, the freedom, and the endless horizon. All of it still called to him.

With a wistful sigh, he was jolted back to the present by a gentle nudge from his horse.

"Quit dawdling Bradley. Even your horse is growing impatient," Adina teased, laughing as she mounted her steed.

Bradley gave his saddle one last check before climbing on. "Dawdling, am I? Well, let's see if you can keep pace with me," he said, his tone playful. Without waiting for a response, he urged his horse forward, galloping out of the stable and towards the open fields.

Adina followed, her laughter ringing out as they raced across the countryside. The wind whipped through their hair as their horses thundered across rolling hills and lush meadows, the landscape a blur of green and gold. For a moment, Adina managed to catch up, and they galloped side by side, their horses moving in perfect harmony.

Eventually, they slowed their pace, laughter fading as they reached a serene meadow. They dismounted and let their horses graze while they spread a blanket on the grass for a picnic. Adina had packed a basket filled with their favourite treats – fresh fruits, cheese, and bread.

"Remember when we used to race to the old oak tree?" Adina asked, a mischievous glint in her eye.

Bradley chuckled. "How could I forget? You always won."

"Only because you let me," she replied, nudging him playfully.

"Oh, how times have changed," Bradley mused. "As much as I love the life I have, I can't deny I miss the ocean. Tell me about your adventures. Satisfy my curiosity."

Adina grinned and sat up straighter, settling into her storytelling. She spoke of ferocious seas and the time her crew faced a massive storm that nearly capsized their ship. She described exotic sea creatures chasing the waves and the breathtaking beauty of uncharted islands. There were tales of treasures and ancient artefacts unearthed in distant lands.

One, in particular, captured Bradley's attention – a solid egg larger than her head and heavier than she could comfortably lift. Its surface was smooth and metallic, etched with intricate patterns that seemed to shift and shimmer in the light. She admitted she didn't know what kind of creature it came from, but the mystery made it irresistible.

"Sounds like paradise," Bradley said wistfully. "I envy you, Adina. The freedom, the adventure…"

Adina placed a hand on his shoulder, her expression softening. "You have your adventures here. A Kingdom to rule, a wife who's… unique, to say the least. She must keep you on your toes?"

Bradley's smile faded. "The situation with Lord Stone had to be dealt with. He has been a thorn in my side for too long. What he did to our ships and crews was unforgivable."

"That may be true," Adina said, her tone measured. "But I've heard things over the years. Rumours about Elinor… how she deals with those she views as the enemy. They often don't live to tell the tale."

Bradley's gaze hardened. "What are you getting at?"

Adina hesitated before speaking. "That your wife is a dangerous woman. Be careful, Bradley. There are people out there waiting for a new monarch to take the throne. I've heard whispers during my travels. There are people out there waiting for the young royals to return."

"And are you among them?"

"Of course not," she blurted. "But rumours are swirling, and Elinor doesn't have the best reputation across the seas. Many fear her, but how much longer will that last if the prince and princess were to come back?"

"No one is returning," Bradley said firmly. "And if they did, she would deal with them."

"She'll be your downfall, Bradley. Mark my words," Adina said, her tone a mix of jest and concern.

Bradley chuckled and shook his head, but Adina's expression remained serious. "A darkness surrounds her, and her time is limited," she said quietly, worry flickering in her eyes.

"She is not my demise," Bradley replied, his voice steady and resolute. "She is my beginning. I see her, and she sees me—the darkness and shadows of our very souls. Together, we'll remake this world. Side by side, to whatever end."

Adina studied him for a moment, her gaze thoughtful. "You're more like Father than I realised. No matter what happens, don't say I didn't warn you. The tides are changing, and you're about to be caught in a tempest you might not escape alive."

"Then I'll die knowing I stood by her side," Bradley replied, his tone unwavering.

Adina sighed, her expression softening. "Just promise me you'll be careful. If you ever need me, I'll be there."

Bradley gave a small nod. "Thank you, but your concern is unwarranted. Elinor and I have everything under control."

The weight of their serious conversation shifted, and they spent the rest of the afternoon sharing stories and enjoying each other's company. Later, they rode back to the castle, where they found Fleur waiting for them. She greeted them warmly, giving Adina a kiss and wrapping an arm around her waist.

"How was your day?" Fleur asked, her smile lighting up her face.

"It was wonderful," Adina replied. "We reminisced about old times and had a great ride through the countryside."

Bradley nodded in agreement. "It was exactly what I needed. Thank you for suggesting it, Fleur."

Fleur's smile deepened. "I'm glad you both had a good time. Now, how about we freshen up and head to dinner? Elinor is waiting for us."

The three of them made their way to their chambers to change. Not long after, they gathered in the private dining room, where Elinor was already seated, looking regal and composed. She greeted them with a nod and a reserved smile.

"Good evening, everyone," she said. "I trust you had a pleasant day?"

"We did," Bradley replied as he took his seat beside her. "Adina and I had a wonderful time catching up."

Elinor's gaze softened as she looked at Adina. "I'm glad to hear that. It's important to cherish these moments with family."

As they settled in, the servants began bringing out the first course. Conversation flowed easily, with tales of the day's exploits and plans for the future. Bradley listened, captivated, as Fleur shared their vision for the business and described the wonders they had encountered during their travels. Adina's earlier stories had barely scratched the surface; it seemed they were truly living the life of explorers – uncovering hidden treasures and navigating uncharted waters.

Elinor's eyes sparkled with interest. "It sounds like you've had quite the adventures. I must admit, I'm a bit envious of your travels."

Fleur smiled warmly. "The journey has been incredible, but it's always nice to come back and share our stories with family."

Adina nodded. "And it's good to be home, even if only for a little while. There's something comforting about the familiar."

As the main course was served, the conversation turned to lighter topics. They laughed over old memories, shared jokes, and enjoyed a delicious meal. Elinor and Bradley spoke of their own plans for the future. Bradley, animated and passionate, shared his vision for the kingdom and his hope for a family of their own. Elinor, her eyes gleaming with ambition, added her dreams of expanding their influence and forging new alliances.

"We have the potential to create a legacy that will be remembered for generations," she said with quiet determination.

Adina listened intently, a small smile playing on her lips. "You both have such grand plans. Your dedication is inspiring to see."

Fleur nodded in agreement. "It's clear you're both committed to making a difference. The kingdom is lucky to have you."

Bradley caught Adina's eye at Fleur's comment. He could tell Adina still harboured reservations about Elinor and their methods, though she was smart enough to keep her concerns to herself in Elinor's presence.

It was interesting to Bradley. Adina had always been much like their father – ambitious and cunning, with an unyielding determination to see her plans through. She had a gift for turning even the most challenging situations to her advantage, whether navigating political intrigue or planning her next adventure on the high seas.

But since meeting Fleur and travelling the world, Adina had changed. The ambition and drive were still there, but her approach had softened. She no longer relied on cutthroat tactics or backstabbing schemes. Instead, she led with compassion and understanding, valuing loyalty and trust above all. Bradley found it difficult to reconcile this change, but he couldn't deny how much happier and more at peace she seemed. It was a transformation he couldn't help but admire.

After dinner, they moved to the sitting room for dessert and a glass of mead. The atmosphere was warm and filled with laughter, a perfect end to a memorable day. Bradley felt a pang of sadness, knowing this time with Adina and Fleur would soon come to an end.

When the evening drew to a close, they bid each other goodnight and retired to their rooms.

The next morning, sunlight spilt gently over the castle, casting a golden glow on the stone walls. Bradley met Adina and Fleur at their chambers, and together they walked to the waiting carriage.

It was time for them to return to the seas, and Bradley felt the ache of parting with his sister. He had enjoyed her company over the past few weeks and wasn't ready to see her go.

"Goodbye, dear brother," Adina said softly, pulling him into a warm embrace. "I'll miss you."

"And I you. Just promise me you'll visit more often. The sea may call to you, but we need you here too," he replied.

"We will," Adina said, her voice muffled against his shoulder. "Take care of yourself, Bradley. I'm serious… change is in the air."

"I intend to," he assured her.

Adina stepped back, a small smile playing on her lips. "And who knows? Maybe one day you'll join us on the seas again."

Before he could respond, Fleur embraced him warmly. "Until next time," she said, her tone gentle.

Bradley smiled as they climbed into the carriage. "Please, give our mother a kiss for me. She left sooner than I expected."

Adina nodded as she settled in, and he stood there watching as the carriage rolled away, his expression tinged with wistfulness. Then, with a deep breath, he turned back towards the castle – his home.

Chapter 13

A Journey for Two

As nervous as she felt, Aevah found the beginning of their journey oddly exhilarating. Neither of them had any idea what was going to happen, but they knew what they had to do. As they neared what they hoped was Burford, Jacob stopped his horse and guided it off the dirt road, onto the grass, away from the other travellers heading towards the town. Aevah followed, reining in her mare behind his. She dismounted and watched as he did the same.

"I'm not convinced this is Burford," Jacob said, scanning the road ahead.

"Oh?" Aevah replied, tilting her head curiously.

"From what Grandfather said, I feel like we still have a while to go."

"Hmm, maybe we should ask someone," she suggested, glancing at the people passing them. Spotting a young pair walking along the road, she called out, "Excuse me!" and jogged towards them.

"Watch it!" a second voice barked as she nearly collided with another traveller on horseback.

"Damn kids," the rider muttered, shaking his head as he rode on. Aevah's heart pounded as she carefully weaved through the crowd, finally reaching the couple she had spotted earlier.

"Pardon me," she said, catching her breath. "Is the town ahead, Burford? My brother and I are travelling there to meet family."

The young woman gave her a kind smile. "No dear, this is Oakridge. But you're not too far away. Follow the path in that direction, and you'll reach Burford in a few hours on horseback."

Aevah looked to where the woman pointed, thanked her, and returned to Jacob, this time more mindful of the other travellers on the road.

"You were right," she admitted. "This isn't Burford. The lady said it's a couple of hours that way." She gestured in the direction the woman had indicated. Climbing onto her mare, she watched Jacob mount his horse, and together they set off once more.

With the route confirmed, Aevah was grateful for the nice weather. Travelling under the sunshine was far more pleasant than enduring the cold and rain, and it made for an easy ride on their first day. It had been a long time since the two of them had spent quality time together, and this journey offered the perfect opportunity to reconnect. They were reminded of how close their bond was and how much they had in common.

There had been no rift between them to create distance – only the natural drift that came with age and differing interests. Jacob had devoted countless hours to woodworking, a craft he loved, while Aevah often disappeared into her books or practised wielding her power under their grandfather's guidance. Unlike Jacob, Aevah had been born with the ability to control it, while he inherited only a faint trace of it, much like their mother. He had needed only a little bit of training for the trickle of power he held and didn't seem to mind that he couldn't wield it as she could.

As children, they had been inseparable. Like many twins, they had developed their own unique language that no one else could understand. Though they no longer needed it, they still remembered it. They had also been notorious for getting into mischief together. As they grew older, their relationship evolved into one of friendly competition. They loved each other deeply, but each was driven to outdo the other in almost everything.

The competitive streak hadn't faded with time. Even now, they often tried to best each other, but it was all in good fun. Despite their rivalry, Aevah admired Jacob's calm, level-headed nature and often turned to him for guidance. In contrast, she was more impulsive and outgoing, which sometimes made her seem bossier. Yet, it was Jacob who tended to lead the way with his thoughtful approach.

As they continued towards Burford, the road widened and became smoother. The dense woods gradually gave way to open farmland. Fields of crops sprouted on one side while sheep and cows roamed on the other. Wooden fences separated the animals from the harvest, ensuring the people's food supply remained untouched.

The flat terrain meant they couldn't see the town yet, but the increasing number of travellers and wagons signalled they were getting closer. The growing activity around them filled the twins with a mix of excitement and nerves. They had never ventured somewhere like this alone before. As children, they had entered cities only with their parents, and even in Sleights, their grandfather had always been by their side. Now, for the first time, they were exploring on their own.

Despite their nerves, the experience was exhilarating. Both felt a thrill at the thought of this newfound independence, even though they were merely passing through for the night.

As the town drew nearer, Aevah glanced at Jacob and offered him a nervous smile.

"Ready?" Jacob asked.

"Yes."

"Then let's do this."

Excitement coursed through Aevah as they approached the town's gatehouse. Unable to contain herself, she urged her mare forward, picking up speed. The late afternoon sun cast long shadows over the large grilled door, which stood open to admit a constant stream of travellers. A crowd bustled on both sides of the entrance. Aevah moved to the left, falling in line with the other travellers, with Jacob following close behind.

As they passed through the gatehouse, they entered the town itself and were immediately engulfed by a throng of bodies.

It was crowded – people were packed together like sardines. Aevah pulled her horse to a stop and glanced at Jacob. She nodded towards him, signalling for them to dismount. Holding her reins tightly, she stepped closer to him and leaned in to hear his voice over the clamour.

"Let's just follow the crowd for now," Jacob suggested. "Hopefully, it will thin out as we move away from the main entrance."

Aevah nodded in agreement and began weaving her way through the congested streets, her eyes darting back often to ensure she didn't lose sight of her brother. Losing him in this crowd would be disastrous – it would be nearly impossible to find him again.

As they ventured deeper into the town, the crowd began to thin slightly, though the streets remained far busier than anywhere they had visited in recent memory. Aevah's grip on her reins tightened. They didn't know anyone here, nor did they have a clear sense of where they were going. The unfamiliarity left her feeling unsteady, and when she felt a hand grip her shoulder, she jumped, spinning around to find Jacob staring at her with a puzzled expression.

"Sorry," he said, "didn't mean to startle you, but you weren't listening."

"Damn it! I was… thinking," she replied defensively.

Jacob sighed. "I think we should ask for directions. We know the name of the inn, and if we don't get help, we'll still be searching come nightfall. This place is much bigger than I expected."

"Agreed," Aevah said. Her eyes scanned the bustling street, searching for someone approachable. She spotted a stall exuding a strong, earthy aroma and walked towards it. A man stood behind the counter, arranging what appeared to be an assortment of spices and herbs. The powerful scent stung her nose, and her eyes watered as she got closer. She dabbed at them with her sleeve before addressing the shopkeeper.

"Excuse me," she said politely, "do you happen to know where *The Lion's Inn* is? My brother and I are meeting family there."

"Visiting, are ye?" the man said with a grin. "It ain't far from 'ere. Just keep on along this road till ye hit tha bakery, then turn right down tha next street. Anotha right past Lady Loom, and ye'll find it. Can't miss tha sign."

He quickly turned his attention to another customer, leaving Aevah to hope he had heard her thanks. She turned back to Jacob and relayed the directions before they set off once more.

As they walked, they took note of the shops and stalls they passed, all the while searching for the inn's sign. The town was far livelier than anything they were used to. The vibrant streets seemed to pull them in, overwhelming their senses with colour, sound, and enticing aromas.

Everywhere they looked, there was activity. Merchants called out their wares, musicians played cheerful tunes, and bursts of laughter and conversation filled the air. The energy was infectious, making it difficult to focus on their destination.

Despite their curiosity, they reminded themselves of their priorities. First, they needed to find the inn and get their horses stabled. They walked on, though at a slightly slower pace, unable to resist soaking in the sights around them.

Eventually, Jacob spotted the large wooden sign hanging above the door, painted with the image of a golden lion. "This has to be the right place," he said. Handing the reins of his horse to Aevah, he stepped inside to check.

The inn's interior was warm and inviting, with red fabrics decorating the walls and furniture, giving the space a cosy ambience. The tables were crowded, with patrons eating, drinking, and talking loudly. Serving girls darted between the tables, balancing trays of full mugs and steaming plates while collecting empty ones. A small band played lively music from a corner of the room, filling the air with cheerful tones.

Jacob soaked it all in, the energy of the place invigorating him. He made his way to the bar, where a young woman was wiping down the counter.

"Excuse me," he said politely, "my sister and I need a room for the night."

"Aye," she replied with a friendly smile. "Ye're in luck. With it bein' harvest season, there's rooms to spare. Follow me, and I'll show ye to one."

"Thank you. We also have two horses. Do you have a stable for them?"

"Aye, we do. Where they be now?"

"Outside, with my sister."

The young woman nodded and led Jacob back out to Aevah, then guided them to the stables, where their horses were handed off to the stable hand for care. Once the horses were settled, they returned to the inn, and Jacob paid for the room.

The woman escorted them up a narrow staircase to the second floor, opening the door to a small but practical room. It contained two single beds, a modest dresser, and a small table with a pitcher of water and a basin. Though simple, it was exactly what they needed – a safe and quiet place to sleep.

"There's a bathroom at tha end of tha hall," the lady said before leaving them to settle in.

After packing away their belongings, Aevah and Jacob decided to explore the town while there was still daylight. Both agreed to return before dark, but for now, the bustling streets were theirs to wander.

Their first stop was a toy shop that caught their eye. Though they were too old for toys, the sight of wooden soldiers, porcelain dolls, and intricately carved animals filled them with nostalgia. The air smelled of fresh wood, and the gentle melody of a music box played in the background, transporting them back to their childhood.

Jacob, fascinated by the craftsmanship, examined the toys closely while the kind elderly shopkeeper shared stories of their creation.

From there, they visited a bakery, where they bought jam-filled pastries and fresh juice. The pastries were crisp and flaky, with sweet, sticky centres that made them savour every bite. The juice was a refreshing complement, and they both indulged in the simple treat.

As they strolled further, they came upon a vibrant clothing shop. Aevah tried on delicate wimples and veils, laughing as Jacob dramatically spun around in a black fur-lined cloak. Nearby, a soap vendor caught their attention. Aevah purchased bath oil and a scented soap bar for her hair. The vendor, a cheerful woman wearing a floral apron, offered Aevah a sample of lavender-scented lotion. Aevah smiled and accepted it, rubbing the fragrant balm into her hands before purchasing a small bottle for herself.

Meanwhile, Jacob was captivated by a nearby stall selling handcrafted wooden trinkets. He was particularly drawn to anything made from wood. As he picked up an intricately carved box, he admired the craftsmanship. He chatted with the vendor, who was also a skilled craftsman until Aevah dragged him away.

Their last stop was an open-air performance on a raised platform. Actors in colourful costumes brought a lively play to life, captivating the audience with animated gestures and exaggerated voices. Aevah and Jacob laughed and clapped along with the crowd, fully immersed in the experience.

As the final act concluded, the setting sun cast a warm glow over the town, and the lanterns began to light the streets. Deciding it was time to return, they headed back to the inn. The streets were quieter now, the energy of the day giving way to the peaceful hum of the evening.

Once back at the inn, they dropped off their purchases in their room and made their way to the crowded bar for dinner. Finding a table by the window, they sat down and ordered a roast and two pints of ale to join in the revelry.

However, drinking the ale was less enjoyable than anticipated. Jacob powered through his pint, alternating sips with bites of food, while Aevah struggled to mask her distaste with each sip. Eventually, she pushed her mug aside and opted for a fruity wine instead, which went down much more easily.

Before long, the wine left Aevah warm and buzzed, and she unwittingly had one drink too many. The room began to spin, and Jacob noticed her growing unsteadiness.

"I think it's time to call it a night," he said, standing to help her.

As they climbed the stairs, Aevah's stomach churned, and she suddenly bolted down the hall to the bathroom. She collapsed to her knees and vomited; her earlier enthusiasm was replaced by utter misery.

From the doorway, Jacob's laughter echoed. "Guess you're not much of a drinker," he teased.

"It's not funny," she snapped between heaves.

After what felt like an eternity, Aevah finally emerged pale and shaky. Back in their room, she crawled into bed, clutching her stomach. Jacob brought her a glass of water and set a bucket beside her bed, still chuckling to himself.

"Here, drink this. It'll help," he said, earning a glare in return.

Taking small sips of water, Aevah swore to herself she would never drink again. Exhausted and feeling miserable, she drifted into an uneasy sleep, her rest frequently interrupted by nausea.

Despite her discomfort, the knowledge that Jacob was nearby offered some comfort. As his soft snores filled the room, she let the exhaustion take over, hoping tomorrow would bring a better day.

Chapter 14

Riddles

As dawn broke, the soft light of morning filtered through the window, casting a gentle glow over the room. Jacob stirred awake, a rare sense of optimism lifting his spirits. Glancing over at his sister, he saw that Aevah was still buried beneath the blankets, only a single foot poking out from underneath. Not wanting to disturb her, he moved quietly, dressing quickly and slipping out of the room after carefully closing the door behind him. His stomach growled – he was famished.

Downstairs, he devoured a hearty breakfast of porridge and toast, savouring every bite. As he ate, his thoughts returned to Aevah. She was bound to wake up hungover, likely regretting the previous night's events. *Should he take her something to eat?* He decided it was better to leave her something comforting, so he left some toast and a cup of tea by her bedside before heading out.

They were supposed to be back on the road by late morning, but Jacob couldn't help wondering how Aevah would manage to ride her horse in a few hours. She hadn't been in great shape the night before, and he had his doubts about whether they would leave on time. Still, there was no point in waiting around. Thanking the lady behind the bar for breakfast, he grabbed his coat and stepped out into the bustling village to pick up supplies.

They didn't know when the next stop would be, so he focussed on buying fresh produce and non-perishable food – things they could eat easily while travelling. The next leg of their journey depended on the notes their grandfather had given them. He had sent them here with only vague instructions, assuring them the answers would lie within the documents he entrusted to them. Neither Jacob nor Aevah had dared to open the sacred scrolls yet. The weight of their importance loomed too large. *What if it all went wrong?*

Even their grandfather hadn't opened the scrolls. He had told them it wasn't his place to interfere. Instead, he had handed over the package, confident they would rise to the challenge ahead. Jacob planned to sit down with Aevah that morning and finally open the scrolls together in the safety of their room. With luck, the documents would reveal a clear destination, and they could set out with a sense of purpose.

On his way back to the inn, Jacob stopped at the bakery and the produce stand, buying a selection of pies, pastries, and fruit to sustain them on the road. He couldn't resist lingering at the wooden craft stall he had admired the day before. The shopkeeper greeted him warmly and demonstrated a few new whittling techniques. To Jacob's delight, the man gifted him a small piece of wood to practice on. Tucking the wood into his bag, Jacob wondered if Aevah was finally up and ready to face the day.

Feeling inspired, Jacob thanked the shopkeeper and made his way back to the inn. When he arrived, the cook was preparing fresh ham sandwiches for them to take on the road. It looked like they would have plenty of food to sustain them for the journey ahead.

Back in their room, he found Aevah sitting on her bed, nibbling on the toast he had left for her. The teacup sat empty on the nightstand. Her head turned towards him slowly as though even that slight movement required great effort. Her complexion was pale, and she looked thoroughly unwell as if she had already been sick that morning.

"What?" she asked, her voice hoarse. She seemed to aim for a sharp tone, but it came out as little more than a croak.

"Just checking in. How are you feeling?" Jacob quipped, the corners of his mouth twitching as he struggled to suppress a grin.

"Better than I was," she muttered, though her expression suggested otherwise.

"Great. So we'll be able to leave within the hour? We have to be out of the room by then and get back on the road," he replied matter-of-factly.

Aevah groaned and flopped back onto the pillows. "Ugh. If I have to, I don't know how I'm supposed to ride a moving horse feeling like this."

"We'll get you some herbal tea before we leave. You'll be as good as new. Maybe next time, don't drink so much." He smirked, dodging just in time as a pillow flew at his head. Laughing, he retreated from the room, Aevah's colourful curses echoing down the hall after him.

Still chuckling, Jacob headed back downstairs to the kitchen. He asked the staff if anyone knew where he could purchase something to cure a hangover. One of the women laughed heartily.

"Aye, lad, ye need but a grotesque-tastin' powder ye mix in water," she said, her accent thick and cheerful. She retrieved a tin from the pantry shelf and opened it, releasing a faint, earthy smell. Grabbing a glass, she filled it with water before adding two heaped spoonfuls of the brown powder. Stirring the concoction vigorously, she handed it to him with a knowing smile.

"Me husband swears by it. Needs a cup regular-like, so I always keep som' on hand."

Jacob thanked her and carried the glass back upstairs. Aevah was still sitting on the bed, looking thoroughly unimpressed, when he handed it to her. Her expression only worsened as she sniffed the mixture.

"Do I *have* to?" she asked, eyeing the murky liquid with disdain.

"Drink it," Jacob insisted, crossing his arms. "It will help."

Grimacing, she raised the glass to her lips and took a tentative sip. Her face contorted into an even deeper scowl as she forced herself to drink it down. Judging by her expression, it tasted just as unpleasant as it looked, but she managed to finish it.

Once she was done, Jacob clapped his hands together. "All right, now that's over with, let's get moving. We have things to do."

***

Aevah woke with her head pounding like a drum. Her mouth was as dry as sand, and every movement sent waves of dizziness spiralling through her. She tried to prop herself up in bed, but the effort only made the queasiness in her empty stomach churn uncomfortably. Groaning, she let herself collapse back against the pillows, pulling the blankets tighter around her.

Of course, Jacob chose that moment to yank the curtains open, flooding the room with blinding daylight. "Good morning!" he announced far too cheerfully, his voice grating like nails on stone.

"Go away," she muttered, retreating further under the covers in an attempt to escape the light – and him.

But Jacob, in true brother fashion, wasn't done tormenting her. As he got ready for the day, he stomped around the room with exaggerated force, rummaging through his things with unnecessary noise. Every clink and clatter felt like a hammer driving into her skull. Aevah's patience, already thin, was on the verge of snapping. She glared daggers at the shape of him moving through the blankets, fantasising about strangling him with her bare hands.

Finally, just as she was ready to explode, Jacob announced he was going to get some breakfast and slammed the door behind him as he left.

Blessed silence. Aevah exhaled and sank back into the mattress, closing her eyes in the hopes of falling asleep again. She whispered a silent prayer to the divine spirit that when she woke, her headache would have miraculously disappeared.

After some time – and the world's slowest bath – she started to feel marginally more human. Scrubbing her teeth until the awful taste of bile was gone helped, as did the tea and toast that had mysteriously appeared while she slept. She didn't know whether to thank Jacob or curse him for his loud morning routine, but she had to admit she felt a little better. The throbbing in her head, however, stubbornly lingered.

When Jacob returned, he handed her a glass filled with some ominous brown liquid. "This will help," he said with infuriating confidence.

She sniffed it and immediately regretted it. "This smells *awful*!"

"Drink it. It works," Jacob insisted, settling himself at the foot of her bed. In his hands, he held the envelope they had yet to open – the one their grandfather had entrusted to them. For a moment, Aevah stared at the drink in her hand, torn between trust and revulsion. Then, with a deep breath, she forced herself to gulp it down. The taste was as horrible as she feared, and her face contorted in disgust.

"This better work," she muttered, pushing the empty glass back towards him.

"It will," Jacob replied, though his attention had already shifted. He turned the envelope over in his hands, his expression uncharacteristically serious. "I guess we should unseal this now."

His voice betrayed a hint of nerves, and for once, Aevah couldn't blame him. Her headache was momentarily forgotten as she watched him break the wax seal and carefully pull out the contents. Inside were a map and four pieces of parchment, which Jacob spread out on the bed between them.

The map immediately caught her attention. It was Ethos, the world she knew, but something about it was subtly off – almost like it was from a different time. She jumped off the bed, but the sudden movement proved to be a mistake. Her stomach rebelled violently, and she froze, clutching her middle until the wave of nausea passed.

Conscious of her still-settling stomach, Aevah walked carefully to her backpack and retrieved their map. Laying it beside the one they already had, she immediately noticed the differences. Many of the roads and towns had different names, and the layouts were far from identical. Three distinct areas on the map were marked with circles. She reached for one of the four additional pieces of parchment and unfolded it. Words were scrawled across its surface, and she read them aloud.

"To find the shards, three riddles await,
a test of resolve to unlock your fate.
Unite all four, and the power is yours.
Though, beware:
Too much power can lead astray,
even the purest souls may lose their way.
With the lines between good and evil thin,
seek us only if you dare begin."

"That sounds like a warning," Jacob said as he picked up the next scroll and began to read.

"I lay atop the highest peak,
above the world if you dare seek.
Brave the cold and icy lands,
where breaths are precious, and strength demands.
Secrets lie hidden for you to find,
but be careful where your footsteps bind.
One wrong step and you might fall,
if true power is what you call.
Tread carefully, for power is a dangerous game,
only one can survive the claim."

Aevah frowned at Jacob as he finished reading the last word. "Is that a riddle?"

"It sounds like it," he replied as he opened the third parchment and read it.

"I am hidden from prying eyes,
in a place where calm and shade arise.
In nature's embrace, I rest,
with secrets buried at their bequest.
Come, lay your head upon my bough,
and seek shelter from the world around.
If you look closely, you shall see,
not everything is as it should be.
Crawl down deep, where roots entwine,
a crystal hidden, yours to find.
In your grasp, you hold it all,
but too much power will steal your soul."

Aevah picked up the fourth and final parchment. She opened it and read the concluding riddle for both of them.

"Long forgotten, I dwell deep below,
in a chamber where water once did flow.
Now, it is dry, dark, and cold.
Not a realm any man would dare to go.
If you find what you truly desire,
remember endless glory do not aspire.
Power and greed will corrupt your soul,

only those with pure minds can control me whole."

Aevah looked at Jacob, a puzzled expression on her face as she held the original map in one hand and the riddle in the other.

"These seem rather ominous, do they not?" she asked.

"Yeah, they don't exactly promise a happy ending for whoever finds them," Jacob replied.

Aevah sighed, her gaze fixed on the old map. "Of course not. Why would finding magical crystal shards involve anything but doom?" Keeping her eyes on the parchment, she pointed at it and continued, "All right, so I guess these circles mark where the perilous crystals of destruction are hidden. And we simply have to find them."

"Yes, but which puzzle corresponds to which crystal? And how do we decide which one to search for first?" Jacob flipped through the riddles, scanning both maps simultaneously. "Plus, the maps aren't identical. What if we can't locate them?"

"Good point. But what if we don't need to solve the riddles just yet?" Aevah tapped the map, pointing to the circle closest to their current location. "Look, this one isn't far from us. If we go there first, we can assess the surroundings and see if any of these riddles make sense in context."

Jacob nodded, though his mind was clearly still processing everything. He was methodical, always needing time to think things before he made a decision. He studied the two maps as if willing them to reveal their secrets. Finally, he exhaled and gave a decisive nod.

"Okay, your plan makes sense. Comparing the maps, it looks like we need to head towards these woods. Once we get there, we can reassess and determine which riddle we need to solve."

Aevah smirked. "Why, thank you. How kind of you to deem my idea worthy." She gave an exaggerated bow.

"You're welcome."

That retort irked her. In response, she shoved him playfully. "Just get ready to leave."

Without waiting for a response, she turned on her heel and started gathering her things. She dressed quickly, packed her essentials, and made her way to the stables. Jacob was already there, waiting by the stalls. As she approached, he wordlessly handed her the reins to her horse.

Saying nothing to her, Jacob led his horse out of the stable. Aevah followed, guiding Whisp behind him. As they moved through the town streets, the rich aroma of freshly baked goods and roasted meats filled the air, making her stomach rumble. After being sick, the emptiness gnawed at her, and she insisted on stopping for food. Without a word, Jacob reached into his pack and handed her a couple of pasties. She shovelled them in hungrily, and with each bite, her hunger subsided.

Once back on the road, Aevah climbed onto her horse. Though her head felt clearer, whatever had been in that drink had done wonders for her hangover. Even so, she set off at a slow trot, wary of triggering another wave of nausea or a pounding headache. She never wanted to experience that misery again.

Fortunately, Whisp seemed to understand and moved steadily beneath her, his gait smooth and controlled.

As they travelled through the countryside, the landscape gradually changed. Rolling hills gave way to dense forests, and the air grew warmer, carrying the scent of damp earth. Aevah took in the sights and sounds, finding an unexpected sense of peace despite the lingering discomfort.

Jacob rode beside her, occasionally glancing her way. "How are you holding up?" he asked, his voice gentle.

"I'm managing," she replied with a small smile. "Thanks for the drink earlier. It really helped."

He nodded, relieved to see her in better spirits. "We'll take it easy today. No need to push ourselves too hard."

Over the next few weeks, they adjusted to life on the road, camping under the stars and adapting to the rhythm of travel. Though Aevah enjoyed the adventure, she could do without the rain. Riding while soaked to the bone was miserable, and tonight looked to be another wet one. Dark clouds loomed ahead, and as the sun dipped below the horizon, they found a suitable spot to make camp.

Aevah dismounted carefully, her legs unsteady from the long day's ride. They set up their tent under a large oak tree, which provided some shelter from the elements. She began gathering firewood, hoping to get a decent flame going before the rain set in. Jacob took care of the horses, making sure they were fed and comfortable.

As they were about to eat, the first droplets began to fall. Aevah quickly led their horses under the tree, tying them securely to its thick trunk. The dense canopy offered some protection from the downpour, and she draped waterproof blankets over their backs to keep them as dry as possible.

Settling inside their tent, they listened to the continuous rhythm of rain drumming against the canvas. They could only hope they wouldn't wake up drenched again and prayed to the divine spirit for drier days to come. Aevah sighed as she adjusted her blanket, shifting to find a comfortable position on the hard ground. The sound of the rain was both soothing and frustrating. She missed the warmth and dryness of a proper bed.

Jacob, seemingly unfazed, chuckled softly. "Remember that time we camped out in the backyard, and it rained all night? We ended up sneaking back into the cottage."

Aevah smiled at the memory. "Yeah. Grandpa wasn't too happy about the muddy footprints we left behind."

They both laughed quietly.

"I wonder how he's doing," Aevah mused after a moment.

Jacob's expression turned thoughtful. "Oh, wonderful, heroic things, I imagine," he said with admiration. "He always had a knack for turning the simplest tasks into grand adventures."

Aevah nodded, her thoughts drifting to their grandfather's fables of magic and daring escapades. "I miss his stories. They made everything seem possible."

Jacob sighed contentedly. "We'll have our own stories to tell soon enough. Just think of all the exploits ahead of us. He'll be enthralled when we meet again."

"Yes, he will," Aevah agreed. Ignoring the creeping cold as best she could, she closed her eyes, letting the gentle rhythm of the rain lull her to sleep, her mind wandering to the adventures that awaited them.

Chapter 15

The Next Stop

"This should be the right spot, according to the map," Jacob said.

Aevah crossed her arms. "That's what you said about the last place we stopped. What makes you so certain now?"

"Because I just am. Now start looking. It's a giant tree… it can't be that hard to miss," he responded.

She rolled her eyes and grabbed onto the oak beside her.

"What are you doing?" he asked.

"Climbing. Last time, you had us wandering around for hours with nothing to show for it. I'm not doing that again. If there's an enormous tree nearby, I'll see it better from up here than from the ground."

"Good point." Jacob followed suit, clambering up the trunk. As Aevah moved to the left, he angled himself to the right. A sharp tug at his leg made him glance down – his pants had snagged on a branch. He cursed under his breath, climbed back down just enough to free himself, and then continued upward.

When he looked ahead, he saw Aevah was still ascending, but his side of the tree had no more sturdy branches to support him. He stopped, balancing himself on a thick bough. Standing upright, he pressed a shoulder against the solid trunk, his feet hovering just past the edge but secure enough not to worry.

The view stretched for miles. Below him, the kingdom unfolded like a living tapestry – miniature cities and villages nestled between sprawling farms, their patchwork fields woven with gold, green, and purple. Smoke curled lazily from distant chimneys, a sign of life humming within the tiny settlements.

He exhaled slowly, struck by a rare moment of contemplation. *What were the lives of those people like? How different were their experiences from his own? What were their stories?*

His father had always spoken about knowing his people – that to rule well, he had to understand them. A king served his subjects, not the other way around. It was a lesson their grandfather had reinforced time and time again: their duty was not just to hold power but to protect and uplift those beneath it.

Standing there, gazing at the vast land before him, the weight of that truth settled deeper into his bones. One day, the kingdom would fall to him or Aevah. And when that day came, he would have to be ready.

If Jacob was honest, he hoped Aevah would take the throne. He had no interest in being king and would be far more content following her lead than giving orders himself.

He scanned the horizon once more, but the so-called great tree was nowhere in sight.

"Any luck?" he called out to her.

"I'm not sure. There might be something over there, but I can't tell. It's pretty far off in the distance."

Unable to see what she was pointing at, Jacob moved closer, circling the tree and climbing across the branches, using the trunk for support. Once he reached her side, he followed her gaze and meticulously studied the landscape. Then he spotted it – a massive tree standing apart from the rest, though it was still a fair distance away. Even if they moved in the right direction, it could take several more days to reach it.

But after weeks of searching, having a clear destination felt like progress. Jacob examined the land between them and the tree, taking note of any notable landmarks that could help guide their way. A small village and a winding river lay ahead. If they kept to the right side of the river, it would serve as a natural guide, ensuring they stayed on course.

"What do you think, then?" Aevah asked.

"I believe that has to be the spot."

They both climbed down, Jacob landing with a soft *thud* before brushing loose bark and twigs from his clothes. He turned towards the path they needed to take. If they retraced their steps and returned to the trail they had left earlier, they could follow it to the next checkpoint. Based on what he had seen, the village wasn't far, followed by a nearby farm. From there, it would only take a brief ride to reach their destination.

Ultimately, the choice came down to where they wanted to stop for the night.

"I think I know where we need to go, but where we rest depends on where you're comfortable staying," he said.

"What are our options?" Aevah asked.

"A village, a farm, or camping in the woods again." Jacob left the choice to his sister this time since she complained about the last few places he had picked. If she ended up dissatisfied with tonight's sleeping arrangements, at least she would have only herself to blame.

"Hmm, I don't know. Let's just get moving, and I'll decide on the way."

With that, they mounted their horses and set off, hoping they were heading in the right direction towards the village. As arduous as their journey had been, Jacob found that, for the most part, riding through the countryside was an enjoyable experience. In just a few short weeks, he had seen more of his own homeland than he had in his entire life.

Much of that enjoyment, he realised, came from his remarkable horse. Both he and Aevah had taken their horses from the guards when they fled home, and both animals had proven to have excellent temperaments. Jacob's horse, a dapple-grey stallion he had named Storm, was particularly exceptional.

Storm had a playful nature and an uncanny ability to sense Jacob's moods. Whether it was a gentle nudge when Jacob was lost in thought or a sudden burst of speed when urgency called for it, the stallion always seemed in tune with him – a valuable trait, especially in unknown territory.

Today, however, was an ordinary day, and after an uneventful ride, they neared what appeared to be another village or town. Jacob pulled out his new map, studying it carefully to determine their location. Judging by the surrounding landmarks, the place ahead seemed to be a farm rather than a proper village.

As they approached, a small farmhouse came into view, nestled at the end of a rocky path. The sun was beginning to dip below the horizon, casting long shadows across the well-kept property. A few chickens pecked at the dirt near the entrance while a couple of cows grazed lazily in a nearby field.

Reaching the front door, Jacob dismounted and knocked. After a moment, the door creaked open to reveal a middle-aged woman with kind eyes and a warm smile.

"Good evening," he said, keeping his tone polite and non-threatening. "My sister and I have been travelling all day. We were hoping we might spend the night here if it's not too much trouble."

The woman studied them for a moment, her gaze lingering on their weary faces and dust-covered clothes.

"I'm Martha," she said at last. "And this is my farm. You're welcome to stay, but you'll have to earn your keep. There's always work to be done around here."

Jacob nodded eagerly. "Of course. We can help with whatever you need."

Martha stepped aside, holding the door open. "Come on, then. I'll show you to the stables first, then where you can sleep."

She led them to the barn to settle their horses for the night. The stables were modest but clean and well-maintained, with fresh hay and water ready for the animals. Jacob and Aevah guided Storm and Whisp into their stalls, making sure they were comfortable before stepping away.

Once their horses were taken care of, Martha ushered them into the farmhouse.

She led them to a small room at the back of the house, simply furnished with two beds and a wooden dresser. "It isn't much, but it's clean," she said. "You can wash up at the pump outside. Dinner will be ready in an hour."

"Thank you," Aevah said, her voice soft with gratitude. "We really appreciate it."

After freshening up, they joined Martha and her husband, Luke, for dinner. The meal was simple but hearty, and the conversation was warm and welcoming. Martha spoke about their life on the farm and how their children had grown and moved to the nearby town. Jacob and Aevah, sticking to their cover, shared a story about travelling to visit family. Everything felt easy and natural.

After eating, Luke took Jacob to the barn to help with the evening chores, while Aevah stayed inside to help Martha with washing dishes and preparing bread for the next day's market. Jacob found comfort in the familiar rhythm of physical labour, the regular tasks of feeding the animals, tidying the barn, and securing the stalls, bringing him a rare sense of peace. Once the chores were finished, he checked on Storm and Whisp one last time, murmuring a quiet goodnight to them before carrying a bundle of firewood into the house.

Later, as they settled into their beds, Jacob turned to Aevah. "We picked a good place to stay. Martha and Luke are lovely people," he said quietly.

She nodded, her eyes already closing. "Yes, I'll be sad to leave here."

***

As morning arrived, Jacob and Aevah bid farewell to their hosts, expressing their gratitude for their generosity. Martha sent them off with fresh bread and eggs, wishing them well on their travels. They rode on through the day, spending long hours in the saddle.

At midday, they took a brief respite in a nearby village for lunch before continuing along their route. By late afternoon, they came upon a suitable campsite – a secluded spot off the road, nestled within dense woods, where a little river meandered through. Though the woodland was compact, a narrow, muddied trail led them to a well-worn patch of grass encircled by stones, evidence of a frequented campsite. Leading their horses in, they set about making camp.

Once the tent was pitched and the fire crackled to life, Jacob, yearning for a moment alone, wandered off to explore. Towering maple trees surrounded him, their leaves still lush but tinged with the first signs of summer ending. Sunlight filtered through the canopy, casting dappled patterns on the forest floor as a warm breeze rustled through the branches. The air was rich with the scent of blooming flowers, accompanied by the melodic harmony of birdsong.

As he ventured deeper, he came upon a fallen tree, its moss-covered trunk dotted with fungi – a perfect spot to sit and whittle. The familiar act stirred memories of his time in the workshop with Larry and Ben, crafting intricate pieces with careful hands. He thought of the necklace Aevah still wore – his most cherished creation. It was an oval-shaped pendant with a hollowed centre, and a rose delicately carved on the back. Her favourite flower. Inside, she kept the small blue gem she used to help her channel.

Settling down on the fallen trunk, Jacob pulled a small block of wood from the forest floor and retrieved his pocket knife. With steady hands, he began shaping a horse, carefully etching details to mirror his own mount.

"Mind if I join you?"

Startled, Jacob looked up to find a young woman standing nearby. She was tall, with dark skin and jet-black curls framing her face.

"I'm Isabella," she said, stepping closer. "My brothers are just beyond the trees. I came to gather firewood." She lifted the small bundle of sticks in her arms as proof, smiling at his silence.

"If I'm honest, I only volunteered for firewood duty to get a break from them," she admitted, taking the lack of response as permission to sit. Lowering the sticks, she eased onto the mossy ground across from him.

Jacob's cheeks warmed at the presence of the striking woman before him. Clearing his throat, he steadied his voice. "I'm Jacob." He continued whittling, his fingers working on the wood. "Nice to meet you, Isabella."

She offered a warm smile, her gaze flicking to the tiny figure in his hands. "What are you making?"

"A horse," he replied, holding it up for her to see. "It's meant to look like mine."

"It's beautiful," she said, leaning in for a closer look. "You have real talent."

Jacob felt his face heat again. "Thanks. It's just something I do to pass the time."

They sat in silence for a moment, Isabella peeling the bark from a twig as Jacob focussed on shaping the horse's ears. Finally, she spoke. "Where are you headed? My brothers and I are on our way home."

"My sister and I are travelling to Belmont," he said. "Exploring the area first before we head there to meet our grandfather."

Isabella looked around. "Where is she?"

"Just beyond the trees, not far. I needed a little time to myself."

"Ah," Isabella said with a knowing grin. "And here I am, disturbing your peace."

Jacob shook his head. "Not at all. That's not what I meant. We've spent a lot of time together lately, and we both needed a break."

She chuckled. "I understand that completely. Well, if you don't mind, I wouldn't mind sitting here for a while."

"Some company would be nice," he admitted with a small smile.

As he continued carving, he noticed Isabella's curiosity. After a moment, he offered her his knife and a spare piece of wood. "Want to give it a try?"

Her eyes lit up. "I'd love to." She took the knife and, under his quiet instruction, carefully began shaping the wood.

They sat together, whittling in companionable silence. For the first time in days, Jacob felt a sense of calm, grateful for the unexpected company. But as the sun dipped lower, a chill settled into the air, reminding him how long he had left Aevah alone.

"I should head back and check on my sister," he said, standing and stretching.

"Of course," Isabella said, rising to her feet. "It was nice to meet you, Jacob."

"And you." With a polite nod, he made his way back through the trees.

When he arrived at their camp, he found Aevah already asleep in their tent. Careful not to wake her, he ate a quiet meal by the fire, finishing his carving until the night grew too dark. When sleep finally pulled at his limbs, he smothered the flames with dirt and then settled in for the night.

Chapter 16

Almost Caught

After several more days of travel and fruitless searching for the shard, Aevah and Jacob neared a town called Silverbrook. Though late summer had set in, the day was cool and windy, forcing them to keep their cloaks wrapped tightly around their bodies. Aevah, weary of the relentless gusts biting at her face, was about to voice her frustration when she spotted a settlement ahead.

"Please tell me that's the place," she exclaimed.

"I think so," Jacob replied, rising to stand briefly in his saddle to get a better look at the town in the distance. It had been days since they had ventured into a populated area, their time spent wandering through dense woods in search of a giant tree.

"Thank the divine spirit," Aevah said and sighed. She longed for a hot meal and a proper bath.

As they entered the town, they dismounted and led their horses through the quiet streets until they found a welcoming establishment. The inn, called *The Blue Lantern*, stood out with its inviting charm. Built from sturdy stone and timber, its ivy-covered walls exuded a rustic elegance. Above the entrance, a large wooden sign, painted in deep teal with gold lettering, bore the inn's name. A lantern illustration, its glow faintly illuminated, added to the allure.

Lanterns swayed gently from the eaves, while flower boxes on the windowsills brought splashes of colour to the façade. The warm sounds of laughter and the clinking of glasses filtered through the air, easing the twins' exhaustion.

Upon entering, Jacob quickly found a worker, arranged for their horses to be stabled, and paid for access to the private bathing chambers. Though they had no intention of staying the night, they both needed to freshen up after days on the road without a proper wash. Without delay, Jacob made his way to the men's chamber while Aevah entered the one designated for women. Fortunately, they had the space to themselves.

The bathing area was unexpectedly spacious. The dimly lit room contained four wooden tubs, each large enough for a single occupant to bathe comfortably. Sturdy benches sat beside each tub, neatly arranged with folded towels and a selection of bathing essentials: a bar of handmade soap, a brush with natural bristles, and a small jar of fragrant oils. A bucket of fresh water stood ready for rinsing, adding to the simple yet thoughtful accommodations.

The air inside was warm and humid, carrying a delicate hint of lavender – a welcome change to the brisk chill outside.

Aevah eased herself into the steaming bath, sighing as the heat enveloped her aching body. The warmth seeped into her weary muscles, loosening their tightness and washing away the fatigue of the travel. The gentle sound of water lapping against the sides of the tub provided a soothing backdrop to her thoughts. She lingered in the comforting embrace of the water before finally reaching for the fragrant soap, working up a rich lather as the refreshing scent of citrus filled the air.

Reluctantly, she emerged from the bath and dried herself with the plush towels, savouring the renewed sense of energy coursing through her limbs. Once dressed, she descended the stairs, her steps lighter than before.

Jacob stood near the bar and engaged in conversation with the staff. Their voices blended with the clinking of glasses and the steady hum of patrons. When he noticed her approach, he wrapped up his discussion and made his way over.

"Ready?" he asked.

"I guess," Aevah said with a wistful sigh. "I could've stayed in that bath forever."

"It felt like you did," Jacob quipped.

She shoved him lightly in response. "Let's look around before we head out."

Jacob nodded, and together, they stepped out of the inn.

The plan was simple: take a walk through Silverbrook, enjoy an early dinner, and move on before nightfall to set up camp. Staying at inns too often was costly, and they had agreed to save their money for food. More often than not, they spent their nights camping in the woods or, when fortune allowed, seeking shelter in farm barns.

They had hoped to locate the crystal shard with ease, but without a proper understanding of the land, every clue felt like another piece in an unsolvable riddle. For now, they sat aside the search, using the next few hours to unwind and enjoy a brief respite from their fruitless quest. There were only so many clusters of trees one could admire before they all started to look the same.

The streets of Silverbrook were a lively contrast to the silence of the wilderness. Throngs of people bustled about, merchants called out to passersby, and street performers filled the air with cheerful melodies. Children darted through the crowds, laughing as they played their games. The energy of the town was infectious.

As they wandered, they passed a flower stall where a vendor carefully arranged vibrant bouquets, their colours striking against the wooden cart. Further along, the rhythmic clanging of a blacksmith's hammer rang through the air, the forge glowing as metal met fire.

For the first time in days, Aevah and Jacob allowed themselves to simply enjoy the world around them.

As they continued their walk, the rich aroma of roasted meats filled the air, making their stomachs rumble in protest. Ready to eat, they turned back towards the inn and settled at a small table for two.

A young woman with a warm smile and curly chestnut hair approached.

"What can I getcha?" she asked, her accent thick with the local dialect.

"I was told earlier the soup was good," Jacob said.

"It is," she confirmed with a nod.

"Then two bowls, please, and just water to drink," he replied.

The waitress disappeared and returned a few minutes later, balancing two steaming bowls of chicken and vegetable soup alongside a basket of crusty bread. Their drinks followed soon after.

The rich scent of the broth stirred Aevah's appetite. She took a sip. The flavour reminded her of cosy winter nights at their grandfather's cottage, though the soup was cooler than she preferred. Without thinking, she grasped the gem in her necklace and channelled a faint pulse of energy into it. A moment later, steam curled from the surface of her bowl. She did the same to Jacob's before picking up her spoon again.

They ate in comfortable silence – until the door of the inn swung open with a forceful bang.

A man in a navy uniform and cloak strode inside. A silver badge gleamed on his coat, though from this distance, Aevah couldn't make its insignia. Even so, a cold shiver raced down her spine the instant his eyes met hers.

A tracker.

His lips curled into a menacing smile as he moved towards them with purposeful strides.

Aevah shot to her feet, her knee knocking against the table and sending her bowl of soup sloshing onto the wood. Across from her, Jacob had already registered the threat. He grabbed her arm and yanked her forward.

"Run!"

With no time to think, she stumbled after him, weaving through the crowded tavern as startled patrons turned to watch. Jacob pulled her between tables, nearly toppling a server carrying plates. Aevah, in her scramble, crashed against another surface, sending their drinks spilling onto the floor.

The tracker was closing in.

With no visible exit nearby, Jacob veered towards the kitchen and dragged her through the entrance. The two of them sprinted past startled workers, dodging hot pans and sacks of flour, before bursting through the back door. Jacob slammed it shut behind them, his chest rising and falling in quick breaths as he glanced around for their next escape route.

No time to hesitate.

Spinning on his heel, he pulled Aevah with him, their boots pounding against the cobbled streets as they ducked into alleyways and wove through the bustling market stalls.

Only when they reached a narrow, shadowed passage did they finally stop to catch their breath.

Aevah felt Jacob's grip on her hand loosen as he relaxed, if only slightly.

She remained tense. Something about the air felt wrong – heavy, charged, as if unseen eyes were searching for her, creeping closer like a mist curling through the streets. A shiver ran down her spine as the sensation intensified.

She turned her head sharply to the right, her instincts screaming a warning.

"Jacob!"

He spun in the direction of her gaze.

The tracker was nearly upon them, his wicked eyes gleaming with the thrill of the chase.

Jacob didn't hesitate. He grabbed Aevah's hand once more.

"Quick, this way!" he urged, yanking her forward.

They tore through the alleyways, their boots pounding against the cobbled streets. The narrow passages twisted and turned, shadows flickering as they wove through them. Aevah felt a sharp stitch forming in her side, her breath coming in ragged gasps. She wanted to stop – needed to – but she had no choice. If the tracker caught her, there was no telling what fate awaited.

Trackers were usually employed to hunt down magic wielders who used their abilities for crime, channelling power through objects to aid in thefts, deceptions, or worse. They worked alongside local guards, their rare ability to sense magic making them invaluable in catching those who would otherwise go undetected.

But some trackers were ambitious.

Some took those they found, especially around their age, straight to Carraton, to the queen. There, they awaited judgement, scrutinised for any resemblance to the long-lost royal children – the niece and nephew the queen had searched for relentlessly. What happened to those taken remained a mystery.

Jacob pulled her down another alley, twisting through snickets and side streets, pushing past startled pedestrians as they fought to stay ahead. The streets blurred together, unfamiliar and winding, until they had no idea where they were.

Finally, Jacob skidded to a halt.

Aevah nearly collapsed beside him, doubling over with her hands on her knees, clutching her side as she wheezed. Her lungs burned, and her pulse thundered in her ears.

For a moment, all she could do was breathe.

Suddenly, the heavy *thud* of approaching footsteps echoed behind them. Aevah's pulse hammered in her ears as she turned – the man was closing in. His eyes locked onto hers, gleaming with a predator's hunger.

"Jacob, he's right behind us!" she gasped.

Without hesitation, Jacob tightened his grip on her hand and yanked her into a narrow alley. They sprinted through the maze of streets, their breaths coming in ragged gasps. But the tracker was persistent. His footsteps grew louder, closing the distance with terrifying speed.

As they rounded a corner, Jacob stumbled, nearly losing his footing. The man lunged, his fingers grazing the edge of Jacob's cloak. Aevah's heart lurched as she saw his hand reaching – so close. In a desperate burst of adrenaline, she wrenched Jacob forward and flung out her free hand. A surge of power shot from her fingertips, striking their pursuer and knocking him backwards.

"Keep running!" Jacob urged. His voice was taut with urgency.

They dashed through the crowded market, weaving between stalls and dodging startled townsfolk. Shouts and curses followed in their wake as merchants scrambled to protect their wares. But the tracker pressed on, his determination unyielding.

Jacob darted into another alley, dragging Aevah behind him. The walls loomed close, the passages barely wide enough for them to squeeze through. He cast a quick glance over his shoulder – too close. The man was right behind them, ruthless.

"This way!" Jacob shouted, pulling her into a side street.

Too late, Aevah realised their mistake.

A dead end.

Her stomach twisted. Trapped.

Jacob's gaze darted around, searching for any way out. Then he spotted it – a stack of crates against the wall.

"Climb up!" he ordered.

Aevah scrambled onto the wooden crates, her hands trembling as she pulled herself higher. Jacob followed close behind, shoving her upward as their pursuer closed in.

Just as the tracker reached the alley, they hauled themselves onto the rooftop, panting and drained. Below, he glared up at them, his face contorted in frustration.

"You can't run forever!" he bellowed, his voice echoing through the streets.

Jacob pulled Aevah to her feet, his jaw set with determination. "We won't have to," he muttered.

They moved swiftly across the rooftops, jumping from one building to the next, creating as much distance as possible between themselves and their pursuer. Aevah's heart pounded as she followed, constantly glancing over her shoulder, half-expecting the tracker to materialise from the shadows and seize her.

At last, Jacob found a ladder affixed to the side of a house and climbed down. She followed, her limbs aching with exhaustion. As soon as her feet touched the ground, Aevah pressed her back against the wall and slid down, burying her face in her hands.

"What if he's still following us?" she whispered.

"He's not," Jacob assured her. "I'm sure of it."

She inhaled sharply, willing her racing heart to slow. As she composed herself, Jacob took a few cautious steps forward, scanning their surroundings. Aevah straightened, drawn to his sudden stillness.

They had emerged in the rougher part of town. The houses were shabbier, some with bordered-up windows, others surrounded by heaps of discarded rubbish. The air smelled stale, thick with the scent of dampness and decay. People slouched against doorways, their clothes worn and threadbare, some walking barefoot on the uneven streets.

Aevah swallowed. This part of Silverbrook was a stark contrast to the bustling market they had fled.

People sat slumped against buildings, some with a tattered hat in front of them if they were lucky – just a piece of cardboard if they weren't – begging for food or coin. Aevah's throat tightened at the sight before her. The tracker was momentarily forgotten. She had always known poverty existed in the kingdom, but seeing it laid bare in front of her was something else entirely.

Especially the children.

They wandered in rags, their bodies skeletal, hollow-eyed and sunken-cheeked. A bag of bones searching the ground for a scrap of food.

"We have to help them," she murmured.

Jacob hesitated. "How?"

Aevah didn't answer. Instead, she stepped towards a frail-looking boy who was poking through the toppled bin with a stick, sifting through the discarded scraps. He froze as she approached, his thin shoulders tensing. Wide, wary eyes met hers, gleaming from a gaunt, dirt-smudged face. He couldn't have been more than eight. And yet, his posture was already that of someone who expected the world to strike him down.

He straightened, gripping his stick like a weapon. "What choo want?" he asked, voice sharp with distrust.

Aevah simply extended her hand, revealing a silver coin resting in her palm. "Here. Take it. Get yourself something to eat."

The boy's gaze flickered between her face and the coin, suspicion etched deep into his features. He stood frozen for a moment, searching for the trick, the catch. Then, in a single swift movement, he snatched the coin and bolted, disappearing into the shadows.

Aevah took a step after him, but he was already gone. A gentle squeeze on her shoulder made her pause.

"We need to leave Aevah," Jacob said quietly. "People are watching, and if we stay much longer, they might turn desperate."

She exhaled slowly, her heart heavy. He was right. These people needed help – but not the kind she or Jacob could offer. And judging by the boy's reaction, the surrounding adults would likely be even more wary. Hunger could make people unpredictable. Desperate.

It wasn't their fault. She couldn't begin to imagine the weight of surviving like this – always hungry, fighting every day for a morsel of food, never knowing if you would wake the next morning or if starvation would finally take you. No one should have to live like that.

They turned back the way they came, but the winding alleys confused them, leading them in circles. Each street looked just as unfamiliar and foreboding as the last, a maze of dark passages and shadowy corners. Aevah's pulse quickened. Every turn felt like a risk, every shadow a potential threat.

Finally, after what felt like an eternity, the surroundings shifted. The narrow, grimy alleyways gave way to wider streets, where homes were brighter and better kept. The contrast was stark – poverty-stricken despair on one side, comfortable affluence on the other. As they stepped onto the main road, the hairs on Aevah's arms prickled. Everything seemed normal, townspeople moved about as usual, but something felt wrong.

"I feel like we're being watched," she whispered. "We need to get out of here."

Jacob looked at her, his expression unreadable. "Is this the power telling you, or just a feeling?"

"The power," she said. "Something isn't right here." She hugged herself, rubbing her arms as an uneasy chill crept over her.

Jacob nodded without question. "Then we grab the horses and leave. If you believe we are unsafe here, I trust you."

Relief flooded through her. "Thank you."

She stayed close to him as they made their way to the stables. The encounter with the tracker had rattled her more than she cared to admit, and she doubted she would feel truly safe until they were far away. One thing was certain – she could no longer afford to use channelled magic, no matter how much easier it was. From now on, she would rely solely on objectless magic, even if it drained her.

She would not be taken.

She would not fall into her aunt's hands.

With the horses saddled, Jacob tucked some food he had bought from the inn's kitchen into their packs. Aevah followed him out of town, glancing over her shoulder one last time before they vanished into the trees.

The tracker was gone. But the feeling of being hunted remained.

Chapter 17

A Change of Pace

Adrian awoke the next day to the sight of Cecilia sleeping beside him. Her features were serene, one arm raised above her head, her face tilted slightly towards his. Even now, it still felt surreal to wake up next to her every morning. If someone had asked him ten years ago what he thought his future might look like, this would not have been his answer. And yet, he didn't mind. The path that had led him here had been messy – largely by his own doing – but despite everything, he was grateful for how things had turned out.

The night he fled Carraton, he had been a whirlwind of confusion and emotion. His past choices had loomed over him, haunting his every thought – his blind devotion to Elinor chief among them. Only when he saw what she became with the power did the illusion shatter, revealing her for what she truly was. The massacre in the dungeons had been the breaking point, sending him fleeing as far as he could. He had ridden through the night in a daze, moving from town to town, replaying every decision, wondering how he had been so blind to her true nature. Infatuation had drawn him in. Desire and ambition had kept him by her side.

Hidden away in Adlington, it had been easy to imagine the glory of taking a kingdom, of serving the future ruler of Ethos. The king and queen had been nothing more than distant figures, abstract obstacles to remove. It was easy to justify treason when you didn't see your victims as flesh and blood. They had become the villains in his mind – the usurpers who had stolen what rightfully belonged to Elinor. Surrounded by those who shared the same belief, it had been natural to fall into the narrative that she was the rightful heir.

So, when they had stormed the castle, he had done it with pride, aiding his queen in reclaiming her throne. But he had been so very wrong. As the months passed, the veil lifted, and he finally saw her for what she was – a vindictive, power-hungry tyrant. A woman whose presence inspired fear, whose temper sent people cowering in silence.

He had seen how she treated those who opposed her, those who recognised her true nature and had tried to stop her – for good reason. He had seen her victims, those she toyed with for amusement, Cecilia among them. Cecilia had endured the mind games, the manipulation. Even now, her children remained in hiding, unable to be safe by their mother's side.

Adrian had tried desperately to understand, to see the virtues he had once believed existed in Elinor, but with each passing day, it became harder. Every decision she made served only her own gain, with no thought for the people of her kingdom. The power had slowly corrupted her already wicked mind. His dwindling hope finally shattered the day he saw the dismembered bodies strewn across the walls. They had not deserved to die like that. All for a crown.

That was not to say he bore no blame. The entire situation rested at his feet. He had helped orchestrate everything Elinor had done, and for that, he would spend the rest of his life trying to make amends.

"Is it morning?" Cecilia asked lazily, rolling towards him and peeking at him with one eye open.

"It is, but since you aren't working today, you have no reason to get up… unless you want to."

She smiled, and her eyes drifted shut again. "Just five more minutes, then."

Adrian couldn't help but smile in return. He pressed a kiss to the top of her head before climbing out of bed. Pulling on a pair of pants, he left the bedroom and ambled down to the kitchen. He retrieved the kettle, filled it with water, and set it on the stove to boil.

Since moving in with Cecilia, his life had changed dramatically – including his profession. Unsure of what to do for work, he had spent days wandering the city's winding streets, searching for inspiration. One day, his aimless steps had led him to the local smithy. As he approached, the rhythmic clanging of metal had drawn him in.

He had stood at the entrance, watching intently as the blacksmith expertly hammered a glowing piece of iron, shaping it into what would become a finely crafted sword. Noticing his interest, the smith had called him over, handing him tools and teaching him the basics. What had begun as mere curiosity quickly grew into a passion. The heat of the forge, the satisfaction of shaping raw metal, and the camaraderie of the seasoned blacksmiths had captivated him.

The job suited him well, allowing him to use his expertise in weapons and armour while keeping a low profile. Most of his tasks revolved around repairing tools, horseshoes, and sharpening knives. But on occasion, he had the chance to craft armour, shields, and swords – those moments brought him the greatest satisfaction.

He also pursued personal projects, typically making edged weapons, as crafting his own sword would have drawn too much scrutiny. Over the years, he had even forged a few daggers for Cecilia and dedicated time to training her in self-defence. At home, he continued to hone his skills, practising primarily indoors to avoid attracting prying eyes or arousing unwanted suspicion.

It had been quite some time since he left, but Adrian knew Elinor still had connections everywhere. One wrong move on his part, and he would find himself at the gallows. Or worse. Knowing what she was capable of, execution would be far too merciful. He had no intention of falling into Elinor's clutches. No, he planned to work with Cecilia to depose her and see one of her children take the throne – Jacob or Aevah, whoever chose to step up and reign.

He had hoped they would have been reunited by now, but with no word from George, Cecilia had been unable to find them. So, they stayed, watching and waiting, hoping for news. But none ever came. Over the years, they had both tried to subtly gather information without drawing attention to themselves.

He knew time was running out. They had to locate the twins soon, even if it meant taking the risk of venturing beyond their safe haven in Adlington. Though their situation remained precarious, they felt relatively secure here, as the locals knew them only by their aliases. Their past lives had become nothing more than distant memories. However, as the years passed, Elinor's determination to find them would only grow stronger.

They were the only genuine threat to her reign. The lords might challenge her, if the rumours were true, but they lacked the strength to overthrow her – unless they gained power from the crystal shards. Yet none of them had access to that magic. Elinor had ensured it by killing the only members of the court who carried even a trace of it in their veins. Even now, she disposed of any children brought before her who displayed the slightest hint of magical ability or bore any resemblance to her niece and nephew.

A cruel, twisted woman, Elinor would stop at nothing to keep her throne. That was why Adrian and Cecilia needed to find the twins. And soon. But convincing Cecilia to leave was another matter entirely. They had discussed it many times, but each time, he heard it in her voice – the worry, the fear. The possibility that, if they left, they might miss the twins coming here in search of her, guided by her father.

So, they stayed. They waited. They hoped.

But no one ever came.

Chapter 18

Adlington

After parting ways with the twins, George set off on a solitary journey towards Adlington. He took the less-travelled routes, weaving through back roads and dense forests to avoid unwanted attention. His progress was steady, and his horse was in good condition.

In just a few more hours, he would reach the city gates. Thanks to his disguise, he had little reason to worry about being recognised; no one could identify him. Still, he remained wary of power trackers, especially near a major capital. These individuals were specially trained to detect those with magical abilities, particularly those who use their skills to alter their appearance. Only a handful of criminals in the largest cities possessed such talents – fortunate enough to have been born with even a trace of magic.

Every city had a few trackers embedded within the local guard. If one of them stumbled upon him, their first instinct would be to apprehend him and strip away his disguise. This wasn't a risk he could afford to take.

Years ago, he had a close call on his way back to the cottage. Fortunately, he had been alone then, with the twins safely within the boundaries, eagerly awaiting his return.

That moment had been the first time in years he had felt true fear – not for himself, but for his grandchildren. If something happened to him, what would become of them? Luckily, he had been more powerful than the tracker and had known how to suppress the man's abilities.

Once his magic signature had vanished from detection, the tracker had moved on, unaware of his presence. That was the way of things for most magic-wielders – the strong could manipulate the weaker if they knew how.

Genuine strength was rare, aside from among the royals. Those who did possess it had typically inherited only a fraction, the result of affairs or fleeting encounters between commoners and nobles. Even then, the magic passed down was little more than a lingering trace.

Some lords and ladies possessed considerable strength, though few could rival the power of the royal bloodline. Only a select few had the ability to wield magic to its full potential. As a direct descendant of that lineage, George held a distinct advantage.

Yet, he was an anomaly. No one else in his family had more than a trickle of power – his daughter Cecilia, among them. If he had been a superstitious man, he might have believed his abilities had been bestowed upon him for a reason.

Continuing his journey, he followed the road leading directly to the city gates. Keeping to the left side and maintaining a composed trot, he navigated the familiar path. Being so close to Adlington, the road bustled with travellers moving in both directions.

As he rode, the landscape shifted from dense forest to open grasslands. In the distance, scattered farms dotted the countryside, and fields of crops stretched towards the horizon. The sight was a welcome change from the endless trees, and for a brief moment, he allowed himself to admire it.

Ahead, the towering city gates came into view, manned by guards who scrutinised each arrival. Those who failed to meet the entry requirements were promptly turned away and forced beyond the walls. As night fell, the gates would close, opening only for those with valid reasons – an effective deterrent against bandits and other unsavoury figures who prowled the darkness in search of easy prey.

Since it was nearly midday, George expected no trouble gaining entry. The guards rarely stopped ordinary travellers, as doing so would slow the flow of people to an unbearable pace. To them, he was just another wanderer with no outstanding warrants. He should be able to pass through without issue and find a modest inn for the night.

After travelling for so long and countless nights spent beneath the stars, he yearned for the comfort of a proper bed and the small luxuries unavailable in the wilderness. Upon reaching the gate, he dismounted, took hold of his horse's reins, and stepped through the walls of Adlington.

The moment he entered, the city engulfed him in a swirl of sound and scent. It was a stark contrast to the peaceful solitude of the country cottage and the quiet village he had called home for the past eight years. Adlington pulsed with energy – people bustling through the streets, voices rising in conversation, gossip spilling between eager tongues.

Merchants haggled over prices, their hands waving animatedly as they sought the best deals. Children darted between carts and vendors, their laughter echoing through the narrow streets. Street performers and beggars competed for attention, some hoping for applause, others for a coin or two from a generous stranger.

George knew that amid the chaos, pickpockets lurked, waiting for an opportunity to strike. But he paid them little mind. What captured his attention was the intoxicating aroma of food, spices, and tea wafting from both sides of the street. The scent alone made his stomach growl, a sharp reminder of how long it had been since his last meal.

Without hesitation, he approached a nearby stall and bought a steaming hot gammon pie. The warmth of it in his hands was a small but welcome comfort.

As he continued walking towards the inn, George ate, his horse trailing obediently beside him. The pastry was rich and flavourful. Each bite was a welcome contrast to the cold meats he had endured over the past week. The crust was perfectly baked – flaky yet firm – while the vegetables were tender, and the meat practically melted in his mouth. The creamy filling made his mouth water with delight. It was exactly what he needed.

By the time he finished his meal, he had reached the inn he had been searching for. Turning down the adjacent alley, he found the stable and handed over the reins to a young boy tending the horses. As a token of appreciation, he flipped a gold coin towards him.

"Take good care of my horse, lad. Shadow's the name, and he's had a bit of a hard ride."

The boy caught the coin and grinned. "Yes sir! The very best care he'll 'ave, mark me words!"

"What's your name, lad?"

"Timmy, sir."

"Nice to meet you, Timmy. Name's George. I trust I can count on you if I need anythin'?"

"Aye, sir. Ye sure can!"

With a tip of his hat, George turned back towards the alley. That would ensure his horse was looked after – and that he had an extra set of eyes should he need any assistance during his stay.

Standing before the inn, he allowed himself a small smile before stepping inside *The Tap House.*

It had been many years since he had last set foot in this place, yet it looked exactly the same. Anyone would have thought they had travelled back in time by a decade or two. The furnishings and décor had certainly not been updated to match the times.

The stone slab stretched across the room, worn and uneven in places. Mismatched wooden tables and chairs were scattered haphazardly, while a few square windows let in just enough daylight to give the space a dim, rustic glow. To the right, the bar was lined with patrons, drinking and talking in low murmurs.

Behind the bar stood none other than Jeff Briars – proud owner of the establishment and the head of the city's secret underground no-rules fight club. It had been years since George had last seen him.

Striding over, he greeted him with a grin. "Jeff, my, my—time has treated you well, I see."

"Feck off with yer sarcasm," Jeff grumbled, wiping a glass with a rag. "I'd say the same, but I know yer hidin' under that mask."

George smirked. "What gave me away?"

Jeff snorted. "Ye have a look and a walk no magic trick can hide."

"Hah, there's no foolin' you."

"Course not. I neva forget a face… or a drink. Usual?"

"Aye."

George settled onto one of the few remaining stools, watching as Jeff poured his beverage. Time had left its mark on the man – his balding head was now streaked with grey, and his face bore the signs of a life hard-lived. He was the only proof that the years had passed in this place.

Jeff slid a pint of ale across the counter, and George took a hearty swig. Say what you would about the inn's outdated décor, but no one could fault the drink. Jeff was one of the few tavern owners who refused to serve ale that was warm or watered down.

The frosty mug had come straight from the tap. Cool and crisp, with a rich, malty flavour, it was bliss on George's tongue. Smacking his lips in satisfaction, he set the glass down.

"Still the finest ale around."

"Aye, only the best 'ere," Jeff said with a nod. "What brings ye back? Been at least fifteen years."

"Visiting a family friend. Be here a while—ye got a room to spare?"

"Aye, got a few left. I'll show ye to one when ye finish yer drink. That all ye got wi' ye?"

"Aye. Horse is in the stable, too."

"No problem. I'll take yer things up now."

George took another sip before adding, "I'll grab a bowl of whatever that delicious smell is from yer kitchen, too, when ye're ready."

"Don't want much, do ye?" Jeff chuckled. "I'll 'ave a bowl brought out soon."

As Jeff disappeared into the back, George continued nursing his drink, his gaze drifting over the patrons. He didn't recognise a single face – not that he had expected to. Like Jeff had said, it had been at least fifteen years.

Jeff, as he remembered, was one of the good ones. He kept his mouth shut and made it a point not to see anything. An important trait for a man running illegal fights for profit.

Ironically, the inn wasn't just a front for his side business. Jeff genuinely loved his little establishment, but it had never been a massive money-maker. That was where the underground fights came in. Those, without a doubt, brought in the real profits.

George had watched a few of these bouts in the past. They were dirty, brutal, and, for the right people, highly lucrative. Those who bet wisely – or knew how to rig a match – could make a fortune. The elite lined their pockets while the rest left with little more than empty hands and broken bones.

As he finished his first pint, a steaming bowl of lamb stew appeared before him, accompanied by a few slices of warm, crusty bread. Eager to eat, George tucked into the hearty dish. Moments later, a fresh tankard of ale was placed in front of him. He took a few sips before returning to his meal. The stew was as good as he remembered – rich, flavourful, and satisfying.

When he had finished, he used the last piece of bread to soak up the remnants in the bowl. Setting his spoon down, he pushed the dish aside and pulled the tankard closer, draining the rest of his ale before placing the empty mug on the counter.

Standing, he turned to Jeff. "I'll head to the room now if ye're good to show me up."

"Course. Follow me."

Jeff led him through the wooden door behind the bar, which opened into a narrow hallway. At the end of the corridor, they reached a staircase and began their ascent. As they climbed, they passed two additional hallways lined with rooms before arriving on the third floor.

Stopping in front of the second door on the right, Jeff unlocked it and pushed it open. Stepping aside, he gestured for George to enter.

George nodded in thanks and stepped inside, taking a quick survey of his surroundings. Much like the tavern downstairs, the room was filled with mismatched but sturdy furniture. Though simple, it was comfortable and functional. A washbasin sat atop a wooden stand – a useful convenience, given that the communal bathhouse was on the lower level.

Knowing he was long overdue for a proper wash, he rummaged through his belongings, pulling out the freshest clothes he had after days on the road. Slinging them over his shoulder, he grabbed his bag of laundry and left the room.

On his way to the bathhouse, he stopped by the laundry area and handed his soiled clothes to the washerwoman. Passing her a coin for the trouble, he continued down the hall towards the bathing chambers. At this time of day, the baths were empty. The room housed six individual tubs, and he chose the nearest one. As the bath filled, he retrieved a towel from the racks and a bar of soap from the cupboard before setting his fresh clothes and essentials aside.

Once the tub was full, he tested the water and then channelled his power to warm it a little more. Satisfied, he climbed in, letting out a deep sigh as the heat seeped into his muscles. The hot water was exactly what he needed after his long journey. As he scrubbed away the grime, he relished the sensation of finally feeling clean again.

Refreshed, he stepped out of the tub and towelled himself dry. Once dressed, he returned to his room, ready to put a plan together.

Though it had been years since his last visit, he still knew this city like the back of his hand. More importantly, he could sense that Cecilia was here, hiding somewhere within its walls. And he needed to find her.

Chapter 19

The Search

George donned his cloak, grabbed a bag of coins, and left his room with a determined stride. Because he knew his daughter well, he was certain she wouldn't seek work in the rougher parts of town. She was more likely in the middle-class area, which was safer and more respectable. This helped narrow his search, but he still needed to pinpoint her exact location.

Thankfully, he had a secret weapon – his power. He could sense her once she was within a certain range. Still, he hoped his new stable hand friend, Timmy, might help locate her.

Heading down to the stables, George found the boy brushing a horse. He approached and greeted him warmly before getting straight to the point.

"Timmy, me lad. How ye be?"

"George! Good, thanks. 'Ow can I 'elp ye?"

"I'm hopin' ye can help me find someone—a woman, 'er thirties, thereabouts. Works in a nearby inn. She's got olive skin and emerald-green eyes. It ain't much t' go on, but it's all I got fer now." He tossed another gold coin to him.

"Aye, I can. I'll let ye know when I find 'er."

"Good lad. Be sure ye don't tell no one, mind."

"Wudn't dream of it."

With Timmy on the lookout as well, George felt more confident that it wouldn't take too long to find her.

As night crept in, he began his own search, hopping from inn to inn, discreetly asking questions about the workers.

The first inn he visited was a bustling place, filled with the laughter and chatter of patrons. George approached the bar and ordered a drink, striking up a casual conversation with the bartender.

"Do ye have any long-term staff here? Anyone who's been around for a few years?" he asked, keeping his tone light.

The bartender shook his head. Most of the team was relatively new, he explained, so George finished his drink and moved on.

The next inn was quieter, its atmosphere more subdued. George repeated his routine, ordering a drink before asking about the workers.

"How goes it with staff here? Is it as hard to keep 'em as it is elsewhere lately?"

The innkeeper, a middle-aged woman with greying hair, nodded thoughtfully. "Aye, it's been tough. We've had a few come and go, but some have stuck around for years. Why?"

George took a sip of his drink, keeping his tone casual. "Just curious. I'm searching for a friend who might have been working in the area for a while."

The innkeeper leaned in, intrigued. "Well, we've got a few long-timers. There's Lucy… she's been with us nearly a decade. An old Joe, he's been 'ere even longer. But if you're lookin' for someone specific, you might wanna check the other inns too. Folks tend t' move around a bit."

George nodded, grateful for the information. "Thanks, I'll do that. Appreciate the help."

As he finished his drink, he glanced at the workers the innkeeper had pointed out. Neither was Cecilia, so he moved on to the next place.

At each stop, he varied his questions slightly, inquiring about long-term staff, recent changes, and whether anyone had seen a woman matching Cecilia's description. So far, he had no luck, but he decided to try one last spot.

Stepping inside the rowdy tavern, George pushed his way towards the bar as a patron sloshed beer over his arm, soaking the sleeve of his coat. He shook his head, wiping at the wet fabric, and pressed through the crowd. The noise was deafening – laughter, shouting, and the clinking of mugs filling the air.

He squeezed between two burly men and caught the bartender's attention.

"Evening," George said, raising his voice over the din. "Busy night?"

The bartender, a grizzled man with a scar running down his cheek, nodded. "Always is. What can I get you?"

"A pint of your best ale," George replied, sliding a coin across the counter. As the bartender poured his drink, George leaned in slightly. "Say, how long have you been working here? Must be tough keeping staff in a place like this."

The bartender chuckled, setting the frothy mug in front of him. "Been here a good ten years myself. Seen a lot of folks come and go. But we've got a few who stick around. Why do you ask?"

George took a sip of his ale, savouring the rich flavour. "Just curious. I'm looking for someone who might have been working in the area for a while. Trying to track down an old friend, you see."

Before the bartender could respond, a loud crash echoed through the tavern as a table was overturned. Shouts and curses filled the air as a brawl erupted in the middle of the room. The chaos swallowed George before he could react. A burly man stumbled into him, knocking him off his stool and sending him sprawling to the floor.

"Watch it!" he shouted, attempting to push the man away. But the fight had already engulfed him. Fists flew, and he dodged punches, struggling to stay on his feet. He landed a few blows of his own, but the sheer number of combatants made it impossible to avoid getting hit.

Just as he thought he might break free from the melee, a particularly large man grabbed him by the collar and hurled him towards the door. George stumbled, barely managing to keep his balance, before being unceremoniously shoved out into the street. He landed hard on the cobblestones. The impact knocked the breath from his lungs.

Coughing and brushing himself off, he stood and glared at the building. The sounds of the brawl still raged inside, but he knew better than to try going back in. With a sigh, he adjusted his cloak and set off down the pathway, deciding to call it a night. Already, a bruise was forming around his left eye, and the metallic taste in his mouth told him his lip was split.

As he walked, the cool night air helped clear his mind. Despite the setback, he remained confident he would find Cecilia – he just needed to be more careful next time. When he reached his inn, hunger and pain settled over him like a heavy weight. He took his supper in his room, eating slowly to avoid irritating his cut lip, then washed up and tended to his wounds.

Lying in bed, his thoughts drifted to his daughter. He pictured her face, her smile, and the sound of her laughter. It had been so long since he last saw her – many months before that fateful night. Even before then, he had disappeared, pretending to leave on a trip so he could secretly keep an eye on Elinor. He had known she was up to something.

Which meant it had been nearly ten years.

He ached to see her again. With luck, he would, even if only for a fleeting moment. Just the sight of her would fill the hollow ache in his heart. He had never intended for her life to take the turn it did.

It haunted him that he hadn't been there when she needed him most. She and James had shared a love so deep, so genuine, that they should have had many more years together. Instead, he had been torn from her so cruelly, and she was forced to live at the mercy of his killer. George could only imagine the suffering she endured – though, in some ways, he understood it all too well.

His own wife had died young, but at least they had seen it coming. Tuberculosis had stolen her away, yet it had also given them time – time to say what needed to be said, to cherish the last fleeting moments. But for Cecilia, it had been sudden. Her entire world had been shattered in an instant. Stripped of everything, her children gone, she had been trapped in an unending cycle of grief.

He was grateful he had got the twins out and kept them safe. It was the only truly good thing he had managed. On that fateful night, when he reached the castle, he had taken a risk, saving his grandchildren in the desperate hope that by morning, Cecilia and James would have thwarted Elinor's coup. But fate had not been so kind.

Now, with Cecilia out of danger, he longed to see her again. Yet, he was apprehensive about how she would react. He knew she would expect her children to be with him, but they had their path to follow, and there was no time to delay. He hoped she would understand that he had done his best – that he had kept them safe all these years, knowing she would be reunited with them soon.

Still, doubt plagued him. *Had he done the right thing, keeping them hidden, even from their mother?* He had asked himself that question every day. He had known for some time that Cecilia had left the castle, having heard whispers in the village about the turmoil in the realm. He had been certain she would seek out the high priestess for help and that they would send her deep into hiding, somewhere unexpected – like Adlington. He could have taken the children and gone to her at any point. But he hadn't.

He told himself it was too dangerous that they needed to remain hidden, safe from anyone who might recognise them. And for years, he had clung to that justification. As each year passed, the temptation to leave gnawed at him. To pack up, find Cecilia, and reunite their family. But he never did. The closest he had come was on the twins' fourteenth name day. They had seemed lost, missing their mother terribly. He had nearly relented. But in the end, he had held firm, insisting that their safety lay in secrecy, in the protection of the cottage.

But had it been for them – or for him?

There was much he had to answer for when he finally faced Cecilia, especially now that he had sent her children off into the world. They would no longer need to fear Elinor. He would make sure of that. The path to the throne would be clear for them –

with their mother's guidance and the crystal shards united, they would be the rulers the kingdom had long needed.

He had never imagined they would remain separated for so many years. He had always believed Elinor's reign would be brief, especially once she began to lose herself to the power. Even now, he could not understand how the high priestess had allowed her to remain queen for so long. *Had she coerced? Or had she her own reasons for permitting such tyranny? What had Elinor done to maintain her grip on the throne?* The whispers and rumours all wove different versions of that fateful night when the priestesses had come to the castle.

So many secrets. So many lies. He might never uncover the full truth. But one thing was certain – Elinor's reign would soon end.

Snapping out of his thoughts, he rolled over and settled into sleep. Tomorrow would be a new day, and his search for Cecilia would begin again. He couldn't change the past, but he could shape the future.

With thoughts of his daughter lingering in his mind, George finally drifted off, ready to face whatever challenges lay ahead.

***

As the sun rose, George woke to the light streaming through the gap in the curtains. It took him a moment to remember where he was. His thoughts drifted back to the cottage – the sound of the twins charging around, their laughter echoing the halls.

But he wasn't at the cottage. He was at the inn.

Shaking off sleep, he got up. Today would be a busy day. He needed to check in with Timmy and start unravelling the local rumour mill. He was determined to uncover what Elinor had really been up to.

To do that, he had to talk to the right people. And to find them, he had to delve into the city's underground world. Fortunately, he had a connection – someone with an inside track. With that in mind, he headed downstairs to speak with Jeff.

It turned out Jeff wasn't a morning person. Gruff and half-asleep, he waved George off with a promise to be back at lunchtime. Left with time to kill, George ate breakfast before making his way to the stables to find Timmy.

Timmy, it seemed, had already set off for town, gathering food and replacement supplies for the stable. George could only hope he was also trying to track down Cecilia, but he would have to wait to find out.

Undeterred by the lack of immediate help, George set off on his own, weaving through the street. The city was already alive with movement. People bustled past, darting from stall to stall, slipping in and out of shops, hurriedly collecting what they needed. This was the part of city life George disliked – the ceaseless rush. Everyone was so focused on getting from one place to another that they never stopped to appreciate the world around them. There was so much to see – though 'beauty' might have been a generous word for this particular part of town. Still, beneath the grime and wear, there were hidden gems for those willing to look.

But few ever did.

They never noticed the small things. The quiet splendour of the world. Flowers thriving in cracks where they shouldn't. A little girl crouched behind an artist, using charcoal on scraps to mimic their painting. A worn-down statue of a long-forgotten hero standing tall despite time's erosion. A choir of students warming their voices in a quiet alley. Workers moving with practised ease, making their daily runs with fresh produce and wares to sell. A fishmonger tossing a fish to a persistent cat.

Life continued all around them, unnoticed. And George, as much as he disliked the city, couldn't help but take it all in.

Everything and everyone were interconnected – a vast domino effect. What one person did inevitably affected the next in ways they could never fully comprehend. The world would not function without its countless, unseen links. People lived their own lives, yet they were all part of something larger, a bigger picture unfolding around them.

It fascinated George.

So he watched for a while, observing as the people around him rushed about, too preoccupied with their daily routines to notice the true beauty of the world they inhabited.

"Can I interest ye in a bite? We got hot pies an' pastries fresh out of the oven, we do."

The voice snapped George from his thoughts. He was a sucker for anything freshly baked, and this stall had it all. To the left, stacks of golden bread and fruit pastries; to the right, steaming meat pies of every kind.

He really shouldn't. He had eaten breakfast not long ago. But how could he say no?

"Aye, I'll take a pie."

Without even asking what was in them, he handed over a coin to the well-rounded vendor. If the man's generous belly was anything to go by, the pies were bound to be good.

His first bite confirmed it – gammon, rich and creamy, just the way he liked it. He took his change, offered a nod of thanks, and struck up a conversation, subtly testing the waters for any useful news. The baker, pleased to have a willing ear, was quick to share the latest gossip.

"Aye, it's been a rough few years for everyone. Wi' taxes risin', folk like meself ain't makin' the coin we used to. The new lord an' lady… aye, they got expensive tastes. An' guess who foots the bill? Not them, that's for sure."

"Seems t' be the same everywhere," George replied, playing along. "I been feelin' the pinch meself. Came back here hopin' for more work… nothin' much happenin' for me in the villages."

The man leaned in, voice dropping.

"Between you an' me, I think somethin's happenin' they don't want us t' know about."

"Aye?"

"Aye. Strange things, they do be happenin' late at night. Secret meetin's an' the like. People disappearin'… poof!... into thin air. Aye, somethin' ain't right these days. Not right at all."

Before George could press for more, the man turned away to serve the next round of customers. Intrigued, George tucked the information away for later and continued his rounds. He spent the next few hours drifting between taverns, much like he had the day before. With the morning still fresh, he kept his inquiries mild – asking about meal times and the quality of the food – while sharpening his focus with his power to find any trace of his daughter.

Each stop yielded nothing. No hints. No leads. But he made sure to thank every worker he spoke to, leaving them with the promise to return for a good meal and a drink later. As the afternoon crept in, George made his way back to *The Tap House*, hoping to catch Jeff. He found him behind the bar, wiping down glassware and stacking it on the shelves.

"George, what can—" Jeff's words faltered as he took in George's face. His brow furrowed. "What happened t' ye?"

George sat down as Jeff poured a scotch and slid it across the counter. He knocked it back in one gulp, placing the glass down with a sharp clink. His posture was stiff, his eyes locked on Jeff.

"Got in the middle of a brawl without meanin' to."

Jeff chuckled, shaking his head as he poured another drink. "Ha! You sure about that?" He grinned. "Well, either way, what can I do for ye?"

George downed the second drink with a grimace before answering.

"I need information. Information on the queen."

He watched Jeff carefully, measuring his reaction. He had to be sure – sure that Jeff was still the man he thought he was. He was calm but prepared. Just in case he was wrong.

Jeff pulled George's empty glass towards him, poured himself a shot, and knocked it back. Then, meeting George's gaze dead-on, he set the glass down and said, "Then to the underground, we go."

Chapter 20

Fight Club

George was ready to go with his disguise in place, but at Jeff's insistence, he remained seated at the bar, waiting until evening. As night fell, they finally set out. He didn't know their exact destination, but he had a good idea. The underground clubs were well known to a select few and completely hidden from those who had no business knowing about them. Having never been inside one himself, he relied on Jeff to lead the way – to get him through the door and in front of the right people, all while ensuring nothing happened to him.

Following Jeff's lead, they crossed the river to the south side, arriving at what appeared to be an abandoned warehouse. It was a notorious spot, a favoured hangout for villains, vagabonds, and thieves. Fistfights, cutpurses, and slit throats were common occurrences here – even on an ordinary night. It's the perfect setting for an illegal fight club.

Inside, the dimly lit space was packed. A makeshift rope ring stood in the centre of the room, its only purpose to keep fighters and onlookers separate. The air was thick with the stench of sweat, blood, and cheap booze.

A crowd had already gathered, voices raised in shouts and cheers as a match got underway. Jeff weaved through the spectators towards the front, and George followed, squeezing past bodies and enduring a few jostles along the way. He finally came to a stop beside Jeff at the edge of the ring, just in time to watch the two men inside exchanging blows with their bare knuckles.

Both were bloodied, but one was clearly faring worse than the other. The blond-haired fighter moved with ease, bouncing lightly on his feet as he circled his dark-haired opponent. The latter struggled to keep up, his movements slower, more sluggish, his focus locked on his adversary to avoid being caught off guard.

But he wasn't quick enough.

A brutal right hook smashed into his jaw, snapping his head back as his body staggered with the impact. Before he could recover, another punch connected with his already bloodshot eye. Blondie grinned, confidence radiating from him as he danced back on his feet, fists raised and ready to strike again.

"Who's your money on?" George asked Jeff.

"Who do you think?" Jeff replied with a nod towards Blondie. "Sam here's one of the best we've got."

The crowd erupted in laughter as Sam's opponent staggered forward, swinging wildly. His punches were slow, weak – drained of power by sheer exhaustion.

"End it!" someone shouted.

"Put 'im outta his misery!"

"Look at 'im! He's gonna drop any second!"

The voices rose into a chaotic din of cheers and jeers, echoing through the warehouse. Sam continued to circle his opponent, his sharp gaze locked on the man before him, waiting for the perfect moment. The punters leaned in, eager to witness the inevitable.

Then, in a blur of movement, Sam struck.

A flurry of four rapid punches landed with sickening force, each one connecting with brutal precision. The final blow crashed into his opponent's face with a resounding crunch, sending blood spraying from his shattered nose.

The man reeled backwards, his vision swimming, his hands instinctively flying to his face as crimson poured down his chin. The crowd winced at the impact, a collective gasp rippling through them.

He dropped to his knees. His body crumpled, arms bracing against the unforgiving concrete, but it wasn't enough. His head hit the floor with a dull *thud*, blood and sweat pooling beneath him.

The crowd roared in approval.

Sam stood over his fallen opponent, chest heaving, bloodied fists raised, and the rush of victory pulsing through him. Around the ring, punters exchanged money, some gloating over their winnings, others cursing under their breath.

Jeff tilted his head towards George, signalling him to follow. Without a word, they slipped through the back of the crowd towards an open door leading into a faintly lit office. Inside, the air was thick with cigar smoke. A slim man with a jagged scar running down his face sat behind a rickety wooden desk, a cigar smouldering between his fingers as he counted stacks of coins.

He didn't even glance their way. Jeff dropped into a chair across from the desk, leaning back with an air of easy confidence. George followed suit, settling into the seat beside him. Silence hung in the room, broken only by the soft clink of coins and the occasional drag of the cigar. They waited.

After a few minutes, the man finally looked their way, his eyes settling on George with a wary expression.

"Jeff, what brings you here?" he asked, his voice rough and gravelly.

"Whisper, this is George. He requires your services," Jeff said, gesturing towards him.

"Aye, does he now?" Whisper exhaled a slow stream of smoke, leaning back in his chair with practised ease. "And what kind of offerings do ye think I have that a fella like you might need?" Though he appeared relaxed, the sharp glint in his eyes and the tautness in his shoulders suggested otherwise. He was ready for anything.

"I hear you deal in secrets… fitting, given your name. I need inside information on the queen and her latest… endeavours." George's hands rested firmly on the table, fingers slightly tensed, making it clear he meant business.

Whisper arched a brow, his fingers drumming lightly against the desk. "That's a bold thing to be askin'. What's a man like you want with such dangerous knowledge?" His gaze flicked between George and Jeff as if weighing whether this was some kind of setup.

"You can trust him, Whisper—on my life," Jeff assured him. "I wouldn't have brought him here if you couldn't."

Whisper studied George a moment longer before snapping his fingers. A boy, no older than ten, appeared soundlessly and poured them each a drink, placing the glasses before them. No one spoke or moved until the boy slipped out, shutting the door behind him.

George lifted his glass and took a slow, deliberate sip, never breaking eye contact. "I know what she does to those who cross her," he said, his voice steady but laced with quiet fury. "She's hunting my family. I need to know what she's planning, so I can stop her."

Whisper leaned forward, cigar smoke curling around his face. "You're playing a dangerous game, old man. The queen's got eyes and ears everywhere. But…" He tapped ash from his cigar, watching it fall. "There's been talk. The same rumours as always… that she's close to finding the shards and the young prince and princess."

"That's nothin' new," George muttered.

"No, but this is—word is, the rumours about her dwindling power are true. And certain lords are ready to help take 'er down if a… suitable replacement can be found." A slow, knowing smile spread across Whisper's face. "Say, a particular set of children?"

George's jaw tightened. His pulse thrummed in his ears. "You know who I am, don't you?"

"Know you?" Whisper's smirk deepened. His eyes gleamed with amusement. "But we just met."

George pushed himself to his feet, planting his palms on the table and leaning in. The room seemed to shrink, the air thick with smoke, tension, and unspoken threats.

"Which lords?" he asked, his voice low and demanding.

Whisper's smile widened, but his eyes remained cold and calculating. "Who do you think?" He took a slow drag from his cigar. "The sly old fox who's never liked her."

George narrowed his eyes, turning the information over in his mind.

Without another word, he reached into his coat, pulled out a small pouch of coins, and set it on the table. "Thanks for the information."

Whisper nodded, his expression difficult to interpret. "Be careful, George. The wolf has teeth sharper than you know," he called out, his laughter trailing after them as George and Jeff left the room.

George moved swiftly through the crowd, eager to leave. Whisper hadn't told him anything he didn't suspect, but at least now he knew who to approach as a potential ally. That was a step in the right direction.

Back at the inn, he nursed a drink, deep in thought. Speaking with Whisper had only solidified what he needed to do next. But before anything else, he had to see his daughter.

As if summoned by his thoughts, Timmy appeared at the bar, breathless and grinning. "Found her," the boy announced, sliding onto the stool next to him.

George tossed him a coin without hesitation. "Directions?"

Timmy rattled them off, and George wasted no time. He strode out of the inn with purpose, following the route through winding streets and shadowed alleys until he reached the establishment.

The moment he stepped inside, he felt her presence before he saw her.

Moving to the bar, he ordered a pint of ale and took a seat at the back of the room, his eyes scanning the space. The inn had a rustic charm – high timber beams, sturdy wooden tables, and a warm, welcoming atmosphere. The workers bustled about, tending to customers with serene smiles and practised efficiency. It suited Cecilia.

He sipped his drink slowly, outwardly composed, but inside, he was a tangle of nerves. She wouldn't recognise him – not with the years that had passed, not with how much had changed – but that didn't matter. He just needed to see her. To know she was safe.

Then, finally, he spotted her.

His heart stuttered.

He blinked, staring as if to make sure his mind wasn't playing tricks on him. She looked different. Her hair was darker, her clothes simpler, but there was no mistaking that familiar spark in her eyes. She moved with quiet confidence, balancing trays, clearing tables, and chatting easily with customers. She was well.

A wave of relief crashed over him, nearly knocking the breath from his lungs.

He stayed until his glass was empty, watching her from the shadows. When he finally stood to leave, he stopped by the owner to ask when they closed.

He needed to talk to her.

With a few hours to spare, he wandered next door and joined a group of workers in a game of poker. He played with half his attention, making idle conversation, passing the time until at last, the evening wound down. Bidding the men farewell, he stepped outside and waited, his eyes fixed on the door.

Soon, she would emerge. And then, after all these years, he would finally speak to her.

Seeing Cecilia slip into the alleyway beside the inn, George's heart pounded in his chest. He moved towards her, his steps heavy with anticipation. By the confusion on her face, it was clear she didn't recognise him. Not wanting to startle her, he let his disguise fall away.

Her eyes widened in shock, but the moment recognition set in, she threw herself into his arms, embracing him tightly. George held her just as fiercely, neither willing to let go. In that instant, years of separation melted away, replaced by the sheer relief and overwhelming joy of reunion.

Cecilia was the first to pull back, staring at him as if she couldn't believe he was real. "You're here," she whispered. "You're actually here."

"I am," George said, his voice thick with emotion. "Oh, it's wonderful to see you. I've missed you more than you could ever know."

"Same," she murmured before suddenly scanning their surroundings with growing anxiety. "But not as much as my babies. Where are they? Are they safe?"

George readjusted his disguise and squeezed her shoulders reassuringly. "They are fine. Let's walk."

They moved through the quiet streets, the silence between them heavy with unspoken words and emotions. When they reached her home, she led him inside and into the kitchen. As she busied herself making tea and checking the house, George sat at the table, taking in the small but cosy space. It suited her – warm, simple, filled with small signs of a life rebuilt.

Cecilia glanced at him as she placed a steaming cup in front of him, her brows furrowed. "You look tired, Father. Have you been unwell?"

He managed a solemn smile. "Nothing serious. Just weary from travelling. I'm not as young as I used to be."

She sat across from him, studying his face. "Well, where do we start?"

He met her gaze. "Why don't you begin? What happened that night?"

Cecilia took a steadying breath before launching into her story, recounting her escape, how she had stolen and hidden the shard in the castle, replacing it with a fake. George listened intently, committing every detail to memory. If the shard was hidden, it could be useful. A new plan would be necessary if it had fallen back into Elinor's hands.

Realising where his mind was wandering, he forced himself to focus. Right now, this moment was about her – about them. They had lost so much time, and he wasn't about to waste what little they had left.

They talked late into the night, their conversation stretching towards dawn. They needed this – both of them. For George, the joy of reunion was overshadowed by something deeper and more painful. Sitting across from his daughter, he saw the damage the years had caused and the wounds his choices had left behind.

And then, Cecilia broke.

Her anger, bottled up for far too long, came spilling out like a flood. Every thought, every ounce of anguish, frustration, and hurt poured from her lips in a torrent of raw emotion. She didn't hold back, and George didn't stop her. He let her say everything she needed to say, listening with a heavy heart as guilt settled deep in his bones.

He had believed he was protecting her. That keeping her and the twins apart had been the only way to ensure their safety. But now, hearing the pain in her voice, he saw the true cost of his decisions.

When she finally fell silent, drained from the outburst, he took a deep breath. "I tried to make the best of a bad situation," he said quietly. "But I see now that I failed you. And for that, I am truly sorry."

His words only seemed to deepen the ache in her eyes. He knew then that part of her might never forgive him – not fully. Some wounds ran too deep to be mended with apologies alone.

Recognising it was time to go, he stood and pulled her into one last embrace. She hesitated before returning the hug, her arms lingering around him for just a moment longer. Then, without another word, he left.

The walk back to the inn felt longer than before, and his mind was weighed down with regret. By the time he reached his room, exhaustion crashed over him like a wave. He barely made it to the bed before sleep claimed him.

***

After he left, Cecilia was a mess. She hadn't realised how much anger she had been harbouring against her father until she began to speak. Then, it all poured out – every bitter thought, every grievance she had buried deep inside. The words tumbled from her lips in a disordered jumble, her voice breaking as tears streamed down her face. She laid her heart bare, revealing the anguish she had carried for years.

Though the situation had begun and ended with Elinor, her father had been a part of it. He was the reason she had been kept from her children for eight long years.

In the beginning, she had lived in constant anticipation, clinging to the hope that a message would arrive, summoning her to them. But the days stretched into weeks, the weeks into months, and as time passed, her hope withered.

Many times, she had come close to leaving – packing her things, preparing to set out blindly in search of them, desperate to find some trace of their existence. But reason had always stopped her. She had convinced herself that her father had kept them away for their own safety, that he knew something she did not.

She had clung to the belief that when the danger had passed, he would come for her. That when Elinor no longer posed a threat, he would reunite her with her children. But he never came.

And now, after all these years, he had returned – empty-handed. The more he spoke, the more her fury built until, at last, she cracked.

"Enough! I do not wish to hear your excuses anymore, Father. Nothing you say will change the fact that you have kept me from my children all these years."

"Cecilia—"

"No!" she snapped, her voice rising. "You protected them, and for that, I am grateful. But then you sent them off into the world on their own! Why not bring them here? I could've helped them. Been there for them. Instead, they are wandering a land they do not know, with danger pursuing them, searching for power they do not understand!"

George opened his mouth to speak, but Cecilia cut him off, her eyes ablaze.

"Do you have any idea what it's like to be kept from your children? To wake up every day not knowing if they are safe or if they are happy? You made that decision without me, and now they are out there, vulnerable and alone!"

George's expression crumbled, the weight of her words striking him like a physical blow. "Cecilia, I thought I was doing what was best for them. I thought—"

"You thought wrong!" she shouted, her voice raw with emotion. "You had no right to make that choice for me. For them. They must think I abandoned them. What kind of mother does that make me?"

A heavy silence hung between them, broken only by Cecilia's ragged breathing.

George swallowed hard, his voice barely above a whisper. "Please, forgive me. I did what I believed was right. But if I had brought them here, then what?"

Cecilia's voice trembled as she answered. "Then I would have my babies back. I would see them. Hold them. After all this time… is it too much to ask?"

George's shoulders slumped, the fight draining from him. With quiet hesitation, he reached out, placing a gentle hand on her arm.

"No, and you will never understand how sorry I am," George said, his voice heavy with regret. "But it had to be done. You need to help them… but not in the way you think. Trust that they are capable. I taught them well. And they have an abundance of goodness in them, both from you and James. I know they're going to be okay."

Frustration rattled within Cecilia as she listened to her father's words. She was too angry to process anything rational, too exhausted to argue any further. A deep, bone-weary fatigue settled over her. With a steadying breath, she pushed her emotions down and rose to her feet, turning to face him.

"It's late. I think it's time to call it a night."

"If that is what you wish." He hesitated before continuing, his gaze softening. "I'll come by tomorrow evening. I know you're furious with me, and you have every right to be. But there is still much we need to discuss."

Cecilia gave him a curt nod and saw him out. The moment the door clicked shut behind her, her composure shattered. Her breath hitched, and the weight of everything she had held back came crashing down. She leaned against the wall, her forehead pressing against the cool surface as tears spilt freely down her cheeks. A sob wracked her body, raw and unrestrained.

She had only ever wanted to hold her children again. To be there for them. To see them grow. And he had stolen that from her – sent them off on some reckless adventure they weren't ready for, shouldn't have been a part of. This was not their fight.

For years, she had longed for them. Missed every milestone, every moment of their lives. *And for what? Because her father had decided they were better off kept hidden?*

A quiet presence behind her made her stiffen. Adrian had kept his distance during her reunion with her father, but now, he stepped forward, his hands resting gently on her shoulders. He turned her to face him, then pulled her into his arms, holding her close in an attempt to soothe her trembling frame.

"What can I do?" he asked softly.

Cecilia's fingers curled into his shirt as she lifted her gaze, her eyes burning with fury and grief. "Bring me my children," she demanded, her voice cracking under the weight of her emotions. She pulled away from him, her breath uneven. "He kept them from me, Adrian. All these years, he thought he was doing the right thing. How could he?"

Adrian cupped the back of her head, pressing a tender kiss to her hair as he stroked her back in a slow, calming motion. "We will find them, my love. I promise you."

But Cecilia's anger refused to fade. She clenched her fists, her entire body trembling. "He sent them into the world alone, without me. They could be in danger, and I'm not there to protect them. How could he make that decision?" Her voice broke again. "What must they think of me? The mother who abandoned them?"

Adrian tightened his embrace, his voice steady and reassuring. "I understand your anger. You have every right to feel this way. But listen to me—they would never believe you abandoned them. They know you love them."

"Do they?" she whispered. "They haven't seen or heard from me in years."

Adrian shook his head. "Your father made a terrible mistake. But I can't believe he would ever let those children think anything other than how much you cherish them. They know, Cecilia. Deep down, they know."

She drew in a shaky breath, struggling to rein in her emotions. "You're right. And we need to help them." Her expression hardened. "But I will never forgive him for what he did. Never."

Adrian met her gaze with quiet understanding. "Then we'll find them," he said, his voice resolute. "And we'll make sure they're safe. Together."

Chapter 21

A Decision to Make

The next day, Cecilia slept in. She didn't even remember going to bed. After the meeting with her father, she had been a mess. She knew dwelling on the previous night would only unravel her further, so she shoved the thoughts aside as she glanced at the time. A jolt of panic shot through her – she was late.

Frantic at the prospect of appearing negligent, she sprang out of bed. After hastily dressing, she bounded into the kitchen, where Adrian sat reading the newspaper.

"I'm late. My gosh, my boss won't be happy."

"Relax and sit down. I already stopped by and told them you were unwell. You need to take the day, Cecilia." He looked at her, concern etched across his face.

She hesitated at his words, but the worry for Aevah and Jacob came rushing back.

"We have to find them, Adrian."

"I know. But from what I overheard last night, it seems George has other plans for you. As difficult as this is, I think we need to wait one more day. Hear him out. Then we leave to search for the twins. No matter what."

He was right. Her father had hinted at an agenda that didn't include Aevah and Jacob. He had everything meticulously planned while she had been left in the dark for years.

She needed to understand his intentions and uncover where her children had gone. Regardless of his expectations, nothing and no one would stop her from reaching them now that they were wandering alone.

"You realise he's going to be very unhappy when he sees you here," she said.

"I know. And no matter what I say, he isn't going to trust me," Adrian replied.

"He'll have no choice if he wants my help. But he's going to be grumpy about it."

As Adrian moved around, her thoughts drifted back to Aevah and Jacob. The day slipped away as she contemplated their whereabouts and how to find them.

That evening, a sudden, forceful knock echoed through the door, making her jump. She rose quickly from her seat and moved to answer it, while Adrian leaned against the kitchen counter. A deep sense of foreboding settled over her. Trouble was inevitable the moment her father laid eyes on him. Taking a steadying breath, she braced herself as she reached the entrance, ready to welcome George inside.

"Father," she said, her tone sharper than intended.

He smiled at her and stepped inside, lingering at her side. Tension crackled between them – her resentment still raw from his decision to send her children away, compounded now by Adrian's presence in the other room.

Before stepping inside, Cecilia turned to her father. "Before we go in, I want to warn you… I have a guest. Someone who might surprise you. Just know he's on my side and has helped me more over the past few years than you could imagine."

She watched his expression shift, his brows furrowing before his eyes widened in realisation.

"Understood," he said after a pause. Then, with a gesture, he motioned for her to lead the way.

Her heart pounded as she stepped into the kitchen. Adrian straightened the moment she entered, his gaze locking onto the man following behind her. The air in the room seemed to shift, the weight of her father's presence pressing against her like a storm about to break.

She moved to stand beside Adrian, facing George. His expression darkened like an approaching thundercloud.

Adrian took a step forward, his stance steady, though a flicker of uncertainty flashed in his eyes.

"George," he said, his voice low but firm.

George's expression hardened, his jaw clenching tight. "Adrian," he replied, the name like a bitter taste on his tongue. He turned to Cecilia, his stare unwavering, demanding answers. "Is this true? Has he really been helping you?"

She nodded, her heartbeat hammering against her ribs. "Yes, Father. He's been invaluable."

Silence settled over them, thick and suffocating. The tension in the room was nearly tangible, an invisible force weighing them down. George's gaze flickered back to Adrian, a storm of emotions passing through his features – anger, betrayal, doubt, and something else. A glimmer of hope.

"I don't trust you," he said at last, his voice rough. "But for Cecilia's sake, I'll hear you out."

Adrian inclined his head, relief and determination mingling in his eyes. "Thank you. I know I have a lot to make up for."

"That you do, boy. Mark my words." George's tone dripped with disdain.

Sensing the tension rising, Cecilia stepped towards the table. "Please, sit down, Father. We have a lot to discuss."

She took a seat first, Adrian settling beside her. George remained standing, his body taut with resistance.

"Father," she urged, her voice softer this time.

Reluctantly, he lowered himself into a chair, though his gaze never wavered from Adrian.

"I suppose I should start with how we first met."

With her father's attention finally on her, she recounted everything – omitting only the details of her and Adrian's relationship. From the look on her father's face, that particular revelation could push him too far.

When she finished, George leaned back, his expression unreadable. Then, with a measured breath, he spoke of his plans, the path he expected her to follow.

"You want me to travel across the country, gathering a rebel army, while my children wander alone, searching for a power they don't understand?"

Cecilia's hands trembled as Adrian placed a reassuring hand on her arm, his fingers squeezing gently. She met his gaze, and with a small nod, he reminded her of their earlier discussion.

Closing her eyes, she inhaled deeply before turning back to her father.

"We all have a duty to perform. If we want to stop Elinor, we each have a role to play."

"And what is yours?" she asked.

George glanced briefly at Adrian before answering. "That is for me to know. As long as you do your part, and the twins theirs, everything will fall into place when the time is right."

Cecilia rolled her eyes but bit her tongue. She only needed to agree to his plan – then she would find her children on her terms.

Forcing a smile, she said, "Fine. We'll do it your way. Where exactly am I supposed to find these rebels?"

George reached into his jacket and pulled out an envelope, sliding it across the table. "Everything you need to know is in here."

She picked it up but didn't open it. A strained silence followed, broken only when George rose from his seat.

"I'd best be off." He exhaled, his expression softening. "I'm sorry, my dear. I truly am. But it's not my fault how this all turned out."

His gaze lingered on Adrian before he continued, "It will all work out, I promise. And you'll have the rest of your life with your children."

Cecilia stood, unsure of what to say, but walked him to the door.

"Goodbye, Cecilia. And good luck. Not that you'll need it. You're capable of anything you set your mind to. You have your mother to thank for that." His voice wavered slightly. "Know that I love you more than anything, and all I ever wanted was for you to be happy. I hope you are. That's all anyone can wish for."

Tears welled in Cecilia's eyes as she pulled him into a tight embrace. He held her for a moment before stepping back. With a final nod, he turned and walked down the path, disappearing around the bend – out of her life once more.

Adrian came up behind her and led her back inside. As evening settled around them, the house grew quiet.

The envelope remained on the table, unopened.

***

The next day was a whirlwind. Cecilia and Adrian spent the morning rushing around, packing the essentials they thought they would need and gathering any remaining supplies from town.

When Cecilia woke, a sense of peace settled over her. She was ready to leave with Adrian and find her children. She understood the importance of finding the rebels, so as they travelled, they would make their way to the locations her father had suggested.

Before leaving, she sent a raven to the temple, notifying the high priestess that she would be vacating the property. The next step was informing their respective places of work that they would not be returning. They used a sick relative in Darlington as their excuse, a simple yet effective story that would prevent further questions and allow them to leave without setting a firm return date.

After double-checking her bag, Cecilia stepped outside, where Adrian was readying their horses. Her mount was a sturdy and dependable Haflinger – the same one she had taken from the farm during her escape. Adrian's was a striking grey Friesian, a horse he had owned for fifteen years, having raised it from a young foal. Both were more than suited for the long journey ahead.

She passed Adrian her bag, then stood in place, mentally running through a checklist of supplies. Suddenly, her eyes widened.

"Oh, the soap!" she exclaimed.

Darting back inside, she grabbed a few last essentials for bathing. If they were going to be travelling and camping often, she still wanted to maintain some semblance of cleanliness. When she returned, Adrian had already divided their packs between the horses.

"Are you ready?" he asked.

"Yes, let's go."

With a final glance at the house, they led their horses through town, stopping at their workplaces to say their goodbyes. Both promised to send word once they returned.

Cecilia's friends, ever kind, sent her off with a bundle of food for the journey. Adrian's associates gifted him a finely crafted hunting knife, a parting gift from the blacksmith.

"Perfect for skinning game, should you need to," the man had said, pressing the weapon into Adrian's hand.

With nothing left to keep them in Adlington, Cecilia and Adrian set off on their journey to find her children. The open road stretched before them, and a surge of excitement swelled within her. Kicking her heels against her horse's sides, she urged him forward. The sturdy Haflinger responded instantly, surging into a gallop, his hooves pounding against the dirt track.

"Wait for me!" Adrian called, laughter in his voice as he spurred his own steed forward.

His grey Friesian gained on her quickly, closing the distance until he was riding alongside her, matching her pace stride for stride. Cecilia let out a carefree laugh, the wind whipping through her hair as exhilaration filled her chest. For the first time in years, she felt truly free.

After a few minutes, Adrian signalled for them to slow. He didn't want to tire out the horses so early in their journey. Reluctantly, Cecilia eased her mount into a trot, and they continued at a steady pace. They stopped briefly for lunch before pressing on until evening.

As nightfall approached, Adrian spotted a secluded clearing, deeming it a suitable campsite. While he set up their shelter, Cecilia unsaddled the horses and fed them their grains, taking care to ensure they were properly watered. Once the animals were settled, she took a lap around the area, scanning for dry materials to build a fire.

Gathering an armful of twigs and kindling, she returned to find Adrian already constructed a fire pit. He was arranging a circle of stones, preparing a safe place for the flames. She dropped the wood beside him and sank onto the ground, watching as he carefully arranged the kindling in a teepee shape.

Sensing her curiosity, Adrian looked up. "Have you ever built a fire out in the woods before?"

Cecilia hesitated before shaking her head. "No. Only in a fireplace, and even then, I always used my power in secret. I never figured out how to make the flame catch on its own." A faint blush rose to her cheeks at the admission.

Adrian chuckled but made sure to demonstrate each step clearly. "This will help the fire catch quickly," he explained, placing additional sticks around the base of the kindling. He struck flint against steel, sending sparks onto the dry tinder. After a few gentle breaths, the embers glowed, flickering to life before igniting into a small, steady flame.

As the flames grew stronger, Adian added larger pieces of wood, carefully ensuring the fire had enough air to breathe. The constant crackling filled the quiet night, casting a warm glow over their campsite. The flickering danced across their surroundings, bringing a sense of comfort and security.

Cecilia moved closer, stretching out her hands towards the heat. It wasn't particularly cold yet, but she savoured the warmth against her skin.

"Hungry?" Adrian asked, glancing over at her.

"Famished," she admitted.

Rising to his feet, Adrian began preparing their meal. Their supplies were light – travelling meant keeping things simple – but they had enough to satisfy them. Without pots or pans for cooking, he laid out a selection of roasted meats, cheese, fruit, nuts, and bread. After dividing the food onto plates, he handed one to Cecilia before settling beside her in front of the fire.

They ate in comfortable silence, savouring each bite. Adrian produced a flask of red wine he had stashed away, and they washed down their meal with slow, measured sips. The warmth of the fire, the richness of the wine, and the quiet intimacy of the moment made it feel almost romantic.

As she finished eating, Cecilia leaned into him, resting against his side. She said nothing, simply watching the flames flicker, content to exist in the peaceful stillness of the night.

***

In the early morning light, Cecilia dressed swiftly before finding an open spot in the camp, waiting for Adrian. She positioned herself in a defensive stance, dagger in hand, her eyes sharp with focus and determined.

A few paces away, Adrian watched her intently. Without warning, he lunged, testing her reflexes. She reacted instantly, leaning back just in time to evade his attack, then countered with a swift, calculated strike aimed at his side.

Adrian spun on his heels, attempting to circle behind her, but Cecilia was quick. She moved with fluid grace, following his motions and swiping at him again, forcing him to duck and retreat.

"Good," he said with a smile, squaring up in front of her. "Now, let's work on your footwork. Staying balanced and agile is crucial."

She nodded, adjusting her stance, watching him carefully, waiting for his next move. In a split second, Adrian closed the distance between them before she had time to react.

"Again."

He reset his stance and advanced once more, this time moving deliberately, demonstrating each step as he went.

“Keep your weight on the balls of your feet,” he instructed, circling her. “Always be ready to pivot. You never know what direction your attacker will strike from.”

He lunged again, and this time, Cecilia sidestepped smoothly, using her dagger to deflect his thrust.

“Good. Now counterattack,” he urged.

She swung her knife in a controlled arc, aiming for his shoulder. He blocked the strike with his forearm and gently pushed her back.

“Remember, use your opponent’s momentum against them.”

They continued their practice, Adrian guiding her through techniques to deflect blows and create openings for counterattacks. He demonstrated a quick disarm manoeuvre, grabbing her wrist and twisting just enough to force her to drop the dagger without causing harm.

“Damn it,” Cecilia muttered, frustrated.

Adrian chuckled. “Relax, it was just a demonstration. You’re doing better than you think.” He retrieved her dagger and handed it back to her. “Now, you try to disarm me now.”

He took his position, and Cecilia mimicked the move he had just shown her. She managed to twist his wrist partially, but not quite enough to make him drop his weapon.

“Excellent,” he praised, passing the blade to her. “Now, let’s do it again, but faster.”

Letting out a steady breath, Cecilia focused her mind and struck again. With each repetition, her confidence grew, her reactions became quicker, and her movements more precise. Adrian's smile widened as he saw her progress.

"You're improving with every session," he said, preparing for another round. But before he was fully ready, Cecilia surprised him. With a manoeuvre he hadn't expected, she slipped behind him, her dagger pressed lightly against his throat.

"Yes, I certainly am," she murmured, a teasing glint in her eyes. "You've proven to be a more competent teacher than I expected."

Keeping the dagger at his throat, she turned slightly to face him. Then, with a playful smirk, she leaned in and kissed him, her lips brushing against his before stepping away.

"Before we leave, I intend to wash up."

Without a backward glance, Cecilia strode towards the water, shedding her clothes before stepping into the ice-cold lake. The shock of the chill sent a shiver through her, but she welcomed it, wading in deeper until she reached the middle. With the soap in hand, she began to cleanse herself, letting the cool water lap against her skin.

She didn't need to turn around to know Adrian would soon follow. Sure enough, moments later, a splash echoed behind her as he entered the lake.

Cecilia continued to glide through the refreshing water until she felt strong arms wrap around her from behind, pulling her close. Adrian's fingers traced over her skin, the water allowing them to slide effortlessly along her breasts. His lips brushed gently against hers, their kiss deepening into something more urgent, more consuming. His hand cradled the back of her head as he pulled her even closer.

A soft sigh escaped her as he trailed his fingertips down her spine, sending shivers of anticipation through her. Instinctively, her legs wrapped around his waist, and he held her effortlessly, carrying her through the shallows as he pressed warm, lingering kisses along her neck, a heat built within her, coiling tighter with each touch.

Reaching the grassy bank, Adrian laid her down, the cool blades of grass tickling her bare skin. His hands roamed her body, tracing the curves that had captivated him for so long. Her breath hitched as she arched into his touch, a deep ache stirring within her.

"Please," she murmured, her voice laced with need as he momentarily pulled away.

With a knowing smile, he parted her thighs, his lips trailing lower, tasting her, teasing her. A soft cry left her lips as waves of pleasure crashed over her, her body trembling beneath his skilled touch.

"Take me now," she whispered, teetering on the edge of bliss.

Adrian grinned with his eyes dark with desire. "As you wish."

With a low groan, he entered her, his movements slow at first, savouring every sensation. With each thrust, his pace quickened, driving deeper, until Cecilia clung to him, lost in the intoxicating rhythm. The tension coiled tighter and tighter until, with a desperate cry of his name, pleasure consumed her.

Her release sent him over the edge, his body tensing before he gave in, claiming her with one final, shuddering surge. Their lips met in a heated, breathless kiss as they rode the last waves of passion together. As the intensity ebbed, they remained tangled in each other's embrace, bodies slick and chests rising and falling in unison. Adrian rested his forehead against hers, and his arms braced on either side of her.

After a long moment, he exhaled a laugh, his voice thick with amusement. "I think we might need to wash up again."

Cecilia chuckled as he pulled her close, wrapping her in his warmth.

Chapter 22

On the Road

All packed up and back on the road, Cecilia rode beside Adrian while she could. Their next stop was a day's ride away, and she was eager for a chance to sleep in a proper bed. According to her father, the location housed a secret faction of rebels who would aid them. The town also lay in the right direction towards her children, reassuring her that she was not straying from the path to finding them.

Before they barged in asking questions, Adrian insisted they stick to the cover story they had prepared, giving them time to determine whom they needed to approach in the town. If they could find the rebels, it would serve them well when the time came to move against Elinor. Cecilia had no desire to act rashly, though – not until she saw her children and knew they were safe.

As they reached the outskirts of Haverford, Adrian led them to an inn called *The Rusty Pin*. Cecilia settled in for the night while he went out to gather information and confirm whether a rebel faction truly existed, as her father had claimed. By morning, he had already left again and returned around midday, his expression alight with excitement.

"I'm certain I have found them," he said.

"Excellent. Then we should meet them." Determination rang in her voice.

They wove through the town's narrow, winding streets, the buildings growing increasingly dilapidated as they went. Finally, they arrived before an old, abandoned house, its windows boarded up and ivy creeping along its crumbling walls.

"This is it," Adrian whispered, glancing around to ensure they weren't being watched.

Cecilia nodded, and they approached the door. Adrian rapped a specific pattern against the wood – a code he had learned from his inquiries. A tense moment passed before the door creaked open, revealing a vaguely lit interior.

"Who are you?" a voice demanded from the shadows.

"We seek the rebels," Adrian stated firmly. "We need your help to stop the usurper."

There was a pause before the figure stepped forward, revealing a stern-faced woman. "Prove it."

Adrian reached into his cloak and withdrew a small, intricately carved token. "A member of your group gave this to us," he explained.

The woman took the token, scrutinising it before biting down on it with her teeth. Satisfied, she gave a curt nod. "Follow me."

She led them deeper into the house, and Cecilia's heart pounded, each beat echoing in her ears. Unease coiled in her stomach as she scanned every shadow and movement, hoping these people could be trusted.

They entered a large room where several rebels had gathered. The tension in the air was palpable, and all eyes turned to Cecilia and Adrian as they stepped inside.

The woman gestured towards them and spoke. "These two claim to seek our help against Queen Elinor."

Adrian stepped forward, his posture both confident and respectful. "My name is Adrian. I was once a knight in the Queen's service."

A murmur of recognition rippled through the room, laced with anger. A burly man with an unkempt beard pushed forward, his expression dark with contempt.

"We know who you are," he spat. "You betrayed the old king and the rightful queen."

Adrian's jaw tightened, his stance bracing as he prepared to respond. But before he could utter a word, the man lunged, his fist connecting with a sickening *thud* against Adrian's face. The force of the blow sent him staggering backwards, blood spilling from his now-broken nose as his vision blurred.

Cecilia gasped, her pulse hammering as she stepped between them, her voice steady and commanding. "Enough! We are here for the same purpose. Fighting among ourselves only serves our enemies."

The woman from earlier narrowed her eyes. "And who are you to tell us what to do?"

Cecilia lifted her chin. "I am Cecilia... your true queen. Adrian's past actions, however regrettable, have been forgiven. Since then, he has dedicated himself to our cause. We need your help to reclaim the throne and bring justice to our land."

A heavy silence settled over the room as the rebels exchanged uncertain glances. The burly man, still seething, turned his glare from Adrian to Cecilia. "And you expect us to trust him? After everything he's done?"

She met his gaze without flinching. "Yes. Because I believe in him, he has proven his loyalty to me time and again. We can't afford to let past grievances divide us when we face a common enemy."

The man hesitated, then gave a slow nod. "If you vouch for him, we'll accept him. But understand this, Adrian—one misstep, and you'll answer to us."

Adrian pinched his nose to stem the bleeding and gave a slight nod. "Understood. Thank you."

The tension in the room eased slightly as the rebels exchanged glances. Then, one by one, they knelt before Cecilia, bowing their heads.

"We have waited a long time for this, Your Majesty. We are at your service," the burly man declared, and the rest of the group erupted into cheers.

As they rose, Cecilia stepped forward. "What's your name?"

"I am Thorne," he replied, his voice firm.

"Nice to meet you, Thorne," she said, offering a modest smile. "Is there somewhere we can sit and discuss our plans?"

Thorne gestured towards a large, worn table, and they gathered around it. Cecilia and Adrian recounted their journey, sharing the information they had received from her father and her intentions to place one of her children on the throne. In turn, Thorne and the other rebels detailed their own struggles, the alliances they had forged, and the growing resistance against Elinor.

They spoke of the queen's movements, her relentless search for the shards, and their covert efforts to rescue as many children as possible from her grasp. As the conversation flowed, a sense of trust began to take root – especially towards Adrian. The rebels, once wary, grew more receptive, eventually revealing the locations of other resistance groups willing to join the cause.

They assured Cecilia that word would be spread and that when the time came, their allies would be ready. Together, they would raise an army and bring down the usurper. Regarding her children, the rebels shared what little intelligence they had, vowing to protect them at all costs and to report any sighting immediately.

With rebel factions spread across the kingdom, they had more support than they had realised. The knowledge filled Cecilia's heart with hope. Encouraged, they turned their focus back to strategy, drafting plans for Elinor's downfall.

Hours later, Cecilia and Adrian stepped out of the rebel stronghold, and their resolve strengthened. With a list of names and locations in hand, their next task was clear – travel across the country, unite the resistance under one banner, and, when the moment was right, lead the attack to reclaim the throne.

Somewhere in the midst of it all, Cecilia held on to the hope that she would find her children, that she would see with her own eyes that they were safe. She believed in them and knew they could endure this, but just because they could didn't mean she wanted them to. This was never the life they were meant to have, but it was the path they walked now. For better or worse, their story had taken shape, and this chapter had to reach its end. She could only pray to the divine spirit that they stood on the right side of history.

As they neared the inn, they turned down a narrow alley, walking in step with one another. The night was calm – until a piercing scream shattered the silence. They jolted apart, their hearts pounding in unison.

A dark figure emerged from the shadows, and their eyes gleamed with malice.

Time seemed to slow as adrenaline surged through their veins.

Before they could react, two more masked figures stepped into view, blocking their path. Cecilia's pulse quickened. Instinctively, her fingers curled around the hilt of her dagger. Beside her, Adrian shifted, stepping in front of her, his stance protective and ready for a fight.

The first attacker lunged at Adrian, a knife flashing in the dim light, but Adrian sidestepped swiftly, driving a solid punch into the assailant's gut. The second attacker swung a club at Cecilia, but she ducked just in time, slashing at his arm with her dagger. Blood spattered. The man howled in pain and stumbled back a step.

The third attacker, larger and more menacing, charged at Adrian. The two grappled, exchanging blows, strength and skill locked in a deadly dance. Cecilia struggled against the second attacker, his relentless strikes forcing her back. His eyes gleamed with a murderous intent.

Adrian slammed the third attacker against the wall, but not before a knife sliced into his side. He grunted in pain, his hand instinctively clutching the wound, but he didn't falter. Gritting his teeth, he tackled the first attacker to the ground, disarming him and knocking him unconscious.

Cecilia, fuelled by a mix of fear and rage, fought with everything she had. Drawing on her power, as feeble as it was, she sent an electric shock coursing through the second attacker. He convulsed, his grip loosening just enough for her to twist free. Seizing the moment, she drove a solid kick into his face. He staggered, dazed. Without hesitation, she plunged her dagger into his shoulder, forcing him to drop his weapon.

The third attacker hesitated, taking in the sight of his fallen comrades.

That was all Adrian needed. Despite his injury, he straightened, his eyes dark with fury. In a swift, ruthless motion, he slit the man's throat.

The attacker's eyes widened in shock. A strangled gurgle escaped his lips as his hands clutched at the deep wound, blood pouring between his fingers. He staggered, strength draining from him before collapsing into a lifeless heap.

Adrian, breathing heavily, wiped the blood from his blade and turned to Cecilia.

"It's time to go," he said, his voice strained but firm. "There could be more of them."

She gave a slight nod, her heart still racing from the encounter, as she rushed to Adrian's side. Her hands trembled as she inspected his wound, her breath quick and unsteady. "We need to get you seen to. This gash is bleeding too much," she said, urgency thick in her voice.

He nodded, wincing as he shifted. "Let's go."

Supporting him as best she could, Cecilia guided him through the darkened streets, her mind clouded with worry. With each step, his movements grew heavier, his strength fading. He stumbled, and she tightened her grip, half-dragging, half-carrying him forward.

By the time they reached the inn, he was barely conscious. Cecilia called for help, her desperate voice echoing through the quiet building.

The innkeeper and a few patrons rushed to their aid, easing Adrian onto a bed and working quickly to tend to his wound. His shirt was soaked in blood, the deep red stark against his pale skin. His breathing was shallow, and his body was weak from the blood loss. The men did what they could to stem the bleeding, but the severity of the injury was clear.

Cecilia's heart pounded as she watched, helplessness tightening around her chest.

"Stay with me, Adrian," she whispered, her voice breaking. She grasped his hand tightly, willing him to remain conscious. His eyes fluttered, and for a brief moment, he met her gaze, a weak smile ghosting his lips before he slipped back into unconsciousness.

The innkeeper, a grizzled man with kind eyes, looked up at her. "He needs a healer and fast. This wound is deep."

Cecilia swallowed hard and nodded. "Where can I find one?"

"There's a woman just a few streets away," the innkeeper said.

"I'll take you," a young man offered, his expression determined.

"Thank you."

Before leaving, she turned back, her heart aching at the sight of Adrian lying motionless. "Hold on. I'll be back soon."

Then, she followed the man into the night, sprinting through the narrow, winding streets. The cool air bit at her skin, her breath coming in ragged gasps. Their hurried footsteps echoed against the cobblestones; each beat a reminder of the urgency pressing down on her. They weaved through the alleys and side streets, the towering buildings around them standing like silent sentinels, watching as she raced against time.

At last, they arrived at a small, unassuming house. The young man knocked, and after a moment, the door creaked open to reveal an elderly woman with kind eyes.

"Please, we need your help," Cecilia pleaded, desperation stiffening her voice. "My friend is badly injured."

The healer took one look at her distressed expression and nodded, already grabbing her bag of supplies. "Lead the way."

They hurried back through the darkened streets, Cecilia's thoughts racing between Adrian and the attack. *Who were those men, and who had sent them?* She shoved the questions aside – there would be time for answers later.

When they reached the inn, the healer moved swiftly to Adrian's side. With experienced hands, she assessed his wound, her gaze sharp and focused.

"Knife?" she asked, her tone calm and professional.

"Yes," Cecilia confirmed, her voice unsteady with worry.

The healer nodded and carefully removed Adrian's blood-soaked shirt. She examined the wound, her brow furrowing in concentration. "It's deep but not fatal. He's lost a lot of blood. I need to clean and stitch this quickly before the bleeding weakens him further."

Cecilia swallowed hard, watching as the healer worked with composed hands, cleaning the wound with practised efficiency. Adrian groaned, his eyes flickering open for a brief moment before slipping back into unconsciousness. Cecilia squeezed his hand, silently willing him to stay strong.

The healer stitched the wound with precise, deliberate movements. "He'll need rest and plenty of fluids," she instructed, her voice gentle but firm. "Keep the wound clean and watch for any signs of infection."

Cecilia nodded, her heart still pounding. "Thank you," she whispered, her words laden with gratitude.

The healer packed up her supplies and offered a reassuring smile. "He'll be alright. Just make sure he doesn't push himself too soon."

As the woman left, Cecilia remained by Adrian's side, her thoughts swirling. *Who had sent the attackers? Was it the queen's doing, or had the rebels betrayed them?* The uncertainty gnawed at her, but for now, she focused on the man who had risked everything to protect her.

By morning, Adrian was awake, though visibly weak. Despite Cecilia's protest, he insisted on continuing their journey.

"We can't afford to lose any more time," he said, determination edging his voice.

"Adrian," she began, her voice firm yet laced with concern. Only yesterday, he had been on death's door. "You need rest. At least give yourself the day. As much as I want to keep moving too, you almost died last night, and I won't risk losing you."

He struggled out of bed, his movements slow and unsteady. With Cecilia's reluctant help, he staggered across the room, slipping into a clean shirt and pants. She muttered under her breath about his stubbornness, but as always, he refused to listen.

"We are going," he insisted, undeterred by her protest.

Cecilia knew arguing was pointless, but as he could barely stand upright, his determination didn't carry him far. He made it only as far as the common room before collapsing into a well-worn armchair, chest rising and falling with laboured breaths. She crossed her arms and watched him, shaking her head.

"Maybe a few hours of rest wouldn't hurt," he admitted grudgingly.

"Glad to see you agree. Let me get you some food."

After ordering breakfast for them both, Cecilia spent the morning watching Adrian stubbornly convince himself he was fine – only to move at a snail's pace and nod off every time he sat down. Eventually, exhaustion won out, and she managed to coax him back into bed, where he fell into a deep, uninterrupted sleep. He didn't stir until the early hours before dawn.

Cecilia felt him shift beside her and sat up abruptly, pulled from her own broken rest. He rose carefully, moving about the room as though testing his own strength.

"How are you feeling?" she asked.

"Better than yesterday. Thank you for convincing me to rest. I needed it."

"You did. How about today?"

His gaze flicked to her hand as it brushed over his wound. "I'm ready. As long as we ride slowly and make sure we have enough supplies, I'll be fine. We can't afford to lose any more time."

Cecilia nodded. "Then let's go."

She got up and readied herself before helping Adrian. He was right – they couldn't afford to waste another day if they could help it.

They had to find the twins and uncover who was behind the attack. With his wound carefully bandaged, they set out, keeping to a slow pace to avoid tearing his stitches.

Their journey took them through villages and towns, and each stop was another thread in the growing web of mystery. They questioned locals, followed leads, and pieced together fragments of information. The attack had left them wary, but it had also strengthened their resolve. They were closer than ever to the truth – and they would not stop until they found it.

One evening, as Cecilia and Adrian sat by the fire in a small inn, a hooded figure approached them.

"I hear you're looking for information," the person said, their voice low and cautious.

Cecilia and Adrian exchanged a wary glance. Adrian's hand instinctively moved to his side, where his weapon remained hidden. "Who are you?" he asked.

The figure pulled back their hood, revealing an older woman with sharp eyes and a determined expression. "My name is Elara. I have information about the twins… and the attack on you."

Cecilia's heart skipped a beat. "What do you know?"

Elara leaned in, her voice barely above a whisper. "The queen has spies everywhere. The assault on you was meant to scare you off, but there's more. Your children are closer than you think, and not everyone within the rebel factions can be trusted."

Adrian's eyes narrowed. "Why should we believe you?"

Elara met his gaze steadily. "Because I want the usurper gone as much as you do. And because I know where the twins are."

Hope surged through Cecilia. "Where are they?"

Elara cast a quick glance around, making sure no one else was listening. "They're safe for now, travelling to a hidden camp no one can find, where the land is sandy, and the air is thick with heat. But you'll need to move quickly. The queen's forces are closing in. If you don't act soon, we're all doomed."

Cecilia's breath caught in her throat. "They are safe? Have you seen them?"

Elara's lips curved into a knowing smile. "I see all."

Before Cecilia could press her further, the woman slipped back into the crowd.

"Wait!" Cecilia called, pushing through the throng after her, but Elara moved too swiftly.

Adrian was already ahead, searching frantically. He bolted outside, Cecilia close behind, but there was no trace of the woman. It was as if she had vanished into thin air.

"Who was that?" Adrian demanded, his voice edged with urgency.

Cecilia shook her head, her eyes scanning the crowd. "I don't know, but she knew about us and the twins. We need to find her."

Adrian's jaw tightened. "We can't let this lead slip away. Let's split up and search the area. She couldn't have gone far."

Cecilia nodded, and they quickly moved in opposite directions, weaving through the streets in search of the mysterious woman. They questioned the locals, scoured alleys, and retraced their steps, but after an hour, there was no sign of her.

Back at the inn, Cecilia sat by the fire, waiting for Adrian to return. Elara's words replayed in her mind. She whispered a silent prayer to the divine spirit, clinging to the hope that her children were safe.

Just as she was about to retire for the night, Adrian stumbled into their room, looking crestfallen.

"She's nowhere to be found. I'm sorry."

Cecilia sighed, her shoulders slumping. "It's okay. If she was telling the truth, then at least I have some comfort knowing Aevah and Jacob are safe."

Adrian's expression softened. "We'll find them, Cecilia. We won't stop until we do."

She managed a small smile, her heart heavy yet resolute. "I know. Thank you, Adrian."

That night, they settled in for a few hours of much-needed rest. Though the danger loomed, and uncertainty clouded their path, Cecilia's determination had been renewed. They were closer than ever to finding the twins – and to uncover the truth behind the attack. No matter what obstacles lay ahead, they would face them together.

One step at a time, they would bring justice to their land and put an end to Elinor's reign once and for all.

Chapter 23

The Plan

Saying goodbye to Cecilia was bittersweet, especially when he believed he would never see her again. He didn't tell her, but he knew there was no walking away from what he had planned. Their paths had diverged. Hers led to the rebels, driven by the hope of securing a better future for her children and the world they would inherit.

His, however, led to the end of Elinor's reign of terror – no matter the cost, even if it meant sacrificing his own life. The challenge ahead was daunting. Elinor's power was formidable, and he understood the near impossibility of what he intended to do. Yet, he remained resolute. Escaping the castle alive was unlikely unless he found allies, and that was where his conversation with Whisper became crucial. He had begun to consider the possibility of persuading Lord Stone, a nobleman, to stand with him against Elinor.

That meant a stop in Geraldton.

With the first light of a new day, he gathered his belongings and left his room. After bidding farewell to Jeff, he made his way to the stables to ready his horse.

"Where you off to, then?" Timmy asked, watching as George double-checked the saddle straps before swinging himself onto the horse.

"Geraldton, laddie. I have business to attend to."

"Wot if I was to come wiv ya? Nofin keepin' me 'ere. A could 'elp ya, I could."

"Sadly, where I'm heading is no place for a young lad like you. More trouble than it's worth, believe me. I wouldn't be going unless I had to," George warned.

"Ah, I ain't scared of nuffin, me. Any bova, an' I'd 'elp ya sort 'em out."

George chuckled. "Oh, I'm sure you would." He tossed Timmy another coin. "Take care, laddie. It was a pleasure meeting you. Until we meet again."

With a nod, he gave his horse a gentle nudge, urging him forward. As he rode away, he settled into the journey alone. For the most part, the road was uneventful – a small mercy. The worst he faced was a few wet stretches of travel. Yet, an unease lingered at the back of his mind. He had the distinct feeling he was being followed.

After a few days on the road, George made camp as usual at his next stop. As he sat by the fire, he called out to the traveller lurking in the dark.

"You planning to sneak behind me all the way, or are you gonna come join me?"

A figure stepped from the shadows of the trees – little Timmy.

"Ow'd choo know I was there?" he asked as he approached the flames, dropping his backpack to the ground and settling beside George, rubbing his hands together against the chill in the air.

"I've known since I left the city, laddie. Been waiting to see if you'd show yourself."

"Dammit. I thought choo'd just send me back if you saw me."

"I would if I thought you'd listen," George said with a chuckle, handing him one of the slightly stale sandwiches he had left. "Bit tough now, but it's food."

Timmy took it without hesitation, devouring it in a few swift bites.

"Hungry?"

"Aye, didn't bring much in the way o' grub," he admitted with a shrug, eagerly accepting the biscuits George passed him next.

"Well, with two of us now, we'll need to stop at a village for more. We're still a good stretch from Geraldton, and I didn't pack enough for us both."

He clapped Timmy on the shoulder, watching the fire dance between them. There was no way he would let the boy follow him all the way to Carraton, but for now – he welcomed the company.

With Timmy by his side, the journey became far more enjoyable. The boy was a mischievous little swine but quick-witted and full of life. More importantly, his street smarts gave him an edge – he had a knack for slipping in and out of trouble, a skill that might prove useful once they reached Geraldton. Lord Stone's associates were much like the man himself: sharp-tongued, cunning, and unpredictable. To deal with them, George would need every advantage he could get.

As they travelled, George found himself growing fond of the boy. Timmy had a way of earning trust, and against his better judgement, George decided to let him in on the truth. As they neared the city, he shared his plans – and, by necessity, his true identity.

"I knew there was sumfin' off about you!" Timmy declared. "Don't choo worry, your secret's safe wiv me."

"Good, because before this is all over, I know I'll need your help," George said.

"Anyfin' you need, Gramps."

"Gramps?"

"Tha's what I'm callin' you now. Gramps," Timmy said confidently.

George just chuckled. "All right then."

As they rode into Geraldton, George continued filling Timmy in on the details. By the time they reached Lord Stone's private manor, the boy knew nearly everything.

The manor was an imposing sight – a grand stone building with miniature turrets that gave it the appearance of a small castle. A massive iron gate enclosed the property, and two sentries stood watch at the entrance.

George approached the pair of guards at the gate, informing them that an old friend had arrived – one who would be most surprised to see him. As he lingered, he let his disguise drop, knowing that Lord Stone needed to recognise him.

After a few minutes of waiting, Lord Stone finally appeared.

"Well, I never…" he muttered, his eyes widening in momentary shock before he quickly masked his reaction with an indifferent expression. "Allow him and the boy to enter," he instructed, stepping aside as the gates swung open.

George and Timmy rode in, dismounting at the base of a winding cobbled path. A stable hand appeared at once, leading their horses away, while Lord Stone guided them towards the gardens outside.

"Forgive me for not inviting you inside my manor, but I expect this visit to be brief. Can't be too careful these days."

"Whatever makes you feel comfortable," George replied.

Lord Stone led them through the pristine grounds, where lush green grass stretched beneath their feet, and a grand fountain stood at the centre, crowned by a statue of the goddess. The entire area exuded perfection, from the meticulously trimmed lawns to the symmetrically arranged flower beds. Not a single leaf was out of place.

He finally stopped at a secluded garden behind the manor, nestled between the trees – just far enough to avoid prying eyes and ears. Timmy stayed near the fountain, waiting for George's return. This conversation needed to be plain and direct, and George knew Lord Stone wouldn't be forthcoming with a child listening in.

"Well, George, why are you here?" Lord Stone asked. "It must be important for you to emerge after all these years in hiding?"

"It is," George said without hesitation. "I may have stayed concealed, but I've heard everything. I know about the animosity between you and Elinor."

"Animosity?" Lord Stone raised an eyebrow. "You're mistaken. We are on excellent terms."

George scoffed. "Ha! Who are you trying to fool? I came here because I thought you might help me. Seems I was wrong."

He turned to leave, but Lord Stone's voice stopped him.

"Wait. Let's say—hypothetically—a certain queen, and I didn't have the most cordial relationship. What kind of assistance are you looking for?"

"Men," George said. "And lots of them."

Lord Stone studied him for a moment before asking, "What exactly are you planning?"

"Give me your word for aid and I will tell you."

Lord Stone remained silent for a long moment, deep in thought. George waited, watching him carefully, hoping he would agree to help.

"I can't," Lord Stone finally said, shaking head.

George's eyes narrowed. "But you want to say yes. What has she got on you?"

"Not what… who," Lord Stone corrected. "She has my daughter. If I make a single move against her, that's it for Rosalind."

George's expression hardened. "When did she take her?"

"Right after I left for the tourney, it would seem. She was safe at home until then. At the very end of the celebration, Elinor brought her out—made it clear what would happen if I ever crossed her again. If I give you my men, I'm signing Rosalind's death warrant."

George racked his brain, trying to find a way to help. He understood all too well what it meant to protect loved ones – he had hidden his grandchildren away for the very same reason. And knowing what Elinor was capable of, he had no doubt that her threat was real.

"I'll bring your daughter home," he vowed. "No soul deserves to be a prisoner to that madwoman."

"If you can get her here safely, I promise you this—your family will sit on the throne once more, where they belong. Mark my words."

George nodded and turned to leave, but Lord Stone spoke again.

"One more thing. I still have spies within the castle walls. They'll know you're coming."

Acknowledging the warning with a nod, George walked away, returning to the fountain where Timmy sat by the water, splashing his hands in an attempt to catch the fish darting beneath the surface. George watched him for a moment – so carefree, so unaware of the true dangers ahead. Just a kid.

He had already made up his mind. On the way to the capital, he would stop by Springhelm Farm, where trusted friends in the rebel alliance could take Timmy in. After speaking with Lord Stone, he was more certain than ever – the boy wouldn't be going anywhere near that castle.

"Ready to leave, laddie?" George called.

"Aye, Gramps. Ow'd it go? Choo get that 'elp you wanted?" Timmy asked, bouncing alongside him as they made their way to the stables, where the horses waited.

"Kind of. Help will be there when I need it."

"Good. So, where to now?"

"To a little place called Springhelm Farm."

***

With the end of summer setting in, the nights had grown colder, and the days were often wet. George was relieved when he finally spotted the small river crossing leading to Springhelm Farm. He guided his horse towards the wooden bridge, walking it across carefully, with Timmy close behind.

Beyond the bridge, fields stretched out before them, surrounding a sturdy stone house at the centre. Smoke billowed from its chimney, promising warmth inside.

As the rain began to fall, George and Timmy quickened their pace, striding briskly up the paved path to the front door. George rapped his knuckles against the wooden frame and waited.

A moment later, the door swung open to reveal a middle-aged man with grey-flecked hair and a sturdy build. His eyes widened in surprise.

"Walter, a long time has passed, old friend," George greeted.

"George! By gosh, it's been years." Walter stepped forward, pulling him into a firm hug. He then turned his attention to Timmy. "And who's this young fella?"

"Timmy. He's been travelling with me," George replied.

"Nice t' meet ya, sir," Timmy said with a respectful nod.

"Likewise," Walter said before glancing at the darkening sky. "Go on inside, lad… warm yourself by the fire. Me and George will see to the horses before the rain sets in. Looks like a storm's brewing."

Timmy hurried inside while the two men led the horses towards the stables just to the right of the house. No sooner had they settled the mares than the skies opened up, and rain poured down in sheets.

"Well, best run for it," Walter said.

"Aye," George agreed. Bracing himself, he followed Walter in a sprint back to the house.

Once inside, George made use of his abilities, drying himself off with a flick of his hand. Walter chuckled. "I'd forgotten you could do that. Help a fella out?"

With another wave of his hand, George dried Walter's clothes as well – though they remained slightly wrinkled.

As they stepped into the living room, they found Timmy sitting comfortably by the fire, a cup of milk and honey warming his hands. Walter's wife, Matilda, sat in her rocking chair, knitting what looked to be the start of a blanket.

Matilda was a woman of both kindness and strength – a true farmer's wife, hardworking and resilient. She ensured that everyone under her roof was fed and cared for. Upon seeing them enter, she set aside her knitting and rose to greet them.

"George, dear, it's wonderful to see you again! And little Timmy here is quite the charmer," Matilda said warmly.

"And you, Matilda, you're looking well," George replied as they embraced.

"Oh, that's one way to describe him," he added with a chuckle, glancing at Timmy. Settling into an armchair, he took a moment to relax before catching them up on everything that had happened – his time in hiding, his plans for the castle, and the dangers that lay ahead.

Walter and Matilda listened intently, amazed but not entirely surprised that George had managed to keep both himself and the twins hidden all these years. They had done their part as well, outwardly maintaining their allegiance to the queen while secretly keeping the hope of rebellion alive. Across the country, small rebel fractions had quietly formed, waiting for the day the true heirs would return. With the twins now nearing adulthood, the movement had grown stronger, their long-awaited return feeling more imminent than ever.

Being close to Carraton, Walter had played a key role in gathering intelligence on the queen's activities, tracking those who were taken to the castle. The fate of these captives was grim – none of them were ever seen again. Determined to put an end to the disappearances, the rebels had made it their mission to intercept prisoner transports and rescue as many as possible, smuggling them to safety where Elinor's reach could not find them.

They spoke late into the night, discussing strategies and the road ahead. Meanwhile, Timmy had curled up by the fire, sleeping soundly.

"What of the boy, George?" Walter asked as the flames crackled softly. "He can't go with you."

"I know," George admitted. "I had hoped he could stay here with you. He's a good lad, and I don't believe he's ever had a real home."

Walter exchanged a glance with Matilda before she nodded with a warm smile. "We would be honoured to take him in."

"Then it's settled," George said with relief. "Timmy will stay here."

Standing, he carefully lifted the sleeping boy into his arms and followed Matilda to the spare room. He tucked Timmy in and then settled onto the other bed, stretching out. He needed a solid night's sleep – his journey was far from over.

By dawn, George rose and prepared for his departure. Over breakfast, he sat Timmy down and explained that he had to leave him behind. The boy's disappointment was evident, but his expression brightened when George assigned him an important task.

"Your job," George told him, "is to help Walter and Matilda with their mission—saving other children from the queen's clutches."

Timmy straightened, his chest puffing out with pride. The thought of having a purpose, of playing a part in something bigger, eased the sting of being left behind.

With everyone on board with his plan, George saddled up his horse and set off, promising to return this way when his mission was complete. Disguised once more, he bid his friends farewell and rode towards Carraton. As he passed through towns and villages, no one paid him any special attention. To the world, he was just another traveller on the road.

It wasn't until he reached Kingsbridge that trouble arose. A tracker was in the area, forcing George to be extra cautious to avoid detection. His magic, drawn directly from the Earth itself rather than through an object, was naturally harder to trace. However, while channelling energy, he became highly visible to others with similar abilities. The more power he used, the brighter he shone, like a beacon at sea.

Unlike those who relied on enchanted objects, George could mask his presence once he released the energy, allowing it to sink back into the ground. But those who carried magical items were far easier to track. Power always lingered in objects, and since most wielders kept their artefacts close, they left behind a constant trail for trackers to follow.

Realising he was being hunted, George abandoned his disguise and pulled his hood lower, doing his best to remain unnoticed by both the people of Kingsbridge and the tracker. He moved quickly, avoiding the main roads as he pressed on towards the city. As far as he could tell, he hadn't been followed.

Still, a sense of unease lingered. A few nights later, he passed a patrol, and one guard stared at him a little too long for comfort. His knuckles whitened on the reins as his heart hammered in his chest. But they didn't stop him. They continued on their way, and he exhaled a slow breath of relief.

Avoiding detection would only grow more difficult the closer he got to Carraton. He could only hope that Lord Stone would make good on his word and provide some assistance in getting into the castle. His disguise would be useless at the royal residence – Elinor undoubtedly had trackers among her staff. There was little he could do about that.

All he could do was press forward, keeping his mind focused on the task at hand and reaching her undetected. So, he rode on, mile after mile, until one day, the city of Carraton finally came into view.

Chapter 24

A Royal Surprise

Elinor had caught wind that George was heading to the city. He wore no disguise, travelling as himself while attempting to remain hidden. Her spies had spotted him several times, but they were under strict orders not to intervene. She wanted him to believe he was one step ahead of her when, in reality, he was walking straight into her trap.

According to the latest report, he was only a week away – perhaps less. Knowing his last known whereabouts, her scouts tracked his movements, ready to alert her the moment he arrived in the city. She also knew he was alone, which made her wonder where the twins were. Guards had already been dispatched to find them. She would have them in her hands soon enough. Over the years, countless children resembling her niece and nephew had been brought before her, but none were truly them. Those individuals had been of no use to her – so she had disposed of them.

Pacing the study, she turned over possibilities in her mind, where the twins might be and what she would do once she had them. A throbbing pain formed at her temple again, and she reached up to massage her head. Lately, she had been more fatigued than usual, yet her appetite remained ravenous. The stress of recent months was beginning to take its toll.

Between the news of George and her ongoing troubles with Lord Stone, it had been a trying time. Thankfully, she had swiftly dealt with the latter by sending him a bloodstained piece of his daughter's dress, accompanied by a chilling note. The message had been unmistakable: if he continued to defy her, his daughter would face a public flogging, followed by the loss of her limbs, one by one.

So far, he had kept his distance, but Elinor knew it was only a matter of time before he tried something foolish. She had to stay ahead of him, which meant preparing for every eventuality. She frowned as the pain in her head flared anew. Unfortunately, preparing for anything didn't account for the persistent headaches that plagued her, yet once again, her own body betrayed her.

Closing her eyes, she rubbed her temples until the throbbing subsided. She needed rest. With that thought, she made her way to her chambers. As soon as she lay down and closed her eyes, the discomfort eased. Drifting into sleep, she hoped she would feel like herself when she woke.

A few hours later, she stirred and turned her head, her gaze landing on Bradley. He was propped up in bed beside her, reading the paper. Seeing that she was awake, he lowered it.

"I think you should see the physician. You haven't been yourself for a while."

"I am fine. It has just been a difficult time lately, leaving me more tired than usual."

"If that's true, then you have nothing to fear from a quick visit," Bradley challenged, a smile playing on his lips.

"Ha! Well done. You have me there."

"Is that a yes to the doctor's appointment?"

"If it stops you from worrying."

"Fantastic, because she will be here within the hour."

When the physician arrived, Elinor felt a wave of unease. She had never been fond of doctors and avoided them whenever possible. There was no rational reason – she simply associated them with illness. As a child, the only time they ever visited was when someone in the family was unwell. Herself included.

So today, she braced herself to be told she had some kind of flu or infection that required bed rest. But the physician's response after examining her was not one she had expected.

"Pregnant? You think I am pregnant?"

"Based on your symptoms and my examination, I am certain. Nearly five moons along. I will take a urine sample to confirm, but I have no doubt."

Elinor was in shock. Pregnant. They hadn't been trying, yet there they were. She wasn't sure how she felt. A part of her was happy, nonetheless, she was also scared. She wasn't sure if she was ready for a baby.

Bradley, however, was ecstatic. It was the one thing they argued about – how to conceive a child. She had never been as concerned as he was. Thanks to her power, her ageing was significantly slower than his, while he aged normally – something he was all too aware of.

Thinking back over the past few months, it all made sense. The constant fatigue, nausea triggered by certain smells, and dizziness throughout the day – not to mention her increased appetite. She hadn't connected the dots, assuming it was just the stress of dealing with Bradley's ships and the tourney.

Resting a hand on her stomach, she felt the slight bump but had chalked it up to weight gain. She turned to Bradley, who hugged her tightly, still rambling about how amazing this was. Not wanting to dampen his excitement, she humoured him. Right now, she was in shock and didn't know how she felt. Maybe once the test results came back, it would feel more real. She took a deep breath, trying to steady her racing thoughts. The uncertainty gnawed at her, but she clung to Bradley's joy, hoping it would be enough to carry her through the next few days.

They were having a baby.

That night, as she got ready for bed, she couldn't help but study her reflection in the mirror. The subtle changes she had missed – or simply refused to see. The firm, small bump that was more than just extra servings of dessert. The curvier figure. The persistent fatigue, no matter how much sleep she got. The bloating. The frequent trips to the bathroom. Now it all seemed so obvious, she couldn't understand how she hadn't pieced it together sooner.

She wondered if she was ready for this – what kind of mother she would even be. Her entire life had been dedicated to becoming queen, and she had always known that producing heirs would be part of that. But it had never truly sunk in that she would have a family of her own. In her mind, she had skipped past the pregnancy and baby stages, always picturing older children trained and prepared to take the throne after her.

Bradley's hands wrapped around her swollen belly as he pressed a kiss to her neck. "You're going to be an amazing mother," he murmured. "I know this might be overwhelming—and certainly a shock, if your expression was anything to go by… but we'll figure it out together. You've always been so strong and resilient. Our child is going to be so lucky to have you."

She leaned back into his embrace, absorbing the warmth of his reassurance. "But what if I'm not ready? What if I don't know what to do?"

Bradley turned her gently to face him, his eyes fixed with unwavering confidence. "No one is ever truly prepared, but you have the heart of a queen. You've led our people with grace and wisdom. You'll bring that same strength to motherhood. And I'll be right here with you, every step of the way."

His words soothed her, easing some of the tension in her chest. "I just… I never really thought about the baby part. I always pictured our children as older, ready to take the throne."

Bradley chuckled softly. "We'll get there, one day at a time. For now, let's focus on this little one and the journey ahead. Everything will fall into place as it's meant to."

She nodded, a faint smile tugging at her lips. "Thank you. I don't know what I'd do without you."

"Well, I am pretty amazing." He grinned, and she swatted his arm.

"I'm joking. Kind of," he added, pulling her close. "But we're in this together, my darling."

He cradled her bump just as she felt a sudden jolt inside her womb. At the same moment, she sensed Bradley tense.

"Was that what I think it was?" he asked, excitement lighting up his voice.

"Yes."

Another *thud* followed, and they both grinned, laughing at the shared moment.

"I don't believe it," he exclaimed, his eyes wide with wonder. "This is incredible."

"That's our baby," Elinor said, her voice filled with awe.

Bradley kissed her forehead, his expression radiant with love and excitement. "We're going to be parents," he whispered, as if speaking the words aloud would make them more real.

She nodded, her heart swelling with a flood of emotions.

"Yes, we are."

Chapter 25

The Showdown

With the city in sight, George halted and took in the sprawling landscape. He had not returned since fleeing with the twins. Now, as he gazed upon it, the grandeur remained unchanged – the towering stone buildings stood as a testament to the skill of the finest builders. Above them all, the castle loomed, an imposing sentinel guarding the capital's history and secrets. Memories rushed through him, quickening his pulse and making his hands tremble.

Forcing his emotions into submission, he pressed forward towards the gates, determined to enter one last time. The main entrance had long since closed due to the late hour, but a smaller metal door remained – a passage he might slip through if he could persuade the night guards. He dismounted, his boots striking the ground with a dull *thud*, and called out.

"Ello? Anyone about? Got turned 'round on the road an' ended up here later than I meant."

A guard emerged from the shadows, torchlight flickering across his face as he stepped closer, scrutinising George. The warm glow illuminated George's sheepish grin as he shrugged and held out his hands in a gesture of harmlessness.

"Please, good sir, I only seek a room for the night. Can't spend another on the cold, damp ground… me back won't survive it." He slipped a gold coin from his pocket, turning it in the firelight just enough for the guard to see.

Suspicion flickered across the watchman's face before his eyes widened at the bribe.

"Aye," the guard murmured, glancing around before nodding. "Can't have a man like yerself spendin' another night in the cold."

Relief washed over George as his tense muscles loosened. He guided his horse through the narrow opening and placed the coin in the guard's waiting hand.

"Much obliged. 'Ave a good night."

"Aye," the guard replied, locking the door behind him and resuming his post, as still and impassive as if he had never moved at all. George knew the man would keep quiet – he wouldn't risk that gold being taken from him.

Swinging himself back into the saddle, George gave his horse a reassuring pat before nudging him forward into a sprint. The empty streets blurred past as he rode. The sooner he reached the castle, the better.

As the looming structure drew near, he slowed, guiding his horse off the main path and into the cover of nearby trees. There, beneath the whispering branches, he dismounted, moving with the caution of a man who knew danger lurked in the dark.

"Well, Dusty, I need to do this next part alone. Can't take you with me," George murmured, patting the horse's sturdy neck. "You stay here till I return, you hear me?"

Dusty let out a low grunt in response. George placed a firm hand on the horse's nose, holding his gaze for a moment before turning away and slipping into the cover of the trees.

He moved carefully, staying within the shadows as he made his way towards the side of the castle. He searched for the section of stonework he remembered, the one with the jutting edges that could be scaled by someone who knew how. The darkness was his ally now, granting him the advantage he needed to reach the castle grounds undetected.

His power was an option, but a dangerous one. If there were trackers nearby, they might notice the pull of energy, even if he wielded objectless magic. He wasn't about to risk exposure – not when he was this close. So, he relied on his hands instead, trailing them along the rough stone wall, feeling rather than seeing his way to the spot he sought.

Minutes passed before his fingertips brushed against a deeper indentation. He stilled, running both palms over the nooks and crannies. This was it. He was certain. Dragging his fingers along the grooves, he dug them in, his nails scraping against the dirt and loose debris as he found his grip.

With a deep breath, he braced his feet against the wall, securing them one at a time in the narrow slips available. They were more difficult to maintain, so he pulled himself upward, reaching for another groove, then another, muscles straining with each ascent. The climb was slow and deliberate, until at last, he hauled himself over the top of the narrow stone wall.

Lying flat on his stomach, George panted hard, his palms raw and stinging, scratched and bloodied from the rough surface. A sharp cramp knotted in his leg, and he clenched his jaw, shaking it off as best he could without losing his balance.

When his breathing steadied, he lifted his head and scanned the area. No movement. No guards patrolling nearby. He knew the hidden paths, the best ways to slip into the castle unseen. For now, he was safe.

Swinging his legs over the edge, he held on with his arms as his toes sought purchase in the slits below. Once secure, he began the descent. It was less taxing on his muscles, but no less perilous in the darkness. With no clear view of the ground beneath him, every movement was cautious and controlled.

When his foot finally touched solid pavement, a wave of relief washed over him. He exhaled sharply, his shoulders sagging as he sank onto the ground. Pulling out his water flask, he took a long swig, letting his pulse settle. The fear of falling had passed – now, his mind could focus on the next stage of his plan.

Before he could take a step, a blade pressed against his throat.

"Hello, George," a male voice whispered.

George froze, hands instinctively rising as he calculated his next move. But just as quickly as the knife had appeared, it vanished. He turned sharply, eyes locking onto a figure clad in armour. A guard.

"Who are you?" George asked, his voice low but firm.

"I'm no one," the man replied. "But a mutual friend told me to look out for you and get you in."

"Give them my thanks."

"It's not that simple," the guard warned. "She knows you're coming. That watchman at the front? He already tipped her off. Men have been following you for weeks, timing your arrival perfectly."

George's jaw tightened. "And your part in this?"

"Giving you a warning." The guard's tone remained even, but there was an urgency in his words. "The castle may seem empty as you move through, but that's deliberate. She wants you to feel safe, and to grow overconfident before you meet her. Be careful."

With that, the man melted back into the shadows, his presence disappearing as swiftly as he had come. George lingered for a moment, his pulse steady but alert. If the guard was telling the truth, then he had to tread carefully. But he wouldn't take a stranger's word at face value – not when the royal watch could be waiting to strike.

Staying concealed, he made his way towards the servants' entrance near the kitchens. No guards stood on duty, and he slipped through the corridors with ease, moving deeper into the castle's secluded hallways.

Despite the late hour, the silence felt unnatural. The oppressive stillness sent a chill down his spine, raising the hairs on his neck. He moved cautiously, peering around corners before stepping forward, pausing to listen before making each turn.

It was too easy. Just as he had been warned.

Still, he pressed on. The only people he passed were a handful of workers tending to their nightly tasks, their heads down as they scrubbed floors and dusted surfaces. A few watchmen patrolled the hallways, but none paid him any mind. Testing his informant's theory, he cleared his throat loudly as he strode past a set of guards.

No reaction.

"Damn it," he muttered under his breath. The warning had been right – Elinor knew he was coming. The only question now was what kind of trap he had just walked into.

As he continued forward, another realisation struck him – he didn't actually know where she was. By now, she should be in her chambers. *Or would she be waiting elsewhere?*

He pivoted, deciding to head towards the royal chambers. But before he could get far, he caught a snippet of conversation between two workers, one of whom was carrying a tray of beverages.

"Who's up at this hour that you're bringin' them tea?"

"The queen, she is. Been up late these past few nights… says she can't sleep much. She's in the throne room again, just sittin' there. Not sure why?"

"Well, who are we to question Her Majesty? Best hurry now. She's not one to be kept waitin'."

George watched as the young worker quickened her pace at her friend's urging, carefully balancing the tray as she moved. Now that he knew where Elinor was – and not wanting the poor woman caught in the middle of whatever was about to unfold – he slowed his steps, giving her ample time to deliver the tea and return to the kitchens unharmed.

As he entered the corridor leading to the throne room, unease settled in his chest. No one stopped him. No night guards blocked his way. It was unnatural. Royals never went anywhere unprotected, and Elinor would be no exception. Yet the hallway stood empty. No guards were stationed outside the doors. No footsteps echoing in the distance.

Where were they?

She had known he was coming. By all logic, there should have been guards posted along these corridors, even if just for show. The complete absence of security reeked of a setup.

Still, George pressed forward, muscles taut, senses sharpened. Whatever trap awaited him, he would face it. He had no choice. Reaching the massive doors, he braced himself, drawing power into his core, and holding onto as much of it as he could. Then he stepped inside.

His eyes swept the vast area, quickly landing on her.

Elinor sat on the throne, fingers curled around a delicate cup of tea, not a single guard in sight. At his arrival, she calmly set the cup down on the tray beside her, then rose, her movements deliberate. A slow, knowing smile stretched across her face – as if she had been waiting for him all along.

Seeing her ignited a fire deep within his bones. Rage clawed its way to the surface, threatening to consume him whole. Memories of everything she had done crashed into him, each one sharpening his fury. His breath came heavy, his body shaking with the effort to restrain himself.

She descended the steps unhurried, and her gaze locked onto his.

George's face was a mask of cold fury as he stepped forward, slow and purposeful, matching her approach. He never broke eye contact. He couldn't afford to.

She was the threat.

And he would end her before she had the chance to destroy his family.

"Hello, George. It's been a while."

"Elinor. I'd say I'm glad to see you, but I was taught not to lie."

"Such a shame because it is *wonderful* to have you here."

"Hah! I don't believe that for a second."

"Oh, but that's the truth," she said, her voice laced with amusement. "I truly thought you'd be dead by now. But from the looks of you, perhaps I wasn't far off." Her gaze swept over him, assessing, calculating. "Especially for someone who wields the power. We tend to age better than most, yet *you*—" She tilted her head, a slow smirk curling her lips. "You look as though you've been ill for some time. I wonder why?"

Her expression glowed with an eerie satisfaction. Her eyes alight with something sinister – like she knew a secret he didn't.

George's body tensed. His mind raced, combing through the past few months, searching for anything unusual, anything that could explain the cruel glint in her eyes. Then, a cold realisation settled in his bones, sending dread crashing into him.

"Where are Aevah and Jacob?"

Elinor sighed, her smirk faltering, just for a moment, before she plastered it back on. "Oh, come now, George, must everything be about *them*? This is about *you*, old man. About your… declining condition." She watched him carefully, relishing the confusion that flickered across his face.

"That's it, George. Think. Can you figure it out?"

He tried. He wanted to ignore her taunts, but the truth was undeniable – his strength *had* waned these past months. His body felt it, even if his mind refused to admit it. Yet nothing in his routine had changed. No wounds, no sickness.

So, what had she done?

Was she testing him? Trying to make him admit weakness? Was she gauging whether she could defeat him outright? Or had she already set something in motion – something far worse – something involving *them*?

"You're playing me, Elinor," he said, forcing his voice to remain composed. "You'll have to try harder than mind games if you want me to believe you've had any effect on my health, which, by the way, is *fine*."

Elinor's smirk widened. "Oh really? Tell me, George, how is Mrs Daleman? I hear she makes a lovely tea… one you drink quite often."

George froze. The name struck him like a hammer to the chest. If she knew *that* – if she knew *who* Mrs Daleman was – then she knew about Sleights. And who knew what else?

"Quite chatty, that woman is. She'll spill anything you want to know," Elinor said, her voice dripping with satisfaction. "She was more than happy to talk about a widowed man and his two children who settled near their quaint little village… right around the time I took the throne. Some might call that an *interesting* coincidence."

George's body trembled, fury and fear warring within him as Elinor watched him with gleeful anticipation, waiting – *relishing* – his reaction. A thousand questions crashed through his mind, each one a demand for answers, but all he could manage was a single word.

"How?" Barely a whisper on his lips.

Elinor's smile widened as she took a slow step forward. "It wasn't easy. I'll give you that." Her eyes never left his, every step deliberate, taunting. "Even now, I *still* can't pinpoint exactly which house you've claimed. But a year ago, my spies *did* stumble upon your little hiding spot… quite by accident."

She was inches from him now, close enough that he could strike, could *end* this, but he needed to hear what she had done.

"One winter's evening, two of my informants were caught in a storm and sought shelter in a nearby village," she continued smoothly, her voice almost conversational. "The innkeeper and his wife welcomed them in, generous hosts that they were. And the wife… well, wasn't *she* just full of interesting little details?" She let out a soft chuckle. "And my spies lingered, listened, and oh, George, they were *not* disappointed."

George's fists clenched so tightly that his nails dug into his palms. His rage burned so hot he swore the very air around him crackled. But his voice – his *voice* – he forced to remain steady.

"Winter has been and gone," he said, his tone as sharp as a blade. "If you knew where I was, why didn't you act?"

A cruel smile tugged at Elinor's lips. She could see it – his anger, his self-reproach. He had grown careless, *too* comfortable. And she had played him for a fool for months.

"Oh, but I *did*—"

"The tea."

The realisation struck him like a physical blow. George surged forward, closing the distance in an instant, towering over her, pure hatred burning in his eyes. "What did you do to the tea?" he demanded, his voice low and dangerous.

Elinor didn't flinch. She merely tilted her head, her smirk deepening.

George's hand twitched at his sides, every fibre of his being screaming to wrap them around her throat, to *end* this now.

But he had to know. Elinor wouldn't live long enough to savour her victory if his carelessness had endangered his grandchildren.

Elinor met his glare with unrestrained glee, her grin stretching wide like a cat that had swallowed the cream.

"Wraith's Whisper," she said.

George's eyes widened in horror.

The name alone was enough to chill his blood. Wraith's Whisper was a poison of an age long past, forgotten by most, and for good reason. Unlike ordinary poisons that killed swiftly, this one was slow and insidious. It could linger in the body for months, silently destroying its victim from the inside out. There were no traces, no telltale signs, only the illusion of mild illness – a little fatigue, a passing weakness. But as time dragged on, the body would wither. Organs would begin to rot, devoured by the unseen toxin, leaving nothing but a husk of the person they once were. Eventually, all that remained was a hollowed corpse.

If caught early, treatment could stop the poison's spread. But if more than a week had passed? There was no hope. Once it had taken hold, the victim was as good as dead.

A thousand frantic thoughts crashed through George's mind, each more desperate than the last.

"Aevah and Jacob," he choked out, his voice breaking with panic. "Did they drink it?"

If they had, it was hopeless. They, like him, would be gone within weeks.

Elinor merely shrugged. "No idea. *You* were the target. Once you're dead, every secret you've been hoarding becomes mine." She paused, then tilted her head, and her smirk deepened. "Though, I won't lie… if they have ingested it, all the better for me. That's three of you out of my way… and only *one* left to find."

The casual, almost bored way she spoke of his grandchildren's deaths sent a murderous fire through George's veins.

Rage overtook him, and he struck out with the power – only for Elinor to counter it instantly, swatting his attack away with ease.

She laughed, a slow, menacing sound, as the two of them circled each other, eyes locked, bodies tense.

George took in his surroundings. Still, there were no guards. No witnesses. No one to intervene. She was so confident in her victory, so sure the poison had weakened him beyond repair.

Let her believe that. He kept moving, watching her, waiting for his moment. Then, with a sudden burst of energy, he struck again.

Elinor blocked it just as swiftly, shattering his attack with frightening precision. He gritted his teeth. She was powerful – more so than he had hoped. *But how much?* Rumours had long whispered that her strength had waned over the years, that she was a mere shadow of what she once had been. Then again, *so was he*. And now he finally understood why.

The question haunted him – did he still have the strength to do what needed to be done? Watching Elinor, he knew he had to try. The fate of the realm depended on it.

Summoning every ounce of courage, George made a daring move to end it all. He feigned a strike, forcing her to counter, and then delivered his true attack – a forceful bind to hold her in place. Moving swiftly, he sliced into his palm, crimson pooling, and seized Elinor's wrist, turning it toward him. He mirrored the cut across her skin and let the knife clatter to the floor.

With a trembling hand, he pulled a gemstone from his pocket, intending to press it between their bloodied palms. His mind was singularly focused; this ancient trick had to work. As their hands met over the gemstone, he felt the force holding Elinor waver. It was now or never.

He poured every last drop of power he had into the jewel, willing it to bind them through their mingling blood – fusing their fates together. What happened to one would befall the other.

Elinor's eyes widened in fury as realisation dawned. An ancient trick – long forgotten. A desperate gambit, either to drag an enemy into death with you or to save your life, knowing the other feared dying.

George strained, channelling every ounce of his energy to seal the bond, but the force shattered. Elinor's hand tore away, her face contorted with rage. The air around them crackled, dark tendrils of energy seeping from her fingers like puffs of smoke.

"How *dare* you!" she snarled, eyes blazing. "You think to destroy me with a pitiful trick like that?"

Without warning, she unleashed her power. Black swirls coiled around George, encasing his body, tightening until he couldn't move. He strained against them, breath growing shallow as his chest compressed painfully. His eyes bulged, his lungs clawing for air as darkness constricted his throat.

Paralysed and completely immobile. He could do nothing but stare at Elinor, her manic smile searing into his vision.

"Only one shall die tonight," he wheezed, forcing the words past his constricted windpipe. His arms were frozen, bound by invisible chains, unable to move an inch. Blood continued to drip from the open wound on his palm, pooling at his feet.

"It's only a matter of time," Elinor taunted, her voice dripping with malice. "Everything you've fought so hard to keep hidden will soon be mine. I can see you struggling, fighting… how futile. All you're doing is hastening your end."

Despite her mocking, George fought with every fibre of his being, gasping desperately, his face flushed, pupils bloodshot and wild. He *had* to break free. His eyes darted downward, catching sight of the knife lying just beyond his reach.

He strained, muscles burning, but his body refused to obey. His consciousness flickered, the world blurring at the edges as his breathing grew more laboured.

Realisation crept into his eyes – she was right. He had failed.

His final thoughts raced, frantic and unfulfilled, as the last breath clawed at his locked throat. His body collapsed to the cold stone floor, and his expression frozen in terror – the grim acceptance that Elinor had won.

Chapter 26

Finding the Cottage

Victory was hers!

Elinor stood over George's lifeless body, nudging it with the tip of her shoe.

"Oh, George," she murmured, tilting her head as if in mock sympathy. "You were a worthy opponent, but alas, you were no match for me."

Satisfied, she turned on her heel and strode out of the room, her steps measured and arrogant. The approaching guards halted at the sight of her, their expressions unreadable. She stopped before them, lifting her chin.

"Put his body on a pike for all to see," she commanded, her voice cold and imperious. "Let everyone know that George is dead. Clean up the mess and prepare for travel. My dear husband and I leave at dawn."

The guards bowed their heads and hurried to obey. Elinor inhaled deeply, a surge of euphoria coursing through her. George

– the elusive, worshipped figure who had plagued her for so long – was finally gone. She had bested him, and soon, the world would know it. The thought of his corpse displayed as a warning sent a dark thrill through her. She had won. There was no one left to challenge her.

She swept through the castle hallways, her pace unhurried yet purposeful, until she reached the study. Something told her this was where she needed to be. It was James's refuge, the one place he retreated to when the weight of rule bore down on him. And if she was right, it was here that she would find what she was looking for.

Crossing the threshold, she paused. Her sharp gaze flickered over the desk, the bookshelves, and the grand map adorning the wall – everything was exactly as she remembered – too perfect. Slowly, deliberately, she moved from wall to wall, fingertips grazing every surface, pressing into creases, searching for something – a secret only revealed now that George was dead.

Turning to the bookshelves, she examined each spine, scanning for a title she didn't recognise. Nothing. Her focus shifted to the map. It was magnificent, the known world unfurled in exquisite detail. Their own country was nothing more than a speck in the vast ocean, insignificant in the grand scheme of things. Yet, as she traced the contours of her homeland, a thought took root.

Her breath quickened.

Whirling, she stormed out of the study and down the corridors, her sudden urgency sending servants scrambling out of her path. She didn't slow. She couldn't.

The library loomed ahead, its doors swinging open at her approach. Without hesitation, she strode inside, heading straight for the cartography section. Scrolls of maps lined the shelves, waiting.

She called out loudly, disregarding the quiet protocol typically observed in this area.

"Erwin? Where are you, Erwin?"

A frail old man emerged from behind a towering shelf, his gait slow and unsteady as he hobbled towards her. Though night had fallen, he wasn't one to keep regular hours. He often stayed in the library long after others had retired, finding solace in the quiet.

"Yes… Your Majesty?" he wheezed, his voice raspy with age.

"I need the map of Ethos. Now. And by that, I mean *THE* map. The one created specifically for this castle."

Erwin blinked at her, then gave a slow nod. "Certainly, my… queen."

Turning, he slowly shuffled towards the cabinet. Elinor followed for only a moment before moving past him, reaching the cabinet first. Resting her fingers against its glass surface, she tapped impatiently, her irritation barely contained.

The cabinet was waist high, with six pull-out drawers beneath the glass pane, designed to showcase a large map in the display section below.

Erwin opened the second drawer with care. Inside, dozens of parchment sheets lay in protective envelopes, safeguarded against moisture, dust, and time itself. These were the oldest charts in the collection, to be handled with the utmost caution. He knew this well. With painstaking precision, he sifted through the stack until he found the one he sought.

Carefully, he laid the wrapped document on the cabinet's glass top. Then, shuffling a step to the right, he retrieved a pair of clear cloves from a nearby drawer. Only once they were properly in place did he extract the map from its protective covering, handling it as though it might crumble beneath his touch.

Elinor remained silent, watching intently. Despite her urgency, she respected the process. The last thing she needed was to be responsible for damaging one of the oldest maps in existence. Still, every second felt agonisingly slow. She held herself poised, ready to pounce the moment Erwin completed his careful setup.

At last, he stepped aside, revealing the aged map beneath the glass barrier.

Elinor leaned in, her hands hovering just above the surface as her eyes darted over the intricate details. She traced the contours with her gaze, searching – waiting – for something to stand out. But nothing did. This chart was old, its name unfamiliar, and its landscapes altered over time.

Her lips pressed into a thin line.

"Bring me a current map," she ordered, her focus never wavering.

Erwin obeyed without question, retrieving a more recent version. The moment he returned, she snatched it from his hands, unrolling it swiftly. Side by side, the maps lay before her, one ancient, one modern.

She scanned them both, eyes shifting between past and present, hunting for a connection. Then, she remembered. Sleights. The small village where her people had found George. Her search narrowed.

She saw it. It was staring back at her – not on the new map, but on the old one, as clear as day.

Middlebeck Farm.

She knew it had to be the place. Middlebeck Farm no longer existed; she had never seen it marked on any modern chart nor heard its name spoken aloud. Yet, there it was. A relic from the past, hidden in plain sight. This had to be it – the concealed secret that had kept the whereabouts of the magical crystal shards obscured all this time.

A rush of exhilaration surged through her.

"Eurika! Spirits blessed it, this is it, Erwin. I have found it at last!"

Overcome with triumph, Elinor thrust the map into his hands and bolted from the library. She had no time for caution – she had to find Bradley. Her pulse thundered in her ears as she raced through the hallways, her excitement propelling her forward. When she finally burst into their chambers, she nearly stumbled in her eagerness.

"I did it, Bradley! I did it!"

Bradley jolted awake at the sound of the door crashing open. Disoriented, he sat up, eyes wide with alarm. "Elinor?" He blinked at her, still half-dazed. "What… what's happened? Why are you so—"

Elinor practically leapt onto the bed, her face alight with elation. "Everything I've been waiting for… it's finally within reach!"

Bradley scrubbed a hand over his face, shaking off the remnants of sleep. "My love, slow down. What have you so eager at this hour?"

She caught his hands in hers, her grip firm with urgency. "George is dead. And soon, all his secrets will be revealed. I know where to go. I know where the crystals are hidden."

His drowsiness vanished in an instant.

"Wait… what?" His gaze sharpened. "George is dead? How? What happened? Who told you?"

Elinor's smile never faltered. "He arrived at the castle not long ago. I knew he was coming and confronted him. It did not end well for him."

Bradley stiffened. "He came here! To the castle? Elinor, why was I not informed? You could have been killed! You—" He hesitated, glancing at her stomach. "There are two of you to think about now."

He threw back the covers, swinging his legs over the side of the bed as if ready to spring into action. But before he could stand, Elinor placed her hands over his, her fingers curling around his in a silent plea.

"I didn't send for you because I had everything under control," she assured him, her voice steady. "My plan with the tea worked. He was already weakened when he arrived. The guards told me he could barely stand."

Bradley's expression remained tight with concern, but she pressed on, squeezing his hands to keep him from arguing.

"If he had been stronger, I would never have faced him alone. But trust me, Bradley. I made the right call. And I was right because here I am. Alive and well. And with everything we've been fighting for finally within our grasp."

Bradley exhaled sharply, his frustration evident. But then his gaze dropped to her palm, and his expression darkened. He turned her hand over, his fingers tracing the thin cut along her skin. The bleeding had slowed, but a fresh trickle still glistened in the dim light.

"Except for this." His voice softened with worry.

Without another word, he reached for the handkerchief on his bedside table and carefully wrapped it around her wound.

"It's nothing," Elinor murmured, brushing off his concern. "George tried something foolish and paid the price." She leaned in, pressing a kiss to his lips.

"I'm fine. The baby is fine. Trust me, my love. Tonight, we celebrate. Bask in this glorious moment with me."

She met his gaze, her sincerity shining through, her smile warm and triumphant. He sighed – that deep, familiar sigh that meant she had won.

Recognising her victory, she seized the moment, pulling him into a firmer kiss.

"Let's enjoy this," she whispered against his lips, her voice laced with promise. "We have a long journey ahead of us tomorrow."

Before he could protest, she kissed him again, this time with undeniable intent. Whatever questions remained could wait. For now, there was only one thing she wanted from Bradley.

***

Morning arrived, and Elinor awoke feeling refreshed and invigorated. The events of the previous night still lingered in her mind, leaving her with a satisfied glow. With George out of the way and a clear path ahead, the day already felt brighter.

Turning to Bradley, she nudged him awake, determined to depart without delay.

"Wake up, my love. We have a long journey ahead of us, and I want to leave immediately."

He groaned, still half-asleep. "Hmm…"

Elinor was undeterred. Springing out of bed, she strode to the door and called for her ladies-in-waiting. Within moments, her main lady, Chloe, entered, flanked by two others.

"My husband and I are leaving later today. We will be gone for several weeks," she announced. "Prepare everything we will need for the journey. Chloe, you will accompany us. See to it that a suitable squire is chosen to assist the king consort."

At her command, the younger ladies hurried off to gather the necessary provisions while Chloe moved towards the adjoining bathroom to draw a bath.

Bradley sat up with a sigh, rubbing the sleep from his eyes before rising to dress. "Has someone finalised the arrangements?"

"Of course. I had the staff begin preparations last night." Elinor gave him a faint smile, already thinking ahead. "I suggest we despatch scouts on horseback ahead of us to secure the location. Find Erwin—he has the map. Have him make a copy of the area our men need to search, then send them on their way."

Bradley nodded. "As you wish, my dear." He stepped forward, placing a brief kiss on her lips before leaving to carry out her orders.

Elinor exhaled, her mind already racing through the logistics of the journey. The cottage was still weeks away by carriage, and while she could cover the distance faster on horseback, she had to acknowledge an inconvenient truth – her pregnancy was already making travel uncomfortable. Riding for extended periods would only worsen the strain.

No, she would take the carriage.

She had no intention of risking her health, nor would she allow a mere inconvenience to jeopardise the mission. Instead, her guards would ride ahead, securing the location before she arrived. An empty cottage was too tempting a prize for thieves and scavengers. If word of its existence had spread, there was no telling what trouble might be waiting.

But she trusted her men. They would ride hard and reach Middlebeck Farm before any looters could. She had waited too long for this moment – nothing would stand in her way now.

With a nod from her lady, Elinor stepped into the bathroom, allowing Chloe to assist her as she eased into the steaming bath. The water was hot, just as she liked it, but for once, she had no intention of lingering.

"This will be a quick wash. I want to leave as soon as everything is in order."

"Yes, Your Majesty."

Chloe efficiently set to work, washing Elinor's hair before preparing her travel attire. By the time Bradley returned, Elinor was nearly dressed, fastening the final ties of her gown with Chloe's assistance.

"Everything is arranged," he announced. "Sir Aldric and his men have already departed, and your carriage is ready whenever you are."

"Thank you." She glanced at him, noting his hesitation. He lingered near the doorway.

"Do I have time to wash up?" he asked.

"If you're quick about it. I want to be gone within the hour, and we still need to eat. I'd rather not attempt breakfast in the carriage… not with how my stomach feels."

Bradley's head peeked around the door, concern etched on his face. "Are you all right?"

"It's just queasiness. Completely normal this far along." She waved off his worry. "Now hurry up. I am ready to go."

"Yes, yes. I'll only be a minute."

"Then I shall meet you in the dining room."

With that, Elinor exited their chambers, Chloe following close behind. Upon entering the dining room, she took her seat as a servant set a tray before her – fresh juice, toasted bread with butter, eggs, and a bowl of mixed fruits. Even the sight of it felt overwhelming, with the nausea still lingering, but she knew better than to skip a meal. Her physician had made that clear.

She started with the berries, their tartness settling her stomach. As her nausea eased, she continued with the rest of the meal. By the time Bradley joined her, taking his seat across the table, she had regained enough appetite to finish most of her plate. He wasted no time beginning his meal, and once both were finished, they made their way outside.

Elinor climbed into the carriage first, accepting Bradley's assistance, followed by Chloe. Once they were settled, the driver gave the reins a flick, and the journey to Middlebeck Farm began.

The hours dragged on. By the end of it, Elinor's patience had worn thin. Restless and irritable, she was eager to stretch her legs.

The moment the carriage came to a halt, she wasted no time stepping out. But as her feet touched the ground and she turned to take in the land before her, she froze.

Her breath hitched.

Charred ruins and the skeletal remains of a fragile structure stood before her, blackened timbers barely holding them together. It looked ready to collapse with the next strong gust of wind.

George had been more cunning than she had realised. To burn the place down – purely out of spite.

Her hands clenched at her sides. He had robbed her of answers even in death.

As anger surged through her, black smoke coiled around her like a living force. A sudden crack of lightning split the sky, striking the ruined cottage with an explosive burst. What little remained ignited once more, flames licking hungrily at the fragile frame.

She spun on her heel, her sharp gaze locking onto the guards standing before her.

"Has anyone dared enter?"

"Yes, Your Majesty," Sir Aldric replied evenly. "There was nothing salvageable."

Elinor closed her eyes, drawing in slow, measured breaths. Still standing there with her fists clenched, she forced them to relax, her nails retracting from the crescents they had pressed into her palms.

"If there's nothing left for us here, then we'll find lodgings for the night. We ride home at first light." Her voice held firm authority, but exhaustion weighed behind it. "I need a break from that cursed carriage."

"There is a village just up the road," Sir Aldric offered. "It has a pleasant inn. It will be comfortable enough for a night's rest."

"By any chance, is this village called Sleights?"

Aldric's brows lifted. "Why, yes, Your Majesty? Have you been before?"

"No," she said, a slow smile curving her lips. "But I have heard wonderful things. Let's go."

George might have burned away her lead, but secrets had a way of surfacing in the most unexpected places. If there was anything left to uncover, she would find it.

Suppressing a groan, Elinor climbed back into the carriage, her hand instinctively resting over the gentle swell of her abdomen. Beside her, Bradley's fingers entwined with hers, offering silent reassurance.

The carriage rumbled forward, following a winding brick road into the heart of Sleights. By now, the late afternoon light had set in, casting long shadows across the quiet village. Elinor stifled a yawn, fatigue settling deep in her bones. This child seemed determined to drain her strength at the most inconvenient moments.

As the carriage rolled to a stop outside a modest inn, Bradley stepped out first, turning to extend his hand. She took it gratefully, allowing him to steady her as she disembarked.

The village was eerily still, with only a few figures moving about. The inn before her was small and unassuming, its timbered frame weathered but welcoming.

Pushing open the door, she stepped inside, immediately greeted by the scent of burning wood and ale. A crackling fire blazed in the hearth, casting a flickering golden light across the rustic wooden tables. A handful of patrons sat nursing drinks, engaged in low conversation.

An elderly man and woman bustled forward from behind the counter, their eyes widening as they took in Elinor's regal bearing. They nearly tripped over themselves in their haste to bow and curtsy, their eager respect bordering on comical.

"Your Majesty, it's a great honour to have you spend the night in our humble inn," the woman said with a deep curtsy, while the man beside her bowed at the waist.

"The pleasure is mine." Elinor inclined her head with a warm but regal nod. "And what are your names?"

"Mr and Mrs Daleman," the man answered.

"It's wonderful to meet you both," she said. "My court and I have had a long journey. If you could show us to our rooms, we would be most grateful."

"Oh, but of course, Your Majesty! Right this way."

Mrs Daleman gestured for them to follow, and Elinor walked alongside Bradley as they ascended the narrow wooden staircase. The few patrons scattered throughout the inn, realising they were in the presence of the queen and king consort, quickly rose from their seats, offering bows and murmured greetings as she passed.

At the top of the stairs, Mrs Daleman led them to a modest, yet well-kept chamber. The room was small but comfortable, with a neatly made bed and a small adjoining washroom.

"Well, this is nice," Bradley mused, stepping further inside. He picked up a delicate pomander box from the bedside table, inhaling the strong scent of lavender before setting it back down. Running a hand along the pillowcase, he tested its softness with an approving nod.

Elinor barely had time to sit before she groaned and pushed herself back to her feet, making her way to the adjoining bathroom.

Another pregnancy nuisance. The baby seemed determined to press against her bladder every time she managed to get comfortable.

When she returned, she sank into the chair with a sigh, grateful to be still for once. The constant jostling of the carriage had worn on her more than usual that day.

Bradley watched her closely, his mouth twitching with concern. "Are we going to talk about what happened at the cottage?"

"What is there to say?" she muttered. "George made sure there was nothing left for me to find. Now, I don't know what to do or where to look. My niece and nephew are gallivanting across the land, no doubt with that information in their pocket. And me?" She let out a bitter laugh. "I'm back at the beginning. Searching blindly. No direction. No plan. Spirits help me!"

She threw her head back, exhaustion and frustration bleeding into her posture.

"I give up."

At her words, Bradley strode towards her and knelt at her feet, taking her hands in his. His grip was firm.

"No, you don't," he said. "You have worked too hard to give up now. You will find them. You just need to look at it from a different angle."

"Oh? And what might that be?" she challenged.

Bradley hesitated.

"See?" she scoffed, pulling her hands away. "Even you have nothing to work with."

Pushing herself up, she trudged towards the bed and collapsed onto the mattress without bothering to remove her shoes or pull back the covers.

"I'm tired," she murmured, eyes already drifting shut. "Wake me in an hour if I haven't stirred."

And with that, she was asleep.

Bradley remained where he was, watching her in silence. Then, with a sigh, he sat and stared at the walls, deep in thought. There had to be something Elinor was missing – something they had overlooked.

Chapter 27

Hidden Clues

"Elinor, wake up."

She stirred at the sound of her name, the rich aroma of beef stew teasing her senses. It took her a moment for her to remember where she was. When she did, she groaned.

Sitting up, she found Bradley smiling at her, a selection of food laid out before her. Despite herself, her lips curled into a smile at the sight of him.

Leaning back against the wooden frame of the bed, she adjusted her posture as he placed the tray over her lap. Her mouth watered, and her stomach growled in response to the feast before her.

A steaming bowl of beef stew, brimming with tender meat and vibrant vegetables, sat beside thick slices of buttery toasted bread. A generous portion of apple pie awaited her, accompanied by a small jug of cream. Without hesitation, she dug in.

The first bite was heavenly. The stew was rich and full of flavour, the bread crisp and warm, and the dessert was a perfect balance of sweet and spiced. She was so ravenous that she finished every last bite.

Bradley watched her with amusement. "So, I know you feel lost on how to find the shards, but I'm here to help. I was thinking… surely, something must be hidden in the castle?"

"I have searched many times," she said, shaking her head. "There's nothing there."

"Ah, but that was before George's death. I implore you—once we return home, search again, this time with my assistance. I believe there must be a clue leading us to them."

She exhaled, unconvinced. "I don't share your faith, but I will humour you. I'll attempt it one last time."

"Perfect. Then it's settled." His grin widened. "Now, while you were napping, I took a short stroll through this village and found a lovely spot for a relaxing walk. Care to join me?"

"It would be pleasant after being cooped up in that carriage for so long."

Taking her arm in his, he led her outside and along the river. The crisp air carried the scent of damp earth and autumn leaves, and the gentle sound of flowing water soothed her restless thoughts. As they walked, the weight of recent events lifted slightly, and a renewed determination settled within her. She would reclaim the shards – no matter what it took.

After completing their loop around the village, Elinor and Bradley returned to the small inn. A relaxing evening and a restful night's sleep left them feeling refreshed for the long journey ahead. As they prepared to depart, they thanked the innkeepers for their hospitality.

"It was our pleasure, Your Majesty," Mrs Daleman said with a warm smile. "If there's anything else you need, please let me know."

"Funny you should say that," Elinor replied, her tone shifting. "Because there are a few questions my guards would like to ask you and the other villagers."

Mrs Daleman's smile faltered. "Oh?" Her eyes flicked nervously between the men advancing towards her.

Elinor clasped her hands behind her back, her expression unreadable. "It seems that, for years, your little village has been harbouring fugitives of the realm. My men won't be leaving until they have answers."

"Fugitives?" Mr Daleman interjected, his voice laced with disbelief. "You must be mistaken, Your Majesty—"

"You dare question your queen?" Elinor cut him off, arching a brow. She stepped forward, lowering her voice just enough to make them strain to hear her next words. "I have it on good authority that a certain 'widow' and his two children have been venturing into your quaint village."

Mrs Daleman paled. "Widow? Do you mean Master Oliver and his precious little ones? Fugitives?"

Elinor let out a short, humourless laugh. "Try the infamous George and the royal twins, Aevah and Jacob, masquerading as villagers right under your noses." She gestured to her guards, their expressions hard as they closed in. "Now, my men will get the answers I seek. Whatever it takes. Understood?"

The Daleman's exchanged a frantic glance, both visibly trembling. "Y… Yes, Your Majesty," they stammered.

Satisfied, Elinor turned on her heel and climbed into the carriage. Already, her muscles tensed at the thought of the long, gruelling ride ahead. But at least she had gained something from this visit. If her guards pried the right information from the villagers, she might finally have an edge in finding her niece and nephew.

For now, she leaned back against the seat, exhaling slowly. The journey home would be tedious, but she could endure it, especially if it brought her one step closer to finding the crystal shards.

***

Back home, Elinor wasted no time scouring the castle for any clue that might lead to the crystals, with Bradley helping her. He pored over old documents in the archives, searching for even the faintest hint of their whereabouts. Meanwhile, she combed through the castle's rooms once more, hoping that something previously overlooked would now reveal itself. A secret hidden by the power only accessible after George's death.

There had to be something here. It was impossible that the only information had been left in that cottage. The princess who had hidden the crystals had remained close to members of the court, ensuring that their family's knowledge was preserved and shared only with monarchs they deemed worthy. At some point, those details must have been recorded and safeguarded.

But where?

Frustrated, Elinor wandered outside, hoping the fresh air would help her clear her mind. She sank onto a stone bench in the garden, tilting her head back to watch the drifting clouds. The hiding place had to be somewhere no one would think to search – somewhere inaccessible, where it wouldn't be discovered by accident, keeping it out of harm's way.

She knew this castle better than anyone. All she had to do was think.

Suddenly, she shot to her feet as if stung by a bee. But it wasn't pain that jolted her – it was a memory. A vivid recollection from her youth surfaced, bringing back a detail she had glimpsed long ago.

It couldn't be… could it?

Heart pounding, she gathered her skirts in her fists and sprinted across the castle grounds as quickly as a pregnant woman could, stopping only when she reached the entrance to the royal crypts. If she was right, everything she sought was hidden within these very walls.

She stepped inside, descending deep into the burial chambers, the flickering torch in her hand casting long shadows across the stone corridors. The air was cool and heavy with the scent of aged stone and dust. Each chamber bore a wooden plaque inscribed with the name of the deceased. Holding the torch higher, she scanned the names carefully until her gaze landed on the one she had been searching for: Garth Maycott.

Her pulse quickened.

Stepping inside, darkness swallowed her. Her feeble flame barely pierced the gloom, a weak flicker against the vast shadowed expanse. Raising her hand, she summoned her power, and flames burst to life in the torches lining the walls. One by one, they ignited, illuminating the chamber's secrets.

A grand crypt stretched before her, filled with imposing stone tombs, each housing a royal family member. Their names were etched upon the stone, their house crest carved beneath. Above each tomb stood a statue of the person buried within, sculpted from the same stone, their expressions solemn yet proud as they stood watch over their mortal remains.

Her eyes moved over the graves. Ingrid, wife of Garth. Then King Garth himself. Others rested beyond – children and noble kin – but they were of no concern to her now. She had found what she needed.

Crouching at the base of Garth's tomb, she focused on the detail that had caught her eye all those years ago – a carving of a crystal, its form broken, just as it was in reality. Each shard was carefully sculpted, but between them lay blank sections of stone as if they could be removed.

Holding her breath, she reached out and carefully pulled free the three empty pieces. Then, with steady hands, she slid together the four remaining pieces, those bearing the etched shards.

They fit perfectly. The crystal was whole once more.

Her heart pounded as she pressed her palm against the image. A deep, resounding *click* echoed through the chamber.

A hidden drawer slid open.

At first, it was barely noticeable, just a faint seam in the stone, but as she tugged at the concealed compartment, it revealed its treasure. Inside lay an ageing envelope, its parchment brittle with time yet still bearing the unmistakable imprint of the royal seal.

She exhaled sharply. The puzzle was nearly complete.

It was a cruel irony that the crystals had been hidden in a secret compartment beside the very king who had spent his life searching for them – only to be buried alongside them for eternity. A final jest from the princess to her brother.

Elinor could appreciate the dark humour of it. And yet, she could scarcely believe they had been here all along, unnoticed by anyone.

Her hands trembled as she broke the ancient seal on the browning envelope, eager to uncover its secrets. Inside, she found four aged parchments, each folded and stamped with the royal emblem. She peeled the seals away and hungrily scanned the pages.

"Riddles… and a map."

Her eyes darted between the documents, trying to decipher their meaning, but the answers remained just out of reach. Frustration mingled with excitement as she carefully folded the papers back into the envelope. Before leaving, she ensured everything was as it had been – the stones replaced, the compartment hidden. No one could suspect what she had found.

Moving swiftly, she emerged from the crypts, blinking against the sudden brightness of the garden. She needed Bradley, but she dared not risk revealing her discovery where others might overhear.

Summoning one of her guards, she sent him to the library with a message: her husband was to meet her in their chambers immediately. It was the safest place for such a revelation.

Once inside her room, Elinor spread the parchments across her writing desk, her fingers smoothing over the fragile paper as she studied the riddles once more.

"Is everything all right? I was told it was urgent," Bradley said, striding in, concern evident in his furrowed brow.

"It's better than all right," she replied, gesturing to the documents before her.

He moved beside her, scanning the letters as his fingers traced the edges of the map. His brows knitted together in concentration.

"Is this what I think it is?"

"Yes. I found them—hidden in a secret compartment within King Garth's tomb."

Bradley exhaled sharply, taking in the weight of her words. He turned his attention to the riddles, reading each one carefully. Then he glanced back at the map, comparing them with the cryptic clues.

"It seems we'll need to solve these to locate the hiding places," Elinor mused, pointing to a marked symbol. "I presume these indicate where the shards are, but they must be well concealed. That's why the riddles exist—to ensure only the worthy can find them."

Bradley nodded. "I believe you're right. The question is, how do you want to approach this? Do you trust others to retrieve the crystal shards for you, or are we about to embark on a quest?"

She met his gaze. "What do you think?"

A slow grin spread across his face. "I'll make preparations for us to leave at daybreak."

This was exactly the kind of adventure he thrived on – a treasure hunt shrouded in mystery, riddles, and danger.

Elinor rested a hand on her ever-expanding bump, a flicker of uncertainty creeping in. Time was against her. She could only retrieve one shard before the baby arrived, and the rest would have to wait.

The plan had always been to give birth in the safety of the castle, not on the road in some unfamiliar inn. With only a few months remaining, she had to be strategic. The locations marked on the map were spread across the kingdom. The closest were Belshire and Almire – either of which she could reach and return from before her time ran out. The one in the Renlands, however, was another matter entirely – too far, too treacherous, buried deep in the snowy mountains.

Still, one shard in her possession would be a start.

As she traced the map, her thoughts drifted to her niece and nephew. *Where would they go first?* Belshire. It was the nearest to their location, making it the most logical choice. After that, they would likely attempt the Renlands, then Almire – moving outward rather than crisscrossing the kingdom.

Having just been to Belshire, frustration gnawed at Elinor. The knowledge that the shard was so close, perhaps even within her grasp, set her on edge. *Did she double back, hoping Aevah and Jacob hadn't found it yet? Or did she move forward to Almire, betting they had already claimed the first shard?*

The twins were being hunted. If they had fallen into her guard's hands, she would soon know whether they possessed the shard from Belshire. But if she pushed ahead and secured the next one first, she would have two shards to their one – a decisive advantage.

She exhaled, turning the possibilities over in her mind before making her decision. Almire. That was where she needed to go.

Bradley took a seat across from her, his gaze steady. "Everything is arranged," he said. "We leave as soon as you're ready tomorrow. Do you have any idea what these riddles might refer to?"

Elinor studied them again before shaking her head. "No, but once we reach Almire, I hope one of them makes sense."

She reread the clues, her eyes scanning the words as if willing them to reveal their secrets. After several fruitless hours, exhaustion overtook her. With Bradley's help, she readied herself for bed. He eased her down onto the mattress, ensuring she was comfortable before returning to the riddles.

She tossed and turned, struggling to find a position that didn't strain her aching back. Sleep, when it finally came, was restless.

The early morning light found her awake once more. Sleep had abandoned her completely, and after a few futile attempts to doze off again, she gave up. Sitting upright, she grasped the bedpost for support and carefully pulled herself to her feet.

Summoning a nearby guard, she instructed him to fetch Lady Chloe to assist her in preparing for the journey.

Minutes later, Chloe arrived, setting about drawing a bath while Elinor cradled her growing bump. The baby was particularly active that morning, tiny limbs shifting beneath her skin. With each kick, small bumps formed across her abdomen – an odd but wondrous sensation she still hadn't quite grown used to.

"Kicking again, Your Majesty?" Chloe asked with a smile.

"Yes, they are most energetic early in the morning," Elinor sighed. "I hope this isn't an omen of what's to come."

Waddling to the large bathtub, she paused. "Pass me your hand."

Chloe hesitated only a moment before placing her palm over the spot where the movement was the strongest. Her eyes widened with delight.

"Oh, that is magical."

"It is," Elinor agreed, "though not when you're trying to sleep."

With Chloe's assistance, she shed her shift and eased into the warm water, sighing as the heat soothed the persistent ache in her hips and lower back. As Chloe bathed her, the two women chatted and exchanged light-hearted jokes, the brief respite easing some of Elinor's tension.

Then Bradley appeared in the doorway.

"Ah, my love," she mused, "could you be a dear and lend me a hand?"

"Certainly, my darling."

He stepped forward, slipping an arm beneath her and carefully guiding her upright and out of the tub. Chloe swiftly wrapped her in a towel, helping her dress while Bradley busied himself with final preparations.

Once they were both dressed and packed, they sat down to a light breakfast before heading out to the carriage.

“Oh, how I look forward to the day when I no longer have to endure weeks of uncomfortable travel in this thing,” Elinor groaned as she climbed inside.

Bradley smirked. “At least this will be our last journey for a while. And it will be worth it.”

“I hope so,” she murmured, her gaze drifting to the passing landscape as the carriage rumbled away from the castle – towards the first hidden crystal shard.

Chapter 28

The Loss

Cecilia sat by the window, gazing out at the busy streets below. The sky hung heavy with dark clouds, and rain pounded the rooftops, drenching townspeople as they hurried through the streets. Despite the downpour, workers pressed on, darting between awnings and doorways in a futile attempt to stay dry. Yet, as she watched the scene unfold, a growing sense of unease settled in her chest. Something was wrong – terribly wrong.

A sharp knock on the door broke her from her thoughts. She turned, her breath catching as she saw Adrian standing in the doorway, his expression grave. Her heart plummeted.

"Cecilia," he whispered, stepping into the room. "I have news."

She rose to her feet, her hands trembling. "What is it? What's happened?"

Adrian drew a slow, heavy breath, sorrow clouding his eyes. "It's your father. George is dead."

The words struck her like a blow. She stood frozen, her mind scrambling for a response, grasping for some reality where this was not true. Her gaze flickered to Adrian's face, searching desperately for a trace of a lie – a cruel joke. But there was none. As the truth settled in, she staggered back, her breath hitching.

"No… it can't be. How?"

Adrian's jaw tightened. "He went to confront Elinor at the castle," he said, his voice thick with grief. "They fought, and she killed him. As a warning to others, she's having his body displayed for all to see."

A strangled sob escaped Cecilia as her vision blurred with tears. "She killed him…"

Adrian stepped forward, wrapping his arms around her. "I'm so sorry, Cecilia."

She buried her face in his shoulder, her body wracked with grief. Time seemed to stand still as she wept for the man who had raised her, who had loved her, and whom she had left in anger. How she wished she had said more to him during their last conversation – told him what he meant to her, how grateful she was that he had cared for her children as if they were his own.

If he hadn't been there that night, her children would likely have died – she might have died along with them. She owed him everything and loved him with all her heart. Yet now, she could never tell him, and the weight of that realisation gnawed at her. Frustration burned within her, believing that if he hadn't been so stubborn, if he had only asked for help, he might still be alive.

"What a fool of a man," she choked out. "Why did he confront her alone? We had a plan. His plan. Why would he throw it away?" She pulled back, shaking her head. "What am I supposed to do without him?"

Adrian held her tighter, his sorrow weighing heavy between them. "He wouldn't have gone unless he believed he could win," he said. "He had faith in his cause. In you. In the future. We have to honour his memory by carrying on the fight."

Cecilia met his gaze, the raw pain in her eyes slowly hardening into resolve. "You're right. We can't let his sacrifice be for nothing. We have to keep going, for him and for everyone who believed in him."

Adrian nodded, his expression set with determination. "We'll gather our forces. We'll make Elinor pay for what she's done. Together, we'll see this through."

Cecilia took a steadying breath, squaring her shoulders. "For my father. For my children. For the future of our kingdom. We will not back down."

As they stood together, Cecilia felt the grief inside her twist into something darker – something fiercer. The pain of her father's loss burned like a brand, but it didn't weaken her. It forged her. Elinor would regret the day she crossed her family. That much, she swore.

***

A chill swept across the nation. News of George's death echoed through the streets, carried by whispers and cries of disbelief. The people mourned the loss of a man beloved by all – a kind soul who had fought for those in need. He was a devoted family man, one who, in the end, had given his life for them. Now, the truth could no longer be denied. The rumours that had circulated for years were real: George had lived in hiding to protect his grandchildren, shielding them from the usurper Elinor's wrath.

In every city, town, and village, candles flickered in his memory. People gathered in town squares, sharing stories of his bravery and big-heartedness. His death had left a void that seemed impossible to fill, and grief hung heavy in the air.

As Cecilia and Adrian continued their journey, sorrow weighed on them. Everywhere they went, they saw the mourning firsthand – faces etched with pain, voices trembling as they spoke of George's kindness. The depth of the people's loss only strengthened their resolve.

Though he had been in hiding for years, no one had forgotten him. They remembered the man he had been, the good he had done. His generosity, his unwavering spirit – these things lived on in the hearts of those he had touched. Even in death, his light burned brighter than ever, a beacon of inspiration that couldn't be extinguished.

The rebels no longer hid in the shadows. Everywhere Cecilia and Adrian went, resistance surged to life. What had once been whispers of defiance became open rebellion. The people looked to Cecilia not just as George's daughter but as a leader in her own right. They saw in her the same strength, the same fire, and they rallied behind her. She vowed to honour her father's legacy – to lead the fight against Elinor with unwavering courage.

Grief and determination united the nation. Elinor's plan had failed. She had hoped George's death would break the spirit of those who opposed her, but instead, she had set ablaze a fire she couldn't control. The voices of the oppressed rose louder, fuelled by the desire for justice for freedom. They would carry on his fight – no matter the cost.

Chapter 29

A Surprise Attack

After veering away from the main roads, Aevah and Jacob had successfully evaded the tracker, stopping only in small villages to gather provisions. They remained cautious, keeping their interactions with others to a minimum and camping in secluded areas far from well-trodden paths.

Jacob believed they were close to finding the first crystal shard – or at least, he hoped so.

"Read the riddle again," he said to Aevah, his mind turning over the words, searching for any connection between the lines and their surroundings.

"I am hidden from prying eyes, in a place where calm and shade arise. In nature's embrace, I rest, with secrets buried at their bequest. Come, lay your head upon my bough, and seek shelter from the world around. If you look closely, you shall see, not everything is as it should be. Crawl down deep, where roots entwine, a crystal hidden, yours to find. In your grasp, you hold it all, but too much power will steal your soul," Aevah responded, her mind working to make sense of the words.

Jacob paced in a slow circle, his eyes scanning their surroundings, hoping to uncover the answer.

"This has to be it! 'A place to rest your head. Roots entwined.' It has to be this giant oak… nothing else fits."

"It does," she agreed, gazing up at the enormous tree. Its sheer size suggested it had stood for hundreds of years.

Jacob moved closer, stepping towards the heart of the massive trunk.

"Whoa!"

"Jacob!" Aevah darted forward just as she saw him slip and vanish. Rushing to the spot where he had disappeared, she spotted a hole at the tree's base, cleverly hidden by the raised roots. The ground was slick with rain, and it was clear he had lost his footing and slid straight below the great oak.

She crouched, peering into the darkness, but the dim light made it impossible to see.

"Jacob, are you all right?"

"A little bruised and scratched up, but I'm okay. It's pretty dark down here, though, and tight. Stay where you are. I'll try searching a bit."

Ignoring his warning, Aevah secured her bag tightly around her and positioned herself at the opening. Sitting with her legs dangling first, she prepared to slide in after him. Lying flat on her back, she manoeuvred carefully to avoid the sharper roots, then pushed herself down the slippery hole.

Vines brushed against her as she descended, one catching her face. The fall lasted only seconds, but it was unnerving, nonetheless. When her feet finally hit solid ground, she lost her balance and stumbled forward onto the wet, squishy earth.

"I thought I told you to stay put," Jacob called from ahead.

"Where's the fun in that?" Aevah shot back, brushing her hands against her jacket in a futile attempt to dry them.

She rummaged in her bag and pulled out a small candle. Holding it at an angle, she pressed it to the damp earth and drew on her power to ignite the wick. No trackers would be alerted here – not this time.

As the candle's glow flickered to life, the tunnel around her became clearer. Soil and roots enclosed the space in a twisting network, an intricate system woven beneath the mighty tree. The air was thick with the scent of moist soil. Damp from the rain trickled in from above, leaving the ground soggy beneath her boots. The passage was narrow, just tall enough for her to crouch, though not comfortably. Crawling was an option, but she wasn't eager to become any more caked in mud than she already was.

Moving forward as fast as she dared, she followed the winding tunnel, waiting to catch up to Jacob. His shadow stretched ahead of her, and as she neared, she quickened her pace until she was right behind him.

“Here, let me take the candle since I’m leading,” he said, reaching back to take it carefully, avoiding the flame.

With the light now guiding him, Jacob picked up speed, and Aevah kept close behind. As she followed, her mind wandered, turning over the possibilities. *What lay at the end of this tunnel? Would they truly find the shard?*

Lost in thought, she walked straight into Jacob, then jerked upright – only to hit her head against the low ceiling.

“Ow! I hope you stopped without warning for a reason.”

“I warned you,” Jacob said dryly. “You just weren’t listening. As usual.”

“No, you didn’t!”

“Yes, I did. Now quit arguing and pay attention. There’s something ahead.”

At his words, the retort on Aevah’s lips vanished. She craned her neck, trying to see past him.

“What is it?” Even with the flickering candlelight, she could only make out shifting shadows and dirt.

“I don’t know. Here, hold this.”

He handed her the candle and stepped forward. Keeping close, Aevah lifted the light higher, and as the glow stretched ahead, she finally saw what he had. The tunnel ended in a solid dirt wall, but nestled within it was a small alcove. Something was tucked inside.

Jacob reached out, carefully grasping the object, then turned to face her, holding it out.

"Do you think the crystal is inside?" he whispered.

Aevah tentatively touched the metal box. It was smooth and ice-cold beneath her fingertips. She half expected it to spring open at her touch – but it didn't. Frowning, she tried lifting the lid, but it refused to budge.

Determined to get it open, she propped the candle against the wall and gripped the box with both hands. She pulled hard – too hard. The container wrenched free from Jacob's grasp, flipping into the air before landing upside down on the muddy ground with a dull *thud*.

Jacob exhaled sharply. "Maybe we should open this on the surface, where we can actually see what we're doing."

She hesitated and then nodded. He was right. The tunnel was too dark and cramped to examine anything properly. Taking the box, she tucked it securely into her bag.

Grabbing the candle again, she led the way back, crouching as they manoeuvred out of the narrow alcove.

When they reached the base of the chasm, Aevah tilted her head back, staring up at the slippery tunnel leading to the surface. Only now did she realise just how difficult climbing out would be.

Passing Jacob the candle, she dug her fingers into the damp earth and hoisted herself up, but the mud gave way beneath her weight. She slid back down immediately, landing with a frustrated sigh. She tried again. And again. Each time, she barely got a foot off the ground before gravity, and the slick surface pulled her back.

"Try gripping the roots in the walls," Jacob suggested, shining the light over the area. He pointed out some of the thicker, sturdier roots that looked strong enough to hold their weight.

Aevah reached for one, wrapping her fingers around it tightly. With a deep breath, she hauled herself into the tunnel, her arms straining as her legs scrambled to find purchase. Below her, she felt Jacob's steady hands grip her ankles, guiding her feet to a stable foothold. With more security, she continued her climb.

The ascent was gruelling. Sweat beaded on her skin, her muscles burned, and by the time she neared the top, her body trembled with exhaustion. With one final push, she heaved herself onto the sodden grass, collapsing onto her back.

Her breath came in quick, ragged gasps, her heart pounding from the effort. Pain throbbed in her hands – stinging, burning, and aching all at once. Right now, though, she was too spent to care.

"A little help here!"

At Jacob's voice, Aevah groaned but forced herself to sit up. He was nearly out, gripping the edge of the hole. Ignoring the protest of her sore muscles, she crawled to him and grabbed him firmly under his arms. With all the strength she could muster, she pulled. They tumbled onto the wet ground in a heap, both panting.

"Let's never do that again," Jacob said between laboured breaths. "That climb was horrendous."

"Agreed."

They were filthy, soaked in mud, and in desperate need of a wash – not to mention some antiseptic lotion for the countless scratches covering them.

Before either could move, a voice cut through the air.

"Well, well, well. If it isn't the royal children."

Both Aevah and Jacob jolted upright, spinning towards the source of the voice.

Two men stepped forward, advancing with slow, deliberate steps. Aevah's pulse thundered in her ears.

Instinct took over. She and Jacob edged back, but she quickly scanned their surroundings. The horses were too far. If they ran, they would be caught before they even had a chance.

Jacob stepped forward, raising his hands in a gesture of peace. Aevah held back, her eyes darting between the approaching figures, her mind racing for an escape. They were trapped.

"Royals? I think you have mistaken us for someone else," Jacob said, forcing his voice to stay calm. "We are merely travellers, passing through."

The first man scoffed, his brows knitting together as he looked them up and down.

"Ye can't fool us, little prince. The queens have been searchin' for ye both a long time and thanks to those kind folk in that lil' village ye liked to visit, she knows exactly what ye look like."

He pulled out two sketches, holding them up for emphasis. They were eerily accurate.

Aevah's stomach dropped. *Someone from the village had given them away*. No – it couldn't be. Their grandfather had been so careful. He had always insisted they were raised as siblings, with Jacob older than her – not as twins. Yet here was undeniable proof that their identities had been compromised.

The first man took a tentative step forward.

Panic surged through Aevah. Her fingers tightened around her necklace as she threw her power outward. A rush of air surged towards him, freezing him in place.

"What did ye do?" the second man snarled.

Then he charged. Jacob barely had time to react before the attacker was on him. He ducked the first punch, but the second grazed his jaw. The third slammed straight into his gut, knocking the wind from his lungs.

Doubling over, Jacob forced himself upright and swung his knife in retaliation. His opponent was faster. He caught Jacob's wrist, twisted hard, and wrenched the blade from his grasp.

"Aevah—help! Freeze him, too!" Jacob gasped.

"I can't," she cried. "It's taking everything just to hold the first one—if I try more, I might lose control!"

Jacob hardly heard her before a sharp, searing pain shot through his arm. A sickening snap echoed in his ears.

Aevah's heart pounded as she watched the attacker's grip tighten around Jacob's throat. She had to act – now.

Snatching up Jacob's fallen knife, she rushed forward. Her hands shook, but she forced herself to act, slashing the blade across the man's upper arm.

He roared in pain, his grip on Jacob loosening as he clutched at the wound. Spinning around, his furious gaze locked onto her.

"Why, you—"

Before he could finish, there was a loud *thwack*.

A thick branch smashed against the side of his head, jerking it sideways. His knees buckled, and he crumbled, dazed but still upright.

From the shadows, a cloaked figure emerged, striding towards the kneeling man. Without hesitation, they grabbed a fistful of his hair, yanked his head back, and pressed a knife firmly against his throat.

"Look away if you're squeamish."

But neither Jacob nor Aevah could. Their eyes remained locked on the hooded figure as they drew their blade across the attacker's throat in one swift, merciless motion. Blood gushed from the wound as the man clutched at his neck, desperate to stop the bleeding. His efforts were futile. Within moments, he collapsed, lifeless.

Aevah's breath hitched. Her skin turned pale, and her wide eyes remained fixed on the cloaked figure, fear rooting her in place.

"Nice trick," the figure said, turning their attention to her. They gestured towards the other man, who still stood frozen in place. Then, without wavering, they dragged the blade across his throat.

Aevah's stomach lurched as crimson poured down the man's chest like a waterfall. But unlike the first man, this attacker didn't fall. The blood slowed, then stopped altogether, yet the man remained standing – an eerie, nightmarish sight.

"You need to release your hold on the power, young one," the figure continued. "Or he'll stand there forever."

Aevah blinked out of her daze, barely registering their words. She forced herself to let go of the power she had been holding. Immediately, exhaustion crashed over her, and she slumped forward, her limbs trembling from the strain.

The frozen man's body crumbled to the ground with a heavy *thud.*

A ragged gasp sounded behind her. Whipping around, she found Jacob hunched over, rubbing his bruised throat as he fought to catch his breath. His other arm hung limp at his side.

Then his expression shifted – his eyes widening as he looked past her. Aevah spun back to the cloaked figure just as they lowered their hood.

"We meet again."

Aevah stared in confusion, but Jacob exhaled sharply. "Isabella. It's you."

"Thank you," he continued, his voice still hoarse. "How did you find us?"

"I've been following you since we met in the woods," Isabella said, sheathing her blade. "My friends moved on to our hideout, but I stayed behind to make sure you were safe."

Aevah's gaze flicked between them, her confusion deepening. "You two know each other?"

"Yes, sorry," Jacob said, glancing between them. "Aevah, this is Isabella. We crossed paths last week at one of our campsites. Isabella, this is my sister, Aevah."

As they exchanged brief pleasantries, Isabella noted Jacob's pained expression. Without wavering, she rummaged through her bag and pulled out a bandage. Spotting a flat piece of bark nearby, she set it on the ground, then reached for his injured arm. Her hands were steady as she carefully set the broken bone, ignoring his sharp winces and weak attempts to pull away.

Once she finished securing the bandage, Jacob let out a breath and nodded. "Thank you."

Aevah, though still wary after witnessing Isabella's brutal efficiency in dealing with their attackers, felt a slight ease settle over her. At the very least, Isabella didn't seem eager to harm them.

With Jacob feeling somewhat better, he recounted his earlier encounter with Isabella and her friends. In return, Isabella revealed that their aunt, Elinor, had known about Sleights for some time. She and her group had been monitoring the area carefully, keeping a low profile while avoiding the guards. They had been waiting for Jacob and Aevah to surface – though they hadn't been sure if it would be in a quiet moment like this or during a much larger fight to keep them out of Elinor's grasp.

The revelation sent a chill through both Jacob and Aevah. Their safe haven had been compromised. The home they thought was hidden was no longer an option. As the weight of that realisation settled, Isabella inquired about their plans – and, more pointedly, how many crystal shards they had.

Aevah stiffened. Her gaze flicked to Jacob, and she gave him a subtle but meaningful look before tilting her head slightly towards Isabella.

Jacob shrugged apologetically to Isabella and stepped towards his sister.

"What are you doing?" Aevah asked.

"What do you mean?"

"How do you know we can trust her or her friends?"

"Well, for starters, she just saved our lives," Jacob answered. "If she wanted to hand us over to our aunt, why kill the guards and help us?"

"It could be a trap," Aevah countered, voice tight. "Befriend us, gain our trust, then steal the shard for herself. Grandpa warned us that people would do anything for that kind of power."

Jacob exhaled, shaking his head. "I believe she's a friend. And I'm asking you to trust my judgement this time." He shot her a small, teasing grin. "If we end up robbed and left for dead in the woods, I'll take full responsibility."

Aevah scowled, clearly unimpressed. Still, with a reluctant sigh, she moved to stand beside him, following his lead – even if every instinct in her screamed to stay on guard.

"We only have the one," Jacob admitted, "but we're planning to search for the next straightaway."

"That's good. Be sure to keep it safe and with you at all times." Isabella's gaze flicked between them. "Do you know how to cloak it?"

Aevah and Jacob exchanged a glance.

"No," they said in unison.

"If you're both willing, I would be happy to take you to my camp. There are a few channellers there, as well as some people you may recognise who are on your side and are family to you. They can teach you things your grandfather didn't know of."

"Where's this place?" Aevah asked, caution still evident in her voice.

"It's deep in the Dunes of Decessus, somewhere no one in their right mind would willingly go. That's exactly why it's safe. And there are many people there ready to support you."

Jacob watched Aevah, waiting for her response. She wouldn't admit it outright, but he caught the flicker of interest in her eyes at the mention of family. He felt it too – the longing for connection, for answers. They had spent their lives in hiding, with only their grandfather to teach them about their past and their abilities. Now, the idea of meeting others like them, of learning more about the crystal shards, was an opportunity they couldn't ignore.

Aevah gave a curt nod. "Okay. Take us to your camp. I would like to meet these friends of yours."

"Excellent," Isabella said with a smile. "First, though, we should deal with the bodies. We don't want anyone stumbling upon them."

Aevah and Isabella worked quickly, dragging the lifeless bodies towards the hole in the tree. With a final heave, they pushed the corpses inside, covering the opening with fallen leaves and branches to conceal them.

Meanwhile, Jacob did his best to pack up their supplies, working methodically despite the pain in his injured arm. His movements were slower than usual, but he managed to secure everything in their bags. When Aevah and Isabela came to help, he gratefully let them take over.

Once they were finished, Aevah wiped the sweat from her brow and looked at Isabella. Despite Jacob's trust in her, she still felt uncertain. The young woman had saved their lives, but the ease with which she had killed those men unsettled her. *Could she truly be trusted?* Aevah wasn't sure – but for now, Isabella was their best chance at safety.

Resigned to putting faith in her, Aevah said, "We're ready to leave."

"Perfect," Isabella said. "Gather your things, and let's get moving." She darted into the woods, disappearing briefly before returning with her horse.

Aevah couldn't help but stare. The animal was breathtaking – its coat a flawless white, while its mane and tail shimmered like silver. It looked almost ethereal.

"This is Moonbeam," Isabella said, patting the mare's neck. "She's got me out of more tangles than I care to admit."

"She's magnificent," Aevah replied before motioning to their own horses. "This is Whisp, and that's Storm," she added, gesturing to hers and Jacob's mounts in turn. "They are war trained. We haven't had to test them much, but if trouble ever comes, I would like to think they will help us through it."

"Let's hope it never comes to that," Isabella said as she swung into her saddle. "Ready?"

Without a second thought, Jacob and Aevah mounted their horses. They urged them into a fast trot, quickly catching up to Isabella.

As they followed her lead, Aevah fought to keep her expression neutral, but she couldn't suppress the excitement building inside her. For the first time in a long while, they weren't just running. They were heading towards something – towards allies, towards answers. Towards family.

Chapter 30

The Dunes of Decessus

As they neared the sands, Aevah felt the temperature shift almost immediately. The air grew drier, and the heat settled against her skin – warmer than what she was accustomed to. Yet, she found it pleasant, a welcome embrace of the sun's warmth. She shrugged off her jacket, savouring the golden light.

The clothing here was different too, more colourful and more revealing than in other parts of the country. The higher temperatures left little need for layers, and the locals dressed accordingly. Loose linens, silk tunics, and flowing dresses draped over bodies in airy, effortless fashion. Children dashed about in light fabrics of every shade, their legs bare and unencumbered. Some had scarves wrapped around their heads, while others wore wide-brimmed hats for shade. Nearly everyone carried a fan, and many were displayed for sale at the market stalls they passed.

Curious, Aevah stopped at one. The table before her held an array of designs – bamboo, silk, and paper, each painted or woven with intricate patterns.

"Need something for the heat, dear?" the stall keeper asked with a warm smile.

"Yes, please," Aevah replied, listening as the woman explained the benefits of each style. After some consideration, she selected a bamboo fan and purchased an extra for Jacob. Isabella already had one. As she tested it out, a wave of cool air brushed her face, offering instant relief.

They continued their journey, the landscape shifting around them. The grass, where it grew, was coarser than the soft greenery of home. Patches of dry, cracked earth spread beneath them, interrupted by bursts of wildflowers – vivid splashes of colour in the flat terrain. Even the plants had an unusual toughness to them, their leaves thick and waxy as if shielding themselves from the relentless sun.

Dust billowed around the horses' hooves as they rode, rising in golden clouds along the parched roads. Sunbaked cobblestones formed a winding path through the town, where white and beige stone houses stood in neat rows beneath sandy-yellow rooftops. Their walls reflected the heat, while the doors and window frames were painted in an array of striking colours, transforming the streets into a living mosaic.

As they walked deeper into town, Isabella paused at a merchant's stall, picking out a thicker scarf for both Aevah and Jacob, along with a headscarf in the same style.

"You'll need these in the desert. When the wind picks up, they'll protect you from the swirling sand."

At another stall, Isabella bought two fine mesh fly masks for the horses, along with lightweight body blankets and protective boots for their hooves.

"They may not like wearing these at first," she admitted, "but they'll shield them from the heat and sand."

Aevah nodded, running a hand over the soft mesh of one of the masks. "How dangerous is the desert?" she asked.

"Very, if you're unprepared," Isabella replied. "The weather is unforgiving, water is scarce, and without proper navigation, you can easily get lost. Many have perished in the desert's belly."

Aevah and Jacob exchanged nervous glances.

"You'll be safe with me," Isabella assured them. "Don't fret. I know these dunes well, and more importantly, I respect the land. That's the key. If you believe yourself to be far greater than nature, it will make you pay—whether through mind games or sandstorms, it always wins."

"Mind games?" Jacob asked, frowning.

"We call them mirage beasts," Isabella explained. "The grains show you what you most desire and lead you astray. It feels like paradise until the sands take you."

"This doesn't sound like a place we should be going," Aevah muttered.

Isabella laughed. "Relax. I tell you this to warn you, not to scare you. Heat, hunger, and thirst can make people see things that aren't there. But no harm will come to you if you listen to me. Deep within the desert, there's a secure village we have built. You'll be safe there."

"And you promise to keep these mirage beasts away from us?" Jacob asked.

Isabella smirked. "Yes, as long as you stay close by my side."

Aevah exhaled and nodded. "All right, then."

"I want to leave shortly, but the horses need proper care before the journey," Isabella said. "While they rest, I'll gather more supplies. You're free to explore in the meantime."

They followed her to a local stable, where the horses were left to eat and rest. A stable hand inspected their hooves, ensuring their shoes were steady enough for the rough, sunbaked terrain they would soon face.

Although Isabella had given them leave to explore, neither Aevah nor Jacob strayed far from her side. The bustling market brimmed with goods familiar and strange. Exotic fruits with spiky rinds and jewel-toned skins sat in woven baskets, their scents thick in the warm air. Vegetables of unusual shapes and textures lay in neat rows, their uses unknown to the twins. They marvelled at the vibrant array, their curiosity outweighing their apprehension – at least for the moment.

Before leaving, Isabella glanced at Jacob, frowning at the poorly wrapped break she had attempted to keep straight.

"Before we go anywhere, you need that bandaged properly. When we reach our destination, one of the healers can mend it, but for now, a firmer wrapping will help."

Jacob nodded, and together they followed her to a small infirmary. Inside, a young healer examined his arm and expertly secured it with a proper bandage, supporting it with a well-shaped wooden splint – far better than Isabella's makeshift attempt.

Aevah watched in fascination, noting from Jacob's expression that the pain head eased significantly now that it was properly set.

"Better?" she asked.

"Much," he replied, offering a genuine smile.

With Jacob's arm tended to, they returned to the stables to check on the horses. Once satisfied with the preparations, Isabella paid the workers and turned to the twins.

"The sands begin a few miles ahead. We should prepare the horses now in case the wind picks up, and the sand catches us early."

Aevah and Jacob watched as Isabella readied her horse, fastening the mesh mask, draping the lightweight blanket, and ensuring the special shoes were fitted to protect against the harsh sun and rough terrain. Following her lead, Aevah carefully prepared her own horse, managing it well with Isabella's guidance. Once she was settled in the saddle, Isabella helped Jacob do the same. Before long, they were on their way once more.

As they rode deeper into the desert, Aevah became acutely aware of the absence of shade. Nothing surrounded them but endless dunes stretching in every direction, the golden waves of sand undisturbed except by the wind. She had never seen a desert before, only read about them in books, and had never truly understood how lifeless they could be. Now, as the vast emptiness closed in around her, she understood why so many had died out here.

The relentless sun bore down on them, her clothes clinging uncomfortably to her sweat-dampened skin. Just as her thoughts began to spiral and exhaustion crept in, Isabella signalled for a stop. With the twins' help, she quickly erected a small shelter, offering a much-needed pocket of shade. They tended to the horses first, making sure they were watered and positioned out of direct sunlight before settling down themselves to eat and drink.

Aevah's thirst was overwhelming, but she resisted the urge to gulp down her water. Isabella had already warned them – drinking too quickly could do more harm than good. Their rations had to last for at least a couple of days before they reached their next destination, and the nearest watering hole was still a long ride away.

"The food we brought will help keep you hydrated," Isabella reassured them. "They'll replace the fluids and salts you're sweating out. Just pace yourself, and your body will adjust."

With no choice but to trust her, Aevah tucked into the provisions she had been given. Alongside dried meat and rice were slices of cucumber and watermelon – refreshing and full of moisture. Isabella had been right; after eating, Aevah felt noticeably better, and the shade provided a welcome respite from the harsh sun.

Beside her, Jacob also seemed more at ease, his earlier fatigue lifting. Neither of them was used to this kind of heat, but they had no choice but to endure it.

As Aevah gazed across the shimmering dunes, something flickered at the edge of her vision. She blinked, rubbed her eyes, and looked again. There it was – a tiny, glimmering shape darting out of the sand before vanishing just as quickly.

"What was that?" Aevah cried out, pointing to the spot where the tiny creature had vanished.

Everyone turned in the direction she indicated, eyes scanning the sand. A moment later, the miniature creature reappeared, its delicate wings fluttering before it dived beneath the surface once more.

"Ah, that's an Ember Drake," Isabella said. "Cute little things, but they can burn you if you're not careful."

The drake hovered near them, its glowing eyes fixed on the food in Aevah's hands. Moving closer, it snatched a piece of dried meat, tossing it into the air before opening its mouth and catching it with precision. Amused, Aevah let out a laugh, but the sound startled the creature. With a frightened squeak, it darted away, disappearing into the sand.

Once they were ready to continue, Aevah and Jacob helped Isabella pack up their supplies and mounted their horses once more. They would ride late into the night, stopping only when they found a natural shelter where they could rest before sunrise. Isabella had planned their route carefully, ensuring they travelled during the cooler hours and rested during the most intense heat of the day. If all went well, they would reach the village by the following nightfall.

As they pressed on, more Ember Drakes emerged, their scales flickering like embers in the sunlight. The tiny creatures flitted about curiously, drawn to the movement of the travellers. They hovered close before darting away as if testing the group's presence.

"They're harmless unless provoked," Isabella explained. "They thrive in this heat, using their fiery breath to hunt small prey. If they don't see you as a threat, they can be quite mischievous."

Aevah and Jacob watched in fascination as a group of Ember Drakes played a game of chase, their flaming tails leaving glowing trails in the air. Despite their small size, they were quick and agile, weaving between the travellers and their horses with ease. Their presence added an unexpected magic to the otherwise gruelling journey, momentarily distracting the twins from the harshness of the desert.

By the time dusk arrived, the temperature had shifted dramatically. The blistering heat had vanished, replaced by an icy chill that crept over the dunes. Aevah shivered, hastily pulling her cloak and wrapping it tightly around her shoulders. She had never imagined a place so scorching by day could turn so frigid by night.

Despite the cold, the desert at night was breathtaking. Above them, the sky stretched endlessly, a sea of stars twinkling like diamonds against the vast darkness. The sand, kissed by starlight, shimmered faintly, reflecting the celestial glow. It was a beauty, unlike anything Aevah had ever seen. If not for the biting cold, it would have been perfect.

After hours of riding, Aevah was utterly exhausted, her body swaying in the saddle as sleep tugged at her. Each time she dozed off without realising it, a sudden jolt would snap her awake. She longed to lie down, if only for a few hours. Thankfully, moments later, Isabella pulled her horse to a stop.

"This is it," she said, dismounting.

With relief flooding her limbs, Aevah slid off her horse, barely able to keep her balance. Moving sluggishly, she followed Isabella's instructions, helping tend to the horses and setting up the shade. The moment her bedroll was unrolled, she collapsed onto it with a grateful sigh. Sleep claimed her instantly.

She didn't stir until she felt someone shaking her awake. Blinking groggily, she opened her eyes to the soft glow of dawn breaking across the horizon – and Isabella's grinning face.

"Wake up, sleepyhead. We need to get moving before the heat becomes unbearable. We'll stop just before midday to take shelter from the worst of the sun."

Rubbing her eyes, Aevah sat up and looked around. Nearby, Jacob crouched beside a small pool of water, splashing his face and neck.

"It's real," Isabella assured her, noticing the disbelief on her face. "An underground spring feeds it."

Without hesitation, Aevah scrambled over, falling to her knees beside Jacob. She drank deeply, relishing the coolness of the water before filling her bottles to the brim.

"I kind of want to stay here," Jacob joked.

"Same," Aevah admitted, wiping her mouth. "Hopefully, the village has springs like this and decent shade from the heat." Her mind drifted, envisioning fresh water and cool stone buildings shielding her from the persistent sun.

"Come on, you two," Isabella called, already preparing her horse. "We don't have hours to waste."

Their horses, too, had taken full advantage of the spring, drinking their fill. Once they had eaten and been saddled, the group was ready to move on. Aevah, however, felt a gnawing apprehension. The day was only going to get hotter.

A breeze stirred the air as they set out. Under normal circumstances, she might have welcomed it, but here, it carried the sand with it. The tiny, stinging grains lashed against her skin and irritated her eyes. Grimacing, she pulled her scarf up over her nose and mouth, shielding herself as best she could from the desert's harsh embrace.

Mounted once more and as protected as possible from the elements, Aevah fell in line behind the others. The journey stretched on in a seemingly endless expanse of shimmering sand, the heat pressing down on them like a physical weight.

By midday, the sun blazed overhead, merciless in its intensity. Finally, Isabella signalled for them to stop. Grateful beyond words, Aevah slid from her saddle and helped set up a shaded rest area. The moment she was out of the direct sunlight, a wave of relief washed over her. She pulled down her scarf, inhaling deeply as she savoured the reprieve.

Jacob seemed to share her sentiments, already lying on his back with his eyes closed, arms sprawled out as he soaked in the brief rest.

Sipping her water, Aevah gazed out over the endless dunes. The desert was a land of contradictions – both beautiful and merciless. By daylight, it was a shimmering golden sea, its rippling sands forming an ever-changing masterpiece against the sky. Yet, to traverse it was to test one's endurance against an unrelenting force. It drained her, challenged her, and left her wondering how anyone could call this place home. She wouldn't wish this journey on her worst enemy.

All too soon, Isabella urged them back into the saddle. "This is the final stretch," she assured them.

With determination, Aevah pressed on, fighting against the whipping sands as the wind howled around them. Each step of her horse sent puffs of dust swirling into the air, making it harder to see. Then, as they neared a towering sand dune, Isabella pointed ahead.

"There," she said. "That's the spot."

Aevah squinted towards the dune's base. For a moment, she thought she was imagining things. A lone figure sat there, unmoving, waiting. She shook her head, convinced it was just another mirage. But as they drew closer, the shape remained – solid and real.

Someone was there.

Chapter 31

New Friends

As they approached, the figure rose to greet them, and Isabella waved in response. When they reached him, she dismounted and embraced the stranger.

Jacob and Aevah climbed down from their horses, waiting to be introduced to Isabella's friend.

"Isabella, you made it, and with new friends," the man said, lowering his mask. Jacob now saw a man in his late forties with a slim, tanned face. Faint wrinkles lined his eyes, deepening when he smiled.

"I did. It's certainly good to be back. I always feel safest here," Isabella replied.

"Many do."

"Jacob, Aevah, I want you to meet Isaac Turner. He is the village leader and a descendant of Grace Turner—the woman who fled with the princess all those years ago."

Jacob stared in awe at the man before him. He knew the story well – the tale of how Princess Mary had escaped with trusted members of the court, seeking refuge from her brother after he seized the throne. It had been a favourite of his and Aevah's, one their grandfather often told.

Yet none of those tales had ever mentioned a hidden village in the Dunes of Decessus. It must have been cleverly concealed if this place had remained a secret for so long, even from his grandfather. *What other secrets lay buried here – secrets unknown even to the priestesses who worshipped the divine spirit in their temples?* If any place could offer them the aid they desperately needed, it was surely this one.

"I'm delighted to meet you both," Isaac said warmly.

"And you," Jacob replied. "We had no idea this place existed."

Isaac smiled knowingly. "It's our little secret—and one that has never been more vital than it is now, with the current queen on the throne. Elinor lacks the values of the past and future royals," he added, his gaze shifting between them.

"We'll talk more inside. Isaac, share your trick with them so they may enter. I, for one, am ready for a nice cold dip in the spring after wandering the desert," Isabella urged, eager to return home.

Isaac chuckled and led them up the sandy hill. The climb proved tricky for Jacob, who kept skidding back with each step. Eventually, though, he managed to stand beside the others. Yet all he could see ahead was more sand. His shoulders sagged at the thought that none of it was real.

Isaac stepped between him and Aevah, extending his hands for them to take. Jacob, intrigued, grasped Isaac's hand first. Aevah hesitated, pulling a sceptical face before reluctantly following suit.

They walked forward, and instantly, the air thickened around them. It was like stepping into an unseen fog, dense and heavy. Each movement felt sluggish as if they were wading through pools of honey, a force actively pushing them back.

Though the barrier was invisible, ripples of wind twisted around Jacob, distorting his surroundings. He pushed forward, muscles straining against the unseen resistance. One hand gripped Isaac's tightly, and the other clung to his horse's reins. Every step was a battle.

After what felt like minutes of struggling, his foot suddenly met solid ground. The shift was so abrupt that when the resistance vanished, he stumbled and fell face-first into the sand.

Sitting up, he coughed and spat out the gritty residue that clung to his tongue. Grabbing his water flask, he took a swig, swirled it in his mouth, and spat it out before wiping his face on the back of his sleeve – the only part of him not covered in dust.

Then he looked up and froze.

Moments ago, there had been nothing but endless dunes. Now, stretching before him was something impossible.

A lush oasis village stood nestled in the heart of the Dunes of Decessus. He blinked, rubbed his eyes, and stared again. But the vision didn't change. It was real.

"Welcome to Dunes Rest," Isaac said, motioning them forward.

Jacob and Aevah followed in stunned silence, with Isabella trailing behind. Wherever Jacob looked, his gaze was filled with wonder. Towering date palms swayed gently in the breeze, their fronds casting dappled shadows on the ground. Olive trees stood in orderly rows, their silvery leaves glinting in the sunlight. Nearby, a sprawling fig tree stretched its broad branches, heavy with ripe, purple fruit. Vibrant citrus groves added splashes of colour with their clusters of oranges and lemons.

The air was rich with the sweet fragrance of desert lilies, their delicate white petals stark against the rugged landscape. Aloe vera plants dotted the terrain, their thick, spiky leaves a testament to life's resilience in the dunes.

The stark contrast between this hidden paradise and the merciless desert beyond was nothing short of breathtaking.

As they walked, the sound of trickling water, birdsong, and children's laughter filled Jacob's ears. Glancing around, he saw youngsters playing and wandering about, many of them appearing to be around his and Aevah's age.

"There are a lot of twins here and children our age in general. Why is that?" he asked.

Issac tensed before answering. "The queen hunts those around your age. Trackers find them and bring them to her if they match your appearance."

Aevah gasped. "What does she do to them?"

"She… disposes of them, just in case."

"No!" Jacob and Aevah exclaimed in unison.

"Unfortunately, yes. Thankfully, rebel groups across the country intercept these travellers when possible, bringing them here to safety."

Jacob studied the faces around him more carefully. Many bore similarities – features that could have easily resembled their own. A chill ran through him at the thought of how far his aunt would go to capture them. His heart ached for those who had already been taken in their place.

"We have to stop her," he said, his voice firm.

Aevah touched his arm. "We will," she added, her eyes reflecting the same unwavering resolve.

As they continued through the village, Jacob's mind raced with thoughts of their homeland and what needed to be done. The lush greenery and vibrant life here made the village feel like a sanctuary, a stark contrast to the unforgiving desert beyond. But people shouldn't have to brave such treacherous lands just to find peace and safety. Knowing what his aunt was doing to children like him and Aevah. He felt an overwhelming urgency to protect this place and its people from her tyranny.

Further into the village, he spotted buffalo grazing peacefully in a grassy enclosure, their massive forms striking against the oasis backdrop. Chickens clucked and pecked at the ground while pigs wallowed contentedly in the shade. The village was a bustling hub of life – an island of abundance and tranquillity in the heart of the desert.

Issac led them to a small stone house, similar to those Jacob had seen in towns along their journey. Isabella took Jacob and Aevah's horses while Isaac welcomed them inside.

The interior was surprisingly cool, spacious, and vibrant. Though it contained fewer traditional furnishings, the open space was adorned with plush pillows and a large circular rug. The walls were decorated with intricate hangings, and a small round table – perfect for someone seated on the floor – held a jug and a couple of empty glasses.

"This is my home. Please, make yourselves comfortable," Isaac said, gesturing for them both to take a seat.

Grateful to be out of the sun, Jacob sank onto a circular purple pillow and removed his scarf and hat, brushing away the lingering flecks of sand clinging to his clothes. Beside him, Aevah did the same.

Isaac brought over fresh, cool water and glasses for them to drink from. Moments later, a woman emerged from an arched doorway carrying a tray of food. She placed it in front of the twins with a warm smile before taking a seat. As Jacob observed, he noticed Isaac making subtle movements with his fingers while looking at her. She responded in kind, using her hands to relay information. This was something Jacob had never seen before.

"Your friend… she is deaf?" Aevah asked Isaac, though she smiled warmly at the woman as she spoke.

"Yes. Apologies, I was about to introduce you all. Jacob, Aevah, this is my wife, Niamh." As he spoke, he signed the words to her, and she signed back.

"She says it's a pleasure to meet you both and hopes you're not too tired from your journey," Isaac translated.

"Thank you. We are grateful for your warm welcome," Jacob said.

"Yes, thank you. You have a beautiful home," Aevah added.

Niamh signed again, and Isaac translated. "She expresses her thanks to you both and says we can all talk later. For now, eat and rest. The desert is a tiring place to travel, especially for those not used to the heat."

Not ones to refuse food, Jacob and Aevah eagerly devoured everything before them. The spread was both refreshing and nourishing, perfectly suited to the tropical climate. Bowls of fragrant rice, infused with a blend of spices and herbs, were topped with tender pieces of grilled lamb. Platters overflowed with juicy dates, figs, and pomegranates, their natural sweetness a welcome indulgence. Freshly baked flatbreads were served alongside creamy hummus and smoky baba ghanoush, complementing the crisp, cool salads of cucumber, tomato, and mint.

Aevah savoured the taste of a ripe mango, its juice trickling down her chin as she bit into it. Meanwhile, Jacob enjoyed a refreshing drink made from chilled coconut water, its natural sweetness quenching his thirst. The meal was a vibrant array of colours and flavours, far richer than what they were accustomed to. He sampled everything, but most of all, he was grateful for the abundance of water after having to ration it in the desert. Encouraged by Niamh, he drank plenty, reassured that their supply was plentiful.

After they finished eating and exchanged light conversation, Isaac showed them where they could wash up before leading them to a guest room they were welcome to use.

Once they had washed and dressed, Jacob and Aevah returned to their seats on the pillows. Soon after, Isabella entered the house and settled beside them. With everyone gathered, they listened as Isaac spoke about the village and the measures taken to keep it hidden, even to this day.

They were both amazed to learn its history, especially the fact that no one could enter without the keeper's guidance the first time. After that, they would be free to come and go as they pleased – but they could never reveal the village's location. The ancient charm cast long ago ensured it.

Isaac's unique lineage, along with the royal bloodline, was bound to this place. However, only the keeper had the power to share its location. Princess Mary had taken precautions to ensure that none of her own family could accidentally find it, knowing the lengths her brother would go to in pursuit of his goals. This made it impossible for Elinor to ever stumble upon the village, especially since Isaac no longer left its safety. The farthest he ever travelled was to the outskirts where he had met them, solely to bring in newcomers.

Despite these restrictions, Issac assured them he didn't mind his circumstances. He lived in a beautiful place, and his presence safeguarded his people – something far more important to him than wandering beyond the village's borders. Unlike him, those granted entry were free to come and go, ensuring that Dunes Rest never lacked anything it needed. Additionally, the protective barrier surrounding the settlement shielded it from the worst of the midday heat and the ferocity of desert sandstorms, making it one of the safest havens in the region.

An underground spring provided a constant supply of fresh water for the villagers. Combined with their ability to channel the power, growing crops was effortless. This allowed them to cultivate food much faster than a traditional farm that relied on natural growth cycles and favourable weather conditions for a good harvest.

Isaac suddenly grinned. "How about a tour? If you're both up to it, I would love to show you around and properly introduce you to my home—Dunes Rest. An apt name, don't you think?"

Jacob looked at Aevah, who was already nodding enthusiastically.

"Yes, please. I would love to see your home. Right, Jacob?"

"Certainly. Let's go."

As everyone rose, Isaac gestured for them to follow him outside. He guided them through the village, describing daily life and the balance the people maintained with the land – taking only what they needed while preserving the ecosystem so it could sustain them for generations to come.

His pride was unmistakable. Jacob could hear it in his voice and see it in the way he interacted with the villagers. He enjoyed meeting everyone, but nothing compared to the moment when he and Aevah encountered familiar faces – members of their own family.

"Aevah, Jacob, I want you to meet some of your relatives… your cousins," Isaac said, gesturing towards the three young adults standing before them.

"You've already met Isabella, and these are Edward and Bryne Goodman," he introduced.

Edward and Bryne bore a strong resemblance to each other, both having olive skin and brown eyes. However, while Bryne had shoulder-length curly hair, Edward's was shaved short. Edward was also a couple of years older and had a bulkier build.

Jacob's eyes widened, his grin stretching from ear to ear. "We're cousins?" he asked, glancing between Edward, Bryne, and Isabella. "Why didn't you say something?"

Isabella hesitated before responding. "I wasn't sure how you would react or if you would even believe me. We haven't seen each other since you were very little. I knew you wouldn't recognise me after all these years."

Bryne stepped forward, extending a hand. "It's nice to finally meet you both."

"Indeed," Edward added. "You were barely seven years old when we last saw you." He smiled warmly as he took in their faces. "You've certainly grown since then." He let out a hearty laugh.

Aevah looked between them all, practically bouncing in excitement. "I can't believe it. This is wonderful!"

"It is," Jacob agreed. "And I think we have a lot to catch up on."

Edward gestured for them to follow. "Come, let's talk at my home."

He led them to a house built in the same style as the others in the village, with white stone walls and beautifully vibrant furnishings that made it feel warm and inviting. Inside, Edward's wife sat reading a book. He introduced her as Sage and gently pointed towards the bassinet where their baby lay peacefully sleeping.

After introductions, they all settled onto the cushions, exchanging stories of their lives since their last meeting. Jacob and Aevah listened with heavy hearts as their cousins spoke of the loss of their parents, while Edward and Bryne, in turn, expressed their sorrow over the death of Jacob and Aevah's father. They also vowed to help in any way they could to find their mother.

The conversation soon shifted to Elinor's reign and the efforts to remove her from power. The Goodmans exchanged glances, seeming to silently agree on something before Edward spoke.

"A group was formed not long after Elinor's coronation. Our family started it."

"It originally focused on keeping tabs on her and trying to find you," he continued. "But your grandfather hid you both so well that no one could track you down. You were safe in the family cottage all these years. Many believed you were dead, and, in a way, that worked to our advantage."

"It allowed the group to operate right under Elinor's nose as she shaped the kingdom in her own image, hunting for the crystal shards and for you," Isabella added.

"And for those who look like us," Jacob muttered, his shoulders slumping under the weight of the truth.

"Yes," Edward acknowledged. "But thanks to our rebel group, many have managed to escape to this village, where they are safe. None of this is your fault, Jacob. This is all Elinor's doing."

Sensing the sombre mood settling over the room, Isabella decided to lighten the atmosphere by sharing humorous stories about their parents from years past. Laughter soon filled the space as everyone took turns telling their own tales and amusing memories. For the first time in what felt like forever, Jacob found himself truly at ease, laughing until his sides ached. Beside him,

Aevah threw her head back, guffawing at one of Bryne's jokes, her entire body shaking with mirth.

As the evening wore on, they eventually said their goodbyes. Walking back to Isaac and Niamh's home, Jacob and Aevah linked arms, enjoying the cool night air. Above them, countless stars twinkled in the sky, a peaceful end to an eventful day.

Chapter 32

Training

Aevah had thought she understood the power, but she had been wrong. There was so much more to it than what her grandfather had taught her – or what she had bothered to take in. Learning from him had felt like a chore, with his lessons rigid and monotonous, filled with endless repetition. She often found herself rolling her eyes, impatient for the lecture to end so she could finally practise.

With Elara, everything was different. She spoke of the elements with a spark of excitement, weaving stories that made the lore come alive. She encouraged Aevah to feel the power, to connect with it on a deeper level rather than simply control it. Each lesson was an adventure, revealing something new every day.

Regret settled in Aevah's chest as she thought back to all the times she had dismissed her grandfather's teachings – the customs she should have honoured. But with Elara, she was determined to make up for lost time. She would master the power, not just for herself, but to prove to her grandfather that she could.

Sometimes, as Elara explained a concept, vague recollections of her grandfather's lessons surfaced in Aevah's mind, fragments of knowledge she had absorbed without realising. She had learned from him – just not as much as she could have. Yet, in only a few short weeks under Elara's guidance, her strength and control had advanced by leaps and bounds. She could wield far more complex techniques without feeling drained after mere minutes.

More than that, she sensed her connection to the land with newfound clarity. The fear that had once held her back had faded, replaced by openness and understanding. Still, the realisation of how little control she had possessed in the beginning filled her with embarrassment. Especially when she struggled with something Elara made look effortless. Frustration often followed, leading to missteps, but she pushed forward, determined to bridge the gap between what she had been and what she was becoming.

One mistake in particular haunted Aevah – the fire from her first week of training.

She had stood in the sand, the morning sun beating down relentlessly. The heat had been oppressive, the dry air making every inhale feel like a struggle. Elara watched her closely, a gentle smile of encouragement on her face.

"Focus, Aevah," Elara said softly. "Remember, fire reflects your inner state. If you are calm, so is the flame."

Aevah took a slow breath, trying to steady her racing heart. She closed her eyes and visualised a tiny spark in her palm. That part was easy. The hard part was keeping it there, shaping it, controlling it. Slowly, a flicker of flame appeared, dancing gently in the air. But the moment doubt crept into her mind, everything unravelled.

The fire spread, surging beyond her grasp. It engulfed her senses, and suddenly, she wasn't standing in the sand anymore. She was back in her childhood, surrounded by flames. The glow of the burning wood, the searing heat licking at her skin, the crackle of destruction – she saw it all as if it were happening again. The fire in her palm flared wildly, more and more sparks forming on the sand. She froze, eyes wide, unable to move. She could still see her grandfather running towards her, his power quelling the inferno before it could consume everything.

Then, just as before, Elara stepped in, swiftly moving around her, mirroring his actions. The flames shrank under her control until they were gone. A heavy silence settled between them as Aevah stood trembling, her breath shallow.

Elara studied her with concern. "Where were you just then?" she asked gently. "You called out for your grandfather. You said you lost control."

Aevah swallowed hard. "I… don't know. I—" Her voice caught in her throat. "A fire. There was a fire when I was a child. I didn't remember it until now."

Elara moved closer, taking Aevah's hands in her own. Her eyes held both sympathy and understanding.

"This could be why you struggled to progress with your grandfather," she said. "It wasn't his teaching that held you back—it was your fear. You buried the memory, but it was still there, keeping you from fully connecting with your power. The more you feared losing control, the weaker your command became."

Frustration boiled up inside Aevah, spilling over before she could stop it. "How am I supposed to control my fear?" she snapped. "You saw what happened. I could kill someone with these flames."

Elara didn't flinch. Instead, she placed a reassuring hand on Aevah's shoulder. "With practice," she said calmly. "It's about learning to overcome your anxieties, to trust in yourself and your abilities. Come, let's try a different approach."

They moved to a safer area, far from the village, and sat in the hot sand. Elara guided her through a series of breathing exercises.

"Inhale peace, exhale tension," she instructed. "Find the calm within you. Trust in yourself. Your past does not define you. You are the creator of your will and the architect of your future. Create it."

Aevah closed her eyes and focused on her breath. Slowly, a sense of tranquillity washed over her. The anger and frustration ebbed, replaced by quiet determination. Elara was right. Without realising it, she had been holding herself back all this time. The fire had been an accident, but if she continued to cling to her fear, she would never move forward.

So, she let go.

She accepted that she was in control of her power – not the other way around.

Opening her eyes, she tried again, this time with a clearer mind. The flame flickered to life, steady and controlled. She shaped it, letting it grow and shrink at will. Then she let it spread around her, guiding it, keeping it contained, preventing it from multiplying. With a deep breath, she drew the fire back into herself, watching as the last embers faded.

Aevah smiled, a surge of confidence rising within her. "I did it," she whispered.

Elara nodded, pride shining in her eyes. "Yes, you did. Fire is a powerful ally, but it demands respect and balance. Keep practising, and you'll master it."

And so, she did.

Over the next few weeks, Aevah dedicated herself to her training. She spent her days learning under Elara's guidance and her mornings meditating with Niamh. At sunrise, she and Niamh would sit in quiet reflection, practising deep breathing, finding peace within herself, and learning to remain calm even in the face of difficulty.

The two teachings intertwined, enhancing not only her control but also her confidence. With each lesson, every breath, and every flicker of flame, she felt herself growing – stronger, steadier, and ready to embrace the power that had once terrified her.

Each day, Aevah became more powerful, her mastery over fire improving as she learned to manage her emotions. Although there were setbacks and moments of doubt when frustration threatened to take hold, she persevered with the unwavering support of her mentors.

A couple of months into her training, as the sun dipped below the desert dunes, she stood before a controlled bonfire, its flames roaring high into the twilight sky. A protective ring of stones encircled the fire, and atop it sat a large black pot, steam rising as rice boiled within.

She took a deep breath, steadying herself. This was a test – not just of skill but of the balance she had cultivated within.

With a focused mind and a calm heart, she extended her hands towards the flame.

The flames responded immediately, bending and swirling in a mesmerising dance. They leapt from stone to stone, growing and shrinking inside at her will. Aevah felt the fire as an extension of herself, no longer a force to be feared but a part of her she had come to understand. Joy surged through her. She had done it. She had mastered fire.

As the flames settled, Elara and Niamh approached, their faces beaming with pride.

"You've come so far, Aevah," Niamh signed, her expression warm. "Your journey is just beginning, but you have proven your strength and resilience."

"Thank you," Aevah said, her smile wide as she pulled them both into a tight embrace. "I couldn't have done it without." She signed the words as best she could. In her short time here, she had picked up a little of Niamh's language, though some of her translations were still clumsy. But Niamh was skilled at reading lips, so even when Aevah's hand signals faltered, she understood.

"We are only guides," Elara said with a gentle smile. "It was your hard work and determination that brought you here."

"Yes," Niamh signed. "Be proud of yourself. You earned this."

Elara nodded, her eyes shining. "And remember, the road ahead may be challenging, but you have the power within you to face whatever comes. Trust in yourself and your abilities."

Niamh added, "And never forget, you are not alone. Even when we are not by your side, your teachings will be."

Aevah smiled, warmth filling her chest. She had come so far, and for the first time, she truly believed in her own strength.

As they sat down to share their meal, the conversation turned to Aevah's progress since she had arrived. Laughter and stories filled the evening, a moment of peace before the challenges to come.

Over the next week, she pushed herself further, determined to refine her abilities and be ready for whatever lay ahead. Each day brought new lessons and fresh obstacles to overcome – but with Elara and Niamh by her side, she felt more capable than ever.

Especially when it came to her aunt, that was one challenge she was ready to face.

***

As Aevah delved deeper into the ways of the power, Jacob focused on his training. For the past couple of months, he had been working tirelessly with Master Arin, honing his skills with the sword. He wasn't a complete novice – his grandfather had taught him the basics – but those lessons had never prepared him for the sheer stamina and strength required to face a real opponent.

Master Arin was determined to make a warrior out of him. From the moment the sun rose, Jacob was put to work, practising with wooden swords. The training was gruelling. His muscles ached relentlessly, and yet, bit by bit, he saw himself improving.

Each morning began with a run, followed by relentless drills until the midday heat made it unbearable. Then came the village tasks – feeding animals, gathering fruit, harvesting crops – before returning to training when the air cooled. Evening sessions focused on building his physical strength and endurance with weight training and more running. By the time he washed up each night, exhaustion had claimed him, and he fell into bed without much thought of anything else.

He and Aevah scarcely saw each other, both caught up in their own rigorous instruction. Still, they made an effort to share their midday meal and catch up when everyone gathered for supper. As difficult as the training was, Jacob found himself enjoying his time in Dunes Rest. Surrounded by so many new faces – his own kin among them – he no longer felt alone. The village reminded him of Sleights, the close-knit community that had once felt like home. But where Sleights had been a place of extended family, Dunes Rest felt like something more. It felt like belonging.

A sudden, searing sting tore through his abdomen, yanking him from his thoughts. He gasped, doubling over as pain radiated from the spot where the wooden sword had struck. His fingers clenched around his upped knee as he tried to redirect the discomfort, his other hand clutching his stomach. The training weapons might not have been real, but they hurt plenty.

"Ow," he gritted out.

"That'll teach you to pay attention." Master Arin's voice was firm but not unkind. "Zone out like that in real combat, and you'd be dead, you would."

Jacob barely had time to recover before the older man took his stance again. "Again. Come at me, but this time, try an' surprise me, eh?"

Jacob straightened, brows furrowed. *Surprise him?* Easier said than done. Master Arin was an expert, impossibly sharp, and more than once, Jacob had been convinced the man could read minds. He always knew what Jacob was about to do before he even did it.

Still, Jacob got into position, his body tensed for the attack. He feigned right, only to shift left at the last moment, but Arin moved with him effortlessly – his form fluid, his strikes precise. They clashed again and again, Jacob's body slick with sweat as he struggled to keep pace.

He was holding his own, but barely. He was on the defensive now, forced to counter each of Arin's strikes rather than make his own.

"Come on, boy! Is that all ye got?" Arin taunted, pressing forward, his attacks growing faster and harder with every swing.

Jacob's muscles screamed in protest. His wrists burned with the effort of keeping hold of his sword, every part of him begging to surrender. But he did not yield.

With the next strike, Jacob let out a fierce yell, putting all his strength into the clash. The swords met with a sharp crack, and though Arin pushed, Jacob held his ground. His feet remained planted, his legs straining, refusing to give way. For the first time, he didn't feel like he was simply enduring. He was fighting.

Master Arin lowered his sword, and Jacob felt the immediate relief as the pressure lifted. His muscles, aching from exertion, finally relaxed, and he let his own weapon slip from his grip, landing with a dull *thud* in the dirt. His legs gave out beneath him, and he dropped to the ground, arms resting on his knees as he panted, his head hanging low.

“Good job, boy. Ye’re gettin’ better every day. Keep at it, an’ you’ll be a master swordsman yet.”

Coming from Arin, that was high praise. Jacob barely had time to process the compliment before a waterskin flew towards him. He caught it and drank greedily, the cool liquid soothing his parched throat. His breathing slowed, and his racing heart gradually steadied.

“Get some food an’ go find Jed. They be needin’ yer help with the animals.”

Jacob nodded, watching as Master Arin strode away. After a moment's rest, he hauled himself up and made his way towards the livestock pens on the far side of the village. His sharp eyes scanned the enclosures, checking that all the animals were where they should be. Despite the sturdy wooden fences, there always seemed to be some escapees – usually the chickens. Sure enough, a few wandered freely, pecking at the ground. He let them be for now, knowing they would find their way back before dark. If not, he would have to chase them down, something he had done more times than he cared to count. At this point, he was convinced they did it on purpose.

The buffalo lay contentedly in the lush grass, lazily flicking their tales. The pigs, on the other hand, were happily wallowing in the mud but perked up the moment they spotted Jed approaching with buckets of food. Aevah followed behind him, carrying two more.

"Jed, Aevah—need some help?" Jacob called as he reached them, watching as they emptied the buckets into the feeding troughs.

"We're nearly done here," Jed replied. "But you can check the henhouse for eggs and take these back."

"On it!"

Jacob crouched low, arms outstretched, and took slow, careful steps towards the first rogue chicken. The bird, spotting him, clucked in alarm and took off.

"Oh no, you don't," Jacob muttered, darting left and right, trying to herd the wayward birds towards the coop.

"Come on, you little rascals!" he called, waving his hands in an attempt to guide them.

One of the hens bolted between his legs, nearly toppling him.

"Whoa!" He wobbled but managed to stay upright, just barely.

With a last desperate lunge, he caught the bird before it could escape again. The second chicken scurried towards the coop on its own, more out of annoyance than obedience. Breathing heavily, Jacob carefully placed the hen in his arms back inside the pen, then secured the gate as the other one strutted in behind it.

"Gotcha!" He grinned triumphantly, wiping the sweat from his brow. He could only hope there wouldn't be any more escapees before nightfall.

Lifting the lid of the henhouse, he peeked inside. Several chickens nestled in the straw, and among them, a good number of eggs waited to be collected. Grabbing the wooden basket, he carefully gathered each one, placing them in the specially carved holders. Once finished, he returned to Jed, handing over the basket before heading off to wash up for dinner.

That night, Jacob and Aevah joined their cousins for a pleasant meal filled with laughter and easy conversation. But soon, the discussion turned serious.

Elinor's pregnancy.

Jacob tensed at the mention of it, the weight of their mission pressing heavily upon him once more. This unexpected news complicated everything. If she had an heir, their task would become even more difficult. *How could they challenge her claim to the throne now?*

Once they were alone, he turned to Aevah, but she spoke first.

"You know," she said solemnly, "as much as I wish we could stay here, we need to leave soon. Our part in all this is just beginning."

Jacob nodded. His expression mirrored her resolve. "I know. I feel the same way. Let's enjoy one more night. Then it's time to move on and find the other crystal shards."

Chapter 33

Deep in the Well

As they travelled towards the shard's possible hiding place, Elinor had ample time to decipher the riddle and its concealed location. She had determined it referred to a well, but which one? According to Julian, there were several in the area. From what she assumed, the well she sought was abandoned, so she had already dispatched trusted guards ahead to scout the nearby wells. Once they found the correct one, the challenge would be reaching it. The riddle made it clear it wouldn't be easy.

"Long forgotten, I dwell deep below, in a chamber where water once did flow. Now, it is dry, dark, and cold. Not a realm any man would dare to go. If you find just what you truly desire, remember endless glory do not aspire. Power and greed will corrupt your soul, only those with pure minds can control me whole." Reading it again, Elinor rolled her eyes.

Corrupt her soul? She had never felt more alive. Her soul wasn't corrupted – it was transformed. It was hers, and she embraced it.

Welcomed it. The darkness was a part of her very being. No, the power didn't consume her; *she was power.*

"Are you certain this is safe for you to do?" Bradley asked.

"We've been through this. Yes, it's perfectly harmless. Besides, none of you can sense the shards. It could take you weeks to find what I could in five minutes. Trust me."

She implored him to believe her, and although he nodded, she doubted he truly did. Still, she knew what she was doing and would never endanger herself – or their baby. As she cradled her growing belly, the carriage slowed. Moments later, Julian rode up to the window.

"My queen, I have received word that three of the nearby wells aren't the ones you seek. However, there is one that looks promising, though it's a two-day ride from here."

"Then let's hope the last option is the right one. Inform the driver. I guess we're going to be travelling a little longer."

"Yes, Your Majesty. I'll send a messenger once we're certain we've found the right location."

Julian rode off, and soon, they were moving again, continuing their journey through the countryside. After another day on the road, a letter arrived by crow, confirming that this well could indeed be the right place. Determined to reach it as soon as possible, Elinor ordered the group to ride later into the night. After only a brief rest at a local inn, they set off again at dawn.

If this was the place, she had to be sure. By mid-morning, the carriage came to a halt. Elinor was eager to escape its confined space for more than one reason. Stretching her limbs, she inhaled deeply before following Julian towards the well.

"It's empty," he informed her. "Been dry for longer than the locals can remember. None of them recall it ever working."

"This is it," Elinor murmured, running her hands along the well's weathered stone edge. A faint pulse of energy thrummed beneath her fingertips. She closed her eyes, drawing in a steady breath as she focused on the shard's presence below. It was weak, buried deep, but unmistakably there.

Behind her, Bradley was overseeing the men as they set up a pulley system with a harness.

"You're sure this is secure?" he asked, peering into the yawning darkness below.

"Yes," Julian replied without hesitation.

"Then let's go. I'm going first. Elinor will follow."

Strapped in, Bradley perched on the well's edge. He shot Elinor a reassuring wink before pushing himself off. The rope creaked as Julian carefully lowered him into the depths. Moments later, Bradley's voice echoed up from below.

"All good! Pull it back up."

Julian retrieved the harness and helped Elinor strap in. Standing at the edge of the dried-up well, she rested a protective hand over her swollen belly. The riddle had led her here, and now the shard was almost within reach. After all these years, she could taste victory. The power called to her, beckoning from the darkness below.

Julian met her gaze, uncertainty flickering across his face. "Are you sure about this?"

Elinor nodded. "I have to do this. That fragment is too important."

With Julian's guidance, she eased herself into the well. The rope held firm as she descended, her breath even, her resolve unshaken. The deeper she went, the cooler the air became, damp and thick with the scent of earth and decay.

At the bottom, darkness enveloped her, but she felt Bradley's strong hands steady her as he unfastened the harness. She exhaled softly, offering him a grateful smile.

"Thank you," she whispered, placing a hand gently against his cheek. "Now, let's find this shard."

"Where do we start?" Bradley asked as he handed her a lantern before raising his own, casting flickering light around them.

The well's interior was narrow, its walls carved from an ancient stone, rough and uneven, long since drained of its moisture. Shadows twisted eerily across the walls, revealing patches of moss clinging stubbornly to the damp bricks. Old cobwebs draped over the corners, and the faint sound of dripping water echoed in the confined space. Small stones and debris littered the floor, crunching beneath their feet as they stepped forward.

Despite the darkness, Elinor could feel the shard's energy pulsing, guiding her every step. It called to her, its presence unmistakable. She stopped in front of the wall, closing her eyes as she let the power hum through the cold, dry air. The pulse grew stronger, beating in rhythm with her own as if the shard were part of her very being.

Guided by the connection, she swept her palm over the rough stone surface until her fingers found the exact spot where it was buried.

"It's here."

Bradley moved closer, lifting his lantern to illuminate the area where her hand rested. "Behind the stone?"

"Yes. We need to pry the bricks out to get to it."

She stepped back as he set his lantern down and reached for his toolkit. His hands hovered briefly before selecting a chisel and hammer.

"Allow me," he said, positioning himself at the spot she had pointed out.

Elinor raised the lantern higher, her anticipation growing as he began chipping away at the mortar. The sound of metal striking stone echoed sharply in the confined space, each impact sending a jolt of excitement through her. With every strike, her pulse quickened, tension coiling in her chest.

The first brick came loose, and Bradley switched to a crowbar, carefully prying it free. One by one, the bricks gave way, revealing a small, shadowed cavity beyond the wall.

"There's something in here," he said, awe in his voice as he stepped aside.

Elinor reached in, her fingers brushing against the smooth wood. She withdrew a small rectangular box, its surface aged but sturdy. With calm hands, she lifted the lid. A faint glow seeped into the darkness, illuminating her face as her eyes locked onto the shard inside.

It was similar to the one in the tower – slender, smooth, with a single pointed end. Though smaller, its energy was just as powerful.

A slow, triumphant smile spread across her lips as she extended a trembling hand. Her fingertips grazed the polished surface, a shiver coursing through her at the raw power emanating from within. Years of searching, scheming, and sacrificing had led to this moment.

"Finally," she whispered, her voice laced with reverence and something darker. "With this, nothing will stop me."

She curled her fingers around the shard, drawing it close as its energy surged through her veins. The lantern light flickered, the well darkening around them as shadows twisted across the stone walls. The shard's glow pulsed, casting an eerie, unnatural radiance over her features.

Her eyes gleamed with dangerous intent as she turned to Bradley.

"Now we can head home and rest easy, knowing we have what we sought. I'll need to conduct the bonding ceremony for the two shards again, which means contacting a high priestess we trust." Elinor carefully placed the shard back into its box, securing it.

"Leave that to me. I know exactly who to contact," Bradley replied as he helped fasten the harness around her. Once she was secure, he gave the rope a firm tug. "I'll see you up there," he said as the pulley system creaked into motion.

With the box resting securely in her lap, Elinor gripped the rope tightly as she was hoisted upwards. The ascent was slow, the depth of the well making every movement deliberate, but the faint light above grew larger and larger until, at last, she emerged.

Julian was there to meet her, extending a hand to steady her as she stepped onto solid ground. "Did you find what you needed, Your Majesty?"

"I did," she confirmed, brushing dust from her dress. "As soon as Bradley is out, we return home and make a plan. There are still two shards left to find."

She settled onto a nearby bench, keeping the box close as she waited for Bradley to appear. Everything was falling into place, but she needed to find the remaining shards before her niece and nephew could get to them. *This was only the beginning.*

When Bradley finally emerged from the well, she rose to her feet, a small smile playing on her lips as she waited for him to be freed from the harness.

"What now, my queen?" he asked.

"Home."

Elinor led them back to the carriage, and Bradley helped her inside before joining her. As Julian organised the guards to keep watch over the possible shard locations, she allowed herself a rare moment of ease. With her baby's arrival drawing near and exhaustion settling deep in her bones, she welcomed the thought of rest.

After several more weeks on the road again, the sight of the castle gates filled her with relief. *Finally*. As the carriage rolled to a stop, she exhaled, eager to return to the comfort of her home.

Settling back into her daily routine, she began delegating many of her usual responsibilities, entrusting Bradley and Julian to manage affairs on her behalf. She had full confidence in them – nothing significant would move forward without her signature. For now, she would conserve her strength. The next phase of her plan would require it.

Bradley and Julian kept a close watch on the lords, particularly Lord Stone and his family. He had been suspiciously quiet lately, and it was only a matter of time before he made a move. *After all, she held his daughter captive*.

Rosalind had settled into her role, obedient and compliant – especially after the public whipping she endured for attempting to escape. The shock of it had broken whatever defiance remained in her. The wounds on her back would be raw and agonising for weeks, a lingering reminder of her place. Unlike the power, where pain faded quickly, her punishment was meant to last. And yet, despite her suffering, she still harboured hope. Elinor could see it in her eyes. Rosalind thought her guard would be down, knowing Elinor was due soon, but there was no one left to help her. Next time, she would think twice before trying anything again.

Despite the minor trouble Rosalind had caused, Elinor found herself at ease as she neared the end of her pregnancy. Moving had become a struggle, so she took comfort in her chambers, resting more often. Her lady-in-waiting, Chloe, insisted on daily walks around the castle grounds, adamant they were beneficial for both her and the baby. Elinor begrudgingly complied, though she despised the way she waddled like a duck. Still, the crisp air was refreshing, even if the effort exhausted her.

Returning from one such stroll, she was desperate to sit down. Her legs ached, and her spine throbbed with every step. The moment she reached her chambers, she collapsed into her velvet-backed chair with a sigh, vowing never to move again.

She fanned her face, feeling overheated. "Why is it so hot in here?" she snapped at one of her maids.

Without delay, they brought her a cool, damp cloth and a glass of water. She pressed the cloth to her forehead, but to her horror, tears welled in her eyes and spilt down her cheeks.

"I'm sorry," she choked out, overwhelmed. "I'm just so exhausted."

Her maid, unfazed by the sudden outburst, offered a comforting squeeze on her arm before continuing to arrange the lavish gifts sent for the baby. Stacks of fine blankets and embroidered gowns sat alongside delicate wooden toys and gleaming jewels – offerings from nobles eager to remain in her favour.

Elinor had begun writing thank-you notes but abandoned the task halfway through. Leaning forward was too uncomfortable, and at this point, *everything* was miserable – except leaning back in this very chair. Even her bed, once a place of comfort, had become a battle to get in and out of on her own.

Sleep had become elusive, her hips ached constantly, and despite reassurances from her physician that everything was progressing normally, the prospect of enduring several more weeks of this felt unbearable. The baby had shifted downward, a sign that the birth was nearing, but until then, all she could do was wait. The midwives remained on standby, prepared to be summoned at a moment's notice.

With her face cooled by the damp cloth, exhaustion overtook her, and she drifted into a light sleep. Now and then, a tightening sensation rippled across her abdomen, but it faded as quickly as it came. Each time, she stirred slightly before slipping back into an uneasy rest, dismissing the discomfort as yet another inconvenience of pregnancy.

As the hours passed, the sensations grew stronger and more frequent. Elinor shifted in her chair, a deep frown creasing her forehead. She had tried to ignore the growing discomfort, but it was becoming impossible to dismiss.

Then, a sudden warmth trickled down her legs. Startled, she looked down, her breath hitching. *Had she wet herself?*

"Oh no," she whispered, her cheeks burning with embarrassment.

She called for her maid, who hurried to her side, assessing the situation with a practised eye.

"My lady," the maid said gently, "your water has broken. The baby is coming."

Elinor's breath caught in her throat. "What?! But—it's too soon." Panic surged through her. "Get Bradley, the midwives, and Lady Chloe. Quickly!"

The maid darted from the room, calling to the guards and sending them in her place. The moment she returned, another contraction struck. The pain was sharper now, more insistent. Elinor gripped the arms of her chair, her nails digging into the velvet as a cry escaped her lips. Her breaths came in short, uneven gasps, the pressure intensifying with each passing moment.

The candlelight flickered, casting shifting shadows across the walls. Distant voices echoed through the hallways as the guards relayed the urgent message. The heavy beat of hurried footsteps approached.

Moments later, the door burst open. Bradley rushed in, his face pale with worry.

"Elinor, I'm here," he said, crossing the room in an instant. He took her hand, his grip firm. "The midwives are on their way."

Elinor clutched his fingers tightly, her knuckles turning white. "It's too soon. I'm not ready."

Bradley knelt beside her. His expression was resolute. "Well, the baby has other ideas, my dear. You're strong, Elinor. You *can* do this."

Lady Chloe entered next, moving with a composed grace that instantly steadied Elinor's nerves. She placed a gentle hand on her shoulder.

"Breathe, my queen," she said softly. "Focus on your breathing. The midwives will be here any moment."

Elinor nodded, though another wave of pain cut through her before she could respond. She squeezed Bradley's hand harder, holding onto his presence as an anchor. The world narrowed to the sound of his voice, the warmth of Lady Chloe's touch, and the unbearable tightening in her abdomen.

The door swung open again, and the midwives swept into the room, their faces calm and focused. With hesitation, they assessed the situation and began preparing for the delivery.

One of them, an older woman with kind eyes, knelt beside Elinor, her voice steady and reassuring. "You're doing wonderfully, my lady," the midwife said. "Just keep breathing and let your body do the work. Now, let's see how far along you are."

Elinor nodded, clinging to the small measure of relief the words provided. She tightened her grip on Bradley's hand, drawing strength from his unchanging presence. The midwife examined her carefully, then looked up with a firm nod.

"The baby will be here within the hour."

The other midwives worked swiftly, preparing for the birth. They spread out warm blankets, arranged bowls of steaming water, and set clean cloths within reach. The scent of lavender filled the air, its calming presence mingling with the faint crackle of the fire. A birthing stool sat nearby, its wood gently warming by the hearth's glow.

Candles flickered in the dim chamber, their soft light casting long shadows along the stone walls. The midwives laid out their simple tools: a sharp knife, thread for binding the cord, and swaddling cloths. One of them, an older woman with a gentle face, approached Elinor with a small pouch of herbs.

"Chew on these, my lady," she instructed. "They will help ease the pain."

Elinor hesitated only a moment before taking them, her fingers trembling as she placed the herbs in her mouth. She cast a glance at Bradley, who met her gaze with unwavering resolve.

"You're doing wonderfully, Elinor," he murmured, his voice calm and full of quiet encouragement. "Just a little longer."

Lady Chloe stood close, whispering a quiet prayer to the divine spirit for a safe delivery. At the midwives' guidance, she tended to Elinor, cooling her flushed skin with damp cloths and pressing a cup of water to her lips when needed.

The contractions came faster now, each one striking with brutal intensity. Elinor gripped the arms of her chair, her breaths ragged as pain surged through her. The main midwife checked her once more before meeting her gaze with a certain nod.

"It's time, Your Majesty. Let's move you to the birthing stool."

Elinor allowed them to help her up, leaning on Bradley for support as they guided her towards the fire's warmth. Lowering herself onto the stool, she gripped its sides, her pulse racing with apprehension.

Then, another contraction tore through her, more powerful than before. A strangled gasp escaped her lips, her eyes widening as the reality of what lay ahead became undeniable.

"This baby needs to come out. NOW!" Elinor cried, her body wracked with another powerful contraction.

Lady Chloe and the midwives gathered closer, their voices a uniform chorus of encouragement.

"You're doing wonderfully, Elinor," Bradley uttered, his grip firm around her hand.

She shot him a glare between laboured breaths. "Easy for you to say. You don't have an entire baby trying to escape your body."

A flicker of amusement crossed his face, but it was quickly replaced by concern as another wave of pain crashed over her. Elinor clenched the handles of the birthing stool, sweat beading on her forehead. The midwives moved efficiently, their calm presence keeping her grounded as she focused on their guidance, her breathing, and the rhythmic surges of her body.

"That's it, Your Majesty," the midwife urged. "One last push, and your baby will be here. Push now!"

Summoning the last of her strength, Elinor squeezed her eyes shut and bore down, a guttural cry escaping her lips. The burning, stretching pain reached its peak – sharp, all-consuming, unbearable. Then, suddenly, a release. A rush of relief swept through her as the midwife caught the newborn, lifting the tiny body into the cool air.

Exhausted, Elinor sagged against the stool, her body trembling. And then, piercing through the heavy silence, the first cries of her child rang out.

"It's a boy," the midwife announced, her voice warm with joy.

Tears blurred Elinor's vision as the newborn was placed into her waiting arms. His tiny body was warm against her chest, his soft cries fading as she held him close. She traced his delicate features with wonder – the downy tufts of hair, the tiny fingers curling instinctively around hers. In that moment, everything else faded. Only this little life, fragile and perfect, mattered.

Bradley leaned in, brushing a tender kiss against her damp forehead. His voice was thick with emotion as he reached out to touch their son's cheek. "You were incredible. Our son is perfect."

Around them, Lady Chloe and the midwives moved quietly, tending to final tasks – cleaning, ensuring mother and child were comfortable. The elder midwife offered Elinor a kind smile. "Rest now, Your Majesty. You and your son are both healthy."

Elinor exhaled, exhaustion washing over her in waves. She turned her gaze to Bradley, her heart impossibly full. "We need to name him," she whispered.

Bradley smiled. "We will. But for now, just rest."

As her eyes fluttered shut, the last thing she saw was Bradley's loving gaze and the peaceful face of their newborn son. And she knew that this moment was the beginning of a new chapter, not just for her but for the entire kingdom.

Chapter 34

The Desert Mirages

After speaking with Isaac the next morning, preparations were made to leave before sunrise the following day. Aevah spent her last afternoon with her cousins, as well as Elara and Niamh. She would miss them all. The thought of returning to the outside world unsettled her, especially knowing that Elinor was hunting them.

Still, the skills she had gained during her time here gave her confidence. And with Elara having placed a shield around the shard she carried, she felt somewhat reassured. Any skilled trackers in the area would be unable to detect its power. However, the shard could still be sensed by the others – since they were drawn to one another. As long as her aunt wasn't nearby wielding the one from the castle, they would be safe. Hopefully.

Knowing they had an early start ahead, Aevah and Jacob spent the evening at Master Arin's residence, having dinner with everyone. The thought of leaving her newfound friends and family was bittersweet. This place and its people had become home to her, and she wasn't ready to say goodbye.

"It's going to be hard parting from you all," she said, her voice thick with emotion as she blinked back tears.

"Well, you'll be happy to know that we're coming with you," Isabella announced with a wide grin.

"Really?" Aevah's eyes widened.

"Yep, all three of us," Isabella confirmed, gesturing towards her brothers, who were both smiling.

"You didn't think we would let you go out there alone, knowing who's hunting you, did you?" Edward said.

Overwhelmed, Aevah found herself unable to speak. Tears spilt down her cheeks, and Jacob responded on both their behalf. "Thank you. Having you with us means everything."

After a brief pause, he hesitated before asking, "But what about Sage and the baby?"

Edward's expression softened. "Leaving them behind is difficult, but given the circumstances, it's necessary. Sage understands, and she's strong. They'll be safe here until I return."

Jacob nodded with a grim expression. It was just another sacrifice forced upon them by his aunt's relentless pursuit.

With their departure looming, the conversation eventually resumed, and everyone bid each other goodnight, knowing they would have plenty of time together in the days ahead.

That night, Aevah struggled to sleep. Her nerves got the better of her, making for a restless night. As a result, morning came too soon, and she found herself sluggish and slow to rise. By the time she was ready, Jacob and the others were already waiting for her.

"Come on, sleepyhead. The sooner we leave, the better. I want to cover as much ground as possible before the midday sun hits," Bryne teased.

"I'm coming," Aevah replied as she secured her belongings to her horse. As she turned, she noticed the adults who had helped them standing in a line along the path ahead, each of them smiling, prepared to bid them farewell. A lump formed in her throat at the sight.

She approached them, her eyes welling with tears. "Thank you all for everything. We wouldn't have come this far without your support."

Isaac returned her gaze with warmth, his own eyes glistening. "You will always be welcome here. Remember, you have friends and allies among us."

Jacob shook hands with Master Arin, his voice steady but heavy with emotion. "We will never forget your kindness. We promise to return once this is all over."

Elara and Niamh stepped forward, their expressions a mix of pride and sorrow. "Stay strong, both of you," Elara said. "Your journey is far from over, but you have the strength and courage to see it through."

Niamh signed, "We believe in you. Go with our blessings and the divine spirits."

With one last look at their friends and allies, Aevah and Jacob mounted their horses. Once they were ready, Bryne took the lead, and the others followed.

As they passed through the barrier, Aevah felt an unnerving sensation, as if she were being repelled by an unseen force. But the moment they emerged on the other side, the feeling vanished. She turned back, expecting to catch one last glimpse of the village – only to find nothing but an endless stretch of barren desert. It was as if the village had simply disappeared.

Taking a deep breath, she turned forward and urged her horse down the hill, following the others as they resumed their journey across the merciless sands.

The first twenty-four hours passed quietly – if enduring scorching temperatures by day, freezing cold by night, and narrowly avoiding a sandstorm could be considered uneventful.

Early on the second morning, as they travelled towards the temple, they realised they were being followed. The revelation unsettled Aevah. In such an open landscape, with nowhere to hide, how had their pursuers remained out of sight? It was Edward who spotted them first – a group of six, one more than their own.

Regardless, they pressed on. The relentless midday sun bore down on them, and though they should have stopped to take shelter from the heat, they had no choice but to keep moving. Their pursuers were closing in.

"We need to keep moving," Bryne said, glancing over his shoulder. "They're getting closer."

"No, we have to make a stand," Isabella countered. "They'll catch us before we reach the safety of the temple. It's still a day away, and without rest, no one will make it out of this desert alive."

"You're right," Bryne admitted. "But just a little farther—we're near the mirages, and I'm hoping they'll turn the sands in our favour."

"Or kill us all," Isabella muttered, shaking her head as they pressed on, trying to keep as much distance as possible between them and their pursuers.

Ahead, the air shimmered, distorting the horizon. Aevah's breath caught as she spotted what appeared to be a small oasis – a pool of water surrounded by trees, with a modest stone house nestled in the middle. "Look!" she cried, pointing towards the mirage.

"It's not real," Isabella warned. "Don't be fooled. I told you the sands play tricks."

Before they could change course, arrows rained down around them, forcing them forward. They had no choice but to continue, herded like cattle in a single direction.

Bryne pulled his horse to an abrupt stop. Edward and Isabella followed suit, and together, the three Goodmans positioned themselves in front of Aevah and Jacob.

"This is where we make our stand," Bryne declared. "If we keep going, we march to our deaths. Edward, Isabella—with me."

"What about us?" Jacob asked.

"Stay back and guard the horses," Bryne instructed. "These men want you alive, so don't engage unless absolutely necessary. Understood?"

He didn't wait for a response before he and his siblings charged towards the six attackers, meeting them head-on.

"Watch out!" one of the men shouted as swords clashed in a brutal frenzy.

The Goodmans fought with fierce determination, their weapons moving in a blur. Sand erupted around them, swirling in the air and obscuring the battle in a shifting haze.

Aevah's heart pounded as she gripped the horses' reins, her knuckles turning white. She watched, tense and helpless, as the fight unfolded. "We can't just stand here," she whispered to Jacob. "They need our help."

Jacob shook his head. "We have to trust them. They know what they're doing."

As Jacob spoke, one of the attackers broke through the line, charging straight for them. Jacob turned just in time, raising his sword to parry the blow. The force of it sent him stumbling back, but he kept his stance.

Aevah moved forward to help, but Jacob shouted, "Stay back!" as he shoved her behind him.

Her heart pounded as she watched him struggle. Blood poured from a deep gash on his arm, his strength wavering against their assailant. Determined to intervene, Aevah reached for the power.

Fixing her gaze on the attacker, she conjured a shield of air between him and Jacob, then summoned a powerful gust of wind. The force propelled the man backwards, straight towards the mirage. He landed on what appeared to be solid ground – only for the illusion to shatter as he sank into the quicksand hidden beneath it.

Aevah stood frozen, watching in horror as the desert swallowed him whole. His screams tore through the air, hands clawing desperately at the sand – until he was gone. A chill ran down her spine. In mere moments, his very existence had vanished beneath the shifting sands.

A sharp cry from her left yanked her back to the fight. The Goodmans were holding their own – two of the attackers already lay lifeless in the sand. But Edward was struggling, being forced back, inch by inch, towards the mirage's treacherous edge.

"Watch out!" Aevah cried.

She watched in horror as he teetered dangerously close to the same fate as the man before him. At the last second, he ducked to the side, levelling himself with his opponent – just as Jacob rushed in to help. A flash of steel, a final strike, and Edward's attacker crumpled to the ground.

Edward grinned in victory, but his expression quickly fell as he realised his mistake. In the heat of battle, he had stepped too close to the mirage's brink. His feet were already sinking.

"No!"

Aevah ran forward as Jacob grabbed Edward's arms, pulling with all his strength. But the sand refused to release him. It clung to him, dragging him deeper. His ankles disappeared, then his calves. His siblings were still locked in combat, unaware of what was happening. By the time they saw, Edward was already waist deep.

Without hesitation, they all rushed in, forming a chain, pulling as hard as they could. It was no use. The sand was winning.

"The power, Aevah—can you do anything with the power?" Isabella pleaded.

"I don't know, but I can try. Everyone, move back," Aevah commanded, stepping forward.

She could feel time slipping away. Edward was already halfway submerged.

"You can do this, Aevah," he said, his voice steady despite the fear in his eyes. "I believe in you."

"That makes one of us," she replied, though she embraced the power, anyway.

Edward grinned at her as if nothing out of the ordinary was happening – as if his life weren't quite literally in her hands. Shaking her head, she pushed aside her nerves and focused on the sand around him, searching for a way to free him.

"Be ready to grab him if this works," she said, not directing it at anyone in particular. Still, she sensed the others shifting closer, poised to act at the moment she gave the signal.

Closing her eyes, Aevah took an intense breath, letting the energy of the power flow through her. She reached out with her mind, connecting with the earth beneath her feet. The sand responded – each grain distinct, yet part of a greater whole.

Slowly, she willed the loose particles beneath Edward's feet to solidify. The quicksand, once a treacherous void, began to firm, creating a stable surface for him to push against.

"Hold on, I'm almost there," she murmured, sweat beading on her forehead from the effort.

The sand around his legs hardened, forming a solid platform.

"Now—pull!" she shouted.

The others sprang into action, gripping Edward's arms and heaving with all their strength. With one final effort, they dragged him free, tumbling onto stable ground.

Edward lay there for a moment, covered in sand but otherwise unharmed. The others fussed over him, brushing off the worst of the grit. As Aevah stepped closer, Edward pushed himself to his feet, shook off the remaining sand, and pulled her into a crushing hug.

"You did it," he said, his voice full of relief and admiration.

"I know. I can't believe it," she admitted breathlessly.

"I can."

With exhaustion setting in, Bryne directed them to move farther from the mirage before setting up camp. They needed rest, and their wounds required tending. Aevah helped Edward transport the bodies, using her power to carry and drop them into the mirage. No evidence could be left behind, just in case.

Back at the shelter, Jacob had been patched up, the horses were tended to, and food was ready. Drained from the battle, they all sat down to eat and recover.

A day's ride still lay ahead before they would reach the temple, and their supplies were running low. After the fight, they had consumed more food and water than they should have – but they needed to regain their strength if they hoped to survive the harsh desert conditions.

Isabella warned them to conserve what little water they had left, though she stayed confident they would make it to their destination in one piece. Just a little thirsty.

After a much-needed rest, Aevah and the group packed up and resumed their journey. Isabella had been right – the heat was relentless. By midmorning, Aevah was hot, sweaty, and parched. Knowing they still had at least another six hours ahead and that her water supply was dwindling, she took only minimal sips. Even so, her lips had begun to crack, and her mouth felt like sandpaper. She had to work hard to produce even a hint of saliva, occasionally swirling a mouthful of water around in a desperate attempt to retain some moisture.

A dull headache throbbed at her temples, and fatigue weighed heavily on her limbs. The sun bore down on them without mercy. She glanced at her companions, all of whom looked just as drained as she felt. No one complained, so neither did she.

"I hope we reach the temple soon," she murmured, her voice hoarse. "I don't know how much longer I can keep this up."

"Not long now," Bryne assured her, handing her a small piece of watermelon. He passed the last of what remained in his pack to everyone, a meagre offering but one they all desperately needed.

Aevah popped the slice into her mouth, savouring the cool, sweet juice as it trickled down her throat. It was a fleeting relief, but it was enough to momentarily ease the dryness that had plagued her. She let the fruit linger on her tongue, reluctant to swallow, sucking on the last traces of moisture until it warmed and dissolved completely.

As they rode on, the temporary relief faded, and soon, Aevah's mouth was as dry as before. She lifted her waterskin to take a sip, but nothing came out. Not even a drop. With a sigh, she let it fall back against her saddle. She refused to ask for more. They were all suffering, and she wouldn't take from someone else when they were just as desperate.

Then, after what felt like an eternity, something appeared in the distance. At first, it was little more than a shimmer on the horizon, but as they drew closer, its form became clear.

"Is that it?" she asked, her voice barely a whisper.

"It is," Bryne confirmed, his own voice rough with thirst. "Another hour's ride, and we'll be there."

Aevah sagged with relief, nearly slumping forward in the saddle. They were almost there. It had been years since she had entered a sacred temple, and never one in this place. *Would it resemble the temple near their home in Carraton?*

As they approached, she could see the familiar grandeur – tall, imposing pillars standing against the sun, a majestic staircase leading up an entrance carved into the stone. Even from a distance, it exuded a quiet power, a sense of refuge amidst the unforgiving desert.

The surrounding landscape was vastly different from what Aevah was accustomed to. The climate had shaped the land into something stark yet striking. Instead of lush green gardens, neatly arranged cacti and succulents formed intricate diamond-shaped patterns, their vibrant hues standing out against the golden sand. Polished stones and glass fragments had been embedded into the pathways, creating dazzling mosaics that caught the sunlight, scattering shimmering reflections across the ground.

Like the temple back home, the walls were adorned with elaborate carvings depicting stories of the past. At the entrance, a grand marble statue of the Divine Spirit stood, outstretched in welcome, its serene expression radiating a sense of peace.

"We made it," Aevah gasped, sliding off her horse. The moment her feet touched the ground, exhaustion overtook her, and she collapsed onto the temple's steps.

The others fared no better, barely managing to dismount before staggering towards the entrance. Two priestesses emerged, their golden-brown cloaks billowing slightly in the dry breeze as they approached the weary travellers. Their faces were hidden beneath their hoods, much like the priestess from home.

"My word, you all look worse for wear," one of them said, lowering her hood. Her warm, deep brown eyes held a kindness that matched the gentle tone of her voice. Soft, dark skin framed a heart-shaped face, her tight curls spilling from beneath the hood. A sympathetic expression settled across her features as she took in their state. She ascended the steps, pausing when she noticed no one had moved. "Come now, you need shade and water."

At the mention of water, Aevah forced her weary body forward, the rest of the party following suit. Behind them, the second priestess had already taken charge of their horses, leading them away to be cared for.

Inside, the temple's layout was familiar, but the décor was unlike anything Aevah had seen before. Unlike the muted tones of the temple in Carraton, this one was a celebration of colour and life. The bright drapes gracefully flowed down the walls, their rich hues beautifully contrasting with the stone. The floor featured intricate mosaics made of brightly coloured tiles.

At the heart of the temple stood a grand altar draped in lively fabrics and adorned with fresh flowers. Petals in shades of pink, orange, and yellow added splashes of colour to the sacred space. A statue of the Divine Spirit stood at its centre, watching over the temple's visitors with an air of quiet reverence.

The priestess led them to a secluded corner where plush pillows and soft throws awaited. Aevah barely had the strength to lower herself onto them before a goblet of water was pressed into her hands. She drank greedily, the cool liquid soothing her parched throat. As soon as she emptied the goblet, it was refilled. This time, she forced herself to sip more slowly, allowing her thirst to ease gradually.

"Thank you," she murmured as the priestess filled it a third time.

"You are welcome, my child," the woman replied gently, her gaze sweeping over the group. "My name is Zuri, and I am the High Priestess of this temple." Her expression turned thoughtful as she studied them more closely. "Tell me, who are you, and what has brought you to our home in such disarray?"

Aevah glanced at Jacob. They needed help. This was a temple of the Divine Spirit – a sanctuary. A safe place.

Jacob gave her a subtle nod, granting permission to reveal the truth. Aevah turned back to the high priestess. Her voice was even despite the weight of her words.

"My name is Aevah Maycott, and this is my brother Jacob." She met Zuri's gaze without faltering. "We are the missing princess and prince of the realm."

Chapter 35

The Temple

Zuri's eyes widened as a gasp escaped her. Jacob rose alongside Aevah, both of them transfixed by the high priestess's stare. Recognition dawned on her face.

"But of course you are," she said. Her gaze lingered on Aevah. "You resemble your mother so much, especially your eyes." Then, turning to Jacob, she added, "And you—well, you could be your father's double."

She bowed her head to them – a mark of respect from the priestesses. Her eyes shifted to their three companions. "You bear the likeness of our dear Lord Goodman. May the divine spirit protect him and welcome him into the eternal embrace."

"Our father," Isabella said.

The priestess's expression softened. "Oh, I am sorry for your loss. He was an honourable man, as was your mother. They deserved so much better than the fate they met."

"Thank you," Isabella replied quietly.

The priestess exhaled, then straightened. "I believe there is a story to tell, but you all need to freshen up and eat first. Rest tonight, sleep well, and we'll speak in the morning."

Jacob and his companions sat as several priestesses brought food to them. Weary from their journey, they ate in silence. When they had finished, they were shown to their rooms and given a place to bathe.

Jacob, Edward, and Bryne shared one chamber while the girls went to another. None of them spoke as they washed away the dust of travel and changed into fresh nightclothes. Exhaustion weighed on them all, and Jacob barely had time to settle his head against the pillow before sleep claimed him. He didn't wake until late morning.

When he stirred, the room was silent. He sat up, his gaze sweeping across the chamber to find it empty. Stretching his arms high above his head, he let out a long yawn before swinging his legs over the side of the bed. Spotting a set of fresh clothes neatly folded on the side table, he dressed and stepped out into the corridor.

He found the others gathered in the same place as the night before, enjoying breakfast.

"There you are," Aevah said with a teasing smirk. "You slept long enough." She nudged him playfully before passing him a plate of fruit as he took the seat beside her.

"You were out cold when we woke up. We thought it best to let you sleep," Edward added.

"Wow. It's usually Aevah who sleeps the day away," Jacob joked as he dished up a portion of fresh fruit.

He barely had time to react before a firm shove nearly sent his food tumbling from his plate. Chuckling, he steadied himself and reached for some flatbread and dates, eating in comfortable silence while washing it all down with hot tea.

As he ate, the others filled him in. The high priestess would be meeting them soon – she wanted to hear their story and see how she could help.

Zuri also had news to share. A great deal had transpired with Elinor during their brief stay at Dunes Rest. Bryne reminded them all, in no uncertain terms, that Dunes Rest had to remain a secret. Even if they never spoke of it outright, revealing its approximate location – by discussing distances or travel times – could still pose a risk. Jacob nodded in agreement. He had a feeling the high priestess wouldn't pry too much, but he would remain cautious, nonetheless.

After breakfast, the group wandered outside, eager for fresh air and a chance to explore the temple grounds. Though surrounded by endless sand, the place held its own hidden beauty. Small springs bubbled up, forming clear pools, each encircled by stone slabs meant to keep the sediment at bay. Yellow pathways wound through the area, dotted with mosaic-covered benches for weary travellers to rest.

The arid landscape was softened by hardy shrubs and clusters of cacti, their green spines offering a contrast to the golden sand. Tiny lizards scurried along the paths or lounged lazily in the sun, soaking up the warmth. As Jacob followed one of the winding trails, his eyes landed on a stunning marble statue of the divine spirit. It stood at the centre of a tranquil pool, the water so clear that the statue's reflection shimmered across its surface. Sunlight danced upon the rippling water, illuminating the figure's serene expression. Jacob lingered there, gazing at the statue, wondering what she would make of the world as it was today.

By midday, the sun had grown too intense to stay outside any longer, so they returned indoors for lunch.

Shortly after, the high priestess arrived. Jacob and Aevah recounted their time with Grandpa George and their unexpected encounter with Isabella. They were careful to omit any details about where they had been since then – something Zuri, to their relief, didn't press. Instead, they spoke of the continued search for the remaining crystal shards.

The high priestess regarded them thoughtfully. "Do you have no inkling, then, of what your aunt has been up to these past few months?"

Jacob exchanged a glance with Aevah before answering. "Only briefly. We know she's still searching for us and for the crystals. And we know what she has been doing to children who bear a resemblance to us over the years."

"Yes, the woman is despicable—and also with child, from what we understand," Aevah said, her frown deepening. Neither she nor Jacob held any warm feelings for their aunt after everything she had done.

The high priestess's expression darkened. "So, you have heard of her… actions of late. I am saddened to confirm that what you have been told is true." She hesitated for a moment, then asked, "Tell me, have you heard anything about your grandfather?"

"No," Aevah replied. "The last time we saw him was the day we parted ways."

"Then I have grave news I must share with you both." Zuri shifted uncomfortably in her seat, her expression heavy with sorrow. "I regret to inform you that your dear Grandpa George is no longer with us. I am so sorry for your loss. I know what he meant to you."

Jacob's face fell, his eyes widening in disbelief. Aevah gasped, her hand flying to her mouth as tears welled in her eyes. The weight of the news crashed over them like a tidal wave, leaving them stunned and heartbroken.

"How?" Jacob whispered.

The high priestess tensed before answering. "Your aunt. He travelled to the castle to confront her… but he never made it out alive."

Jacob trembled, his hands shaking as he turned to Aevah. Her skin had gone pale, and tears streamed down her face as she clutched her head in her hands, rocking back and forth in her seat. He reached out, resting a hand on her back, but she suddenly sat up, her wild, tear-filled eyes locking onto the high priestess.

"No… this can't be," she cried, her voice cracking with anguish.

The sight of her grief mirrored Jacob's own, but while she wept, all he could feel was blind, seething rage.

A heavy silence fell over the room, broken only by Aevah's sobs. Jacob swallowed hard, his own vision blurring as tears finally slipped free. He reached for Aevah, and she clung to him. Together, they mourned the man who had raised them, protected them, and loved them as his own.

Memories flooded their minds – the warmth of his smile, the way he brought their bedtime stories to life with different voices, how he let them win at games, and the endless stash of treats he always shared. He had been a guiding light, a figure of kindness and strength, someone the world would sorely miss.

After a long moment, they slowly pulled apart, both wiping away their tears as they turned to the high priestess once more.

When they were ready, she continued, revealing more of what their aunt had been up to in recent months. From the tourney to the pirates to her relentless search for the crystal shards, Elinor had left a trail of chaos in her wake. Zuri couldn't confirm whether she had found what she sought, but she knew the queen had searched extensively around Almire before returning to the castle – just in time to prepare for the arrival of her and Bradley's first child.

"Already?" Aevah asked, her voice laced with shock.

"Yes," Zuri confirmed. "She is expected to give birth any day now. We have yet to receive any news, but once she has an heir, her reign will be further secured."

Jacob turned to the high priestess. "What do we do?"

"You keep going," she said firmly. "Find the crystals. Challenge her for the throne. She is a usurper, and there are many who long to see her removed. One of you belongs in her place."

"Yes," Isabella agreed. "Many still stand against her. Becoming a mother won't erase the suffering she has caused—the lives she has taken, both young and old, just to hold on to the power."

The high priestess nodded. "We need you to do your part. When the time is right, support will be there. You have more allies than you realise, and the priestesses of the realm stand behind you."

Jacob inclined his head, then turned to Aevah. He saw it – the fire in her eyes, the unwavering determination etched into her expression.

"We will not fail," Aevah declared. "But we must be careful. We don't know if she has the other crystal or how many she has managed to claim. No doubt her spies are still searching for us."

Jacob placed a reassuring hand on her shoulder. "We can do this. For our people. For our future. For Grandpa and Father."

"And you won't be alone," Isabella said as she stepped forward. "We will stand with you. Whatever it takes. Both our families deserved better."

Jacob nodded, remembering the pain the Goodmans had endured at Elinor's hands.

Zuri smiled, warmth and conviction in her eyes. "Then go with the blessings of the divine spirit. May your path be clear and your hearts stay true."

She rose from her seat and walked over to Aevah, resting a gentle hand on her shoulder. "Before you face the queen and before you retrieve the remaining shards, you must bring them to one of our temples. The priestesses will perform the bonding ceremony to link you to them. It's the only way to defeat her."

She turned to the rest of the group, her expression resolute. "Good luck to you all. And remember—when the time comes, the priestesses of the realm will be there when you need us most."

"Thank you," Aevah said as the others nodded their gratitude before leaving the room. With nothing more to be gained by staying at the temple, Jacob and the group packed their belongings, eager to continue their search for the other crystal shards. With Elinor back in Carraton and occupied for the time being, it was the perfect opportunity to move.

Though it was already later in the day, leaving now meant avoiding the worst of the heat. Bryne reassured them that they had travelled far enough from the desert's edge to encounter villages along the way. There was no longer any risk of getting lost without water or shelter.

As they prepared to leave, they quickly agreed on their general route, but choosing which crystal to pursue first caused a disagreement. Aevah insisted on heading to the mountains to find the shard they were certain Elinor hadn't seized. Jacob, however, wanted to go towards Almire, knowing Elinor had been there, to check if the shard had already been taken. Neither was willing to back down, and each was convinced their plan was the right one.

"Look, we haven't even left the temple yet. Why don't you both put this minor disagreement on hold?" Edward interrupted as Aevah started to argue her point again. "When we reach the next town, you can decide."

"Fine. But I'm right," Aevah shot back.

Jacob opened his mouth to retort, but Edward raised his hands in surrender, silently warning him to let it go. Jacob exhaled sharply but held his tongue.

"Let's go," he said instead, resisting the urge to make a witty remark.

With their decision postponed, the group thanked the high priestess once more and set off. As they left the desert behind, their journey became far more bearable. The further they travelled, the cooler the weather became. Autumn had already begun in the rest of the country, forcing Jacob to swap his light clothing for warmer layers, especially in the evenings. After weeks of camping outdoors, the sudden drop in temperature was a shock to the system. He couldn't decide which was worse – being too hot or too cold.

When Edward suggested they spend the night at an inn, Jacob eagerly agreed. The sky had taken on a heavy, ominous hue, and the rising winds carried an eerie silence that signalled an approaching storm. By the time they reached the inn, it was packed with travellers, no doubt seeking refuge from the worsening weather.

The innkeeper informed them that only two small rooms remained, each with space for two. That meant one of them would have to sleep on the floor. Before anyone could argue, Bryne shrugged.

"I'll take the floor," he volunteered without hesitation.

Once they had settled in, the girls entered the boys' room, discussing their next move. Outside, the storm raged on, rain pelting the window in steady sheets. Aevah stood by the glass, absentmindedly turning the crystal shard in her hands, ignoring Jacob's question. He watched her for a moment, the shard glimmering under the dim candlelight. Its clear surface refracted rainbow hues, making it mesmerising to look at.

One shard in their possession, another in Carraton, and two more yet to be found – if Elinor hadn't claimed them already.

"Aevah, we need to decide where we're going next. The mountains or Almire," Jacob said.

She turned at the sound of her name. "Both," she replied simply.

Jacob frowned. "Both? And how exactly are we supposed to do that?"

"We split up," she said, as if it were the most obvious solution in the world. "I'll go to the mountains, and you head to Almire. It's the only way to get to them both before Elinor does."

Jacob stared at her, his heart and mind battling for an answer. He wanted them to stay together, but a part of him knew she was right. Splitting up meant a better chance at securing both shards before Elinor. Staying together risked losing valuable time – and possibly one of the crystals – if she got there first.

"You can't go into the mountains alone," he argued.

"She won't," Isabella said, standing up. "I'll be with her. These two can go with you." She gestured to her brothers.

Jacob remained silent, jaw tightening. He knew this was the right call, but that didn't mean he had to like it. He had grown to appreciate their time together as a group, and though he hated to admit it, he feared what might happen once they split up. But it had to be done.

"Fine," he relented with a sigh. "Tomorrow, we split up and try to find a crystal shard each—before Elinor."

"Agreed," Aevah said and then nodded. Their cousins chimed in their own agreements, and they decided to reunite at Springhelm Farm once their mission was complete. Their grandfather had once mentioned a man named Walter who lived there – an ally who could offer them shelter and protection.

With the plan set, no one wanted to dwell on the weight of their decision. Talk shifted to food instead, and after a quiet meal, they all retired early.

Jacob lay awake, staring at the ceiling. His thoughts swirled, doubts creeping in. *Was splitting up really the right choice?* He knew, deep down, it was their only chance. They had to find the crystal shards before Elinor. Everything depended on it. As sleep finally overtook him, he whispered a silent prayer to the divine spirit to watch over them all – especially Aevah and Isabella. The mountains would be treacherous.

The next morning, Jacob was the first to wake. He dressed quickly as his cousins stirred around him. As he finished packing, Edward sat up, groggy and half-aware.

"Ow—watch where you're walking!" Bryne groaned from the floor.

"Sorry, forgot you were down there," Edward muttered, offering a hand to his brother. Bryne waved him off and sat up, rubbing his shoulder.

Jacob chuckled. "I'll meet you both downstairs."

He left the room and made his way to the common area, where Aevah and Isabella were already seated, eating breakfast with their bags beside them.

Joining them at the table, he ate a bowl of porridge and fruit while one of the kitchen staff handed them several packets of food for the road. By the time they finished, Edward and Bryne had finally come downstairs. As the girls grabbed their belongings, Jacob followed them to the stables to ready their horses. The boys joined them soon after, having eaten a quick meal.

With everything packed and their horses saddled, they rode out of town, following the winding road until they reached a fork in the path. There, they dismounted.

The air was heavy with unspoken words as they exchanged goodbyes. Aevah threw her arms around Jacob, holding him tightly. He returned the embrace just as fiercely, reluctant to let go. *Once they parted, who knew how long it would be before they saw each other again?*

"Good luck, Aevah. We'll reunite soon. I promise."

"I know," she said, forcing a small smile. "Remember—Springhelm Farm. I expect I'll be waiting for you as usual." Her voice was light, but her eyes shone with unshed tears.

Jacob let out a quiet laugh. "Ha, I'm sure you will." He squeezed her hand before mounting his horse. "Love you."

"Love you more," Aevah called back.

Jacob watched as Aevah and Isabella rode away, their figures growing smaller in the distance. Swallowing the lump in his throat, he turned his horse towards the road ahead and spurred it forward. Bryne and Edward followed close behind. Their separate journeys had begun.

Epilogue

In the temple near Carraton, High Priestess Zara paced her office, a crumbled note clenched in her hand. The parchment detailed Elinor's most recent actions – each more brazen and ruthless than the last.

"She has gone too far this time," Zara said, her voice laced with fury. "The pirates, George, all the children, and now Lord Stone's daughter. When will it end? She is killing anyone who stands in her way, and with an heir to the throne, she is about to become unstoppable if we don't do something."

Her words echoed through the chamber, filled with a mix of anger and resolve. The other priestesses around her nodded solemnly, their expressions grim.

"We must act swiftly," one of them said. "Elinor's reign of terror can't continue. We have to gather our forces and strike before she consolidates her power further."

Zara raised a hand, silencing the murmurs. "If she retrieves the shards as well, we'll be no match for her. Our last encounter proved that, and she was only bonded to one then. We need allies—both old and new. The rebel faction has already shown their willingness to fight, and we must seek support from the other temples. The time has come to unite against her tyranny. It's our duty to protect the innocent and restore peace to our land. By the light of the divine spirit."

A hushed debate broke out among the priestesses, discussing where to begin and how to locate the scattered rebel factions. Before they could act, they needed agreement from all the high priestesses. No one wanted a repeat of their last disastrous attempt. Too many lives had been lost that night.

Zara herself still bore the scars of that fateful battle. The immense power she had wielded had left her physically weakened, her once steady hands now trembling slightly. The toll on her body was a constant reminder of the price they had paid. Her energy wasn't what it once was, and even the simplest tasks left her fatigued. The memories haunted her – the faces of the fallen flashing before her eyes whenever she closed them.

"High Priestess, what do you think?" Priestess Nala asked, pulling Zara from her thoughts.

Zara exhaled, then met Nala's gaze. "We need to reach out to the other temples and summon them here as soon as possible. We must bring in the rebels' commander, Walter of Springhelm Farm. His support will be vital in our fight against Elinor. I also believe he knows more about this situation than we do."

Nala nodded. "It shall be done, and I agree. There is something about the rebels we don't fully understand. With

Walter here, we may finally get the answers we have sought for years."

"We can only hope," Zara said firmly. "For too long, even the priestesses have been kept in the dark. If we are to unite, we must share knowledge freely. The time for half-truths and hidden agendas is over. Transparency and trust will be our greatest weapon against Elinor."

Determination shone in Nala's eyes. "I will send word to the other temples immediately and arrange for Walter's safe passage. We must act swiftly."

As Nala left to carry out her orders, Zara turned to the remaining priestesses. "Prepare the temple for our allies. We must be ready to receive them and provide a secure environment for our discussions. This is our chance to unite and reclaim our land from Elinor's tyranny."

The priestesses bowed their heads in agreement. As the meeting concluded, they rose from their seats and dispersed to begin their preparations.

Zara made her way to her chambers, the weight of their discussion heavy on her mind. As she walked through the dimly lit corridors of the temple, an eerie glow caught her attention. It emanated from the direction of the library – a place she had visited countless times, yet never before had she seen such a light.

Curiosity piqued, she followed the glow, her footsteps echoing softly against the stone floor. The light led her to a secluded corner of the library, where an ornate, locked box sat on a pedestal. Zara had never seen it before, and its presence filled her with an inexplicable sense of foreboding.

She reached out, fingers tracing the intricate carvings adorning the box's surface. Summoning her power, she unlocked it. The lid creaked open, revealing an ancient scroll.

With trembling hands, Zara unrolled the parchment, her eyes scanning the glowing text. Her heart pounded. The scroll contained a prophecy – one that spoke of two fates. A prophecy hidden away for centuries, known to no one.

"We must succeed," she whispered, fear creeping into her soul as the burden of the future pressed upon her.

***

In another temple, an opposing High Priestess, Liora, stood before her followers, her eyes gleaming with conviction. "Elinor has proven herself a powerful ally. With the pirates, George, and now Lord Stone's daughter under her control, she is closer than ever to securing her reign. We must ensure she remains on the throne and captures the twins to solidify her power."

The surrounding priestesses nodded in agreement, their expressions resolute.

"We'll come to her aid," one of them said. "With our support, Elinor will be unstoppable."

Liora's lips curled into a knowing smile, her eyes narrowing. "I intend to visit our queen myself, under the guise of the newborn. She possesses the two shards, and with my help, she will bond with them—regaining not only the control she once wielded but even more."

"Perfect, High Priestess. Before you leave, we received a letter from High Priestess Zara. She requests your presence to discuss matters of the realm."

"No doubt concerning our queen." Liora's expression darkened briefly before she turned to Thalia. "Thank you, Thalia. Send word that I shall be there. This presents an opportunity—I can uncover the other priestesses' plans while securing my own. I will not allow them to interfere. Elinor will remain in power, whatever the cost."

Thalia bowed and hurried off to carry out her orders. Liora turned to the remaining priestesses. "Prepare the temple for my absence. Everything must run smoothly while I am away. We can't afford mistakes."

The priestesses inclined their heads before going off to perform their duties. Liora stood for a moment, collecting her thoughts, her mind racing with possibilities. She knew that Zara and the other priestesses would be formidable if they united against Elinor. But she also recognised the queen's growing power. With the shards, Elinor would be unstoppable.

As Liora prepared to leave, an uneasy feeling settled in her chest. This meeting with Zara would be pivotal. She would have to tread carefully and play her cards with precision. The fate of the realm teetered on the edge, and she was determined to ensure that Elinor emerged victorious.

Acknowledgements

Wow, I can't believe book two is here! It feels like I was writing this section for book one just yesterday, yet here we are. Working on book two has been so much fun, and this time around, the process has felt much more seamless. Continuing from book one means I know my world and characters better, and this familiarity has allowed me to dive deeper into their stories and add new dimensions to their journeys. Though, if I'm honest, the characters run the show and do as they please, I simply follow their lead, writing what they tell me.

I want to extend my heartfelt gratitude to everyone who has supported me throughout my writing journey. To my husband, family, and friends, your unwavering encouragement and love have been my anchor. Thank you for believing in me and my dreams.

A special thank you to my editor, Carien. Once again, your guidance and support have had a significant impact on me, my writing, and my ability to navigate through this series. I'm so grateful to have met you!

To my loyal readers, your enthusiasm and support mean the world to me. Thank you for joining me on this adventure and for your continued encouragement. Your excitement and feedback have been a constant source of motivation.

Lastly, I'm excited to share that I'm hard at work on book three, which will be out soon. I can't wait to see how this series concludes and to bring you all along for the wild ride.

With heartfelt gratitude,

Abigail Mader

About the Author

Since the release of book one, Abigail has been deeply immersed in the world of writing, continuing to work on this series while also discovering a whole new community of indie authors like herself. This journey has been incredibly enriching, allowing her to connect with fellow writers, share experiences, and find inspiration in their stories.

Abigail's passion for storytelling has only grown stronger, and she remains dedicated to honing her craft and exploring new creative avenues. Beyond writing, she has loved engaging with readers through book clubs, podcasts, and author interviews, helping to foster a vibrant community of book lovers.

When she isn't writing, Abigail enjoys immersing herself in nature, drawing inspiration from the world around her. She believes that every experience, no matter how small, has the potential to spark a new idea or add depth to her characters and plots.

Connect with Abigail on:

Website

www.abigailmaderauthor.com.au

Instagram

https://www.instagram.com/abigail.mader_author/

Threads

https://www.threads.net/@abigail.mader_author

www.ingramcontent.com/pod-product-compliance
Lightning Source LLC
Chambersburg PA
CBHW030603310726
48979CB00003B/549

* 9 7 8 1 7 6 3 5 7 4 0 4 5 *